# Blood Tail

A lieutenant Beaudry novel

Michael Kent

## MEZZO PUBLICATIONS

Montreal Canada

Copyright © 2015 Michael Kent

All rights reserved.

ISBN:
ISBN-13: 978-0-9937131-2-5

Cover art by Tirzah's Book Covers

# DEDICATION

For Louise who puts up with me, and my other passion, writing.

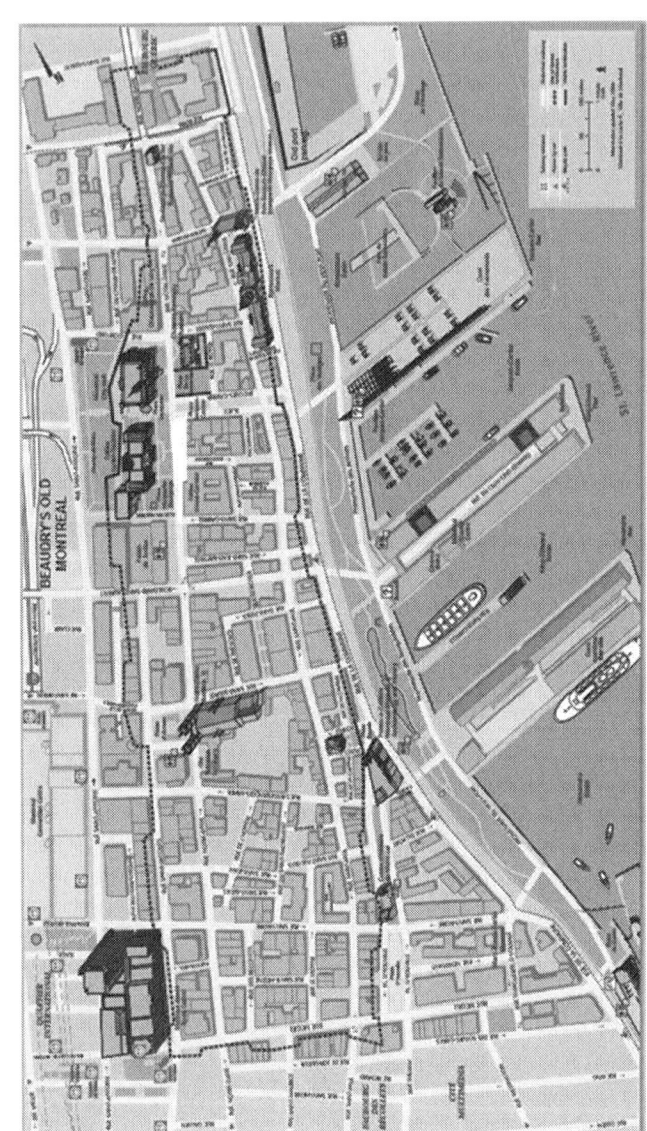

# ACKNOWLEDGMENTS

My grateful appreciation to Jacqueline M. Franklin and all the other reviewers on The Next Big Writer, for their insights, suggestions, and continued support.

Thanks to Michael Carr, whose skillful editing keeps Beaudry's adventures on track.

Blood Tail is a work of fiction. Names, characters, and incidents are products of the author's imagination and are used fictitiously. Any resemblance to actual events, locales, or persons is entirely coincidental.

Copyright ©Michael Kent, 2016
All rights reserved. No part of this product may be reproduced, scanned, or distributed in any printed or electronic form without permission. Please do not participate in or encourage piracy of copyrighted materiel in violation of the author's rights.

*Women and cats will do as they please, and men and dogs should relax and get used to the idea.*
—Robert A. Heinlein

# ONE

I swirled my glass of pinot noir, the little magenta wave aerating and intensifying the bouquet of raspberry and light spices with every turn. I raised it to the light, admiring the color and that dubious signpost of quality known as the wine's "legs." We were in Old Montreal, having a late supper at our favorite French restaurant.

"I've decided to take the promotion," she said.

Now she had my full attention. "That's the posting in Ottawa?"

"It is. You're not home half the time, anyway, and you spend more time with murderers and criminals than with me. You're married to your job, not to me. We've had this conversation before. It just isn't working out." Colleen looked past me, took a micro sip of wine, and puckered as if she had

bitten into an unripe persimmon. She put her glass to the side and said, "I prefer the Silver Oaks cab."

I used to think her spoiled-little-girl pout was cute, but after a year of living together, it had begun to pall.

I plunked my glass down on the table, spotting the restaurant's starched white cloth with a single crimson teardrop.

I felt a lump forming in my gut. She was right: this wasn't our first conversation about my chaotic work schedule. I took a deep breath and let it out slowly. "I'm a cop, it's my job. You knew that when you married me."

"Don't get mad; my decision is made."

"I'm not mad; I'm upset. There's a difference. I thought we were trying to work things out. Now you drop a bomb on me."

"You're turning your wineglass back and forth, and your forehead is all crinkly. You *look* mad." Colleen refolded her napkin into a precise square, hem inside. "I told you about the offer last week, and nothing's changed since then. The governor general's staff is a big opportunity for me. I'll meet diplomats and dignitaries from all over the world. I'll be where the action is, in charge of planning all the official functions, balls, and events. You've got your career as a famous detective. I have a right to some limelight, too."

A bitter taste had moved up to my throat. I swallowed hard and stopped fiddling with my wineglass.

"I've always supported your career," I said. "I know you love planning big events. You're good at that type of stuff. I'm just disturbed that you're moving to Ottawa so suddenly."

"It's only two hours away. You could come up and see me sometimes," she said with a strange smile.

Alarm bells went off in my detective's brain. I looked into her eyes. They were light blue but broken with an orange segment, like a pie with a slice gone, revealing a contrasting plate underneath. A hereditary condition called sectoral heterochromia iridis. Her odd eye color had drawn my attention from the start.

"Is there somebody else?"

Her eyebrows clenched together for a millisecond, and she stopped squaring her napkin to touch the corner of her mouth with her forefinger. "Robert Beaudry, why would you say such a thing?" She swallowed and looked down and to the right, into her wineglass. "Of course not. Don't be silly. Besides, I wouldn't have time. Like you, I'm way too busy at work."

Working twelve to sixteen hours a day on several cases for the past month or so, I had often

come home in the early morning, just as she was leaving for her job at the Canadian Immigration office. I knew she was unhappy with my working weekends or late into the night—mostly because it kept me from attending her parties and social events.

She loved parading my linebacker frame around friends and coworkers, sometimes introducing me with a coy wink as her "bodyguard lover."

Her nonverbal cues, and speaking my full name, told more truth than her words, those exotic eyes that had first seduced me now unwittingly saying what she couldn't voice. The late-October evening chill had somehow wafted from outside to engulf our table. My romantic night out was now frosted by the knowledge that my relationship with my tall blonde had run its course. I had planned this tête-à-tête because my detective's radar had sensed that something was going awry. The subject of separation had come up a few times, and I had thought I could charm her back. But it was too little, too late—the felon offering to make amends before the sentencing judge.

I felt as if I had been summarily fired without getting my two weeks' notice. And yet, somewhere under the bad feeling was a glimmer of relief. The guilty awareness of newfound freedom served as a

painful admission of wrong choices in my life.

Colleen was needy. It had always been a high-maintenance relationship, and getting married had been my response to her complaints that I was flirty and that we weren't close enough as a couple. To her, the ring on my finger was more a sign of ownership than a statement of undying love.

If we had had the gold bands engraved, mine would have read, "You wore me down."

Luc, the founder and owner, enhanced his bistro's reputation for world-class service with an uncanny expertise at reading the body language of his guests. In his establishment, one had but to raise an eyebrow to summon a waiter. Subconsciously aware of the sudden chill surrounding Colleen and me, he glided up to our table. "Is everything to your satisfaction, Lieutenant?"

Before I could answer, Colleen clicked into her public relations mode, her downturned mouth snapping into an automatic smile. *"Tout est merveilleux, Luc, merci de votre attention."*

Luc's sixth sense told him that not all was marvelous at our table. He touched the side of his crooked nose and looked at me, the question mark in his gaze subtle but unmistakable.

I shrugged. "Love that comes crashing in on the crest of a wave sometimes departs quietly on the outgoing tide."

He gave us a sad little smile. "Ah, monsieur is always quoting some poetic verse. Who was that from?"

"Me."

I was a regular patron of his little bistro. Having served me and many of my amorous interests over the years, Luc was a knowing witness to my up-and-down love life.

He tilted his head a little to the side. *"Ah, bon courage, mon lieutenant."*

Courage I had. It was patience that always seemed in such short supply.

My smartphone cut off my potential reply with a drum roll, breaking the tension of the moment. Luc gave a little bow and pivoted gracefully away to another table. I fished the phone out of my jacket pocket as Colleen shook her head, her mouth back in its default downturn.

"I hate that tune. That's your job calling, isn't it?"

I swiped the screen awake and answered. "Beaudry."

She was right; that ring tone was dedicated to Homicide Captain Jean O'Neil, my boss.

"Robert, I need you here ten minutes ago. I'm in the middle of a bloodbath in Upper Westmount."

Colleen recognized the look on my face: that of a hockey player called off the bench by the coach and headed into action on the ice. She picked up her purse and slid out of the booth. "Just go, Robert. I'm going to pack some things. I'll be in Ottawa tomorrow, apartment hunting with some friends. I'll call you Friday."

The captain gave me the crime scene address as Colleen walked out of the restaurant and my life.

Michael Kent

# TWO

My mind had drifted, and I wasn't focused on my driving. Still reeling from Colleen's bombshell, I reviewed our fractured relationship and keelhauling myself for my "job first, home life second" priorities. My brooding got me lost in the winding, self-intersecting mountain roads, dead ends, and twisting crescents of upper Westmount, the older posh neighborhood of Montreal and the richest postal code in Canada. Rescued by my offline Google map, ten minutes later I parked across from the address Jean had given me. My sixty-seven GTO became the maroon-and-chrome exclamation point at the end of a long row of white and blue police cars and tech-squad vans. The sheer number of official vehicles and the several-million-dollar property I was headed for warned me that this was going to be a high-profile case.

In another three weeks, the 1920s stone mansion across the street would be the perfect

setting for a Halloween party. The gibbous moon hung just left of the chimney, a wisp of cloud softening its outline. Two dormer upper windows and the vaulted main entrance were lit, giving the place the appearance of a monstrous jack-o-lantern. The "do not cross" police tape draped around the property lent an added theatrical touch. I sucked in a breath of cool night air and opened the front door.

In the foyer, a patrol officer had me sign the logbook. Nobody entered a crime scene without their name and badge number or authorization in the register. He handed me a pair of paper painter's booties to put over my shoes. I also left my jacket and scarf with him. I had learned years ago that contamination of a crime scene could let a guilty man walk. The breadth of my shoulders, augmented by a sport jacket, made it easy to brush against evidence. I threaded my way carefully into the living room.

There was no mistaking who ran the show here. Captain Jean O'Neil dominated the scene, and not only because his six feet six put him half a head above anyone else. Like a military general, he seemed to be the psychic vortex for all the action swirling about him. He didn't just walk into a room; he took possession of all thought and movement therein. Sitting or standing, he seemed forever at rigid attention, his lean body taut, ready to pounce on

any sloppiness of method or procedure. My loose interpretation of the rule book often put me at odds with my boss, but redemption always came with getting the job done. I had the highest homicide clearance rate in the department.

"Holy crap," I said, "you weren't kidding about a bloodbath. It looks like a war zone. Where's all the bodies?"

"About time you showed up. Did you walk?"

Jean regarded me with his usual accusatory look, his little gray mustache edged down in disapproval. He nodded toward the entrance to the dining room. "Two vics—one in the corner under the sheet. The other, the owner of the house, Paul Landry, the eminent lawyer and TV host, we found slumped here against the wall."

I rotated my gaze slowly, splitting the room into four segments and trying to get a feel for what happened here. Nothing broken, no furniture out of place, the TV still on but muted, everything looking almost normal, aside from the outlines of two bodies—Jackson Pollock drip abstracts in monotone crimson. We didn't really need a chalk drawing to show the location of the bodies; the blood-spray shadow showed it clearly enough. Most of the east side of the living room—floor, walls, ceiling, furniture, and lamps—was marred with dark-red arcs, streaks, dots, and splashes. It spoke of rage and

unrestrained violence.

Blood-spatter analysis is a science and an art form. Normally, you can deduce what happened at the scene.
Sometimes, you can even recreate the chronology of the event. In this case, it was information overkill.

"What's your first thought, Beaudry?"

The use of my last name—another sign that my hour and sixteen minutes to get here didn't quite square with his meaning of "I need you ten minutes ago."

I ignored the unspoken rebuke. "Only one bullet hole in the wall, yet there's blood all over," I said. "Looks as if the ghost of Lizzie Borden came back with a hatchet and a chainsaw."

"Close, but no cigar." Jean turned from me and crooked one finger to summon a technical officer, who was snapping pictures of everything in sight. The undernourished, spiky-haired kid with old-school horn-rim glasses minced over to us on tiptoes and balls of feet, deftly avoiding the array of tags, markers, and gore on the floor.

With a nod to each of us, the captain made the formal introductions. "Tristan Dobson, Robert Beaudry. You two get to work; I have to be back downtown."

He handed me his notes and the preliminary identification sheet, indicating that I was now in

charge. Then, cinching up his immaculate Burberry, he parade turned on his right heel and headed for the exit.

I would have guessed Dobson's age at 27-ish.

I'd be turning 40 on the next page of this year's calendar, and now it seemed that anyone under 30 was a kid.

We shook hands. "I've heard a lot about you, Lieutenant," he said. "You really are built like Schwarzenegger."

"All the bad stuff you heard is slander and innuendo; all the good stuff is true," I said without a smile.

"What good stuff?" he deadpanned.

The kid had a sense of humor. We were going to get along fine.

I made a horizontal circle with my index finger and double-barreled my questions. "So who called it in, and what happened?"

"A passing jogger heard screams and called it in." Dobson gave me the sly smile of a shell-game artist asking the rube, *where's the pea?* "It's a real mess. What do you think, Lieutenant?"

"My first interpretation would be a surprise attack by a bunch of crazed Benihana waiters, or maybe knife-wielding zombies."

Dobson raised an eyebrow and gave me a lopsided smile. "Well, you're partially right. No

zombies, but there was more than one attacker, and a blade or blades were used." With a slow, dramatic sweep of the arm, Dobson indicated the spatter on the wall. His hand paused over the floor in front of us.

"This is probably the blood from the first sword blow. See? The projected droplets are mostly the same size—around four millimeters—some skeletonized and dry. And the distribution pattern is in a tight group—a circle with a part missing. I'd say an outside slash to the knee or lower leg."

Before he rattled off the whole blood-spatter analysis manual, I touched his shoulder.

"Sword?"

"Yes. Not very sharp, and not more than twelve inches. Longer would have given more impact speed. See here? The drops have little tails—medium velocity, probably in the twenty-feet-per-second range. The cuts on the victims vary in depth and angle. I don't think they were martial artists with the blade, eh. Seems more your basic hack-and-chop."

I touched his shoulder again. "Superior analysis, Dr. Watson. Can I get the crib notes on that?"

He turned to me, eyes wide as if I had woken him suddenly. "It's Dobson, not Watson."

"Joke, Tristan. I trust your technical expertise. Just give me your movie version of the scene."

He gave a Donnie-and-Marie smile of orthodontic perfection. The tone of his voice deepened, and he strung his words together like a horse-race-announcer as he mimed the actions.

"Everything happened fast. I see two assailants, each with two short swords.

One of them got the chauffeur-bodyguard as he opened the door, before he could draw his weapon. As the chauffeur reached for his belt holster, one of the attackers pinned his move with a straight stab through the hand and belly. Then slashes left and right to both legs with the other sword brought him to his knees. A final upward swing gutted him open. Nearly the same method for the primary target: slash to the legs, then chops here and there to put the guy out of action but not kill him outright. Then a third attacker came into play. He pistol-whipped the lawyer's face to hamburger, then a put the gun in his mouth and pulled the trigger."

I unconsciously clenched my eyes. "Ouch, Tristan! That was an explicit-violence movie clip. It looks like our dead lawyer had a singularly unhappy client."

"Lieutenant, nobody uses my first name—

everybody calls me Dobson. And, eh, incredibly, the lawyer was still alive when we got here. I sent him to a doctor friend of mine—specialist in head trauma at the Jewish General."

I took a step back and made a fast grab for the pen that had slipped from my hand, *"Still alive?"* I said, as my pen hit the floor.

"I'd guess he had a neck spasm as the trigger was pulled. Bullet went through his cheek. The beating is what saved him—so far, anyway.

The guy's face was such a mess, it was hard to see the exit wound, so they left him for dead."

I retrieved my pen that had rolled next to Dobson's foot.

"You believe there was a third aggressor, because a swordsman wouldn't use a gun, and vice versa?"

"Eh, yes, exactly, Lieutenant."

Dobson had moved away from me while acting out the swordplay. Sidestepping a puddle of blood, I moved closer to him.

"The living room's a mess," I said. "What about the rest of the house—anything of interest?"

"The rest of the house is immaculate. In fact, it feels to me like it was staged to sell. Everything's in its place. No clutter, no family pictures. Not what you'd call a lived-in home—more like a room at the

Intercontinental."

I scribbled my shorthand version of Dobson's comments in my notepad. "Did you find suitcases or anything else to indicate that he was moving out?"

"I thought of that. No, there's food in the fridge for more than a week. The master suite is the only area that looks lived in. One walk-in closet is empty, eh, no women's clothes anywhere in the house. The bodyguard had a room next to the master suite. He had a suitcase, but most of his stuff was in the dresser—sundries all in the hall powder room."

I looked up from my notepad.

"Sundries?"

"Shampoo, shaving stuff, medicine. He has—eh, *had*—a lot of pills: meds for heart problem and high cholesterol."

"Who would hire a heart attack-prone bodyguard? That's no good."

Dobson gave me his toothy grin as I mimed shooting myself in the head with my index finger and thumb.

"How'd they get in—any sign of forced entry?"

"No. The house has bars on the windows, and the alarm system is an upgrade on Fort Knox. Looks like the killers were expected visitors."

"So he knew them. If Landry can talk, I may be able to close this case real fast. I'd best get myself

over to Jewish General."

Dobson shook his head, his lower lip in a downward curl. "Not tonight. If he makes it—and that's a sizable *if*—he'll be in tremendous pain. They'll keep him so doped up, he won't be able to make a straight sentence—certainly not one that'll stand up in court."

"Okay," I said, "the hospital's on my list for tomorrow. Give me the name of your doctor friend, and keep me informed of Landry's condition if anything changes. Call me anytime."

We traded cell phone numbers as we picked our way back to the hallway.

"Anything else, Dr. Watson?"

Dobson gave me his signature toothy smile.

"No, Lieutenant Sherlock, we're just waiting for the Humane Society to pick up the guy's cat. Then my team will finish up the evidence collection."

"Uh . . . cat?"

"We followed a trail of blood down the hall. It turned out to be more of a blood *tail* than a blood trail. There was this huge cat with its big, fluffy tail soaked in the bodyguard's blood. It's hiding in the hall closet. It was licking itself clean when one of the patrol officers tried to pick it up. He nearly got his hand clawed off. The captain had to send him to the local clinic."

"Now, that's a cat I'd like to see." I took Dobson by the elbow and steered him toward the closet.

He opened the mirrored door gingerly. Two dots of fluorescent green shone out from behind a row of winter jackets and coats. The cat's growl told me it was not amused at the intrusion. I opened the door wider, and Dobson jumped back as the growl rose in volume. I slid the coats to one side, exposing a big, fluffy black and white cat.

I bent down on one knee. "Hi, Fluffy Face. What's the problem?"

The cat stopped his panther imitation and sauntered out to sniff my hand.

"You must be a cat whisperer, Lieutenant," Dobson said. "Everybody was scared to go near this thing."

I picked it up and cradled it in my arms. It had a spot on a whisker; the tail and one back paw were damp from its grooming. "This *thing* is a probably a thoroughbred Maine coon. I like animals, and they must feel it—they come to me like I'm a magnet. If I had the same luck with women, I'd be Don Juan.

I let the big purring cat climb to my shoulder, Dobson reached out to pet it. The purr modulated to a hiss, and the cat dug all its rear claws into my arm for purchase as it tried to swat Dobson.

I tugged him by the scruff of the neck. "Whoa, Tiger! Down, boy." The cat instantly sheathed his claws, but he stayed glued to me like a twenty-pound appliqué. We headed back to the foyer as a round, red-nosed man walked in with an animal cage.

He nodded at the living stole draped on my shoulder. "Is this the cat to be euthanized?"

In a modified tai chi move, I blocked his leading foot with mine and swiveled my catless side to pin him against the wall.

"Are you the guy I'm going to arrest for interfering with a police investigation? He's a witness in my custody." I said this in a tone closely approximating the growl of the cat, who was now in full dudgeon and trying to climb my head for a better swat at the shocked animal-control guy.

Dobson jumped in and herded the man back to the entrance. "It's a mistake," he said. "We won't be needing your services. Sorry for the bother."

I gave another light tug to the scruff of the cat's neck, and it went quiet. Dobson turned back to me but stayed well away from the fluffy fiend nestled in the crook of my arm.

"Eh, I guess you're taking care of the cat, then, Lieutenant. What's your instructions?"

"Finish up here. You said there's no evidence of forced entry. If you find an agenda or anything

that points to him meeting someone here, let me know. I'm going to his office first thing in the morning. Whoever made this mess has big anger-management issues and wanted to pay back our lawyer with some real pain. It's best if we keep everything below the radar."

"I get your drift: no news to anybody but you and the captain. Do we put a guard on his hospital room, or will that attract attention?"

"No guard. I'll touch base with you in the morning."

I wrapped the cat in my scarf, and Dobson helped me with my jacket. As I headed to the door, the crazy cat gave him one last farewell hiss.

"Dobson, get your doctor friend to write up Landry as DOA, and temporarily register the patient as a John Doe. I've got a bad feeling that if the killers find he's still breathing, they'll make another run at him."

Michael Kent

# THREE

It was a perfect evening for a drive: cold and clear, a starry sky, and little traffic. I normally reveled in the throaty rumble of the tuned V-8. I had perhaps a month or less before the snow season would force me to put my maroon classic in winter storage. It had taken me two painstaking years of parts hunting and grease under the fingernails to restore my 1967 Pontiac GTO coupe to its original muscle-car status. It had been worth the effort.

I could have enjoyed every second of the drive home, but I was still disturbed by Colleen's news and the telltale signs of another man in her life.

I had proposed to her under duress—a shotgun wedding, of sorts. "We get married or I'm gone" was her version of a double-barrel twelve-gauge leveled at my chest.

I had discussed Colleen's wedding ultimatum with a minister and longtime friend. Alex, a philosopher by nature and a man of God by calling, had often been my sounding board. He taught me to look at things and events from different angles before making a decision. His admonition had been "Robert, use your brain, not your brawn. I think all those years of weightlifting may hinder more than help you. You charge into situations like a bulldozer with the throttle stuck open. Well, don't. Slide in quietly by a side door and take a fast mental snapshot. What you see in that instant—more importantly, what you *feel* in that nanosecond flash—will be the truthful voice of the still, silent place within you."

I admitted my doubts to him. Colleen wasn't my perfect, self-assured, self-reliant woman. We couldn't just enjoy the day together; we had to be constantly *doing* something: restaurants, clubbing, parties. If I couldn't be there, I was doing something wrong. Conversely, the break-the-headboard-and-rattle-the-walls sex helped me overlook the more problematic aspects of our life together.

Alex reminded me that a healthy sex life was essential to a secure and happy relationship, but that by itself, it made a shaky foundation to build on. I figured we could work things out and that once we

were married, Colleen would feel more secure. But this was wishful thinking. Within a few short weeks of the honeymoon, she was more possessive and demanding than ever. The moral of that story, of course, is that you can't strengthen a weak relationship by marriage; you can only make it worse.

On the drive home, the cat had jumped into the back of the car, where he patrolled the rear window ledge while giving a purring, growling running commentary on passing cars, pedestrians, and my driving skills. Dobson had called me a cat whisperer, and although I did have a persuasive way with animals, I didn't speak cat. The Maine coon had a surprising vocabulary, from the traditional meow to a weird chittering, birdlike sound. I was silently grateful for the big cat's funny antics. They kept the dark feelings over Colleen's departure from overwhelming my mind.

Jean's call had ended my dinner at the restaurant before it began, and by the time I got home, I was starving. I poured myself a pint of Smithwick's Irish Ale—the remnant of a St. Patrick's Day party with some friends from the vice squad—and tossed a quick meal together. When I dropped a can of tuna onto the salad greens, my furry new roomie turned into a meth addict on a two-week binge. He sped back from inspecting his new digs

and, with a running start, leaped up onto the kitchen counter and pounced, all four feet first, into the bowl, knocking over my beer glass as he pawed aside the salad and gulped down the fish. All this mayhem happened in less than six seconds but took fifteen minutes to clean up. It appeared that the cat was hungrier than I.

I surrendered the salad and made myself a mushroom omelet.

After supper, the furry monster resumed his house inspection while I went over the captain's notes. My boss wrote impeccably, with well-chosen words and elegant calligraphy. I, was his polar opposite. I had my own brand of shorthand, scrawling notes fast and often on the fly. Weeks later, I routinely had trouble deciphering my own scribbles. This month, our department was in the midst of something called an operational communications audit. My impenetrable scrawls in the case files had gotten me a written complaint from a Sergeant Lorne Trehearne, a pencil pusher from Internal Affairs who had volunteered for the audit assignment.

Tonight, I had to admit that Jean's penmanship and lucid prose did make my job easier. His description of the scene was as clear as a photograph. He had also done a fast background

check on the victims. Paul Landry was a well-known corporate lawyer in the firm of Landry, Bertoni, Brown, and Levinsky, otherwise known as "LBBL." He was also the host of the television show *The Law and You*. He had gained a reputation as the go-to guy in difficult or unusual litigations, representing high-profile clients in civil, family, and corporate matters. From the carnage at the scene, I would have expected a link to a criminal case, but that wasn't Landry's line of work. The only hint of violence in corporate law is the use of a shotgun clause in a partner buyout, and even there they don't use a real shotgun. Maybe a vitriolic divorce case with a homicidal ex-husband? His having a bodyguard indicated that Landry had feared for his life before the attack. I would start the interviews with his business associates, but my instincts told me I'd have to widen the pool to friends and family. The attack had to be something personal. That the assailants destroyed his face would normally be an indication of a deep, visceral hatred of the victim. It raised questions about the parts of his life that weren't strictly business.

The ID and wallet documents of the second victim showed him to be a former provincial police officer and a professional bodyguard. He had a valid RCMP authorization certificate for his weapon. In Quebec, where it seems you must fill out a ream of

paperwork to purchase a slingshot, this was quite unusual. Also, his Ruger SP101 .357 Magnum revolver with the two-and-a-quarter-inch barrel was on the list of firearms prohibited in Canada. To cut through all the red tape and get the authorizations signed off on for his concealed-carry permit, somebody had serious political weight. Working my way back through this anomaly was on my growing list of things to do in the morning.

A small addendum at the bottom of Jean's note read, "Robert, I remember reading about a messy divorce for Landry a year or so ago. Interview ex-wife."

Not only did my boss write well, he also had a USB flash drive embedded in his brain. The man could remember in minute detail anything he had ever read or seen. If you made a mistake, it might be forgiven, but it could never be erased. This called for creative editing of my reports *before* handing them over to my boss.

Naturally, his note reminded me of my own dissolving marriage, and my mind drifted back to my last conversation with Colleen. I decided to call it a night. Sufficient unto tomorrow were the evils thereof.

# FOUR

My morning started at pre-dawn, with the sixty-grit surface of a feline tongue rasping away at the tip of my nose, and a paw working to pry open my right eyelid.

"Aw, go back to sleep, cat!"

He didn't, and after fending off several attacks on my toes and anything else that moved under the sheets, I gave up. Still half asleep, I plodded to the kitchen to feed him. He tried to climb my pajama leg as I opened a new can of tuna.

"Get off me, you nutcase!"

This early in the morning, the smell of fish was nauseating. The cat, on the other hand, was ecstatic, rolling on the floor and purring like a souped-up Volkswagen.

"Your 'cute' show isn't going to work," I muttered. "Don't expect to be fed this expensive stuff every morning."

When I stepped into the washroom, the stench jolted me fully awake.

He had left a present in the shower. "Oops, my fault," I said to the cat, who was rubbing against my legs. "I forgot to give you a litter box last night." At least his aim was good: a bull's-eye on the floor drain.

I found some bathroom disinfectant and turned the shower to medium scalding; erasing the smelly offering as I came to understand that what goes into a cat must eventually make its way *through* the cat. While I cleaned his mess, the cat playfully spun the toilet paper, unrolling it into a pile on the floor. Shouted warnings of "Stop that, you crazy beast!" only egged him on. I lost the game when I made a last-ditch grab at him and he ran off with several feet of two-ply quilted tissue fluttering like a battle ensign in his wake.

Dressed at last, I walked out into a crisp, cold morning. At the local convenience store, I picked up a couple of breakfast muffins, cat food, and a bag of Everfresh kitty litter. Then I went back to my apartment, filled the cat's food dish, wolfed down the tasty but no doubt artery-clogging French breakfast pastries, and set up a litter bin in the corner of the bathroom. It was nearly nine by the time I got on the road, headed for the LBBL offices.

\* \* \*

Landry's law firm occupied a full floor in one of the prestigious aluminum-and-glass boxes on downtown René Lévesque Boulevard. A plaque in the lobby announced that the building had a LEED gold certification for environmental design and had won the BOMA Building of the Year award in 2010. Although I couldn't have cared less, it surely made some owner or architect very proud.

The receptionist was a well-proportioned middle-aged brunette of stern visage. Smiling, I presented my badge and credentials.

"I need to speak with the partners, Messieurs Bertoni, Brown, and Levinsky."

The credentials didn't impress her, and my smile bounced right off. The stern look darkened to a full scowl.

"Mr. Brown is semiretired and is at his Florida residence, Mr. Levinsky is in court all day today, and you should have made an appointment to see Mr. Bertoni."

I was born impatient and have gotten worse with age. I now score a negative four on the patience scale. I leaned over her desk and dangled my badge an inch from her nose.

"I'm not making an appointment, and you're on the ragged edge of hindering an official police

investigation. I need to see the partners *now.*"

scowl wavered a bit, and she peeked up at me over the badge. "Investigation? What are you talking about?"

I flipped my badge case shut and pocketed it. "Paul Landry was brutally attacked last night." Her eyes went wide, and she folded in the middle, as if her office chair had been traveling forward at high speed and suddenly stopped.

"Wha . . . wha, what?"

I pointed to the many-buttoned telephone on her desk. "Bertoni. Now."

Her hand shook reaching for the phone. "Sylvia, I need you in front."

She seemed weak in the knees when she grabbed the edge of the desk and pulled herself out of her chair. She said, "Follow me to Maître Bertoni's office," emphasizing her request with a beckoning index and middle finger.

I followed her down a carpeted mahogany-wainscoted hallway to the next-to-last door. For a woman in her forties, she had a good stride, and the view from my vantage point was captivating. She knocked once, didn't wait for a reply, and walked in ahead of me.

The occupant was leaning back in his office chair, Gucci-shod feet propped on his polished desk. He was reading a page from a large sheaf of papers.

A Harvard Law School diploma on a side wall proclaimed that this was indeed Matteo Bertoni, Juris Doctor. He had short-cropped blond hair and piercing blue eyes—an odd pairing with such a thoroughly Italian name.

"This policeman says that Paul was attacked last night," said the scowler, plopping down in one of the client chairs.

I did the badge-flip thing again.

"I'm Lieutenant Robert Beaudry," I said. "I need to speak with you in private."

With the barest of movements, Bertoni shook his head. "She stays." He tossed the papers onto his desk and waved at the other client chair. "I don't do interviews without a witness."

I smiled and said as I sat down, "I wouldn't expect anything less from a lawyer. As I indicated to your receptionist—"

"Executive assistant," Stern face corrected.

"Mr. Landry was murdered late last evening."

"*Murdered?*" said Bertoni.

I sat back in the chair. "Beaten to a pulp and then shot in the face."

Stern Face folded from the middle again. This time, her eyes rolled back and she fainted forward off the chair, to land on the plush carpet, hair over her face, lovely bottom in the air, as if she

were crawling on hands and knees. I bent to check her carotid pulse and found a steady beat. Either her blood sugar had bottomed out, or my news had hit her hard. This was probably the first real clue in the case.

# FIVE

We were back in Bertoni's office, facing each other over his cherrywood desk. Stern Face, whom I now knew to be Angela, had been driven home for the day by a long-haired, freckle-faced blonde who could easily have chosen modeling instead of paralegal work. We had managed to revive Angela, and between sobs and tears, she admitted to a more than strictly professional relationship with Landry.

"Did you know that Angela was having an affair with your partner?" I said.

"Yes, Paul had confided in me," Bertoni said. "His wife, Suzanne, suspected something, so she had a private detective follow him."

"Go on."

"The detective snapped a few pictures of the couple holding hands in a restaurant, and again, locked in a passionate kiss in Angela's Volvo. He tried to blackmail Paul. That's when Paul came to

me for advice."

"Which was?"

"Pay him double what he was getting from Suzanne, and have him follow *her* around. Suzanne is a very good-looking woman, but she's a spoiled brat from a well-to-do family. She has a reputation as a round-heeled tramp."

"She sounds like trouble," I said.

Bertoni gave an infinitesimal nod. "Quite so. Her father's a friend of mine. He wanted to keep her busy and get her away from some questionable friends she was hanging around with. I gave her a job as a receptionist. Paul was infatuated with her from day one. *She* was infatuated with his Learjet and his Lamborghini."

"Private jet and a half-million-dollar car," I said. "Your firm seems to be doing well in a poor economy, and you seem to have more than the normal ratio of pretty women around. What's your secret?"

Bertoni ignored the comment and continued. "She set her sights on him. He didn't stand a chance. They got married six months later."

"I thought Landry was a smart lawyer."

Bertoni gave a crooked smile, one corner of his mouth curling up slightly.

"The big head? Yeah, smart as a whip. But he was thinking with the little one. You haven't met Suzanne yet."

I said, "I think it was Neil Gaiman who said something like 'Love is horrible. It makes you so vulnerable. It opens your heart and it means that someone can get inside and mess you up.'" I shook my head, smiling. "Now I understand that she's suing him for his infidelity with Angela."

"That'll be for the court to decide," Bertoni said. "When she insisted on separate bedrooms, Paul realized that his new wife had married for money, not love."

"What happened with the detective you put on Suzanne?"

"A few weeks after the arrangement to spy for Paul instead of Suzanne, the private eye gave him very incriminating pictures of her with two different lovers. Joe Vissani—that's the low-life detective—tried to blackmail both of them. That's another mess that came out in the discovery when she filed for divorce. Then, when that didn't work, he tried to get them into a bidding war for his favorable testimony in court."

I made a sour face. "Not an especially savory character, this Vissani."

"Paul set a trap for him with one of our legal researchers. He secretly recorded a meeting in Paul's

office, then had Vissani arrested for attempted blackmail and extortion. Vissani swore he'd get back at Paul."

"I wondered why Landry had a bodyguard."

Bertoni straightened in his chair.

"Where was André? He should have saved Paul."

"Wasn't much help. They're both dead. At least, now I have a suspect."

Bertoni gave another all-but-subliminal head shake. "Afraid not, Lieutenant. Vissani was killed by another inmate in a holding cell a few months ago."

"Rats."

"Who knows about Paul's death?" Bertoni said, reaching for the phone.

"Whoa, no phone calls. No news to anyone. I'm keeping this under wraps for now."

"I have to tell his uncle. He's the one that provided the bodyguard."

"Who's the uncle? And no, you don't tell a soul until you get an okay from me. We won't release the body for a few days, until the tox report and autopsy are complete."

"His uncle is Jean Landry, a fellow lawyer I went to school with—very politically connected and related to an ex-premier of Quebec."

"That explains it."

"Explains what?"

I made a waving motion. "Never mind. What cases was Landry working on? Any recently divorced husbands who had a grudge against him? Or some ugly and expensive corporate problem that could have provoked his murder?"

Bertoni shook his head for real this time.

"I'm at a loss for words. Can't think of anything."

He looked down at his desk blotter and grew silent and pensive for a moment, as if measuring his words before speaking.

"Paul didn't have many cases in the past few months. The bad publicity surrounding his divorce has scared clients off."

"I remember something inane on the evening news a few weeks ago," I said. "Something about the wife demanding custody of a picture album."

Bertoni waved his hand dismissively. "The press blew everything out of proportion. Suzanne is terribly vain—wanted all the pictures of Paul and her with various famous people on trips and at parties. Paul told her that when he found out about her infidelity, he threw her picture album into the fireplace. She went ballistic. It overflowed to the outside of this building, where, surprisingly, reporters were waiting."

I stopped scribbling in my notepad. "Who tipped off the press?"

"Paul thinks Suzanne did it to get favorable news coverage."

"You seem hesitant in saying that."

"There wasn't much time between Paul's admission at the discovery meeting here in the boardroom and Suzanne's storming out of the building. The reporters had to have been called in way before."

"Somebody else tipped them off?" I said. "This is getting twisted. You're certain you can't think of anything in his case files that would lead to the attack? I'd like a peek at a list of his clients."

"As I said, Paul hasn't been very active lately. After his divorce hit the newspapers, he took a leave of absence. I'm stuck taking care of most of his clients." Bertoni stood up as if to indicate that the interview was over.

"I have a few more questions, Mr. Bertoni." Bertoni pointed to his law diploma.

"*Maître* Bertoni," he said with a sudden snap
in his tone. "I have to get back to work. In any case, our files are off limits to you. I can't tell you anything without a court order. Our work is confidential."

My jaw tightened. "Never mind the client-confidentiality crap. I didn't ask for details. It's a yes-or-no answer: is there anything that could have

provoked his murder?"

Bertoni's face tinged pink, and his voice dropped a full octave. "No." The temperature in the room seemed to drop a few degrees—the interview was over.

I beat him to the punch. "That's enough for today," I said. "I'll let you get back to work, but I'll be back with more questions."

Michael Kent

# SIX

On my drive to the hospital, I called Dobson.
"Anything new from the crime scene, Dr. Watson?"

"Partial footprints at the scene confirm there were three assailants. No fingerprints—they wore gloves."

"Criminals must buy surgical gloves wholesale now," I said. "I can't remember the last case with latent prints coming up. Any good news at all?"

"Eh, I experimented on a gelatin slab with a number of blades. The one that comes closest to both victims' wounds is a Vietnamese haxit, a sort of chopped-off machete. I'm trying to find how available that type of weapon is in Montreal."

"And you're going to tell me it's a ten-inch blade, as you predicted."

"As it happens, eh, yes."

"Did you find an agenda or memo book indicating a meeting with someone that day?"

"Nope. You're going to have to do some more Sherlocking, Lieutenant. But this may interest you. In his desk, he had a printout for the rental of a sixty-two-foot Azimut Flybridge out of south Florida, for three weeks from now. But I, eh, didn't find plane tickets to Miami."

I made a mental note to question the stern-faced Angela about this little southern adventure.

"The guy didn't need a plane ticket," I said. "He has his own jet, with a side of Lamborghini to go. There seems to be no shortage of money around this case."

"I reported to our boss, eh. He had notes on Landry's divorce. The wife is asking for a twelve-million-dollar settlement."

"Can you dig up his tax records, his financial background? Do the same on his LBBL partners. All this luxury for a small law firm doesn't smell right."

"I'll get somebody on that. By the way, Lieutenant, with all due respect, I'm CSI, not your secretary."

"Not a secretary, Dobson—a partner. On my side, I found out Landry's well connected politically. His family name should have rung a bell for me. While he had, or is having, an affair with one of his associates' executive assistant, he has proof that his

wife was doing some horizontal dancing with at least two other partners. I'm not sure she should be banking on the twelve million just yet.

Brush your teeth and comb your hair. This mess is going to make the headlines for sure."

"Eh, sorry for the comment. None of the other detectives keep me in the loop. I'm just a lab rat for them."

"Well, then comb your hair and brush your tail. We're a team. I get in the news, so do you. I'm headed to the hospital. I'll check back with you later, Dr. Watson."

"Roger, Lieutenant." I could tell from the timbre of his voice that he had that toothy grin.

Dobson's comment that nobody gave him feedback was a surprise. It must be unrewarding to provide all the technical data and then never find out what happened to the case or even what his contribution had been. My treating him as an associate instead of an underling brought up sad memories for me. I had lost my partner of seven years to prostate cancer some six months back. The captain had yet to find someone I could work with, and so, with my usual disrespect for hierarchy and protocol, I had decided to latch on to Dobson. If they saw him as just a lab rat, they were underestimating his skills.

The visitors' lot at the hospital had a "full" sign. While parking is a problem in most large cities, in Montreal it's a near impossibility. Between all the construction cones, streets blocked off for repair, and too few parking lots, you have to be creative in finding somewhere close and safe to put your car. I parked in the reserved-for-customers area of a pharmacy across the street from the hospital and stuck my "official police vehicle" sign on the dashboard, hoping it would give the towing contractor second thoughts.

At the reception desk, an elderly woman with parchment-gray skin and lipstick the color of venous blood directed me to Dobson's friend, Dr. Blain. As in most hospitals, I had to navigate a maze of identical-looking corridors. I asked for directions at a floor station, saying I wasn't lost, just navigationally confused. A pretty nurse with pale skin and big bright-green eyes smiled and pointed me in the right direction.

Dr. Blain's hospital office was slightly larger than a modest-size pantry. He sat on a stool, clutching an iPad. I sat sideways on the corner of his patient chair, my right elbow brushing the pale-avocado wall.

At five feet nine and a half inches and with a long lineage of broad-shouldered farmers, and years of serious weightlifting, I have, as some of my police

colleagues are fond of saying, the dimensions of a walking refrigerator.

"Good thing I'm not claustrophobic," I said.

"It's temporary—renovations again."

Blain was pale of face, round of cheek, and sparse of hair. He did have soft brown, trustworthy eyes—surely an asset for a doctor.

So far, everyone in this hospital seemed pallid, as if they had given up trying to find their way out of the corridor maze and into the sunlight.

"I'd like to see our John Doe," I said. "I understand he was in pretty bad condition when they brought him in."

"If, by 'pretty bad,' you mean his face looked like a side of beef dragged over a quarter mile of bad road, then yes, he was. But I've seen worse. It's mostly superficial. Once the swelling goes down, he'll be left with a few pockmarks on the face—nothing a touch of plastic surgery can't take care of."

"So the prognosis is good?"

Blain gave me a fast Gallic chin shrug, his lower lip in a pout.

"The head trauma's the problem. He'll survive, but I don't know about permanent brain damage yet."

"Can I see him?"

"I'm nearly finished with my rounds, and I'm not due at my clinic for another forty minutes. I've

hidden him upstairs in geriatrics. I'll walk you there."

***

Blain had finished his examinations and was scribbling in Doctorese on his iPad patient file. On the other side of Landry's bed, I was sweltering in the overwarm room.

"Am I running a fever, or is it steamier than a devil's fart in here?"

Blain smiled. "Geriatrics is kept a bit warmer than the other floors."

"A *bit* warmer'?" I slipped off my leather jacket. "It's like high noon on the sunny side of Mercury."

With his head bandaged up completely, and holes for his eyes and mouth, Paul Landry looked like the invisible man. Tubes and wires snaked between him and various bags and bottles and to a bank of machines behind his bed.

"With all the plumbing and stuff you have plugged into him, he looks like a terminal case," I said. "I can never understand how one person could hurt another so badly. Years as a cop, and I still have trouble comprehending that an instant of rage can turn a human being into a vicious animal."

Blain made another pouting shrug. "Actually, he's in pretty good shape. The brain-wave data is

good on the last EEG. I've reduced the meds. It's just a matter of time before he wakes up."

"How much time?"

"In these cases, hard to say. Could be in the next fifteen minutes, could be fifteen days. The sooner he wakes, the better the prognosis."
Blain finished his notes and headed to the door. "You want to follow me out?"

"No, I think I'll stay a while. Maybe he'll snap out of it and I can solve my case in the next fifteen minutes."

The doc wished me luck as I headed for the visitor's chair to mentally rehash what I knew about the case so far.

The warm, stuffy room must have gotten to me. A woman's yelp jolted me awake. I stood up to face a tall nurse in nicely fitting pale-blue scrubs. She yelped again.

"I'm sorry, did I scare you?" I said. Flipping my badge holder open, I noted the "M. Zotti" on her name tag and nothing on her left ring finger.

She took a step back, taking time to look me over. "Surprised, mostly. It's not every day I find a big brute of a man—wearing a gun, no less—in one of my patient rooms."

I crossed my arms in mock indignation. "'Big brute of a man'—now, is that a compliment, or a slur on my size?"

"No slur at all," she said with a demure smile but also a seductive tilt of the head. "You have that handsome, rugged look." Her eyes glowed like warm honey.

I ogled away as she checked IV levels and monitors. Her every movement flowed like a dancer's. Or maybe it was just deprivation—in the past few months before my breakup, there had been no romance. Nurse M. Zotti exuded a sexual energy that made the already warm room seem downright tropical.

Reaching over the bed to inspect an intravenous drip, she turned her head and looked me in the eyes. "Bold, too. I caught you staring at my ass."

"I'm a trained observer. You have no panty lines."

She grinned. "You don't know that for certain."

"That would require a more thorough investigation," I said, giving her my full-power smile.

She stood facing me, a look of silent appraisal on her face. Pretending to stare over her short dark auburn curls at one of the patient monitor screens, I felt frozen in time, awaiting her next words.

"I get off at seven thirty. I sometimes drop

into McCarold's before heading home. It's about three blocks west of here."

My blood pressure rose another notch, and I cleared my throat. "Okay, seven thirty sounds good," I said in the best baritone I could manage. "I'll hold off on the APB until eight."

She licked her lips and gave her hair a subtle toss. "Well, I'd love to chat more, but I have to finish my rounds."

I stood at attention. "And I have to get back to chasing criminals."

I picked up my jacket and wiped a bead of sweat from my upper lip as she glided out of the room.

Michael Kent

# SEVEN

I got back to my car just in time to see a heavyset tow truck driver hooking it up.

"Whoa, buddy! Didn't you see my 'police vehicle' sign on the dash?"

"Big deal. You can get one of those for two bucks."

"Trust me, this one is real. Unhook the car."

He gave me the middle-finger salute. "Read the sign on the wall, pal."

The obscene gesture was half the mistake; the other half was making it while standing within arm's reach of me. I latched on to the upraised digit. He grabbed my wrist to break the hold, but this had no effect on the slow backward bending of his finger.

"This finger has committed an offense against an officer of the law," I said. "I may have to break it off and bring it downtown as evidence."

He tried to twist around to relieve the painful pressure, but nothing worked.

He wound up on his knees, with tears in his eyes. With my free hand, I flashed my badge.

"Sorry, sorry, Detective," he said in a strained voice. "It didn't look like a police vehicle. My mistake."

"I'll have to give you that one, buddy" I said, letting go.

"Tony," he said. "Antonio Borsellino."

I got a hint of a smile when I said, "Sounds like a movie star name."

While he massaged his tender hand, I took the liberty of pressing one of the levers on his truck and unhooking my Pontiac.

Not needing another complaint in my file, I said, "Sorry about this little misunderstanding." I fished a business card from my jacket pocket. "You ever get yourself in a situation, give me a call. I'll see what I can do."

I wrote my cell phone number on the back of the card and gave it to him.
Like a Japanese businessman, he took the card in both hands.

"You serious?"

"No joke, Tony. If you ever get a tit in the wringer, call me. By the way, I like the snake tat down the side of your neck—good three-D effect." I got into my car, fired it up, and gave him a wave as I cut into traffic.

A half block down the road, my cell phone started making impatient electronic-rattlesnake pulsations in my pocket. There's no Bluetooth in a sixty-seven GTO, so I slid into a space in front of a hydrant. It was an unknown private number.

"Beaudry."

"Lieutenant Beaudry, this is Eli Kraus from Revenu Québec."

"I paid my taxes," I said. "Call my accountant; I'll give you his number."

"No, no, you're misunderstanding. I got your number from a Mr. Dobson. You're asking for financial information on several people. I'm a tax inspector. Your investigation is crossing mine. I think we should meet."

I sighed. "Sorry I was quick on the trigger. Quebec taxes are a sore point with me. Remind me, your name again?"

"Eli Kraus, special investigations unit, Revenu Québec. Are you free for lunch today?"

I chuckled. "Huh! Seems I'm not the only one fast on the trigger. Lunch where? What time?"

We agreed on a time, and he named a downtown Lebanese restaurant. My instincts on LBBL's ostentatious show of expensive toys seemed to be on target. Nine and a half times out of ten, a murder is about a woman or money. This one was probably both.

The second I put my phone down, it drummed its little tune again. This time, it was a number I knew.

"Hey, Nico."

"*Come stai,* big guy?"

"I'm good. What's up?"

"We're about to raid Jimmy Stevens, the drug dealer. It's on Ontario Street, where you had a body on the sidewalk last month. I remember you telling me he was a less-than-cooperative witness. Thought you might want to join in."

"It was a drive-by shooting from a rival street gang," I said. "I got the perp. He had the poor judgment to dis his girlfriend; she gave him up."

"More corroboration doesn't hurt your case," Nico said.

"Good point. When's showtime?"

"Tomorrow morning, just before lunch."

"Okay, I'm on. Jimmy pissed me off. A body on his doorstep, nine shots fired. Three hit the victim, one a parked car, two the front door, three his living-room window—one of these punching a hole in his wide-screen Sanyo—but Mr. Stevens didn't hear a thing, didn't know nuttin'."

"He may open up a bit more when he's in custody," Nico said before signing off. "Metal around the wrists often seems to jog the memory."

Sergeant Nico Di Lalla of the vice squad was a longtime friend and a good cop. Unfortunately,

some members of his immediate family were on the other side of the badge, which hindered his chances of promotions. On the plus side, his uncle Mario had a direct line to the local don, and the crime boss had often given me information on cases where it suited his organization.

I put the car back in gear, enjoying the throaty burble of the big V-8 as I headed to the office and the reams of paperwork piling up on my desk.

Michael Kent

# EIGHT

I had nearly made it to my office when the disembodied voice of my boss resonated down the corridor.

"Beaudry, I need to see you."

No one could sneak into the building without his knowing it.

I backtracked two offices. "Jean, either you have an IP camera hidden somewhere in the woodwork, or you're a true psychic."

"My door is always open, and your heavy footsteps are unmistakable." Jean pointed to the ratty old guest chair. "Sit."

"Wazzup, boss?"

"That's my question." Jean tilted back and put his hands on top of his head, squishing down his immaculate brush cut. "Last night, we had a dead bodyguard and a nearly dead lawyer. This morning, Sergeant Dobson informed me that Paul Landry is

doing better, this just minutes after I received a hostile phone call from one of his law partners, telling me that you bullied his whole office while informing them that Landry was murdered."

I groaned. "You didn't tell him otherwise, did you?"

"No, I told him Landry was critically wounded and that I hadn't checked with the hospital yet, and I'd get back to him with some news. So, Beaudry, I'd appreciate knowing what your plan is on this."

"What makes you think I have a plan?"

"*Sacramentos*, don't tell me this is about to blow up into a publicity nightmare again." Jean didn't upset easily, but when he did, he always added his modified version of French profanities.

"No, no news to anybody. The guy was beat up worse than the cheating husband of a female cage fighter. I figured somebody really wanted him squashed like a bug. I'm trying to protect him until he wakes up. I'm playing this by ear."

"*Calvase*, your politically incorrect play by ear always generates aggravation for me. The news media will blow this all out of proportion: 'Famous lawyer dies and comes back to life.' Are you insane, Robert? You're going to make us look like idiots—again."

I put my hands up in surrender. "You can't

leave that little fender bender alone, can you? You're going to hang that over my head for all eternity?"

"Yes, because we'll be in court for all eternity. You stole a snowplow, managed to rip the front off a police cruiser, and sideswiped six civilian cars."

"The guy had just murdered the Vietnamese storekeeper. I wasn't about to let him escape. Besides, I only *borrowed* the snowplow—gave it back with barely a scratch."

Jean double-stabbed the desk blotter with his middle finger. "Let's get back to the Landry situation. Fix it, Robert. Bring him back to life and smooth things over with his law firm, *period*."

"Okay, okay." I dropped my hands. "Speaking of his law firm, they're replete with private jets and fancy cars. My intuition tells me something's fishy. In fact, I just got a call from an agent from Revenu Québec. He's investigating LBBL and wants a meet."

"Beaudry, *facts* solve the case. Intuition, on the other hand, is what generally gets you in the middle of a shootout. And now that other agencies are involved, I can predict this is going to turn ugly. So keep me informed *as things happen,* not two days later." Jean picked up a report and moved it to the center of his desk. I was getting pretty good at picking up the signs that a meeting was over.

"Have a good day, boss," I said as I left.

I fired up my outdated office computer and opened an e-mail from Dobson. It confirmed what he had told me over the phone.

He also added something new that piqued my interest: his last paragraph was a summary of an interview with Landry's housekeeper, confirming that he was planning a vacation and that she was preparing to close up the house for an indefinite period. I queried the database and found the address and phone number for Angela Andreadis, Mr. Landry's office paramour. Then I mounted a halfhearted attack on the growing pile of papers on my desk. I cleared up a few late reports, then headed to my meeting with Kraus, the tax guy.

# NINE

This time, I opted for a parking lot. The scraggly-bearded attendant with a Slavic accent was dressed as if he had just escaped from the gulag. He complimented me on my car, but I still had to pay the stiff fee in advance and leave my keys.

"Can you please take special care of it?"

"I'll treat it like my own," he managed to say with a straight face. It didn't comfort me.

I walked down a block to Maisonneuve Boulevard and the Lebanese restaurant. As I entered, a slim fiftyish man with salt-and-pepper hair waved at me from a table at the rear of the small dining room. He was sitting with a spectacular raven-haired young woman who looked to be of Mediterranean descent.

"How did you recognize me?" I asked, staring past Kraus to the dark-haired beauty seated beside him.

"Sergeant Dobson told me to look for a wide

Schwarzenegger type with blond hair."

I sat down across from him and extended my hand to the woman beside him.

"This is my colleague Zafirah," Kraus said with a smile. We shook hands all around. They had solid grips, looked me straight in the eyes, then both handed me their business cards.

"Kraus—isn't that Jewish German?" I said. "And you favor a Lebanese restaurant?"

"I favor good food. Besides, I have to practice my Arabic—it's one of the ten languages I speak," Kraus added with a subtle grin.

"Only eight fluently," Zafirah observed.

Kraus gave her a gentle push with his shoulder. "Enough with the chitchat. Let's get business out of the way so we can enjoy the food. I understand that Paul Landry was murdered and that you're in charge of the investigation."

"This meeting is confidential, we agree?" I got affirming nods from both. "Murdered' may have been a bit of an exaggeration on my part. He's in bad shape—in a coma but still breathing. I have him hidden in case somebody tries to have another go at him."

"It's good you have him secreted away," said Kraus. "The Russians will try again if they know he's still alive."

"Russians?"

Zafirah closed her eyes momentarily, and the corners of her mouth turned down. *"Mitri Korisky."*

Kraus continued the thread. "We're ninety percent sure that LBBL is laundering money for the Russian mob. Korisky is the local rep and enforcer—a sadistic killer who likes to make bloody examples of people who annoy him. A story on the street is that a waitress once spilled hot soup on his lap. He had her kidnapped abused her for two days then cut off one of her fingers as a reminder."

"The doc said Landry's face looked like undercooked hamburger," I said. "That sounds like the same type of handiwork to me."

"Zafirah made friends with an executive assistant in LBBL," Kraus said. "She was supposed to talk Landry into a meeting with us. Korisky may have found out."

"Angela—Landry's mistress," I said.

Zafirah gave me a sideways smile. "You know?"

"To be quite honest," Kraus said in a hushed voice, "we were leveraging Paul's illicit relationship to get him to cooperate."

"Blackmailing the informant," I said to Kraus. "Sneaky and underhanded. I'm beginning to like you already."

The waiter interrupted our conversation to recite the daily specials. Once we placed our orders,

we turned back to business. Zafirah pulled out folded sheets from a soft leather Hermes purse big enough to hold a full-size laptop.

"This is a list"—she made a side-to-side rotating motion with her open hand—"totaling, we think, forty-six million dollars of real estate transactions made in the past two years. Purchases by Korisco, Kor holdings, MKR development, and Mitroco Financial—all companies incorporated with the help of Charles Brown, Esquire, who is also legal counsel for all of them."

"All companies that list Mitri Korisky as principal shareholder," Kraus added.

"Forty-six million, more or less?" I said.

Zafirah made the same hand motion again. "Could be double that. They have intercompany loans, transfers, and a number of irregular financial transactions. And, they may have sold some assets that we're not aware of."

Zafirah slid the list back into her expensive bag as our waiter appeared with the lavish meal that Kraus had ordered for the table.

While we ate copious lunch, Kraus and Zafirah gave me a crash course in real estate fraud: overvaluing and flipping, undervaluing schemes, called "flopping," and various other ways of defrauding banks or laundering illicit funds. Both tax investigators impressed me with their eagerness and

knowledge. The bottom line was that they had a lot of incriminating data pointing to LBBL's being partners with the Russian mob, and they were fiercely determined to nail Korisky and the crooked lawyers.

The bank rip-off lessons over, Kraus ordered a honey-dripping baklava, and Zafirah ordered Turkish kahvesi for herself and me.

"This coffee is delicious—probably the strongest I've ever had," I said. "I'll be up all night."

It surprised me when demure Zafirah raised her cup in salute and said, "Hopefully, not alone."

Kraus pushed aside the flaky remnants of his dessert. "What's our next step?"

"My CSI partner found a reservation for a yacht trip. It looks like Landry was either planning a long romantic getaway or running away from something. I'm going to question Angela. I'll keep you informed. In the meantime, send your data to Dobson. We'll see if we can find something that will allow a subpoena of Landry's files."

"We were already going that route," said Kraus. "But a judge is going to look kindlier on a wide subpoena for a murder case than for fraud. Better still, I can use your info on the trip to show intent to flee. Our department has shortcuts to seizures and confiscation; let's just coordinate beforehand. I don't want to give the partners any

warning."

"You're right," I said. "At this point, we're not sure who's involved at LBBL: all of them or just some of them."

"Our department motto is, 'When in doubt, seize everything,'" Kraus said.

"And you also have a bit of a rep for shooting first and asking questions later. We should get along fine."

"My reputation is exaggerated, though I get the job done . . ." I reached over the table to shake his hand. ". . . with the help of friends."

After I paid the bill, Zafirah burrowed in her purse and handed me a summary of LBBL transactions for Korisky and company, then gave me a high five and a wink.

As we left, I promised to call them back after my meeting with Angela.

# TEN

At 3:20 in the afternoon, I was crawling along in second gear in the northbound center lane of Decarie Boulevard. Today, it resembled a funeral procession more than an expressway.

My GPS dash cam setup hinted that I should double my twenty-minute estimate to Angela's house in suburban Saint-Laurent. In the car ahead of me, a young woman was bobbing her head in a familiar rhythm. A texting beat: look down to the phone in her lap, then back up to make sure she didn't bump into the slow-moving procession ahead of her.

I reached for my phone. Dobson answered on the first ring.

"Hi, I just finished my meeting with Kraus the tax guy and his stunning associate. I can't even describe her; you'll have to see for yourself."

"I wouldn't be interested. In case you haven't Sherlocked it already, I'm gay."

"Dr. Watson, that doesn't change your skill sets. No difference to me, but I thank you for your straightforwardness. It shows trust."

He paused a beat, then said, "I, eh, enjoy working on this case with you, Lieutenant. I didn't want my orientation to interfere with our teamwork."

"Working relationships are independent of gender," I said. "They work or they don't. In my case, my wife just dumped me for another guy, so if I act impatient, you'll know I'm just in a lousy mood these days."

"Ah, eh, okay. Honesty begets honesty. I didn't expect you to share that."

"Back to business. The tax investigators suspect that LBBL is laundering money for the Russian mafia. They were trying to get Landry to turn informer, and they implied that Mitri Korisky, the local mob enforcer, may be responsible for his attempted murder."

"Eh, I'll search the databases for info on Korisky. What else do you need?"

"In the spirit of cooperation, can you e-mail Landry's yacht reservation to Kraus? He'll use it to show risk of flight and ask for a writ of seizure on Landry's office files."

"Done. I have an e-mail from Kraus with his office info."

Movement in the left-side mirror caught my eye. A provincial Sûreté motorcycle patrolman pulled alongside and waved me over to the emergency lane.

"I'm being pulled over for talking while driving," I said. "I'll touch base after I meet with Angela. Keep the boss informed." I hung up on Dobson and flashed my badge at the cop next to me, impressing myself with my flip speed. If could get to my holster that fast, I'd be the fastest gun in Dodge. I caught his eye and tilted my head toward the still-texting woman in the car ahead. He got the message and moved up with his flashers on. The traffic was clearing, and I moved the Hurst T-bar shifter up to third gear and swung into a spot in the fast lane.

\* \* \*

Angela lived in new Saint-Laurent. I hadn't been in this part of the island for a few years. Row condominiums and high-end houses had sprouted like mushrooms after a week of rain. Her housing complex had the units arranged in a horseshoe facing a common green, where a maintenance man seemed to be inspecting some bushes. I crossed to her address on the inside of the crescent.

She opened her door at the first ring, as if she was expecting someone.

"Oh, it's you!"

"Who were you waiting for?"

"A delivery—they never tell you what time. What do you want?"

I looked down into her reddened eyes. "I came to apologize for this morning."

She shuffled her feet. "Come in."

I sat in the middle of her low couch, and she perched on the edge of a brass-studded leather side chair perpendicular to me. Tears welled in her eyes.

"You weren't exactly diplomatic, but I guess you were just doing your job."

I clumsily bumped one of her accent cushions to the floor as I slid closer to her. "This morning, I told you and Bertoni that Paul was dead. In truth, he isn't."

For an instant, she became a statue of herself. Then she said, "What . . . ? Where's Paul? Is he okay? Why would you do that? Is this a bad joke?"

"Slow down," I said. "Paul is in the hospital, in a coma, but the prognosis seems good. His attackers think he's dead. I wanted to protect him and get the reactions of his partners—surprise is hard to fake."

"We're *suspects*? Why would you think anyone in the office would hurt Paul? Are you unwell?"

"I've just had lunch with Kraus and Zafirah.

We need to talk."

"Are you arresting me?" Angela clasped her shaking hands together and sucked in her lips.

"Whoa, you lost me on that one. Why would I arrest you?"

"I've known for over a year that Charles is laundering money. Until I, uh, told Paul, I didn't have the guts to say anything about it. Eli Kraus says I'm an accomplice and I might be prosecuted."

"Charles?"

"Brown, Mr. B-Brown."

Afraid she was about to fall apart on me again, I moved closer and held her forearms loosely.

"Relax, Angela. Nobody's going to arrest you. Take a deep breath. You're as nervous as a long-tailed cat in a room full of rocking chairs."
My dad's old saying made her crack a strained smile, but I still felt her trembling.

"This is all just too much for me," she said. "A tear rolled down her cheek. "I'm so confused."

She went limp, and I dropped to one knee in front of her. She bent forward, her head resting between my neck and shoulder. For a long while, I held her in my arms while she sobbed in silence.

Michael Kent

# ELEVEN

Angela was on the sofa, legs tucked under her, both hands wrapped around a mug of coffee.

"When can I see Paul?"

I put my canned soda down on a little zebra-patterned side table beside me.

"As soon as he wakes up," I said. "I don't want visitors attracting attention to the location. He's safer that way. Kraus thinks the Russians may try and finish him off."

"Russians?"

"The laundered money—it's for the Russian mafia."

"Oh, no, no, no." Angela started to wobble, and I caught her tilting coffee cup as she teared up again.

"Enough with the blubbering," I said. "Shape up. You have to help me get these people so Paul and you can stay safe."

"I . . . I just thought that . . . that it was crooked financiers. It's all my fault for getting Paul involved with this."

"Take a deep breath," I said, "and tell me everything from the beginning."

Angela gave me chapter and verse on her work with law partner Charles Brown, his initial Florida meeting with Korisky, and the setting up of his various companies. In the first few months, the operations seemed legitimate as Brown had Angela transfer more and more funds from international banks and financial institutions to local corporate accounts. But when intercompany sales and substantiating documents were missing or prepared retroactive to the transfers, it made her curious. Her curiosity turned to suspicion when she collated the fiscal year's figures. It was apparent to Angela that Korisky's companies were grossly overbilled. When she questioned Brown on a particular invoice, he promoted her to executive assistant for Bertoni and Landry. She never got an answer on the trumped-up invoice.

"We worked late hours together, Paul and I, "Angela said. "He started confiding in me about his marital problems, and one thing led to another until I realized I was in love with him. Now he's been

beaten half to death and it's my fault."

"Don't point a finger at yourself," I said. "We don't know what happened yet."

"Last week, after we had, um, an evening together, I told Paul about the overbilling and the strange transactions. He was to meet Charles to talk about it."

"You think Brown is the only one involved in this?"

"I don't know what to think anymore." Angela shook her head slowly. "Matteo asked me questions about my work with Charles, but I don't think he's involved. Charles is the managing partner and founder of the firm. He does pretty well what he pleases. Nobody complains, and we get substantial cash bonuses each year."

"Cash?"

"Well, Quebec taxes are brutal. Cash is king."

I wasn't surprised. Quebec had always had whole separate under-the-table economy, which the government was fighting hard to eradicate, with limited success.

The doorbell chimed, ending our discussion. A courier asked for Angela's signature and handed her a carton the size of a shoe box.

She came back to the sofa holding the box tightly to her chest. The shipping label was upside down but faced me.

"A package from LBBL?" I said. "What's in it?"

Her cheeks flushed. "Do I have to tell you?"

"Angela, I thought we were being open and honest. You're squeezing that box hard enough to bruise it."

"It's Paul's bonus. A hundred and twenty-three thousand from his office safe. I mailed it to myself." She placed the box on the coffee table and swallowed.

"He asked me to hide it." Her voice fell to a whisper. "His wife is after everything he owns."

"Does this have anything to do with the Florida trip?"

Angela backed up and flopped onto the sofa.

"We're trying to get away from Suzanne. She has people following us daily, and her lawyer is trying to find all of Paul's assets to build up a claim. Paul comes from a very wealthy family. I think his wife's new boyfriend is pushing her to get millions that she doesn't deserve. We just wanted to get away, get some peace and some time together."

"Angela, don't go back to the office," I said. "Take some time off. I'll call you with news on Paul later today."

"Her face went pale. "Am I in danger?"

"I don't know at this point. Just don't take chances." I left her my cell number and Dobson's. She stood up and hugged me tight before I left. She seemed relieved to have gotten the story out.

Michael Kent

# TWELVE

It was a little before six in the afternoon, my big lunch had long since digested, and I was starving again. At my size, it takes a fair amount of daily caloric intake to keep the motor humming. I was driving back downtown for my date with Nurse Zotti, hoping for a decent meal, and perhaps, with her as dessert. At this hour, Decarie would be a parking lot. I was on a side street, avoiding the slowdown, when I remembered that I had to resurrect Landry from the dead before my boss launched into another fit of French swearing. Whipping into a fast-food parking lot, I pulled out Bertoni's business card and punched in his cell number. To my surprise, he answered on the second ring.

I used the polite French form of address for a lawyer. "*Maître* Bertoni, sorry to disturb you. This is Lieutenant Beaudry."

"Go ahead; I was just leaving the office."

"I just came out of the hospital," I lied. "Paul was officially dead on arrival in the emergency room, but miraculously, they managed to revive him. He's still in a coma, and they aren't sure of the outcome. I just wanted to let you know."

"That's great news. Thank you, Lieutenant. What hospital is he in?"

"He may still be in danger, so I have him incommunicado for now. He's off limits to everyone, and his whereabouts are confidential." I could hear the smirk in my voice.

"That's unacceptable. I want to know where he is."

"You needn't bother calling my boss," I said. "He doesn't know, either. I'll keep you informed of his condition. You can rely on me."

Bertoni hung up without a word.

"What's good for the goose . . . ," I said to the dead line.

\* \* \*

I walked into Miss Zotti's after-work hangout at fourteen minutes to seven. The place was a cozy, nicely done imitation of a Dublin pub. I opted for the bar so I could monitor the front door. I sat at the last stool, taking up roughly twice the space of a normal-size customer.

The barmaid was a leggy brunette in a nicely filled white blouse and way-too-short tight black skirt. She kept tugging her hem down as if she had a nervous tick. She made her way toward me, with every straight male eye at the bar following her.

"What can I get you, honey?" she asked.

"The embroidery on your blouse says 'Jasmine,'" I said. "Doesn't sound all that Irish."

"It's not my real name, and I'm Lebanese. The drinks are all authentic Irish, though. What'll it be?"

"Well, your cheeks glow like an Irish girl's. You have beautiful skin."

"I'm good with makeup. You here to flirt or you want a drink?"

"In keeping with the Gaelic atmosphere, I'll go with a Smithwick's."

She went to the tap, poured, let the foam settle, and then added a little more, scraping off the excess head with a little wood ruler.

"Good choice of beer," she said, setting the brimming glass delicately in front of me. "And you have a pretty good line."

"Just practicing. I'm meeting a pretty nurse here."

Jasmine nodded sideways. "Half the crowd is from the hospital. Good luck, honey."

I raised my glass in salute as she took off to serve another patron.

Two beers later, Nurse Zotti glided in the front door and came toward me with that same smooth, catlike walk.

I said, "Miss Zotti, you're so graceful, you don't walk; you just sort of *flow* across a room."

"Ten years of yoga, my charming sir."

She unbuttoned her gray leather coat. The wait was worth it, every minute. She wore a three-quarter-sleeve red dress that fit her like a wet T-shirt.

"Wow—uh, I mean, hello." I stood up and took another look at her. "No, on second thought, I'll leave it at 'wow.'"

The barmaid came around to hug Nurse Zotti. "Zee, watch out for this guy," she said. "He's a big flirt."

"I know. So am I." She kissed Jasmine on both cheeks and added one for good measure.

"Zee?" I said.

"My given name is Marizza. Combined with 'Zotti,' it's a lot of 'z's."

Jasmine pointed to a secluded table. "I reserved it for you," she said to Zee.

We moved to the table at the end of the bar.

"I wasn't sure you'd show up," I said. "I'm glad you did."

"I wasn't sure, either. It's very unusual for

me to be interested in a man so fast."

"It's my magnetic personality," I said. "Then again, magnets repel as well as attract. I lost a wife this week but gained a big furry cat."

"If you like cats, you can't be all bad. But I see I'm a rebound flirtation."

"Not really. It had been sliding downhill for a while. She just made it official yesterday."

Zee reached for my hand. "Ah, so the big guy got dumped, poor dear."

"I'm sure she's been on the north side of cheating for a while. Hard to keep a relationship—I sometimes work around the clock."

"North side of cheating?"

"She has someone up in Ottawa."

Jasmine brought the menu, a white wine for Zee, and another beer for me.

I slid the menu to Zee. She slid it back to me. "Rania knows to get me my usual," she said.

"So Jasmine's real name is Rania."

"Can't hide much from a detective," she said, again with that delicious grin. "I may as well give you my story, too. I came out of a two-year relationship six weeks ago. I work irregular hours and sometimes double shifts, and yeah, it's hard on relationships. But I was the dumper, not the dumpee."

"So we're both on the rebound." I smiled.

"And free to flirt away."

Zee fluffed her hair "Uh, that requires a more thorough investigation. Let's regain our strength first. I recommend any of the pub sandwiches or the black velvet ribs."

She was on target with the ribs. I enjoyed the meal, and Zee's company even more. She talked about her job; I talked a bit about my police work.

We quickly moved on to personal histories and feelings. I had her giggling like a schoolgirl over my misadventures with the newly adopted kitty.

"All cats are crackers," Zee said. "They have a daily crazy hour."

"*Crackers*—that describes him perfectly! You just named my furry fiend."

As the evening progressed, Zee grew less talkative. She seemed introspective, and it occurred to me that I may not have interested her enough for a second date. Then she surprised me.

"Robert, you're very open and honest. I want to be, too. I'm not interested in a serious relationship right now in my life. I really enjoy being with you, and you turn me on—something I haven't felt with a man in years."

"I think we're on the same page, Zee. I just came out of a big mistake, and I'm not about to jump into anything binding, either. As for the physical attraction, I stand by my original 'wow.'"

"I'd like to tell you more about myself, but I think I'll quit while I'm still *wow*. I live in the inner city, and I need a big brute of a man to walk me home. Know anybody?"

Her eyes glowed like warm honey again. What could I say?

Michael Kent

# THIRTEEN

I was parked within a block of the bar. It had rained, and the GTO's maroon metal-flake paint shimmered under the streetlamp. I nodded toward the car and said, "I'd enjoy walking with you, but I can't leave my toy here."

She gaped, then grinned. "Speaking of wow, I would have expected a duller sort of unmarked police car at best—say, a Ford Crown Vic. This is nice!"

I opened the passenger door. "Took me two years to restore it."

"So you're a craftsman."

I gave her a sly smile as she slid into the seat. "I have skilled hands."

"That's a reckless claim that will surely require a more thorough investigation," she deadpanned. I felt my heartbeat kick up a notch.

We drove to her house, talking about nothing: the weather, traffic in Montreal. There was

an underlying tension in the car.

When we parked across the street from her apartment, she said, "Maybe you should come up and check in case there's a knife-wielding maniac hiding behind my shower curtain."

"Absolutely. I'd be remiss as a detective if I didn't check that shower."

Zee's place was four and a half rooms on the top floor of a triplex, decorated in modern contemporary. Everything was color coordinated and immaculate.

"Nice layout," I said. "I like the geometrics on the wing chair—it makes a bold statement and ties everything together."

"A cop with decorating sense—I'm awed."

"I'm multifaceted," I said with a grin.

Again she gave me that demure look with the lascivious subtext. "I usually take a shower when I get back from work. You didn't check for lurking bad guys yet."

"I think I'm the only lurker here, but I can check."

"In that case, maybe you want to jump in at the same time. It's a roomy shower. You can soap my back."

"I'm all for ecology and saving water, and I'm even better at fronts than backs."

What followed is the stuff of fond memories,

scented with Dove body wash.

\*\*\*

Next morning, I raided Zee's refrigerator and whipped up French toast for both of us while she changed the mangled bedclothes. I hadn't slept much, and it had nothing to do with the strong coffee I had at lunch. Zee's yogic flexibility, combined with a certain bold openness, had kept my heart rate up for most of the night. I could skip my tai chi routine for today.

I drove her to work. "I really loved our time together," I said. "But neither of us wants to get into serious commitments, so if you give me your cell number, I promise not to put it in my favorites."

"We'll exchange numbers, but you'd *better* put me in favorites, she said, with an arch glare. "I do remember you telling me, sometime in the predawn, that we had beaten your personal best by at least an hour. That alone warrants my number in bold and in *favorites*."

My answer was a long good-bye kiss and a promise to call her later in the day.

Michael Kent

# FOURTEEN

I headed home to feed Crackers. I had muted my phone while in the bar with Zee, and it had drained away without a whimper. I plugged it into the USB port that had replaced the useless cigarette lighter—the no-smoking law in my car was strictly enforced. My phone came to life, pinging that I had messages and voice mails.

The first text was from Angela: *"Tried 2call U, no answer. Some1 broke in apart while I ws shopping."*

The second was from Dobson: *"Angela called, can't reach you. Going to her place with the patrols, call me."*

I called Dobson, and he answered on the fourth ring. "Thanks ever so much, Beaudry. It's ten past seven; *now* you call."

"I was out following a lead and forgot to charge the phone."

"Eh, if you say so, Lieutenant. Angela called around ten in the evening. She was in a panic. Her apartment was ransacked."

"Did they find the box?"

"What box? She didn't mention a box."

"Never mind. We need to put—"

As if reading my mind, Dobson said, "She's safe. I have her in a hotel."

"Okay, great. Can you tell the boss I'm meeting a contact from the vice squad? I'm trying to get info on the Russians."

"Why am *I* calling him?"

"I'm just covering my ass," I said. "I'm doing a raid with the vice squad. Getting permission is too complicated—easier just to do it and ask forgiveness later."

"I'm not going to get in trouble, am I?"

"Never," I lied. "I'll call you back later. Thanks, pard."

We hung up, and I punched in Angela's number from my phone log. She answered on the first ring.

"Lieutenant . . . I was about to call you."

"Sorry you couldn't reach me yesterday," I said. "I had problems with my phone. These things happen . . ." The excuse sounded feeble even to me. "Did they get the box?"

"No, garbage day is next Tuesday. I had it

hidden in the bottom of my trash bin. I have it with me."

"Who would know about the money?"

"Only Paul and I," Angela said. "I'm not sure they were after the money. They may have been after information on Paul. The only thing that seems to be missing is a picture of him and me."

"Did the officers check if any of your neighbors saw or heard anything?"

"Brahm, next door, said he saw a man dressed as a gardener, in the afternoon."

"I saw him when I went to see you," I said. "Asian, wearing blue bib overalls."

"The gardeners finish end of September," Angela said. "Now it's just the snow removal guys. Brahm said it looked suspicious because the guy had no tools."

I felt like a moron for not catching that, but all I said was, "I'll make sure that's followed up."

I suggested that she put the cash in the hotel safe and promised to call her back later with news of Paul.

\* \* \*

At home, I fed Crackers and washed out the shower again. He had ignored the litter box. It seemed I would never find out whether Everfresh lived up to the hype on its bag.

"You're fittingly named, *Crackers*," I said to

the cat. "You shredded another roll of toilet paper, and what do you suppose happened to the fern in the corner?"

True to his criminal nature, he ignored my questions and pawed at the patio door, asking to be let out.

*"Mrrr, mrrr."*

"Don't try to sweet-talk your way out of the mess you've made," I muttered, then slid the door open for him anyway.

I made myself another breakfast, updated my notes, checked my e-mail and texts, and then cleaned the mess in the hallway, bathroom, and living room. I was repotting the fern when Nico called.

"You still on for our visit to Stevens's drug boutique?"

"Meet you there," I said. "I need a little favor from your uncle. I'd like to know if the family has business with the Russians in Montreal."

"Offhand, I don't think so. The family tries to avoid those who have no sense of honor. But I'll ask. Someone will call you back."

"Okay. Thanks. I'll see you on Ontario Street."

"We'll be in a white Express Chevy van, Dahan Electrician stenciled in black underlined with a red lightning bolt." Nico said before hanging up.

# FIFTEEN

I found Nico's surveillance van on a side street. I had to park a block and a half away and hoof it back.

"You've got a good view of Mr. Drug Dealer's front door," I said. "What about the back?"

Roger, Nico's longtime partner, answered. "We have a team with a video setup. They're in a shed across the lane." He handed me a small-screen lap pad that showed a view of the back of the house.

"Nice toys you guys have," I said.

"We have to—our work is more surveillance than shoot-'em-up," Roger said with a smirk.

Roger and I had different views on police work, and he often ribbed me on my rather too-public gun fights. Roger "Professor Lucky" Lamont had a background in criminal psychology and was one of the smartest people I knew. He always dressed like a frumpy, eccentric university professor—the sartorial opposite to Nico's just-

stepped-out-of-*GQ* workday attire.

"Not much action yet," Nico said. "The average drug user is not really a morning person. We're waiting until he has a client or two before we hit."

"I hate doing stakeout duty," I said. "I get bored, and my ass falls asleep."

"Speaking of sleep," Nico said, looking sideways at me, "you look like you spent the night hung out on a clothesline."

"I'd tell you where and how comfortable I was, but you'd turn green with envy," I retorted. "And *that* would clash with your fancy blue sport coat and daring powder-blue shoes."

Roger steered the subject back to his original comment. "Our business in vice is ninety-nine percent lazy stakeouts, interspersed with one percent heart-racing action to make the collar," he said. "You guys in homicide start off with a body that's bleeding evidence. A bullet, a wound that matches the murder weapon, fingerprints, DNA samples. Hell, the tech squad probably solves half your cases. In vice and drugs, the evidence is already up somebody's nose or vein, and nobody wants to report a crime. It's always '*What* bag of coke? Never saw it before, and I haven't a clue how it got in my toilet bowl. I didn't know she was underage, and besides, I was just helping her with her homework . .

. human anatomy—yeah, that's it.' The only way we solve anything is by building a case with our surveillance toys."

Nico added, "Not to mention informants.
I must have spent sixty percent of my law-enforcement career sitting in a car, watching and waiting, or parked in some back alley with an informant who was terrified to be seen talking to me."

"Yeah, CSI does help," I said. "But I don't agree with your statistics. We still have to hit the streets to catch our bad guys."

"I have to admit that your *clients* are more often the violent type," Roger said. "Ours lean toward pleading and wheedling, trying to rat somebody out to get a better deal in court."

"I still can't figure out how you guys don't go loopy," I groaned. "Staring out of a tinted windshield for hours on end."

"It's easy," Roger said. "We talk. We talk to our partner about love, politics, kids, family, money, the stock market, solving world hunger, the vagaries of the feminine psyche. When we've solved all of life's problems, *voilà!* It's time to retire."

I nodded. "I know what you mean. We didn't do that much car sitting, but Paul and I used to talk about everything. I miss his smart-assed comments."

Roger shuffled in his seat, turning to see me better. His eyes wrinkled up smaller, and his lips set in a straight line. "I was at the funeral, and I wanted to offer you my condolences, but you didn't look in too good a shape, so I let you be. I should have said something. I worked with Paul years ago when we were cops on the beat. I liked the guy. He was really smart—could see through people's bullshit stories like he had X-ray vision. It was uncanny sometimes."

"Paul never told me he worked with you," I said.

"We were on the beat together for only ten months before he aced the sergeants' exam. But he didn't drop his old friends. That's why the church was overflowing at his funeral. He would call me now and then for a lunch. I hadn't heard from him in over a year. It was a shock finding out about the cancer."

I looked down at the leather pocket on the back of Roger's seat. I didn't want him to see my eyes misting up. "A shock—more like a bomb blast, really. I haven't gotten over it yet. Let's talk about something else. How'd you get the nickname Lucky?"

Roger was about to say something, but Nico jumped in before he could get a word out. "He has a horseshoe up his ass, right next to the rabbit's foot.

He's been shot at five times and never once hit. Friggin' Wyatt Earp, I tell ya. Last time, the perp was two feet away, firing an Uzi, and a round jammed as he swung it towards Roger. How shithouse lucky can you get!"

Roger held up his hand, fingers out, and mouthed silently, "Five feet away."

Their computer whistled softly, and everybody turned to the picture on the screen. Three men were at the drug dealer's back door.

Nico spoke into his walkie-talkie, ordering the backup team into action. "Rock and roll. Keep your eyes open, guys. They'll be jumping out of windows."

It wasn't my type of hard entry. Professor Roger gently picked open the front door, and we sneaked in unheard and headed straight to the kitchen, where literally *everything* was on the table.

I had my gun drawn and held down by my side. Nico and Roger, badges hung around their necks, guns holstered, strode in as if they owned the place.

"Good morning, gentlemen," Nico said. "We interrupting anything?"

Roger took a picture of the group with the dope on the table. He pushed one of the customers to the side and swept up the folds and fingers into a large evidence bag.

"I like the stamp of the young girl on your folds of coke," Nico said. "It stands for what, exactly?"

One of the addicts, head bent down and trying to avoid eye contact, mumbled, "Virgin."

Roger opened the back door for the two plainclothes backup guys. "Bundle these fellows off to uptown," he said, pointing to the three customers, "while we have a little chat with our host."

The backup detectives were off to headquarters with the three addicts. Roger was listing the tally of paper packages of coke and the latex "finger" tubes of heroin.

Jimmy Stevens was sitting tie-wrapped to one of his kitchen chairs, his right knee pumping up and down like a sewing machine.

"I like your cocaine branding," Nico said. "'Virgin' is a nice touch—offsets the notion that it's been stepped on more times than a whorehouse front doorstep. Unfortunately, your competition's jealous of your success, and they ratted you out. So . . . you want to return the favor? We're looking for even bigger fish than you, Jimmy."

Jimmy opened his mouth but was interrupted by a scraping sound from the front of the house. Nico and I looked at each other with the same thought in mind: *Shit, we didn't clear the front rooms!* Roger headed toward the noise with a speed

and agility belying his age. I rushed to keep up with him. As he turned into the living room, a shotgun blast ripped chunks of plaster, lath, and a six-inch strip of molding from the door frame next to him. I reached the doorway just as a teenager with spiked blue hair was racking another round into a Winchester twelve-gauge. Roger was groping for his weapon when I tripped him aside. With no time to aim, I fired twice from the hip, in time with the second blast. One of my bullets hit the youth, and he dropped his weapon.

Through the ringing in my ears, I could just barely hear him screaming, "You shot me! You *shot* me!"

Blood was seeping out of his right jeans leg. I kicked the shotgun aside, grabbed his shoulder, and swung him into the wall. "Relax, numb nuts, it went thru your ass cheek," I said. "You're lucky I didn't have time to aim for center mass."

"I'm bleeding!" he cried. "cripes, it burns!"

"Yeah, usually happens when you catch a poorly aimed bullet. With better aim, you get no pain, just permanent darkness."

Nico rushed into the living room, gun out. Roger was leaning unsteadily against the doorjamb. "Beaudry saved my life. My head was here," he said, pointing to a fist-size hole in the wall to his left.

Nico shook his head. "*Gavone,* be careful.

You're gonna run out of lives one day. Even a cat only has nine."

Nico was checking Roger like a mother running her hands over a child who has fallen off his tricycle.

"Nico, if you can stop groping your partner for a minute, you'd best come here," I said. "The kid and I are the only ones bleeding here." The left side of my head was afire, and I could smell the coppery scent of my blood as a warm wetness dripped down my neck.

Nico looked at my wound. "Just a scrape. You have a three-inch long slice of hair missing just above your ear." He plucked something from my scalp. "A little triangle of plastic," he said. "No pellets—you just caught a piece of the wad."

"Rats! There goes my fresh haircut," I said, holding my scarf to my head.

Roger left to check on Jimmy and get a towel for the kid, who was leaking blood and tears at roughly the same rate.

"I thought you guys were here to rob my uncle—didn't know you were cops, I swear," the kid said.

"What's your name, and how old are you?" Roger said in a deep, menacing tone.

The kid stopped sniveling. "Kenny. Seventeen next month. Am I in trouble?"

"Well, you did try to kill two policemen, so, in a word, yes. You're in deep shit, in fact. Why aren't you in school, anyway, you little prick?"

"You didn't say 'police' or anything. The big guy just *shot* me. That's not right!"

"Kenny, it's just a flesh wound," I said. "In a week, you'll be boasting about it. All the girls will want to look at your scar. Of course, so will some of the guys . . ."

Roger came back with Jimmy and a towel for Kenny to sit on. His tears had stopped, and the bleeding had slowed.

"This is a bit of a mess," said Nico. "I have to call it in. Let's get our stories straight."

Roger said, "I owe you one, Robert. Let me take the heat on this."

We built our scenario around Jimmy's cooperation to implicate one of his suppliers. Kenny was more than willing to go along with anything we wanted. He was too pretty not to attract the wrong type of cell mate, and he knew it. The kid wanted very badly to stay out of juvie.

Nico called his boss, and I called Jean, who, during our short conversation, managed to use nine French swear words that were entirely new to me. We both were instructed to stay put and wait for Internal Affairs.

Michael Kent

# SIXTEEN

Everybody had their parts rehearsed. Roger had shot the floorboards in line with Kenny's wound to give us a reasonable forensic backup. My spent bullets, hiding somewhere in Jimmy's stained and tattered living-room sofa, were the only potential glitch in our story.

Nico's boss, Captain Falco, arrived before Internal Affairs, giving us time to brief him on our version of the truth.

"Vice is a favorite target for Internal Affairs," Falco said. "I have a love-hate relationship with them, weighted somewhat toward the latter, and it's reciprocal. All of you, listen to me." He seemed to look everyone in the eyes at once. "Shut up. You talk only when I tell you to talk. I'm in charge. Follow my lead."

We went over our story again, each doing our little solo, with Falco as the orchestra conductor.

The Urgences-Santé medics had patched up Kenny and were cleaning me up when IA Sergeant Lorne Trehearne and his rotund partner, Simon, came into the room. They both seemed out of breath. "Lorne, you have to stop shuffling all those useless reports and get out more," I said. "You're wheezing; you look out of shape." Falco gave me a searing look, and I shut up.

"Shots fired," Trehearne said. "Why am I not surprised to see you, Detective Beaudry?"

I put both palms up toward him and shook my head but didn't respond verbally.

\* \* \*

Kenny and I had refused transport to the hospital. Both of us had follow-up appointments at the local outpatient health facility. I was sitting on the potentially incriminating sofa, next to Nico. Simon was taking notes on his laptop, fat little fingers hunting and pecking away. Both Kenny and Jimmy were ensconced in high-backed wing chairs, Kenny favoring his right buttock. Falco and Roger were standing facing Trehearne.

"This is the second time we go over the events, Trehearne," said Falco. "I won't repeat myself again. We got a tip that Jimmy Stevens was dealing drugs. When Sergeant Di Lalla contacted

Jimmy, he requested that Lieutenant Beaudry be present."

Falco looked at Jimmy, who took his cue.

"I have a drug problem, but I'm getting help for my addiction. I met Detective Beaudry last month when somebody got shot in front of my place. I was a bit high at the time, but Beaudry was sympathetic. He was okay with me; I trust him. I didn't want to discuss my old suppliers without him being here."

Falco continued, "When they met here at lunchtime, some other users were present. They had to be cleared out before Jimmy agreed to talk. The noise of the back door opening and closing woke Kenny, who was sleeping unseen on the living-room sofa."

At Falco's eye signal, Kenny jumped in like a seasoned thespian. "My uncle's been robbed twice. I heard slamming doors and loud voices. I was scared, naturally, so I grabbed Jimmy's shotgun and yelled 'Get out of the house!' and fired a warning shot to scare the robbers away." Kenny's voice trembled like a scared kid's would. I wasn't sure whether it was real or part of the act.

"A man appeared in the doorway. I told him to get out of the house and fired another warning. The wad from my shell accidentally hit the other cop that came in behind the first one."

Falco moved his gaze over to Roger, who picked up the thread.

"Kenny looked panicked. I didn't know if he was on drugs. I fired at the same time he fired, as I yelled, 'Stop, police!' I'm not a great shot. There was no time . . . I nicked Kenny."

"The coke found was user quantity," Falco lied. "Nobody's pressing charges. Jimmy is under police protection as a confidential informant. End of story."

"It's end of story when I say end of story," Trehearne replied. "We're going over this on a one-by-one interview before I complete my report. It will go to the Provincial Police, who will then do their follow-up."

"You can write your report in prose or in rhyme," Falco said. "Hell, you can write it in Esperanto or ancient Cretan Linear A, for all I care. But it better match mine, period. End of discussion. I'm headed back downtown, and I want my people back on the street fast, so move your butt, Trehearne."

Trehearne had nearly finished with me when my phone chimed. It was Zee's number. I interrupted his last question to take the call. "Sorry, this is important," I said as I stepped away from the kitchen table.

"Beaudry. Talk to me," I said in a serious tone.

"I take it you're on the job," Zee said.

"Yup. Was going to call you later."

"Well, this is a business call. Our mutual patient just woke up."

"Good news," I said. "I would have been calling you about something else."

"I have to work late tonight, but you have an invitation for supper at my place tomorrow, seven thirty."

"Even better news. I'll drop in at the hospital soon as I finish here."

Trehearne was tapping his pen impatiently on the tabletop when I hung up.

"I have a victim in the hospital who just came out of a coma," I said. "I have to talk to him urgently—he may not survive his wounds. So we need to wrap this up fast."

We did, and I headed to the hospital in good humor. Everything was moving in the right direction. Roger had taken the heat from IA. My boss would now modulate his swearing to a murmur, sticking to expletives I already knew as he brought up my past peccadilloes. I had a cute nurse to take care of me, and Paul Landry would probably give me all the information I needed to close my case. What could possibly go wrong? I was on top of my game.

Michael Kent

# SEVENTEEN

Sticking the police sign on the dashboard, I left my car in the pharmacy parking lot again. This time, I managed to find Paul Landry's room, deep in the hospital labyrinth, after only one wrong turn.

He was sitting up in bed, hemmed in by the chrome side gates and still plugged into a few wires and an IV. He looked tired and fragile, but the bandages were off.

I stuck out my hand. "Paul Landry, I'm Lieutenant Robert Beaudry."

He took my hand in a weak grasp and looked at me with vacant eyes. "Do I know you?"

"I'm in charge of your case," I said. "You were unconscious when I first saw you. You had bandages all over your face. You're a bit black and blue and you have some swelling, but you look pretty good for a guy who's been chopped, beaten, and shot."

A tear ran down his cheek on the side facing me. "The doctors told me I was attacked, but I can't remember the event.

Even my name doesn't sound right. They said it was caused by trauma to the head. I'm lost . . . My life is gone. I feel so empty."

"You have amnesia?"

"The doctors think my memory loss is temporary. They were happy with all the other tests . . . I'm sure not." Tears trickled from both eyes. "In this state, I may as well be dead. I'm nobody—no name, no history, no friends."

"Aw, rats!" I said. "I counted my chickens before the eggs were hatched."

"What chickens?"

I shook my head. "Never mind. Just talking to myself. Do you feel strong enough to talk with me?"

"About what? I'm telling you, I don't remember a thing."

"I'll do the talking. I'll tell you everything I know about you and others around you. It may jog your memory. In any case, you'll find out that you do have a history—and friends."

"A discovery of sorts, and this will be germane to the *actus reus* against me. Good thinking, Lieutenant."

"See? Things are coming back to you

already," I said. "You haven't forgotten your legalese: *actus reus*—the guilty act."

He cracked a thin smile, and his eyes opened wider. "Yes, Dr. Blain tells me I'm a well-known lawyer. Tell me about the famous Paul Landry, please."

I gave Paul a half-hour bedtime story, all that I knew and maybe some conjecture here and there. He threw in an occasional question but mostly just lay there taking it all in, trying to absorb my review of his life. Sometime during our conversation, Zee peeked into the room. I turned toward her, but she had already discreetly disappeared.

By the end of my story, Paul looked drawn and strained, but his eyes had a lively glow. I could detect a fighting spirit starting to climb out.

"Angela, Angela . . . yes!" he said, brightening. "I don't see her face, but I have a good feeling attached to her name. I know that I trust her. Suzanne brings bad feelings, and I do remember her sulking face. She looks like an angel but has the heart of a demon."

"The good news is that you're in the process of getting a divorce from her," I said.

"I'd better get well fast. I seem to have a few problems that need attending to. The mention of divorce brings a bad taste to my mouth. There's something dark and foreboding in the back of my

mind, but I can't reach it. Frustrating . . . *very* frustrating indeed."

"Relax, Paul," I said. "Take it slow. We've jogged your memory enough for today. Don't worry about your problems. That's *my* job. Just try and get some rest.

John Steinbeck said, *"It is a common experience that a problem difficult at night is resolved in the morning after the committee of sleep has worked on it."*

Landry smiled. *"Maybe all of my life is but a dream. 'For often, when one is asleep, there is something in consciousness which declares that what then presents itself is but a dream.' That I do remember, from Aristotle."*

"Good." I said. "See? You're getting better hour by hour. Now, get some sleep. That's an order. I'll stick by your bedside for a while."

\* \* \*

The overwarm room got to me again. My phone woke me. It was Zee. "Hi," I said. "I fell asleep in Landry's room."

"This is beginning to be a habit, Robert—but a cute one."

"Way too hot in here," I said.

"It's about to get warmer," Zee said. "Dr. Blain just got an urgent call from the security agent

downstairs. There's a woman at reception making a scene. She insists on seeing Mr. Landry. Says she's his wife."

"Rats and double rats! How the hell did she find him? I'd better go down and take care of this."

"I looked in on you, but you were in deep conversation with Mr. Landry and I didn't want to disturb. Did I see a bandage on your head?"

"A small scratch in the line of duty," I said. "I hope it won't affect my sensual good looks."

"Well, maybe I'll have to check you out tomorrow at supper."

She hung up without saying good-bye.

While Paul and I slept, one of his problems had sneaked up on us. I headed out into the maze of corridors and down to the reception area, to confront Suzanne.

# EIGHTEEN

Paul Landry had warned me that Suzanne had the face of an angel, but the heart and morals of a devil. I couldn't comment on the second part of his characterization yet, but even across a wide lobby, I could see that he was spot-on about the first part. A bottle blonde, no doubt, but with a face and a body that made heads turn. Though she had clearly begun to pall on the exasperated-looking security officer standing beside her, she probably could pull most men to the cheating side of town with a profile view and a bat of the lashes.

Too bad she had to open her mouth and burst my bubble. At the moment, she was spewing vitriol at Dr. Blain. He stood before her, eyes to the floor and head shaking slowly from side to side. The raspy voice made the drawn-out Valley-girl enunciation doubly grating.

"I kno-o-ow Paul is here. I insist on seeing

him im-m-mediately."

"For the third time," Blain said, "Mr. Landry has been moved from the neurological center to a private wing. I'm not letting anyone see him till he's off the critical list. No visitors, *period*."

Before Suzanne could go another round with him, her phone rang with a cacophonous tune every bit as jarring as her voice. Disregarding the sign directly above her prohibiting cell phone usage, she put it to her ear.

"No, no, the *do-o-octor* tells me they've moved him and—"

In a slow, gentle move, the lanky security officer plucked the offending device from her hand and turned it off.

"Ma'am, I tole ya foah times, no cell phones here."

"Oh . . . my . . . God! Oh, my *God,* did you just do that?" Suzanne yanked the phone out of his hand and made a telegraphed swat at his face, which he casually blocked. Then she confirmed the second part of Landry's characterization: "You ghetto piece of shit, I'll sue you. And I'll sue you, too, you little prick of a doctor." Then, giving both of them a middle-finger farewell, she turned and stormed toward the exit. As I followed her past Dr. Blain, I heard the guard murmur, "Be okay, maybe, if she just keep that nasty mouth shut."

As her hips swayed down the corridor, most heads, both male and female, turned to watch her pass, some blatantly, some more discreetly. If they only knew . . .

By the time she reached the hospital lobby, Suzanne had her phone back in hand. I closed the gap between us as she stepped outside. She headed toward a black Mercedes AMG parked in a spot reserved for ambulances, where a slim, well-dressed Eurasian man was nose to nose arguing with a security officer. Ignoring both antagonists, Suzanne yanked the passenger door open and plopped ungracefully inside. She managed to show a nice bit of leg before slamming the door. Mr. Handsome Eurasian backed off a couple of feet and spat on the security guard's boot, flipped him the bird, turned and got in the driver's side, and gunned the car in reverse. As he turned it toward the exit, I grabbed my pen and jotted the plate number on the back of my hand.

Maybe today was Nasty Middle Finger Day and I hadn't got the memo. The couple in the speeding car seemed a perfect pair. I'd have to find out more about Suzanne and her chauffeur.

I speed-dialed Dobson, who again picked up on the first ring. "Landry just woke up," I said. "He has amnesia. Doesn't remember shit about the attack."

"Is he confused, eh? Can he talk cohesively?"

"Talks okay. Said he didn't remember his name or anything about his past. He wasn't faking; he was in tears. I told him what I knew about him, and things started coming back.

It's frustrating to have a witness who can solve my case, and not be able to get the information out of him."

"Eh, could be physical, due to the concussion, or could be psychogenic amnesia due to the shock of the attack. Sounds anterograde to me. Did they give you a SCAT-three score?"

"Psycho *what*? Scat what? Dobson, where does this Doctorese come from?"

"Eh, I was a trauma nurse before CSI, Lieutenant, and I have a medical degree."

"So I had you pegged right at 'Dr. Watson.' What's the bottom line?"

"SCAT-three is the sport commission assessment tool for concussion. Your bottom line is that if he's not confused and is talking well, his memory loss may be very temporary. Within a day or two, you may have your answers."

"I hope you're right, Watson. In the meantime, I have a plate number I want you to run. Text me the info, okay?"

"Lieutenant, Angela wants to go to her condo to get some more clothes and stuff. I told her you'd pick her up."

He gave me the hotel and room number, and I gave him the plate number of Suzanne's friend's AMG. We hung up, and I turned back toward the hospital entrance.

I found Dr. Blain waiting for me in the lobby.

"The hospital administration won't like this type of situation," he said. "I'm not exactly following official protocols here. I'm going to move him to my private clinic in Town of Mount Royal."

"Good. But I'd like to know how Suzanne found out about Paul being here. I thought only you and I knew."

His eyes narrowed. "Don't look at me like that. The leak could have come from your side."

"Okay, okay," I said. "Don't get all huffy. I'll look into it. Call me im-m-mediately if Paul's memory improves."

My Suzanne imitation got a crooked smile from Blain. We shook hands, and I headed back to my car.

# NINETEEN

In the parking lot, Tony, the towing guy of yesterday's misunderstanding, faced off with three angry gangbanger types. Their scratched gold lowrider was strapped to the truck bed. He had his back against a front fender of his Freightliner and a jack handle held down against his thigh. The mouthiest of the three was growling that if their ride wasn't on the ground in the next minute, real trouble would happen. The other two were moving left and right of Tony in some apparent pincer move. Walking carefully, I managed to position myself unobtrusively behind Growling Man.

I said, "Yo, Tony, can you get that piece of crap out of here so I can move my car?"

My voice, coming from a foot away, so startled the guy, he nearly jumped out of his sagging pants.

He tried to turn toward me but moved too

slow and too late. I already had my hand clamped on the pressure point just above his elbow.

"Get outta my face, muscle head," he unwisely snarled, inciting me to dig my fingers into his arm at the "policeman's notch" and step on the arch of his foot. Hitting two pressure points at the same time flashed major pain signals up and down that side of his body. A little added tug to the side toppled him at my feet. He wound up on the ground, leaning against my legs, his arm and foot useless for the moment. I reached down over him to the front of his neck and sank my two first fingertips into his collarbone pocket. He tried to get up, and I pressed on another sensitive spot. Looking like a Mr. Spock Vulcan move, it was nearly as effective in restraining an aggressor without inflicting permanent damage. The other two bangers had gone for Tony. One threw a punch that lost out to an upraised tire iron, and he now danced a merry jig, howling and cupping his smashed knuckles against his chest. The other lay on the asphalt, rubbing his kneecap. I released the guy at my feet and helped him up.

"Why don't we settle this the easy way?" I said. "What's the tow charge, Tony?"

"A hundred."

"A hunnud? You *nuts*?" the guy rubbing his knuckles said. "It took, like, two minutes to put it on the truck."

I put my hands up in a sign of peace. "How about fifty and we forget any of this happened."

The goon in front of me suggested that Tony do something to himself that was physically impossible. I took a step toward him, and he had a sudden change of heart.

"Okay, damn! Ease up, man. Vincent, you got bank; give the man his fitty."

The transaction over, the gangsters-in-training drove off, middle fingers waving vigorously from the car windows as they peeled out.

"I really didn't get the memo," I said.

"What memo?"

"Just talking to myself, Tony," I said. "You handle that tire iron like a nunchuk. You may want to use open-hand techniques next time. Self-defense notwithstanding, they were unarmed, which means you could be looking at assault with a deadly weapon."

"So what are you sayin'? The criminals get off and I get in trouble?" Tony dropped the tire iron into the truck cab. "What kinda justice is that?"

I said, "In my business, I learned fast that the legal system's one thing and justice is another. Luckily, they meet every now and then."

Tony gave a snort. "You can use your karate moves or whatever that was, but I have to defend

myself however I can."

"Ah, Tony, Tony," I said, shaking my head. "I used to get in trouble a lot. Every time a perp resisted arrest, I'd deliver him bruised and bleeding.

I was forced to attend a police-sponsored seminar on pressure points. Since then, no muss, no fuss."

"I was with the Royal Engineers," Tony said. "My training was in EOD. But it doesn't help me defuse the crazies I meet every damn day. People love the tow truck driver when we pull 'em out of the snow bank, but they want to kill us when we tow their illegally parked ride."

"Bomb disposal—that's gutsy. Look, I lost my gym partner a while back. You want to join me sometime, I'll show you the basics."

"I may take you up on that, Lieutenant."

Out of the parking lot, Tony went left and I went right. I wasn't sure why I had invited a stranger to my gym routine. Maybe because he was Italian and I missed my ex-partner, Paul Tondino, more than I knew.

# TWENTY

I hadn't gone but a few blocks when my phone chimed. I angled into a spot in front of a fire hydrant. The phone's display showed "Revenu Québec." Another phone call from Eli Kraus, and on the same street as last time, and probably in front of the same hydrant. Déjà vu.

"Beaudry," I said. "Talk to me."

"It's Agent Kraus. I'm at LBBL with the Provincial Police. We're executing a search and seizure. I would have called you before, but the Provincials were adamant about not tipping off *anybody* before the raid."

"It's okay," I said. "I'm used to interagency noncooperation, and besides, I'm busy on other stuff. Did you find anything that relates to the attack on Landry?"

"Nothing yet, but I understand that yesterday some woman, purportedly from the police

department, called Maître Charles Brown in Florida to get him to return promptly to Montreal due to an attempted break-in at his Westmount house. It's always nice to avoid extradition complications. His secretary tells me he's booked on Air Canada Four-Oh-Two, arriving at nine fifteen this evening. Maybe you want a meet and greet?"

"Sounds like a plan, but I suggest you talk to Zafirah about the legal implications of impersonating an officer. Just saying."

Kraus ignored my warning. "I have a team that'll pull an all-nighter sorting out the files we've got on all of the Korisky transactions. We'll probably have enough for an arrest warrant on Brown in the next few days. So you still have first dibs on him. I hope it helps you on the Landry case."

In the background, I heard someone calling for Kraus. "Gotta go," he said, and hung up.

I texted Dobson, asking him to meet me at the airport for Brown's arrival. I didn't need backup, but I did need a witness.

I headed to the hotel to pick up Angela. A quarter to six in the afternoon, and the sun was already dipping low. I wasn't looking forward to another Quebec winter. I wondered if Angela and Paul were going to be stuck with the yacht rental out of Miami. Maybe I could wangle my way on as a deckhand.

\* \* \*

The cold October rain pelted down as Angela and I made the hundred-foot dash from the hotel entrance to the corner where I had parked my GTO. We both were now trickling onto my pleather seats.

"I don't mind rain in the springtime," I said. "But I don't like it in the fall. I know the clouds are just practicing for snow."

"Based on last winter," Angela said, "I don't think that they need any more practice."

I used my jacket sleeve to swab ineffectively at the drops on the wood-grain console and on the edge of her seat. Angela pulled out a soft tissue pack from her purse and handed me one; then she pulled out another and dabbed at her face while I tried to sponge off the side panel of my door.

"Men and their cars," she said. "You remind me of Paul when he fawns over his little collection of classics."

"Ah, a man of discriminating tastes. I liked Paul the moment I met him," I said, meaning it. "What's he got?"

"A Camaro Z-Twenty-Eight, two Fords—one of them a sixty-four-and-a-half Mustang that he loves probably more than me, and some purple monstrosity with a big wing-thingy on the trunk."

"Wing on the back. I'd guess a Plymouth Roadrunner." I smiled. "Paul's into muscle cars big-time."

Angela snapped her seat belt on. "I don't want to turn your smile over, but I need to get out of that cheap, dingy hotel you put me in. I appreciate that you want to keep me safe, but I'll probably catch some awful disease in that place, or one of the rats will pull a knife on me. Everything is dirty, and the facilities are disgusting."

"The police budget for this is limited," I said. "I guess Dobson did the best he could."

"I'll pay my own way. I have money."

Getting onto the Decarie Expressway ramp, I slid between a slow Camry and a plumbing truck, with inches to spare. Angela braced a hand on the dashboard.

"I know," I said. "A hundred and twenty-three thousand."

"No, no, that's Paul's. I pay my own way. You've got me confused with Suzanne. You know something, Lieutenant? I'm insulted that you'd think I would take advantage of Paul's wealth."

"Sorry, I didn't mean that at all. And I would never confuse you with Suzanne. I had the displeasure of seeing the lady in action today. And I use 'lady' in the loosest possible sense."

On the road to her condo, it was apparent that something was bothering Angela. Or maybe she was still miffed about my comment. She hadn't spoken a word. I had tried small talk but gave up when I got only grunts in reply.

The rain had eased up from raging torrent to persistent drizzle. On the wet asphalt, the fat Dunlops made that butter-in-a-hot-skillet sound, and the wipers thumped a regular beat. It was the only relief from the cold silence between us.

By the time I turned onto her street, Angela had thawed out a bit.

"Don't go by the front," she said. "Take the next left. There's another parking area that's closer to my back door."

"Okay." As I responded, we passed a white van idling at the curb. The driver, phone in hand, was intent on texting. I caught only a glimpse, but his Asian features seemed familiar.

Angela directed me through a back lane to a private parking lot reserved for the condo owners.

When we passed her back door, she said, as if exhaling a long-held breath, "Ooh . . . somebody's been in my house again. I closed my kitchen curtains before I left."

For some reason, turning off the ignition triggered my memory. "Rats! The gardener."

"*What* gardener?"

"Never mind," I said. "Do you have a key on you to your patio door?"

Angela pointed to a sloped entrance leading to a wide garage door at the side of her building.

"No, but we can go up by the basement parking."

"Not *we,* Miss Andreadis. Before I let you go in, first I check whether someone is still there." I held out my open palm. She fished out keys and a pass card from the depths of her purse and dropped them in my hand.

"Am I . . . safe here?"

"Can you drive a standard shift?"

"Yes," she said. "Paul taught me on the Mustang. I can even double-clutch to downshift." She looked at me sideways, her head tilted proudly up.

"I'm mightily impressed," I said. "Change places with me. I'll leave the keys in the ignition. If you see anyone other than me headed for the car, scoot out of here and call Dobson."

Angela gave a little shudder but said, "Yes, okay."

# TWENTY-ONE

Hugging the wall, I swiped the garage door open. From where I stood, partly hidden by the corner of the building, I saw only the front of the hood of the white van but not the fake-gardener driver. If I couldn't see him, then from his vantage point, he couldn't see me, either.

On one side, the garage was zoned into outlined parking spaces assigned to the specific condo owners; on the other was a row of numbered steel doors. The key Angela had given me bore the number 2. Her door opened with the grind of a rusty spring being pulled taut, then made the same noise in closing. So much for a stealthy entrance.

I climbed a flight of stairs up to a little mud room. Women's galoshes and winter boots were aligned in a row on a rubber mat. A polka-dot raincoat and a big, misshapen woolly sweater hung from brass pegs above the boots. I couldn't picture

pert, proper Angela wearing something so floppy and unflattering. Ahead of me, a pocket door led probably to the kitchen. Afraid to make any more noise, I slid it open a millimeter at a time. I was right about the layout.

Gun drawn, I stepped into the kitchen and inched around the cooking island, toward the living room. From my side of the hallway, I could see down to the other end. A pair of work-booted feet, crossed at the ankles, rested on the coffee table where yesterday Angela had placed the little box that held Paul's generous cash bonus. Above the boots, I could see six inches or so of light-blue trouser legs. The wearer of the boots was installed on the two-seater sofa from where I had interviewed Angela.

I moved down the center line of the corridor, imitating Crackers whenever he stalked any bird foolish enough to preen itself on my rear balcony. *Creep forward, freeze for a few seconds, creep forward . . .* Halfway down the corridor, I glanced through the partly open door of the bedroom. Nothing untoward. Continuing to channel Crackers, I sidestepped slowly left at the edge of the hallway. I could see into the living room. The young Asian sitting on the sofa had long, forward-angling spiked hair and, like the gardener, was dressed in light-blue bib coveralls.

"Police," I snapped. "Don't move."

My surprise entrance didn't seem to faze him. Casually turning his head toward me, he slowly raised his hands to the top of his head, though he seemed to be looking somewhere behind me. His face remained passive, but his eyes suddenly smiled.

Years of training, instinct, pure dumb luck, or maybe all those things saved my life in that moment. I went loose and flopped to the floor like a marionette with its strings cut. I felt the wind ruffle my hair as the guy behind me swung. It was weird; he seemed to have popped out of nowhere. The force of the strike drove his short sword through the drywall at the level where my neck had been.

My fight-or-flee instincts kicked into overdrive, and events unfolded in slow motion as the adrenaline flooded in. I rolled onto my side, pointed up, and pulled the trigger. The round caught him under the chin. He froze for an instant, then bowed gradually over me. In the same moment, the guy with the spiky do had sprung off the sofa and was now on his knees behind the coffee table, pointing a large-caliber revolver in my direction. I shot twice, so fast it sounded like one extended blast. With my assailant mostly behind the coffee table, I had gone for the head shot. He bent forward at the waist, arms outstretched in front of him, and the weapon dropped to the floor. He lay cheek to tabletop, blood seeping from under his face.

With my ears still ringing, I rolled his partner off me, stood up, and took a few deep breaths, trying to calm down. I checked out the guy at my feet: no carotid pulse, empty eyes.

He was deader than disco. Apart from my single shot, he had an entrance wound in the middle of his forehead. I surmised that Spike must have shot at me in the same instant that I fired, and hit his falling partner instead.

Gun still in hand, I moved to the coffee table. I bent to check for a pulse but stopped when I saw the puddle under the table.

I remembered a scene from my first days on the beat. My partner and I had responded to a 911 call, arriving at the same time as the first-responder firemen. The guy's wife told us that her husband got up from his chair, said he needed fresh air, then looked at her with wide eyes and wet his pants before pitching over on his face. The young fireman went through the motions but told me later that the guy was dead of a massive heart attack before he hit the carpet.

"When life leaves, the body goes slack and voids," the firefighter told me. "Like the portrait of the Grim Reaper, sudden death does not show a pretty face."

My head started to clear, and I noticed a warm wetness oozing down my left arm. I looked at my hand. Blood was dripping off my thumb and index finger. *Rats.* I guess we both fired twice. A little wobbly on my feet, I sat down on the sofa and dialed Angela.

"Stay where you are," I said. "A couple of guys were waiting to ambush you."

"Are you okay, Lieutenant? I called nine-one-one when I heard shots." Angela's voice was shaky and half an octave higher than usual. I hoped she wouldn't go into one of her fainting spells.

"I'm fine," I lied. "I'll go to you when the officers get here. Take a deep breath and stay put."

I hung up and hit the speed dial for Dobson. The call went to voice mail.

"I'm at Angela's place," I said. "Two guys were waiting for her. I had to shoot both of them. Get down here as soon as you get this message."

I peeled off my jacket to look at the line of peeled-back skin on the outside of my left arm. It looked as if someone had worked a groove using a rattail file on my biceps. Feeling around the wound to make sure the bullet had just skimmed and sliced, set up a fiery throbbing. I shouldn't have probed—what you don't know doesn't hurt as bad. I laid the P99 on the sofa beside me, decocked it, and pressed my palm over the gash on my arm. I had made quite

a mess. Why were those two after Angela?

The situation didn't make any sense. Korisky wouldn't yet know about the raid. Besides, he would use Russian trigger men, not Asians.

Before I could come up with anything plausible, the patrol officers were banging on the front door.

# TWENTY-TWO

Dobson had taken charge of Angela, the medics had finished my temporary field dressing, Captain O'Neil was on his way, and Sergeant Trehearne, reliably, was in my face again. He sat across from me, his trusty aluminum clipboard and forms poised to record any procedural peccadillo he could nail me with.

"My, my, Beaudry," he said, "this is a record even for you—two shootings in the same week! You've managed to get to number one on our Internal Affairs best-customer list."

"Just doing my job on the streets, Lorne. Real shit can happen when you're not pushing a pencil around all day."

"You can wisecrack all you want, Beaudry. If I had any say in it, you'd be off the streets. But it's not my call. I make my report, and the Provincial

Police will take over the rest of the investigation. They aren't going to be happy, either.

All you bring with your gunslinger attitude is bad publicity for the department."

I pointed to the machete still half buried in the wall. "Sorry to have let the department down. Probably if he had lopped off my head, it would have been better PR—poor cop dead on the job, instead of a criminal getting what he deserves."

Trehearne jumped to attention as my boss strode in.

"Beaudry, you okay?" I gave him a thumbs-up as he walked toward us.

"You didn't have to stand up, Lorne," I said. "You were already at perfect ass-kissing height."

"I can see you two are at it again," Jean said. *"Té dans quelle merde, Robert?"*

In answer to his question about just what manner of shit I had gotten myself into this time, I gave the captain a summary of events leading up to here and now. Like a court stenographer on meth, Trehearne scribbled away as I recounted my day. I told them about my unproductive hospital meeting with Landry and my observations of Suzanne. I left out my opinion of her and, of course, my helping Tony in the parking lot.

I had reached the point where Angela wanted to come and get some clothes from her condo, when

Trehearne interrupted. "You have her in a hotel at the department's expense? Was this approved?"

"Lorne, she's germane to the investigation,"

I said. "Look around you. Her house was ransacked, with two scumbags lying in wait. You wanted her *here*? She was in danger and scared. I put her in a safe environment."

"We're getting off track," Jean said. "I'm sure I saw Robert's requisition somewhere on my desk."

Although I often exasperated my boss, he always stood up for me. Someday, I'd have to buy him a beer and tell him how much I appreciated that from him.

After I finished my story of the shoot-out, Jean and Trehearne left me alone for a face-to-face in the kitchen. Jean came back from the impromptu meeting with a look on his kisser that told me that I had just saved the cost of a beer.

"I can see by the crease on your forehead and the southerly turn of your mustache that you're about to give me some bad news," I said.

"You're riding a desk for a week, or until IA finishes their investigation."

"Thanks for the vote of confidence, boss," I said. "You *know* this was a clean shoot."

"It's *always* a clean shoot, Robert, but the sheer number of them is tipping the scales."

"I didn't know I had a quota on how many times I was allowed to protect my or somebody else's life."

"I can do without the snarky ripostes, Robert. You're supposed to *find out who caused* a dead body, not create more of them. You don't know how much flak this is going to generate. The Landry case is in the political spotlight. If you find the guilty party, I'd really appreciate it if, just this once, you bring him in *alive*."

"Putting me on a desk while Lorne and his minions generate reams of reports isn't going to solve the case," I said. "That's just inefficient."

Jean's six-foot-six frame suddenly invaded my space. In a boot camp sergeant major's tone, he said, "Get the job done—with brains, not bullets—and do it quick. You can continue your misuse of CSI Dobson—*this time,* with my permission."

I gave him a crisp military salute. "Yes, Captain. Thank you very much, sir."

He stared down at me for a few seconds. I could feel his warm breath on my face as he struggled to compose himself. He suddenly turned his glare onto Trehearne.

"Shelve the smirk. You better be working this weekend. I want a copy of your report on my desk by midweek."

I knew that Jean was out of line with his demand to Trehearne. I guess it was to balance the dressing-down he had just given me. Maybe he would get that free beer after all.

As my boss headed to the front door, Dobson walked in. Jean said a few words to him, then marched out of the condo.

Dobson dropped onto the sofa, beside me.

"Is Angela okay?" I asked.

"She's installed at the Downtown Westin. The clerks at reception were tripping over themselves when she pulled out the black stainless steel VISA card."

"The legal profession is in a different tax bracket than us poor cops."

As I spoke, Trehearne sat down across from us. "Speaking of poor cops," he said, "better get yourself to the Lakeshore General to take care of your wound. I've already called; they're expecting you."

"Why the sudden interest in my health, Lorne?"

"Can't lose my best client, now, can I?" he said, putting on a sad face. "You think I have something against you, Beaudry, but you're wrong. I'm here to make sure we follow correct procedures so you're not kicked out of court when you bring the

criminal to justice. I may do my job with pencils and you do yours with handcuffs and a gun, but we're on the same team."

Trehearne got up and walked away without a backward glance. I looked at Dobson, who looked as mystified as I felt.

"That was weird." I said.

Dobson's phone rang. He stood up and walked to the kitchen to take the call. A minute later, he came back, his phone still on his ear, and waving his other hand as if his fingers were on fire.

"*¿Qué pasó?*" I said.

Instead of an answer, Dobson handed me his phone.

"Lieutenant Robert Beaudry speaking," I said. "What's this about?"

"Lieutenant, this is Shift Commander Méndez, Palm Beach Police. Your department has a request for information on a Canadian citizen who has a home in our jurisdiction. A Mr. Charles Brown."

"Yes, it concerns a homicide investigation. Why are you calling at this hour?"

"Brown was found facedown in his pool this afternoon. He wasn't snorkeling."

"Rats, rats, rats!"

"Come again?"

"It's just my expression of surprise. What happened?"

"The pool-cleaning guy found him. Our preliminary indicates that Brown was in the water for several hours. He had blunt trauma to the side of his head."

"Are you calling it accident or homicide?"

"Waiting for the medical examiner's report."

"I can tell you that on our side, he was under investigation for money laundering, and I wanted to question him in a murder investigation," I said. "We're also looking at one Mitri Korisky, a suspected Russian mafia enforcer who had dealings with Brown and also, coincidentally, has a residence in Palm Beach."

"You're telling me we should dig deeper into this?"

"No, I'm sure your investigators will go with the evidence that they have. It's just for your information."

"Okay, Lieutenant. Thanks for the heads-up."

"If you need any other info, don't be shy about calling CSI Dobson."

We hung up, and Dobson said, "Eh, not sure we can discuss a current investigation that openly. I think the captain wants this low profile."

"Look at the positive side," I said. "We just saved ourselves a trip to the airport, *and* we made a new friend in Florida."

"I'm getting a better picture of how you manage to antagonize IA," Dobson said. "Let's take Lorne's suggestion and get a doctor to patch you up properly. Leave your car here. I'll drive."

"Don't bother, I'm okay."

"Eh, sure, drive stick shift and try to handle steering with a crippled wing. The 'I'm driving' was not a suggestion, Lieutenant."

I was too tired to argue. As we headed to the door, Trehearne said, "My office, ten in the morning. I'd like to go over a few details so as to get my report out as fast as possible."

"Make that eleven and you got a deal," I said.

The day was getting weirder by the minute. The adrenaline high had long gone, and I was looking forward to getting home.

# TWENTY-THREE

After I was patched up, Dobson dropped me off with the promise to pick me up in the morning for my meeting with the IA geeks. I opened my door to Cracker's imitation of the bloodcurdling yowl of a cougar. It was way past his six p.m. supper time. I was not used to juggling a feeding schedule on my daily to-do list.

The caterwauling abruptly stopped as soon as I pulled out Crackers's favorite fishy supper from the kitchen pantry.

"Okay, okay, relax." I said as he tried to climb my leg and claw open the food can himself. "You made a mess of the house again. You keep this up, and I'll toss you out on your furry butt. What did that poor fern ever do to you, anyway?"

I swept up the broken teacup, repotted the fern in the living room, and collected the piles of shredded toilet paper in the hallway and bathroom. I hadn't the courage to check out the bedroom.

With the cat fed, now it was my turn. I decided on barbecue chicken. It reminded me of Colleen—not the chicken so much, but ordering food at ten at night. She had been to Paris twice and had adopted the snobby French custom of late suppers and made it her own. This was but another incompatibility between us. I surely spent more energy during my workday than she. She did office work while I was on the street, chasing down witnesses and bad guys all day. By the end of my shift, I was starving. By seven, I was gnawing on the tabletop. But in Colleen's world, it was somehow uncouth to eat before nine in the evening.

When I picked up the phone to order, the bland female computer voice informed me that I had a message. Colleen had said she would call today. Bad vibes held my finger floating in hesitation over the phone keys until, with an effort of will, I punched in the retrieval code, certain that her message would cap off my weird day. I heard the sound of party laughter and people talking loudly in the background. By the ambient noise alone, I knew that the call was from her before she said a word.

"A friend found me an upscale furnished suite within walking distance of Parliament Hill. It even has a rooftop terrace. I need my clothes and personal stuff from your apartment, but barely anything will fit in my Cooper. I need a small favor,

Robert. I'd have to borrow your car. I'm in Montreal Tuesday to transfer files to my replacement.

We can switch cars then. I'll call you to tell you what time. Bye for now."

Along with body language interpretation, detectives learn to listen not only to the story but also to the tone of voice, choice of words, small hesitations, breathing rhythm, and, often, the words *not* said. Among other clues, no "hello, how are you," an unnamed friend, the commitment to upscale living arrangements, and the use of "*your* apartment," not "*our* apartment" told me that this was the last nail in the coffin of my marriage. Grudgingly, I had to give her an A for "audacity"—not only was she dumping me, but she wanted to borrow my car to empty her stuff from our apartment—correction, *my* apartment. Loaning my car to *anyone* was, for me, a favor far removed from the descriptor "small." In the emotional mix of sad, disappointed, and angry, I nearly called her back to say rent a van—even got as far as looking up the number for U-Haul—but I had done enough battling for one day.

* * *

With the table cleaned off, Crackers hidden somewhere with a stolen chicken leg, and green tea cooling in my cup, I moved to the living room. I

clicked the Bose to my latest jazz CD, then plunked into the overstuffed leather chair to recapitulate my day. I was now certain that not one but two gangs were in play.

The attack on Landry had nothing to do with the money laundering. I decided that the late Charles Brown, as well as Mitri Korisky's schemes, was off my investigation list. I'd leave all that in the crosshairs of the tax fraud investigators. Mr. Kraus and his team would, I was sure, soon bring that house of cards down on the guilty.

My instincts told me that the Asians lying in wait for Angela probably belonged to Mr. Handsome Eurasian, Suzanne's chauffeur and, perhaps, boyfriend. A little warning bell sounded in my head as I recalled Jean's note from the crime scene: *"Robert, I remember reading about a messy divorce for Landry a year or so ago. Interview ex-wife."* Ah, rats, I should have done that days ago. Maybe today would have played out differently.

I was glad to have come out vertical and not horizontal from the gunfight, but I was disturbed about having taken two lives. It brought back memories of the first time I had to use my weapon. With only sixteen months on the street as a beat officer, and by pure luck—not necessarily the good kind—my partner, Armand, and I were passing a Saint Lawrence Street Royal Bank branch just as a

ski-masked robber, keen on a fast exit, popped out the front door. He took one panicked look at us and jumped back into the bank. In today's world, we would have had to hold down the fort, call for backup, and wait for the negotiator and the SWAT team to arrive. In those days, we *were* the swat team. Instinctively and without much thought, we pulled out our sidearms and followed on his heels.

A male teller had stepped to the door—I suppose, to see what direction the robber had headed. As we entered the scene, the would-be Dillinger promptly took him hostage. With no time to grab the teller from behind, he stood beside him, holding him by one arm, and pointing his revolver at the man's chest. In retrospect, all the participants were young, inexperienced, cranked on adrenaline, and in a panic situation. The robber accidently pulled the trigger, and this brought an automatic response from Armand and me. Two of my bullets were found in the robber's chest, and one of my partner's rounds was in his neck. To this day, I don't remember aiming or firing my weapon. I had nightmares for weeks and relived the event during waking hours, trying to figure out what else we could have done. This evening was the same: one of those nights when nothing feels exactly right and you second-guess everything you did.

At the hospital, I had asked whether I could drink alcohol with the antibiotics they gave. There were no contraindications, but the nurse suggested that moderation was always the best route. I lived life to the fullest every day, not that I did anything to excess, but "moderation" probably wasn't part of the usual lexicon used to describe my personality.

I traded my cold tea for a generous tumbler of Glenrothes Select Reserve single malt.

Somewhere after my first glass, I heard Crackers's *I want to be let out now* meow. I dragged myself out of my comfortable reverie to slide open the patio door for him. I was in the middle of an Internal Affairs shooting investigation. Again. I hadn't followed Jean's advice or paid attention to Colleen's needs, and I was probably not bringing my A game to Zee, either. I stood in the doorway, glass in hand, letting the crisp night air clear the images of my weird day. Hopefully, a night's sleep would let me start the morning a bit wiser than I was today.

# TWENTY-FOUR

My emotionally troubled cat woke me an hour and a half before dawn. I struggled to lift the weight of my eyelids. My eyes felt as if they weren't properly seated in their sockets—the result of last night's slight overindulgence in expensive whisky. I managed to focus on the furry creature intent on stomping a hole in my chest.

"You just spoiled a great dream of Zee," I growled.

*"Mrrrr, prrrr, mrrrrr."*

"Give me a break. It's still dark out."

The beast had a built-in alarm clock. I didn't even need the one on the nightstand. He insisted on breakfast at ten to six every morning. I'd have to get an automatic cat food dispenser or go to bed earlier. He sniffed my nose, jumped off, and ran out of the room. I guess my breath bore evidence of the three-scotch night. Or was it four? I tried a jump-twist exit

from the bed but had to grab the dresser for support.

I fed Crackers and myself, let him out, and started my tai chi routine. Somewhere after "cloud hands," I had to let Crackers back in. By the end of "needle at the sea bottom," he wanted out again. Impenetrable cat logic.

I cleaned up another of Crackers's toilet paper shred fests, showered with cling wrap protecting the bandage on my arm. When got my cell phone from the charger, I saw it indicated two text messages. The first was from Tony the towing guy, who wanted to take me up on my pressure point training offer. I answered with the address of my gym, saying to meet me at two thirty. The second was a reminder from Zee: *"Supper 2nite 7.30 dnt bring xthing just U appetite."* I figured that in another ten years, we all would be talking the way we texted—an ignominious end for the English language. I laid out a Michael Kors sport jacket and color-coordinated shirt and slacks for my date but pulled on jeans and a leather jacket for my meeting with IA. My gym bag was already in my parked car at Angela's. *Rats.* It reminded me of last night's phone message. I felt ill at ease loaning my car to Colleen. She drove her Cooper around town as if she were immortal and on a race track. I shook the bad thoughts from my mind and headed out into the bright, sunny fall day.

\* \* \*

Dobson turned into my street within a minute of his promised time. I folded myself into his little lime-green hybrid.

"Too nice a day for work," I said. "*I* have to go in, but you're free to do something else. You could drive me to my car instead of to headquarters."

"No problem," my CSI wunderkind replied. "I often go to the office on Saturday morning. Few people around, no interruptions—perfect for catching up with all my paperwork."

"Will you have time to drop me off after? I have a date tonight and I need my car."

Dobson gave me a curious sideways glance. "Didn't you tell me earlier this week that your wife just left you? You bounce back fast."

"Just happened to meet a cute nurse. One of those magical occurrences when everything clicks."

"I know what you mean," Dobson said. "It was the same for me. Also a nurse. We've been together six years. André's finished med. He's an intern at the Children's. Now that they changed the law to permit same-sex marriage, we're thinking of making it official next summer."

"Congratulations," I said. "But at the risk of seeming indiscrete, couldn't that cause some harassment for you in the department?"

I had unleashed a flood of personal information from Dobson.

By the time we reached headquarters, I realized just how difficult it had been for him to be gay in an over-macho police environment. The presence of more and more females on the force had dialed back the discrimination, but it still popped up on occasion. Generally, men seem to compartmentalize situations. Business is business, and home life and personal feelings are separate. Women have a more holistic view of things. There are no pigeonholes; everything's all in one big drawer. Statistics show that women are consistently more accepting of homosexuality than men. They let facts and feelings mix, and it often gives a more nuanced picture of events and situations. Then again, I'm biased; I love having women around.

At headquarters, we agreed that whoever finished first would call the other, and then we each headed in different directions. I had great respect for Dobson's work skills and, now, also for his moral tenacity and commitment to his life partner. I had to wonder, if I knew more about Sergeant Trehearne, would it temper my opinion of him?

# TWENTY-FIVE

Trehearne's desk was a disaster area. In lieu of files, he had piles: papers and photographs stacked into perilous towers. Rows of Jenga games waiting to topple.

I pointed to his work area. "If an earthquake strikes, you're going to be in big trouble."

"Good morning, Lieutenant. We get perhaps three or four earthquakes per year, but invariably two or less in magnitude—not seismically significant. But you're right: I have to clean up. It looks like I'm hoarding."

"It *is* a good morning, Lorne," I said. "Way too nice to be stuck in an office. So let's get this show on the road. I'm impatient to get out of here."

"Sit down, Beaudry. Your impatience is one of the things I want to talk about. You have me worried."

"Worried?" I said. "Yesterday you shocked

me with your concern over my health. Are you for real?"

"You understand nothing, Beaudry. And yes, I'm worried for your life. Sit down and let me talk."

I took his swivel chair, and Trehearne perched on a little bare corner of his desk.

"You were involved in two shootings in the same week."

"I know, I know, but I was the shooter in only one"—*as far as you know.*

Trehearne put both hands out as if he felt an uncontrollable urge to strangle me. "Please shut up and let me talk. In both cases, you barged in with your usual bravado, full speed ahead and damn the torpedoes—or bullets. Absolutely no regard for proper procedure."

"Ah, you're going to give me the procedure speech again," I said.

Trehearne's face flushed pink. "Please, *please,* shut up and listen."

I was taken aback. He looked minutes away from a stroke. I shut my yap and sat back. The swivel chair tilted rearward with my movement, and I made a grab to steady myself. "Sorry," I said, releasing his knee and giving it a pat.

In full preacher mode now, he ignored my antics. "I'm worried that the next time I get called for you, it will be 'officer down.' You don't take my

comments seriously. I'll repeat myself: you made the same mistake twice, and both times it nearly got you killed. You failed to clear the area properly.

You and the vice cops walked right by the living room where Kenny slept with a very visible shotgun in the corner next to him."

"You're right on that one," I said. "I was senior officer. I should have done it by the book."

"Yesterday, you told me you peeked into the bedroom," Trehearne said. "You forgot the washroom, where your sword-wielding criminal was. I can use your entry techniques as part of a course at the police academy—great examples of what *not* to do."

"He was in the bathroom?"

"*Yes*, and they weren't there to kill Angela. They were there to kidnap her."

"Kidnap?"

"No question about it, Beaudry. The guy was in the en-suite preparing a hypodermic from a vial. I sent it down this morning to your buddy Dobson. He'll figure out what the liquid is. They had a packsack with duct tape, tie wraps, nylon rope, and a hood in it."

"Crap, you're right. A rape kit, or kidnap—same thing," I said.

"I read—or, I should say, *deciphered*—some of your reports to Captain O'Neil." Trehearne held

his chin cupped in his hand, as if deep in reflection. "You were wrong. In the break-in to her apartment, they weren't searching for something. The mess they left was probably just to shake her up, to scare her into running to Landry.

They wanted to find out where *he* was, probably to finish the job."

"Well, they seem to have found out where he is," I said. "Suzanne popped up at the hospital. I haven't figured out who gave her the info."

"Yes, you told us about Suzanne yesterday," Trehearne said. "I looked into that on my own. Lawyer Bertoni is on the hospital's board of directors. He found out easily where you stashed Landry. He must have inadvertently divulged it to Suzanne, or perhaps he's involved ab initio."

"Divulged? Ab initio? Jeez, Lorne, you just got an attack of lawyerspeak. You've got it bad, I fear."

"Sorry. Had to take some procedural law courses for this job."

"I don't think the attack on Landry has anything to do with the Russian money laundering," I said. "I think the Asians belong to Suzanne's boyfriend."

"I concur with that, Lieutenant. The question is, why do they want Landry dead?"

"I haven't figured out the why yet," I said.

"Suzanne hit Paul with a twelve-million-dollar lawsuit. I don't see what she would gain by having him killed."

Trehearne aimed his index finger upward as if using it as an exclamation point. "From your notes on file, it's uncertain that Suzanne will win the court case. Paul has evidence that she was fooling around, probably before his own dalliance.

There is other money in play. He has to be killed before he can change something—probably his will. Or, better, an insurance policy, before he can change the beneficiary. Often, in a corporation, they have partners' insurance. In the event of a sudden death, the corporation can pay the wife or the heirs the value of the inherited shares. The partners don't want the wife of the deceased as a director or participant in the running of the business, so the insurance pays the heirs and they stay out of the picture. You should check that out, Beaudry. Also, you need to get the report from what's-his-name, the private detective. That may hold the answer."

"Vissani—his name was Vissani," I said. "I'm duly impressed, Lorne. I'll never ride you about the pencil pushing again."

Trehearne handed me a soft-gel pen. "I'm sure you can solve this case without the use of firearms. Let's go over some ambiguous points in your report. I'll ask questions, and you write your

reply, as legibly as possible. I'll attach your notes to my report and send it to the Provincials and up the line, copy to Captain O'Neil. You'll be back 'on the streets,' as you say, Tuesday morning.

With a newfound respect, I followed Trehearne's lead through the IA analysis of the scene. I added clarifications and comments where he needed them.

We were on the last pages when Dobson called. He told me he was coming up to the Internal Affairs office with the analysis Trehearne had requested on the vial's contents.

Trehearne stopped clipping my notes to his draft report when Dobson knocked on the glass door. He let him in, and Dobson handed him a document.

"Flunitrazepam in a saline solution," Dobson said.

"Just as I thought: Rohypnol," Trehearne replied with another finger exclamation point.

"Gentlemen, that's enough legalese and scientific jargon on an otherwise nice Saturday," I said. "Now, I'm hungry, and I know an excellent little French pastry shop and bistro a couple of blocks from here. Anybody interested? My treat."

Dobson jumped at the invitation, but Lorne said that he had brought his lunch and wanted to finish up before heading home to pick up his son for an interschool soccer game.

I realized that I was missing a lot of people skills. I had never asked if Lorne had a family or what his interests were. I had pigeonholed him as a nerdy pencil pusher because he worked in an office, not on street duty—as if that made him less than a real cop. I was wrong about him, and I probably should mention it to him someday.

\* \* \*

I had the bakery's morning special: a heaping late of mixed fruit and cinnamon toast. Dobson went for an almond croissant and a cappuccino.

"I saw Trehearne in a whole new light this morning," I said. "He actually helped me with the case, and he's rushing his paperwork to get me back on the streets."

"People are many-faceted, Robert, eh. Not just good guys and bad guys, you know."

"This is the first time you call me *Robert*. This one of those many facets you speak of?"

Dobson shrugged. "Roger texted me this morning. Paul is installed in his private clinic."

"Roger?"

"Eh, Blain. He says that Paul is beginning to recover his memory. Might be good to drop in and see how he's doing. Perhaps, call Angela to see if she needs a lift."

I nodded, picked up my phone, and dialed Angela. The call went to voice mail. "Angela, this is Lieutenant Beaudry," I said. "I forgot to thank you for the nine-one-one call yesterday. Thank you. I understand that Paul has moved to the clinic in Town of Mount Royal. I'd like to visit him. If you need a lift, I can pick you up. Call me when you can."

"Let me know how your meeting with Paul goes," Dobson said. "You can text me anytime. The captain told me I'm working as your backup on this."

"Well, Dr. Watson," I said, "I'm not sure who is backing who on this. Just to say, I'm really glad to have you on the case."

Dobson's cryptic half smile appeared and vanished in the same second, as if he had caught himself doing something wrong—an uncomfortable show of emotion, maybe, a body tell announcing that he was not used to getting anything remotely akin to an attaboy or a compliment. He put his cup down and fished a notepad from his corduroy jacket.

"The two at Angela's had empty pockets—no wallets, ID, or anything. I ran the fingerprints. Got one hit from an arrest sheet after an altercation between drivers involved in a car accident. I found a Nguyen Bào Quân in the system, but the mug shot isn't of the guy I fingerprinted. I'm lost on this one."

"Computers aren't always right," I said. "The *garbage in* adage has basis. 'Nguyen' is the Vietnamese equivalent of 'Smith' in North America. Try a given-name and middle-name search. Those guys were pros. The nothing in the pockets tells a story. Unless they recently arrived from another country, my guess is, they have a rap sheet somewhere."

Dobson smiled as he flipped a page of his notebook. "I scored better on the Mercedes license plate. The car's registered to T and T Performance, an aftermarket car parts manufacturing company. They have a plant in the East End of Montreal. The owner is Pham Thuan Trung, a.k.a. Thomas Thuan."

"Thomas Thuan—he's a race car driver," I said. "I remember the 'T n T' emblem on his jumpsuit.

I saw him on the podium at a car show a few years back. Not sure the man I saw escorting Suzanne was him, though."

"Well, he still thinks he's a race car driver," Dobson said. "He's got a list of speeding and aggressive-driving violations on record. Eh, also involved in a few bar and nightclub brawls."

Dobson gave me the phone number and GPS coordinates for Thuan Trung's business.

I paid for lunch, and we headed to Angela's to pick up my GTO.

Michael Kent

# TWENTY-SIX

I found my windshield decorated with a glued-on 8" x 11" sticker warning that I was parked in a reserved-for-owners area and subject to towing fees. In our city, as in most major metropolitan areas in North America, one of the new symbols of success, right up there with how fashionably you dress and what exotic car you drive, is a private parking space, reserved for your use only, protected by closed-circuit cameras and monitored by sticker-wielding security personnel.

In my car trunk, I keep a scraper and an extra bottle of windshield-washer fluid—insurance for those frosty Montreal mornings. Several minutes of elbow grease later, I concluded that the intractable bond paper was stuck on with some insidious blend of Crazy Glue and epoxy. I called and left a message for Tony, explaining that I was stuck with something and would be late.

He called as I backed out of the parking slot.

"Lieutenant, I got your message. In any case, I have to cancel. I just inherited a three-car mess on the Decarie Boulevard service road."

We hung up after I told him he had an open rain check. The phone rang while still in my hand. Angela's name scrolled on the screen.

"Good morning, Miss Andreadis."

"Good morning, Lieutenant Beaudry. I picked up your message. I spoke to Paul this morning, and he wants to see you, so your offer is perfect timing."

"He wants to see me? Anything special?"

"Paul knows who attacked him."

"His memory is back?" I breathed, as if saying it too loud might break the spell and erase the precious recollection.

"He told me his faculties are one hundred percent. He can't wait to get out of the hospital."

"Knowing the attackers' identity is one thing," I said. "Making sure they're no longer in a position to harm anyone is another. We need to consider his safety and yours before he gets discharged from the hospital."

"I'll let you and Paul discuss it, but I know he wants to go back to his home."

"I can be downtown in twenty minutes. Is that okay?"

"I had a late brunch in my room. I still have to dress. I need at least an hour."

"Okay, I'll call you from the lobby."

The GTO was high on the power-to-weight ratio but low on the fuel economy scale. With the gauge headed for E and with some spare time available before I picked up Angela, I stopped at a corner gas station. One look at today's announced gouge rate told me I should be driving a company car. I had chosen to drive my own because police vehicles had to be returned at the end of the shift, never to be used for personal activities. Driving my GTO ensured that it was not recognizable as an unmarked car—an asset in certain situations—and it gave me flexibility in my work hours and for running personal errands during the day. The purse strings on the city budget were so tight that my boss never pushed the issue. Looking at the dials spin up more than the monthly payment back when the car rolled off the showroom floor, I reconsidered my initial choice. I'd have to discuss options with Jean—when he was in a good mood, if that should ever occur.

Sunday drivers were out a day early, and the main boulevards to downtown were as congested as on a weekday. The stream of cars trickled me downtown at glacial speed but without actually stopping. When I got to the hotel, a sleight-of-hand twenty in the hotel valet's hand convinced him to

leave my car in one of the fifteen-minute "for check-in only" slots.

I was exactly on time at the reception desk. I dialed Angela's cell phone three times in as many minutes, only to be shuttled to voice mail after six rings. *Strange,* I thought. If she was on the phone, the system would transfer to message after the first or second ring. Suddenly worried, I made my way to the front desk.

I pointed to a house phone on the marble counter and asked the young man at reception to connect me to Angela's room.

He never looked up—another slave to the glowing screen. "Can you spell the last name for me, sir?"

"Angela Andreadis," I repeated, then spelled it out slowly for him.

"I'm sorry, but we don't seem to have a guest registered under that name, sir," he said, finally managing to rip his attention from his monitor and look up at me. "Are you sure you have the right hotel?"

I did the badge flip. "This *is* the hotel. Can you double-check for me?"

"Uh, I've found a file." His Adam's apple undulated rhythmically as he cleared his throat twice. "Just one moment, sir."

He reached for his desk phone and punched up a speed-dial number. "I have someone at reception for you," he murmured, and then hung up.

"Is she coming down to the lobby?"

"Just one moment, sir." Again his Adam's apple betrayed the swallow.

Before I could ask what was going on, I spotted a well-dressed, muscular gentleman walking briskly toward me. Instinctively I turned to face him while assuming a nonchalant but action-ready stance.

He held out his hand. "Lieutenant Beaudry, I'm sorry for the inconvenience."

For a muscular guy, he had uncalloused hands and impeccably manicured nails.

"How do you know my name?"

"You've been on television and the news more than a few times," he said. "My name is Naren Naidoo. I'm head of security for the hotel. It's part of my job to keep up with police intelligence."

"What's this about? Did anything happen to Miss Andreadis?

A busload of people and wheeled suitcases had queued up behind us. He nodded to the left, toward a little alcove and two high-backed upholstered chairs. "Let's step out of the reception area, where we can talk."

Following him, I could see the fabric of his bespoke suit tighten in the shoulders and back as his

muscles flexed. I dropped into one of the chairs, and he did the same, only more gracefully.

"So give," I said. "You've got me worried about my witness."

"No worries in this hotel," Mr. Naidoo said. "We take good care of our guests. Moments after Miss Andreadis checked in, a man dressed in dirty coveralls asked for her room number. We never give out room numbers. The front desk clerk asked if he wanted to phone her room. The man declined, said he'd call her later, and left in a hurry. The clerk thought it suspicious because, when Miss Andreadis checked in, a police officer accompanied her. He left his card with the clerk and wanted to make sure we had security cameras in the corridor of her floor. The clerk called me, and I had him upgrade Miss Andreadis to a suite, and we also put her under another name. She's registered as Mrs. A. Dobson, though she doesn't know it."

"*Rats, rats.* Dobson must have been followed. I forgot about the gardener."

"Lieutenant, never mention that word in a hotel."

"'Gardener'?"

"No, the first words."

"Very funny, Naren. I use the "R" word in place of the "F" word. It was a deal I had with my ex-wife. Sometimes, even a good habit is hard to

break. Now, back to Angela. I'm surprised you're so proactive on security."

"We cater to hockey teams, grand prix drivers, and celebrities who value their privacy. I have to be on top of things. I use outside contractors when I need extra protection for the guests.
Would that apply to Miss Andreadis, Lieutenant?"

"I don't think I need a team of mercenaries. We have it under control."

"I prefer the term '*contractors,*'" Naren said as he handed me his card. "You need anything, call me."

We stood up as Angela walked to the front desk. I headed to her, with Naren three steps behind me. I overheard her explain to the desk clerk that she left her room card and cell phone on the bed and had locked herself out of her room. I was certain that the room rates in this upscale hotel were on the high side of my budget, but the service was worth it. Naren took charge and instructed a bellhop to fetch Angela's missing card and phone while he led us to a dining alcove with complimentary coffee and little pastry bites. We sat in comfortable wing chairs facing each other over a low coffee table.

"Paul didn't tell you who his attacker was, did he?" I said.

"No, we talked about, um, *other* things."

I nodded as I sipped my coffee. Angela fairly

glowed. She looked as if she was really in love and eager to see her "back in shape" paramour. I, too, looked forward to seeing Paul—and, the gods willing, solving this case with no further gunplay. A few minutes later, Naren Naidoo returned with Angela's missing phone and card key. Before we left, he reminded me once more to call him if I needed anything.

# TWENTY-SEVEN

Dr. Blain's clinic looked like a sterile copy of a downtown luxury hotel. A private security guard ushered us into the suite. Landry rose from an overstuffed armchair and rushed to hug Angela. The hug quickly escalated to ardent kissing.

Before it developed into tonsil hockey, I said, "Maybe I should step out of the room."

With flushed cheeks, Angela broke free long enough to send a displeased look my way. Paul laughed and pointed me to one of the armchairs. "I'm glad to be alive, and I feel fine. Thank you for saving Angela's life yesterday, by the way. I owe you."

I sat down in the offered chair. Paul sat in the other, with Angela perched on the arm and caressing the back of his neck. They looked like love-smitten teenagers. My thoughts drifted to my date with Zee later tonight. I shook my head and refocused.

"I was just doing my job," I said. "And I don't think they wanted to *kill* Angela. We think it was a kidnap attempt."

Angela made a little gasping sound and tilted toward Paul. He slipped his arm around her waist and pulled her onto his lap.

"Why?" he said.

"Let's back up a notch first. Who attacked you?"

"Suzanne's boyfriend, Thomas."

"Thomas Thuan, the race car driver?"

"Thuan's not a race car driver. He's a wastrel who's managed to spend his inheritance on fast cars and faster women."

"Why does he want you dead?" I said. "It's not going to help Suzanne in her case against you. What am I missing here?"

"I can't tell you why he wanted me dead. What I can tell you is, the guy's obsessive—a real nutcase. His henchmen wanted me to give them a report, but I didn't know what they were alluding to. Thomas came in a few minutes later, didn't say a word, just started swearing and hitting me. I lost consciousness—didn't even know he'd shot me till Dr. Blain explained my injuries."

Angela went teary eyed. "It's a miracle you're okay," she said, burrowing her face into his neck. Paul moved his hand a little higher on

Angela's thigh. I was definitely a third wheel here.

"I'll have my partner, Dobson, come and take a statement from you. You okay with that?"

"Yes, no problem," Paul said. "I want that psycho out of our lives. He should be locked up."

"I *had* figured out that the attack had nothing to do with the money laundering that your partner, or partners, are doing for the Russian mob," I said. "But that scenario was my first assumption. Did you confront them on this?"

"Partner, not partners. Only Charles is involved, and the *only* reason is that he needed some fast cash to pay off his houses and some debts he had accumulated."

"Dealing with the Russians can only get you deeper in trouble," I said. "It wasn't a good solution. For a smart lawyer, he should have known better. He's part of an in-depth tax investigation that may now rub off on your firm."

"No," Paul said. "he acted independently from the firm. And there's more to the story. Two winters past, Charles lost his wife to cancer. Seven months ago, he was diagnosed with stage-four lung cancer. They were both heavy smokers. He didn't want to go through all the chemo and suffering that his wife had. He opted instead to put all his affairs in order and let nature take its course. He's paid off his houses, provided for his children, and been generous

with his partners."

I unfolded myself from the chair and avoiding Angela's legs circled closer to the lovebirds.

"Well, I guess he made a good decision after all," I said. "It makes it easier for me to tell you some bad news. I'm afraid that Mr. Brown died yesterday at his Florida home."

I spared them the details, as well as my suspicions about Brown's demise. They could find out later without spoiling the cuddly mood of the moment.

"For your statement on Thomas," I said, "I'll have Dobson call on Angela's phone before he comes to see you. Now I'll go to the office and have a warrant issued for Thuan's arrest."

"It's Saturday. If you have a problem finding a justice, call my golf partner, Judge Daniels. Tell him my story. He'll sign your warrant."

"I have my own list, but thanks for the advice. I do need something from you, though. Can you get me a copy of the report from your PI, Vissani?"

"Why do you need that?"

"Just tying up some loose ends," I said. "The warrant will get Thuan in our hands for questioning, but he'll probably lawyer up and then make bail. On the loose again, he'll surely be a danger to you and Angela."

"We have to circumvent that possibility," Paul said. "I want to go home and get on with my life. I'll not cower for the likes of him."

"I agree with the attitude," I said. "As the inspirational Orison S. Marden wrote; 'Most of our obstacles would melt away if, instead of cowering before them, we should make up our minds to walk boldly through them.' But in this case, you also have your lady to look after."

"I don't want to go back to my place," Angela said. "I couldn't sleep knowing there had been two dead bodies in my living room. It would give me nightmares. This morning, Paul and I agreed: I'm moving in with him."

"From the way you two look at each other, I'd say it's a logical decision," I said. And it certainly makes security easier. I'm sorry about the unavoidable mayhem in your house."

"It's okay," Paul said. "We know you were defending Angela, but I guess police protection can go only so far. I presume I'll have to source my own security as soon as I leave the clinic."

I ambled back to the wing chair as Angela left Paul's lap to rearrange the flowers in a vase on the night table. Fishing my phone out of my jacket pocket, I said, "You presume correctly, but I can help you with arrangements."

I dialed Naren Naidoo, the security guy from the downtown Westin. "Naren, this is Lieutenant Robert Beaudry. You said call you if I needed something. I'm calling."

"No problem at all. I'm pleased to be of service." Naren sounded sincere and willing to help. I gave him the abridged story of Paul and Angela's security needs, and Paul's home address. He offered to contact the VIP bodyguard service himself. I gave him Angela's cell number before thanking him and ending the call.

"You go above and way beyond the call of duty, Lieutenant," Paul said. "I can't thank you enough."

"That reminds me," I said. "I'm taking care of your cat. I saved him from the pound and brought him home with me."

Paul laughed. "I'm not really fond of cats. It's Suzanne's. She said she didn't want it anymore—said it shouldn't have grown so big—and dumped it on me. If you want, you can keep him. It's another favor I owe you. I'd really like to do something for you. I appreciate all your kindness."

"You let me visit your car collection someday, and we'll be square."

"I'm out of here on Monday," Paul said. "Anytime after that, whenever you're available, Lieutenant, we can go for a ride to my country place.

That's where I keep my collection. Angela tells me you drive a vintage GTO."

"We can compare man toys next week," I said. "If you feel up to it, you can drive my car to your country place."

"I'd love to, but Blain forbade me to drive for at least a month, until he's sure there are no vestigial problems with my cognitive abilities."

I unfolded myself from the overstuffed chair. "I'm headed to my office. You enjoy the rest of the day."

Paul gave me a wink before I turned to the door. It got me thinking of Zee again.

# TWENTY-EIGHT

I phoned Dobson as I headed for the office. I'd have to get myself some kind of Bluetooth accessory. It didn't bode well for a representative of the law to be in constant violation of the new no-cell-phone-in-hand-while-driving law. With a hundred and fifteen dollar fine and four demerit points, I'd spend my pay and my license would be suspended within a week.

Dobson answered on the first half ring. "Hate to bug you on the weekend," I said, "but Lawyer Landry's memory is back on track. He says Thomas Thuan is his attacker."

"That's another fast close for you, Lieutenant, and it's no bother—I'm still at the shop."

"For *us,* partner. I need you to get a steno, go to the clinic, and take an official statement from him. We need to back up an arrest warrant."

"I was just about to call you," Dobson said,

his voice oozing excitement. "The lab struck gold with those two you shot at Angela's. Traces of blood on one guy's shoes match the bodyguard André Tisseur's blood type. I've got a rush on DNA analysis. I'm ninety-eight percent sure it'll put them both at the crime scene."

"Good news. If we can tie them in with Thuan, we're on the right track."

"Eh, hold on a minute. The captain just walked into the lab."

I heard muffled words as if Dobson had his hand over the phone. Then the voice of my boss assailed my ear.

"Beaudry, what the hell are you doing at the hospital! I told you, you're on a desk. *Sapristi,* are you deaf?"

"Not deaf, but that may change if you keep yelling at me. It's the weekend; I'm on my own time. Just visited a friend in the hospital. I'm on my way back home."

"Beaudry, save the horse pucky for someone who doesn't recognize the smell. Dobson just told me you need a criminal warrant for Landry's attacker. I'll take care of it myself, and you stay out of the arrest—I need a *living* culprit on this case. Is that clear, or should I send you a text?"

"Crystal, and thanks for the vote of confidence."

"I'm just protecting you from yourself. If you go and get yourself killed, I'd have to suspend you indefinitely."

"Okay, yeah, I get it. You don't want to see me, but you still love me."

The captain handed the phone back to Dobson. "Eh, Lieutenant, I caught one side of that conversation. Don't worry, I'll follow up for you."

"Starting something and not being able to finish," I said. "Very frustrating."

"Eh, know the feeling."

"Still a lot of loose ends," I said. "The attack on Landry makes no sense. We have victims and guilty parties, but no motive. A talented defense attorney could fly loops with a 747 through the holes in our case. I'm not happy with this at all."

Lieutenant, I'm not even going to ask what you're planning. But good luck."

We hung up. I was antsy about my date with Zee, not sure what I was getting into. I felt upset about Colleen's brusque departure, disappointed by my boss's mistrust of my ability to make a simple arrest without shooting someone, and unsure whether my case was ready to send to the prosecutor. My gut feeling said trouble was coming my way. Before I could sort out my muddle, the drumroll on my phone announced a call from the captain.

"I'm still on my way home," I said in place of my usual "Beaudry." "I heard you the first time: I'll stay away. Honest, boss."

"No, no, never mind that. Charlie and his partner are at a domestic dispute gone bad. Kids and wife stabbed. Everybody else on the team's unreachable for the weekend. You're the only one I can send. Patrols just called in a homicide at a bar."

"Aw, crap, Jean, you'll owe me some time off."

The captain gave me directions to the scene. He didn't have any information on the fight, other that it had ended in a death. It was three minutes from my location. I couldn't in good conscience say no. One muddle, two muddles—why not? I made an illegal left turn, cut off two cars, and headed to the bar. In the background, the almost musical sound of blaring car horns.

# TWENTY-NINE

The patrols had cordoned off the area. Canary-yellow polyethylene strips with black print proclaiming in French, "*Barrage de Police - Accès Interdit*," strung between lampposts, utility pole, and squad cars. I passed a group of curiosity seekers convened across the street. In the crowd, a pale young girl in a hoodie and pyjama bottoms soothed a crying baby by rolling the stroller back and forth. She held hands with formidable black woman dressed in Day-Glo green and purple spandex. Two youths in baggy pants were jostling for a better view behind a homeless man's heavily laden shopping cart. Others in the crowd were busy snapping cell phone pictures of the bar entrance and the cops guarding the door. *Welcome to West Sherbrooke Street,* I mused as I slid the hood of my Pontiac under the police tape and between two blue-and-whites. I swiped my phone to Zee's number.

She answered, as Dobson had, on the first ring.

"You keep your phone right there in your hot little hand, Zee?" I said.

"Just about to call you before you send out an APB."

"Uh, what's up?"

"They need a qualified nurse in the ER—kid with stab wounds. You okay for a late supper?"

"No problem," I said. "Do what you must do. I'm used to having supper past nine. I was calling you to say I may be late myself, but I'm *really* looking forward to see you again."

"Okay, eight forty-ish. And, uh, bring your *appetite*. Sorry, have to go." She hung up. No cell phones in moving cars, no cell phones in a hospital. We were both terrible at keeping to the rules. Maybe that was part of our attraction.

The beat officers had done a good job: body roped off, area well secured, and evidence left untrampled. But for the unnatural angle of the neck, the two-hundred-pound guy with a wrestler's build looked comfortably asleep on the scuffed hardwood floor. The bar and poolroom patrons were lined up on one side of the room. The EMT Urgences-Santé team, looking weary and sad faced, stood near the victim's feet.

"You try to revive him?" I said.

The taller and more mournful of the two medical technicians lowered his head as if peering over a pair of glasses or, perhaps, addressing a fool.

"Can't revive a broken neck."

"Somebody broke his neck?"

"Died in a few minutes from spinal shock—neck snapped probably at C-three or C-four. Dunno about the 'somebody,' though; that's the cops' job, not ours."

"Yeah, I'm the cop, and it's '*Lieutenant*' cop. You stick around till the coroner gets here."

"Ah, crap, our shift was finished."

"My feelings exactly," I said. "I was heading home myself. Did you touch anything else?"

The technician pointed across the room. "No, the big cop told us not to move from here."

The big cop was indeed large of girth—a sergeant in conversation with one of the bar patrons. I moved to them. His name tag read "B. Phillips"; the officers at the door had called him Bernie. With a smile on his face, he explained to me what he understood of the situation.

"The ugly guy on the floor is Cesar Bauer, a.k.a. Bully Bauer." Bernie flipped his thumb over his shoulder, not bothering to look at the body behind him. "He worked hard for that moniker. He

was on my short list of assholes. It was only a matter of time before somebody put him out of everyone's misery."

"Sergeant, you seem a little too pleased that he finally met somebody bigger and meaner than he was," I said. "I'm getting a sense that you didn't like the guy."

"He put a lot of hardworking people in the hospital and always seemed to get away with it. He provoked and provoked till his victim finally took a swing at him; then he beat the crap out of them, claiming self defense."

Bernie's smile turned into a big, silly grin. "This is the guy that did him in—accidentally, as it happens."

I turned to the skinny little man next to Bernie. A line of dried blood ran from his nose down to his chin. The stain reappeared just below his collar and ended in a half circle at the bottom of his shirt pocket.

"Are you pulling my leg, Bernie?"

His smile got wider, his eyes merrier. "Nope, Lieutenant, that's the hero."

"Hero, not culprit," I said. "I can see whose side you're on."

Bernie introduced me. "Lieutenant, this is an old schoolteacher of mine, Professor Leger."

Leger is a common enough French surname,

but it also means "lightweight." I restrained myself from making a jest that he surely had heard a thousand times and no longer found amusing. The guy was five feet and a finger width tall and weighed all of 110 pounds after a big supper. He appeared to be in his late sixties, and his white frizzy do recalled Einstein in his latter years.

He had his suit jacket draped over his arm. I took it, patted it and him down, then walked him by the arm toward the unhappy tavern keeper fidgeting behind the bar.

"Okay if I use your office for a few interviews?" I said in a way that suggested he didn't have much choice. "It'll speed things up. Otherwise, I have to drag *everyone* downtown."

The bartender stopped nervously wiping a sparkling-clean glass and sighed. "Yeah, yeah, sure. The faster I get back to business, the better. Go ahead, the door's not locked."

I sat Leger in a chair and myself on the desk, notebook in hand.

"You're not under arrest," I said. For now, you're a material witness. I'm going to ask for your version of what happened, but anything you say may wind up used against you in a court of law. Do you understand?"

He answered in a surprisingly deep, resounding voice. "I understand perfectly. Even if no criminal charges are laid, your notes may be subpoenaed in a civil case against me."

"Uh, yes. You wouldn't be a *law* professor, would you?"

"No, I'm Professor Adrian Leger, U of M. My specialties are applied mathematics and geometry. Bernie has all my personal information. Let's get to the facts of the case. First, what's your name, Officer?"

I did the badge flip in slow motion, giving him time to read the credentials.

"Okay, Professor, what are the facts?

"I come here once in a while to play pool—such an elegant combined application of geometry and physics. When BB was present, if he wasn't busy baiting his next mark or arm wrestling some other Neanderthal, he would make fun of me and anyone who played with me."

"'BB'—that's Bauer?"

"Bully Bauer is—er, *was*—BB." His voice dropped from tent-meeting preacher volume to a near whisper. "It was an unfortunate accident. I was lucky. He wasn't."

The professor looked at the floor and seemed to shrink into himself. If he didn't stop soon, there wouldn't be much of a witness to question.

"You okay?" I said. "Can you continue? You need a drink?"

He gave his head a vigorous shake like a dog getting out of the water, which fluffed his hair out even more. He straightened and looked up at me.

"I don't drink. I just come to play pool. Normally, BB makes a few ill-placed jokes about my appearance or my lineage, then moves on to his favorite victims. Today, he decided on me. But I didn't just let it ride as I usually do. I answered back, matching him one for one, eventually challenging him, in front of all the patrons, to a duel of sorts: eight ball. I win, he shuts up and leaves me alone; he wins, I never set foot in this establishment again."

"For such a small frame, you have a powerful voice," I said. "I'm guessing he took the challenge."

"I need volume and resonance to reach the class lazies in the back row. And yes, he did. People in the bar were clapping and goading him on. He couldn't back down without looking silly. To show off, BB added twenty dollars a game to my challenge. After I had pocketed eighty, he started accusing me of cheating and made me change cues. When I won the fifth game, he came undone."

"Undone?"

"Totally insane. Swearing, spitting insults, trying to provoke me into a fistfight. I had seen some of his antics before, and regardless of what he said, I

wasn't dumb enough to fall into his trap."

"If you didn't fight him, then who punched his ticket?"

"That's the funny thing. Nobody."

I put down my pen and pad. "Nobody. Is this a replay of 'Who's on first'?"

"No, no. He grabbed my stick, broke it in two as easily as snapping a pencil, and then started poking me in the chest with the big end." The professor unbuttoned his shirt as he spoke. "I'm sure I have bruises.

"Whoa, horsey, I'm missing something here. He started hitting *you*. Nobody hit him, and yet, *he's* dead on the floor."

"You're too impatient. I hadn't finished. He scored a few hits on me, but he always dropped a shoulder before lunging. I could read it coming and I'd back up or swipe the cue away. He kept on missing, and it enraged him. He lunged at me one last time. I ducked; his wild swing put him out of balance. He skidded on the small end of the cue, which he had tossed to the floor, fell backwards, and hit his head on the corner of the pool table. You'll find the broken cue under him."

"That's a good what-goes-around-comes-around story," I said. "The bully finally getting what he deserved. Am I going to get corroborating statements from the other patrons?"

"I'm sure of it, Lieutenant Beaudry In any case, you have the tapes."

"What tapes?"

"The two hidden cameras in the bar. Jimmy doesn't trust his bartenders, nor does he enjoy hearing complaints about somebody's missing wallet." The professor pointed somewhere behind me. "The monitor is on the desk. No pickpockets in the place since he put the system up last year."

"Does Bernie know about the surveillance system?"

"He's the one that recommended it to Jimmy. He didn't tell you?"

I stepped to the door and barked that I wanted Jimmy and Bernie in the office.

The bartender walked in with a scowl, followed by Bernie, wearing his silly grin.

"Bernie, you neglected to tell me about the closed-circuit video. If I were of a suspicious nature, I might think you're enjoying this." I spread my hands out, palms up, as if to say, *what gives?*

"Bauer was in my class from fifth grade to high school. I got into law enforcement to stop bullies, thieves, and abusers of all kinds. The shrinks will tell you that I'm compensating for years of abuse and ridicule. Me, I just enjoy my job. I get to see famous detectives solving crimes from up close."

"Okay smarty pants, I get that Bauer bullied you for years—probably gave you some demeaning nickname."

The corners of Bernie's mouth flipped from up to down, and in a low voice, he said, "Fluffy."

"Fluffy—that's not so bad."

"There was usually another 'F' word before the 'Fluffy.'"

"Well, I'll invite you for a beer sometime and we can trade stories about who had the worst childhood," I said. "For now, let's do a reset and get back to the job. We need to play back the videos."

Jimmy, the owner, didn't have to be told. He swiveled the screen to the front, unlocked a file drawer, and pressed a couple of buttons.

The show was a dramatic enactment of Professor Leger's story. From one camera angle, it showed Bauer slipping on the broken-off small end of the pool cue, striking his head, and dropping the other half of the stick, which then rolled under the pool table. The other angle was a good shot of the professor getting clipped on the nose by Bauer's last lunge. As far as I was concerned, apart from Bernie's snide remark about detectives, no wrong was done and I had no wrongdoers to arrest.

Pulling out my phone, I pointed to Bernie and then to the floor in front of me. Bernie waddled up as the captain answered. I put the call on speaker.

"Captain, I'm winding up at the bar fight. The victim slipped on a cue that was on the floor. Going down, his head struck the edge of a pool table, cracking vertebra C-two or C-three, causing transection of the spinal cord. End of story. We have witnesses up the wazoo, and video disks of the accident. I'm working with patrol Sergeant Bernie Phillips, a senior officer who knows what he's doing. I'm leaving him in charge of finishing up with the forensic team, getting statements, and handing over the video disks to the evidence locker. You okay with that?"

"For an accidental death, no problem on my end. We'll let the coroner rule on that one. Let me speak to the sergeant."

I handed the phone to Bernie as I heard the forensic identification team come in the front door.

I mouthed "*CSI is here*" to Bernie as I walked over to greet them.

The CSI team took pictures from all corners and then from the center of the room looking outward. They stuck little rulers and ID tags next to various objects and fixtures and made measurements up, down, and sideways. I commented on their professionalism but reminded them that this was not a murder case. They reminded me that their official designation was not "CSI" but "FIS"—Forensic Identification Service. We left it at that.

I delegated responsibility for the scene to Bernie, who thanked me for my confidence in him. I gave him my card and cell number and reiterated my offer to grab a beer sometime. When I left, he still had a big smile plastered on his face.

# THIRTY

I was back on the road to home. I liked Zee's "*dnt bring xthing just U appetite*" text, though I wasn't entirely sure what appetite she was hoping I'd bring. I had to stop and get some flowers, change clothes, and feed the cat, with no time to waste. The traffic-jam demon must have hacked directly into my thinking process.

Some idiot in a mad rush zoomed out of a service station entrance and got T-boned by a city bus. His jacked-up truck flipped a hundred and eighty degrees, its rotation stopped by the powder-blue Maserati ahead of it when one of the oversize all-terrain tires crushed its trunk. I could picture the insurance adjuster weeping at signing off on the claim cheque for the damage to a city bus and a quarter of a million dollar sport car.

I put my blue light on the dash, flipped the hidden switch under the dash, and sirened my way

over to the sidewalk and into the gas station parking area.

I hurried over to the truck and saw no blood. The driver seemed dazed but unhurt. Bless the roll bars that he had probably installed just for show. I badged a few rubbernecks, telling them to move away from the scene, and helped the pickup driver crawl out of his smashed windshield. A well-dressed woman of mature years stood by the open driver's door of the Maserati, tears running down her cheeks.

"You okay, ma'am?"

She shook her head. "Not even close. My husband will kill me."

I walked to her and handed her my card. "Have him call me before he goes violent. It wasn't your fault."

She stared at the card. "I wasn't serious about him killing me. I didn't mean *kill* kill."

"Just the same, have him call me."

I went back to the young driver of the truck. He looked a bit wobbly. To steady himself, he held on to a mud flap, now at head height on the upturned truck.

"You look a bit shook up," I said. "Did you hit your head?"

"No, no, I'm fine, fine. No problemo. No-o-o problemo."

His pupils weren't dilated, but his reply

smelled like a recently imbibed six-pack. I phoned 911 asking for backup at the accident scene, and dispatch told me patrols were already on the way.

From the leather case on my belt, I pulled out a rarely used pair of handcuffs.

"Can you put your hands behind your back for me?"

"I din't do nothin'—had maybe two beers." He looked rearward from where he stood, telegraphing his intention. I let him turn, then kicked him behind the knee. He folded and then tried to bound up as a patrol officer hurried toward us. I showed my badge and asked the officer in French slang to do a Breathalyzer test on the driver.

"*Passe lui la balloune,*" I said, pointing to my guy, who was trying to go around the officer. He got no farther than the officer's nightstick reached. It guided him back to his responsibilities.

The unlucky drunk sat in the squad car, sweating, blowing in the balloon, and rubbing his kneecap. I gave the patrolman's partner the story as I saw it. The screen on the tester showed an alcohol concentration well over the limit. I looked down at the young driver.

"BAC of point one-oh-three. Maybe two beers, maybe you forgot to mention the two shots they were chasing."

I got my cuffs back and headed back home as

other patrolmen unsnarled traffic and directed a tow truck to pick up the bent metal. It was a different service from Antonio's company.

The city was segmented into districts, with different towing companies having priority in different zones.

The woman's comment about a husband who might get violent over his precious Maserati rang a sad note for me. I scrolled down my phone contacts to Charlie Harmsen. I let it ring forever, figuring his cell would eventually go to voice mail. He finally answered, sounding out of breath.

"Bo, Beaudry?"

"Chief sent me to a body in a bar, told me you guys were stuck with a bad domestic. What's your situation? Need backup?"

"Thanks, we're just wrapping up. Situation was shit. Not good, not good at all. Husband a manic-depressive off his meds. I wish we could have got here sooner. Stabbed his wife maybe forty times, his son and daughter another twenty. Then he tried suicide by cops on us."

"Aw, shit, did you have to put him down?"

"Tased him to the ground. Only good part of the day. For your ears only: I might've aimed a bit low. He may have trouble getting it up for a while."

"I have a friend in the Jewish said they were working on a kid with stab wounds," I said.

I heard Charlie take a couple of deep breaths. "The twelve-year-old daughter stood in front of her younger brother, trying to protect him. He was a mess, but alive when we put him in the wagon.

Let me know how if he makes it, Robert. I'm going home to hug my kids; then I'll have a stiff drink."

"Take it easy, buddy; I'll get you some news."

I drove with a lump in my throat, but no other traffic-jam goblins interfered along the way. I made it to my corner florist minutes before closing time.

\*\*\*

In a record thirty-eight minutes, Crackers was fed and let out and I was back on the road. I had managed to reduce my house cleanup chores—no more toilet paper confetti strewn along the hall. This morning, I had decided that from now on, unless I had guests, I would remove the double roll of Ultrasoft from the dispenser and hide the *Nephrolepis exaltata* fern in the bedroom. I was a bit worried about where else he might transfer his perverse attentions, but that would wait for another day.

Tonight, I motored to Zee's dressed as a guy going on a hot date, but with sadness in my heart and worries in my head.

# THIRTY-ONE

Zee opened her door, and smells of fresh bread and something sautéing in garlic wafted out to me. She wore a knee-length white kitchen apron that had seen some action.

"It smells great, and the hot chef has splashes of tomato sauce on her apron," I said. "A clue that we're eating Italian, perhaps?"

"Welcome to Trattoria Zotti—and it's not a bring-your-own-wine establishment, you bum."

She took the flowers and led me into the dining room, where I put the bottle on the table.

"Valdicava Brunello di Montalcino 2010 *riserva*. Whoa! I snared a big spender." She gave me a fast peck on the cheek. "Sit down; you look beat. I'll get a vase."

I pulled out a chair, took off my jacket, and hung it on the back. Then I dropped my tired butt on the seat. I forced a smile when she came back.

She looked over her shoulder at me while arranging the flowers. "You really look bummed, Lieutenant. Put the badge away and send Robert out."

"Sorry, sorry, Zee," I said. "I feel as if I've spent the day dredging the sewers of Montreal."

"Well, my day wasn't exactly life affirming, either. I have my special *bruschetta con funghi* in the oven. Let's have the appetizers and your fancy wine. You moan about your day, and I'll whine about mine. Then, when all that's out of the way, we enjoy the farfalle, spicy sausage, and each other's company."

"That sounds like a fine plan."

I gave Zee the story of my day, working backward from the drunken idiot driver who, but for the grace of God, could easily have killed a few people, to the body in the bar, back to my meeting with Paul, seeking a warrant for his attacker, and my boss's orders against getting any further involved in that case.

"So you're unhappy not to be in on the final chapter," Zee said, refilling both our glasses.

"No, he's right. Others on the team can take over. It was just a slap to my ego to find that he thought I couldn't wrap things up without shooting someone or creating a mess. But considering my

history, I really can't fault him. I killed two perps this week, and I'm sure I could have avoided that confrontation by following procedure and not rushing in with my red cape flapping in the wind. I'm really not at ease with how that ended."

"I understand. It can weigh heavy on you. I'm always upset about losing a patient, even when I know there was nothing I could have done about it. I think you're down because you're disturbed about more than just the job."

"'Disturbed' may be the right word. I feel like crying and laughing at the same time. I'm not the strong, silent hero cop the media makes me out to be. I'm just in bad shape right now and I don't want to let people down—especially you."

"Don't jump off the boat just yet, sailor. We said we were taking things easy and loose. Don't go all mournful on me now."

"You're right," I said. "I think the last few weeks just caught up with me. Wife gone with someone else. I'm pissed and relieved at the same time. I'm not good at admitting my mistakes, but that marriage was stupid from the get-go. The last few days, I've been sloppy on the job, and it nearly got me killed twice."

Zee took my hand and slapped me hard on the wrist. "Just because I'm a nurse doesn't mean I'm going to bandage you up when you get sloppy,

you big oaf."

She had a frown, but her eyes had that warm-honey glow again. I pulled my hand back and made a show of rubbing it.

"Domestic violence—I could handcuff you for that."

"Promises, promises," she said, topping up our wine glasses yet again.

I tried to sound less serious than I felt. "Speaking of domestic violence how did the kid with stab wounds make out?"

"He's going to be okay. Was that domestic violence? I thought it was a gang fight."

"Dad went off his meds. Killed the wife, then went after the kids."

"Oh, shit, no wonder you're fucked."

"It wasn't mine. I was at an accidental death in a bar. But one of my buddies took it hard. The daughter put herself in front of her little brother, trying to save him. My friend has two kids the same age. He felt real bad he didn't make in time to save them. You sure the boy will be okay?"

"Now we're getting to the rotten part of my day. The surgeon on duty was sloppy. You would have sworn he just got out of med school. He was making such a mess, I had to call the head surgeon and insist that he get his ass to the operating room."

"So you did what you had to," I said. "Kid was lucky you were there."

"You don't understand the politics. A nurse—even a supernurse like me—can't go around questioning a doctor's procedures. I made a scene in the ER and held the doctor back until the boss showed up. Even though I was right, I'm liable to be disciplined."

"That's stupid."

"Apparently, it would have been better if I'd let the kid bleed out. Screw the system."

"I guess I'm not the only one with a red cape flapping in the wind, *Supernurse.*"

"'Licensed nurse practitioner' is the official designation. I'm one of about twenty or so in Quebec with the added degree, but it's worthless. Docs have a stranglehold on the health-care system, and they don't give an inch."

"So bottom line: the boy will be okay?"

"The head surgeon had problems with a lot of bleeders but managed to plug everything up. He may have to go in again if something pops loose, but I doubt it. Dr. Vineberg's meticulous. The kid's arm will be scarred for life, but for the rest he's going to be fine."

"I'm going to call my buddy and let him know, okay?"

Zee had a penetrating look on her face. "I think your heart's as wide as your shoulders. Robert." She kissed me hard on the lips.

\* \* \*

The farfalle with sausage, tomato, and basil was mouthwatering. Fortified with another good bottle of vino from Zee's pantry, we were feeling no pain by the time we got to cappuccino and dessert.

Pointing to the remnants of the lemon curd and mascarpone parfait in front of me, I put my index finger to my cheek and made a twisting motion—Italian body language for delicious.

"*Tutti molto sapporito, bella,*" I said.

"That's sweet. Didn't know you spoke Italian."

"My best friend is first generation. I understand most sentences but need a lot of practice speaking it. The plural exceptions with adjectives and those irregular verbs are murder. Not to mention the variations in pronunciation that every little village has."

"You came to the right place to practice your Italian flirting. Anything else you'd like to work on?"

"Well, now that you mention it, we should probably do some movement to digest our supper."

*"Aspettare qui bello."* She told me to wait as she walked to the bedroom.

I snuffed the candles on the table and rinsed the wineglasses out. A few minutes later, she called from the bedroom.

"I need a detective to check under the bed. You never know . . ."

"A man's work is never done," I replied.

She was dressed—barely—in a sheer black babydoll.

"I think I should check the top of the bed first. You never know," I said, peeling off my clothes.

We cuddled together, and within minutes, the wine took its toll. I heard soft snoring as Zee went softer in the crook of my arm. Oh, well, there was really no rush. Nobody had to be at work in the morning. I hugged her tighter and closed my eyes.

Michael Kent

# THIRTY-TWO

I woke before Zee, slid my arm deftly out from under her, and went to the washroom. I found toothpaste and finger-brushed the wine breath from my mouth. When I got back, she was on her tummy and had lost the short negligee. She did a languorous yogic sort of stretch, arcing her backside up in a fetching way.

"I think we should get back to what we started last night," she said.

"I don't think we had time to start anything."

"Must have been in my dream, then."

"If I'm not mistaken," I said, "Anaïs Nin wrote, 'Dreams pass into the reality of action. From the actions stems the dream again; and this interdependence produces the highest form of living.'"

"She wrote erotic literature, didn't she?"

"Some of her work, yes."

Zee flipped onto her back and did the arching

move again. It was even more spectacular from this new angle.

"We should verify her statement, Detective."

\* \* \*

After some mildly strenuous but invigorating team yoga, I made breakfast. Zee came back from the shower dressed in jeans and a form-fitting green sweater.

It was sunny, with no rain in the forecast, so we jumped in the car and went adventuring to the Eastern Townships. No schedule, no commitments."

I took the freeway to the eastern townships then 112/108 towards Vermont before exiting onto winding back roads towards Lac Magog and Massawippi we passed through some of the prettiest villages in Quebec. Patches of maroon and ochre-gold leaves clung on here and there, but it was a bit late in the season for the full autumn color show. We didn't care, jacket collars up and the windows down, telling each other silly jokes and enjoying the fresh country air.

"We've cleansed the serious-detective face from you," Zee said. "You look happy and relaxed."

"Fresh air and yoga must be the secret."

"Typical male answer," she said, shaking her head. "Cars and sex rule the world. I don't think you're that superficial. You probably have a poem or

some deep thought on driving with the wind in our hair."

When stuck for something exquisite, you can do worse than Yeats. *"Faeries, come take me out of this dull world, for I would ride with you upon the wind, run on the top of the disheveled tide, and dance upon the mountains like a flame."*

"Robert, you're an interesting, complex man, but a little bit scary."

"Now who's getting too serious? Why would you say that?"

"You act like a goofy teenager, then, in the next instant, the cultivated aesthete, reciting gorgeous poetry, but your eyes always look like a predator's."

"Acting silly is how I stay sane. I've seen horrors I can't unsee. Maybe my eyes reflect my job: tracking down deadly rages that are often hidden behind ordinary, bland faces."

We passed a faded blue farmhouse, a weather-beaten sign advertized brown eggs for sale. Crude wood stands stacked with pumpkins fronted the roadway. On the horizon the silvery spire of a village church foretold of a village.

"So your eyes reflect your job?" Zee said.

"Nah, it's just the gleam of lust. I only have eyes for you."

"Good, we're back to silly. All this fresh air is getting me hungry. A late lunch would be nice."

Fifteen minutes later, we entered North Hatley. We found the local pub at the entrance of the main street bridge. Zee took one look and shook her head. Pure luck and a detour down School Street found us nicer bistro. The dining room in this heritage home had floor to ceiling bookcases on both sides of the fireplace. Tall windows and crisp white tablecloths offset the dark red walls.

Our soup was an in-season cream of pumpkin, carrot, and some spice that defied our taste buds. The service was genial, and the chef, surprisingly open with her secret ingredient. When I told the young server that we couldn't identify the subtle taste she asked her mother to come and explain the recipe. Zee chose the sliced duck breast, and I went with the Roasted Halibut.

"A day with you is like a week's vacation," I said.

Zee gave me a silly and suggestive grin. "And wake-up sex with you is like a weekend binge without the calories or the hangover."

"Now who's the poet?"

"I don't think I want to go back to work tomorrow," Zee said. "It's too nice here."

"I'm tied to a desk. No rush to go in early. When does your shift start?"

"Two p.m., but I have to work late."

"I have to go feed my cat; then maybe we can have supper somewhere near my place?"

"You've talked a lot about your crazy cat," she said. "I'll finally get to see him."

We motored back toward reality, Zee leaning over the console with her head on my shoulder. For the last six months of my marriage, I had been living alone with someone. Now I had found a quiet, tender synergy with Zee. I could get used to this. The little voice in my head warned me. Both of us had said "no long-term commitment," but I knew that somewhere down the line, heartache awaited.

Michael Kent

# THIRTY-THREE

My home is in a row house much like a New Orleans veranda building. The first apartment is at street level. Then the typical Montreal wrought-iron curved staircase up to a second-floor balcony, a door for the second apartment, and another door to an interior flight of steps up to my place on the third. Crackers peeked down at us from under the second-floor railing as we stepped out of the car. He announced his displeasure with a wildcat's growl.

"Crackers doesn't like to stay outside all day," I said.

"You named him Crackers?"

We reached the top of the stairs. "I took your suggestion—fits him perfectly." I pointed with my chin at the hissing, humpbacked furry monster jumping sideways in little spurts toward us.

"More predator eyes," Zee said. She slipped her purse around her neck and, in a fluid move, bent over, grabbed him by the scruff of the neck, and

flipped him upside down into the crook of one arm.

"Not afraid of you; not afraid of him."

She put her other hand under the cat's neck, preventing him from nipping at her while she scratched behind his ear. He seemed crestfallen that his wildcat exhibition hadn't impressed Zee. I unlocked the front door, and she followed me up the stairs with Crackers, nestled like an enormous docile kitten in her arms. She plunked him down in the living room, and he galloped into the kitchen. His supper was late. I filled his dry food bowl as he milled impatiently around my legs.

I gave Zee a tour of the apartment. "My dad passed last year," I said. "I inherited this triplex and an old farm that I rent out."

"I'm sorry to hear that," she said. "Your mom still alive?"

"Died when I was eight—victim of a botched bank robbery. Then and there, I decided to become a policeman."

"Following in Dad's footsteps?"

"No, he was well off and successful—a plumber by trade. I'm the only one in the family who turned out badly."

"Still in silly mode, I see. You have a cozy bedroom with a king-size, but the walk-in full of women's clothes is a bit of a turn-off."

"She's borrowing my car on Tuesday to cart everything out to her new digs."

This brought a scowl to her face. "I told you your heart is as wide as your shoulders," she said. "You should have thrown everything in the street."

"The thought did occur to me, but hey, I'm a cop. I have to be a good example for my neighbors."

"Would it be a bad example if you walked out with a few things packed for tomorrow and slept over at my place tonight?"

"Nah, that's just living the Boy Scout motto: 'be prepared.'"

Michael Kent

# THIRTY-FOUR

A little starry eyed after another joint stretching wake-up shag, I drove Zee to work. A hug and a kiss later, I aimed the GTO toward Thomas Thuan's T&T factory. I had a message from Dobson telling me there was an APB out on Thuan but he was still on the loose. The raids on his workplace and home had yielded nothing. I then phoned my boss to report in. Happily, I got his voice mail.

"I'll be at my desk later today," I said. "Gotta pick up some parts for the Pontiac. You owe me time off, anyhow. My cell is open if anybody needs me."

The trip was fast—light traffic on a Monday just after lunch. I turned into the reserved-for-visitors plant parking.

The receptionist, a wispy, very young-looking blonde, was multitasking between the phone system, her computer, and a pile of mail. Her eyes had the faraway look of a teenager ignoring an adult.

I cleared my throat and did the badge flip. "Need to talk to Thomas Thuan, or whoever's in charge."

The young girl had attitude. "Thomas isn't here; *still* don't know where he is. There were a bunch of cops here yesterday asking for him. Don't you guys talk to each other?"

"Well, we're still looking for him. Sorry to disturb your important work, but I need to talk to someone in charge—*now*."

"Dwayne Hollis is the boss. He's busy and you don't have an appointment."

"Two choices: he talks to me here or downtown in an interrogation room. You ask him which he prefers. And by the way, you're already on the ragged edge of interfering with an ongoing murder investigation. Maybe I should extend the ride-downtown invitation to you, too."

She stared at me with eyes of disgust and contempt—a look that teenage girls can master perfectly. She left everything on her desk and walked away in a huff. I wasn't sure she'd be back.

A slim, fit-looking man came into the reception area, followed by Miss Attitude. His salt-and-pepper brush cut and ramrod-straight walk reminded me of a Royal Air Force officer I had once met.

"Your SWAT people were here yesterday," he said. "We wasted hours. What is it now?"

I showed him my power smile and my ID card. "I'm really sorry to disturb you," I said. "There's been a murder, an attempted murder, and an attempted kidnapping. I think you can really help me stop another death from happening. I'm trying to protect a potential victim, and I absolutely must talk to you."

"Ah, well, come into my office," he said. "I'm in a meeting, but I'll be with you in five."

He was true to his word. He stared haughtily across his big desk to where I sat, on an armless visitor chair.

I stood up so I could look down at him. "I know that Thomas is involved in a murder," I said, "but I can't reason why. I have to learn more about his personality, attitudes, and such from someone who knows him well—someone like you. I need to figure out his next move. The situation is worsening by the hour, and I foresee a few more bodies if *we* don't act fast."

Hollis seemed to look right through me. Trying to ignore people must be a company trait. "I don't know what to tell you."

I moved closer, forcing him to focus on me. "We start from the beginning. What's your relationship with Thomas?"

"We're—or we were—business partners."

"*Were* business partners?" I said. "Start at the beginning."

"Sit down, Lieutenant, you're making me nervous. Thomas has always been a spoiled playboy. His Vietnamese family is wealthy—old money from before the conflict. Thomas is very bright. From his experience in racing, he developed performance-enhancing parts for car enthusiasts. His problem is that he has a short fuse and zero people skills. He hired me to set up and run the plant. Then, when he needed money, I bought in as a partner."

"Needed money?"

Hollis shook his head. His face reflected disapproval. "His father died, and now he has a limited stipend, not the old man's generous cheques. Thomas isn't good at managing money, and he's addicted to racing. He bought a two-hundred-thousand-dollar Gallardo and sank another hundred thou fitting it for competition."

"Racing hot-stuff Lamborghinis costs," I said. "Did it win?"

"Didn't last long. He destroyed it during practice and promptly purchased a new one. He was hemorrhaging company money to the point of ruin. I had to step in to protect my investment—offered to buy him out."

"Ah, invoked the shotgun clause." I said. " He must have loved that. I'm surprised he didn't go violent on you.

"Anything happens to me, he'll lose the company. I have a law degree and an MBA in international business. There's two pages of fine print in my contract with him."

"Didn't he have a lawyer go over the contract?" I said. "He should have questioned the fine print."

"The fat slug didn't understand half my clauses. I think Thomas hired him because he can get him to do some dirty dealing."

"The clause, however well written, normally let's him buy *you* out for the same amount," I said.

"He's pissed away all his money on women and cars. He acts like an asshole and has a reputation for aggressive behavior. Nobody'll lend him a dime; banks won't even talk to him."

"I've heard that story before."

"He has to come up with two million plus in the next eight days or accept my lowball offer," Hollis said with a mean grin.

"The mess he's got himself into wouldn't have gotten him a bent dime," I said. "I don't understand his thinking."

"Rational behaviour is not his forte." Hollis got up and took a few steps away from his desk. "Is there anything else? I have to get back to work."

"He's on the run," I said. "Do you have any idea where he might be holed up? We have his North Shore house under surveillance, but he's a no-show."

"Here, let me give you his lawyer's card. He might be in contact with Thomas."

"Thanks for the card and your time." We shook hands, but I continued probing. "Does he own any other properties, anywhere else he'd go to ground?"

"If he hasn't left the country, he'll be using a woman, hiding out at her place or house-sitting for one of her out-of-town friends." Hollis walked me to his office door. "Don't let the craziness fool you. He's smart, and dangerous as a cornered wolverine."

"While I'm here," I said, "would you guys have extended valve-cover bolts for a sixty-seven GTO four hundred engine?"

"Probably. Ask Catherine at reception."

"Ouch. That kid has attitude."

Hollis gave me a crooked smile. "My daughter. You should hear her at home."

I got my parts, and Miss Attitude turned into Miss Nasty—charged me full retail even though I was picking up at the factory.

As soon as I got to my car, I called Dobson. His phone went to voice mail. "Hi, partner, I'll be in a little later and give you an update. In the meantime, got an address for Suzanne, Paul Landry's soon-to-be ex-wife? Appreciate if you could text me."

I swiped the map app on my phone and typed in the address from the lawyer's card that Hollis had given me.

\* \* \*

The office was in an East End gold-tinted glass tower that was part of a large shopping mall complex. I stepped out of the elevator on the fifth floor, home to six small companies. One of the listings on the board read, "Étude Légale, Dulac-Radino-Yu. The card I held read "Me. Phillip Yu, LL.B."

I had no appointment. I hoped the receptionist would be more understanding than T&T's Little Miss Attitude.

I did the usual drill: give power smile, show credentials, lie to receptionist. "I apologize for cutting into Maître Yu's schedule," I said. "It's a last-minute thing. Mr. Hollis told me to rush over."

She pressed one of the buttons on her phone system and mumbled into her headset microphone. "I have someone here from Hollis, says it's urgent."

It appeared his calendar wasn't full. He couldn't have whisked into the reception area any faster if Scotty himself had beamed him in. Neither handsome nor hideous, Yu looked like a pear-shaped, bald Buddha, with wrinkles around his eyes and a wide smile on his face.

He looked at me for a second, put his hand out, palm down, and wiggled his fingers as if typing on an invisible keypad. As I stepped forward to shake his hand, he turned and said, "Yes, yes, come," and headed down the corridor. I followed.

His office looked like an unkempt warehouse for a paper distributor. Piles of documents and banker's boxes stacked to waist level filled most of the room.

He pointed to an orange plastic chair for me while leaning himself against a huge, intricately carved desk that was also covered in reams of stapled documents.

I didn't think the flimsy chair would hold my weight. We stood face-to-face, arm's length apart. "I just came from T and T," I said. "Mister Hollis indicated that you may be in contact with Thomas Thuan. I have to speak to Thomas urgently."

"Not know, not know."

I stepped a bit closer into his space and raised my voice. "Bullshit. You're Thuan's lawyer. I have

to find him before he gets into more trouble."

My impertinence bounced right off his beaming smile. He nodded enthusiastically while answering, "Thomas gone. Not know."

I backed off a foot and shook my head. "You're a scholarly person, a lawyer," I said in a sad tone. "You're surly aware that if I find out that you knew where Thomas is hiding, you could be charged with harboring a criminal or interfering with an investigation. Probably get you disbarred."

The smile remained painted on his mouth, but it was gone from his eyes. I caught his nervous glance toward something on his desk.

"Do I call officers to take your office apart?"

"Thomas gone with lady friend. Not know, not know."

"Thomas is gone with Suzanne, but you don't know where?"

This time, he shook his head slightly. "Not know where."

I shifted my weight to the right. "Has he left the country?"

Yu sidestepped left as if to block my view of his desk. I put my left foot on his right, preventing him from taking another step, my hands in a low tai chi defensive position. His mouth opened slightly and his eyes went wide. A bead of sweat broke free and trickled down the side of his face. I was sure he

had something on his desk that he didn't want me to see.

"Give it to me," I said.

Rolling his belly over the edge of his desk, he reached to the center to retrieve an envelope. He handed it to me.

"Not know where he now. Not know."

The legal-size envelope had small Chinese characters down one side and "Hold for Thomas Thuan" printed in bold script. I opened it. Inside were documents requesting a visa for a several-month stay in China. Other documents were undecipherable, but from the letterheads, they appeared to be from Chinese firms. At the bottom of the envelope was Thuan's Canadian passport.

"What's this about?"

"Thomas go suppliers China next week. Not come get documents. Not know."

I was beginning to believe him. "When was Thomas supposed to pick up his documents?"

"Tuesday."

"Tomorrow?"

"Last week, the Tuesday last week."

"I'm going to hang on to this," I said. "I appreciate your helping. I'll mention it to my captain."

Of course I had no intention of doing so, but I wanted to confiscate the passport without a yard of

paperwork. He nodded and appeared relieved. I took it as my cue to get out.

\* \* \*

As I stepped out of the elevator, my phone played a note indicating a message. I waited till I was back in the car to read the text from Dobson. It was Suzanne's address. I added the entry into my GPS map app and fired up the GTO.

I spotted the unmarked car parked two houses away from Suzanne's. Fat cop tires, shitty hub caps, and an antenna on the trunk of an off-white Ford. On a residential street of expensive row houses, it blended in like a fire truck. This was not a discreet, inconspicuous stakeout. Probably patrol officers on temporary duty and just glad to be in civvies for a change. I parked on a side street behind their position. From the trunk, I grabbed my delivery man disguise: stenciled brown jacket, cap, clipboard, and fake UPS special delivery parcel. I walked up to Suzanne's address and rang the doorbell, not expecting to get an answer. I wasn't disappointed. I promptly went next door to her neighbor on the right. Again no answer. Maybe, in these fancy houses, both parents were working to afford the mortgage payments. I tried the left-side neighbour and got the same result. I crossed the street and rang another doorbell. A frowzy-haired woman in her

golden years came to the door. She had more makeup than a Kabuki dancer and held something furry and alive in her arms. A dog that looked for all the world like an Angora rat started yipping and ran to the back of the house the moment she put it down.

I pointed over my shoulder to Suzanne's door. "I'm delivering a package across the street," I said. "Do you know if they'll be home later?"

She looked me up and down and motioned me into the foyer. "You're not the regular UPS guy."

"Special-delivery package—she's gotta sign for it."

"I don't think Suzanne will be back for a while, and good riddance."

I took off my cap. "What makes you say that?"

"She's not a very nice person. George's car is an older Cadillac. I have trouble getting it into the garage, so I leave it in front of her house sometimes. Can't park on this side of the street Tuesdays or Thursdays—have to park it on her side. She rang my door asking me to get it out from in front of her house. I won't repeat her nasty words." She mimed closing a zipper over her lips. "And it's not true that George's car is rusted. He always took care of it. Washed it every week, even when he went for the cancer treatment."

I held my hands up in a T for "time-out."

"I meant, what makes you say she won't be back for a while?"

"Oh, they left with a pile of luggage—didn't all fit in the trunk. The Chinaman threw some of her cases on the backseat and they took off like the Devil was chasing them. He didn't look too happy, if you ask me. Actually, neither did she, as if I give a darn, pardon my French."

I made another time-out sign. "When was this?"

"Some morning last week . . . must have been Wednesday, because my car was on this side of the street."

The barking rat started up again. "Stop that, Mooky!" she yelled.

I excused myself, saying I was late for my other deliveries, and thanked her as I made my escape.

I walked by the stakeout car and tipped my cap. They should have wondered about a delivery man with no truck, and I could have told them about the luggage, but why spoil a nice break for them?

The heavily spackled, powdered, and rouged lady gave me another part of the puzzle. I learnt that Thuan had packed to leave with Suzanne on the same morning as the attack on Landry and his

bodyguard. My problem was that I now had plenty of puzzle pieces, but none of them fit together. Why would Thuan be in a rush to escape *before* he committed a crime, and why did he miss his appointment to pick up his travel documents from lawyer Yu on the day before. The sequence of events seemed in reverse order. Paul had fingered Thuan as his attacker, but I still hadn't discovered a motive for the brutal attack. There was something happening behind the scenes that I couldn't yet grasp. Maybe I had discarded the Russians a little too easily.

# THIRTY-FIVE

In the nursery rhyme, Tuesday's child is full of grace, whereas Wednesday's is full of woe. I was a day early with the woe. I had come back from the office late last night, grabbed a quick bite, then headed to the gym to meet Tony the tow truck driver and teach him some pressure-point moves. When I got home, I just crashed.

At seven this morning, I retrieved yesterday's message from Colleen: *"I'll be at your place around eight. I have help to move, so it shouldn't take long. If you're not in, leave your car keys on the kitchen table. I'll do the same with mine. I still have a house key."*

I'll face drug-crazed, gun-wielding felons before breakfast, but I just didn't feel up to facing the aggravation that Colleen dispensed so effortlessly. I took a few things from the bedroom

and kitchen that I didn't want her to mistake for *her* stuff, and put them in a locked travel chest I have in the back room.

I left the GTO keys as a paperweight on a note telling her I had inherited a big, pushy cat that would certainly want to be let back in, but not to listen to his complaints and to leave him outside.

I opted to avoid the annoyance of interacting with Colleen and walk to a restaurant a few blocks down. I'd disappear for a couple of hours and treat myself to a leisurely breakfast. I carried an oversize envelope, sent from Paul Landry's office that landed in my office mail yesterday. In a fast meeting, the captain had confirmed that *officially* I was still tied down to a desk. I took it to mean that my leash was fairly long and that he didn't expect to see me at my desk for my entire shift. Our internal people had accepted last week's shooting as occurring in the line of duty, but the Provincial Police had yet to sign off. At this point, it was paperwork formality, and I was expected to be back on the street in a day or so.

I had a longer meet with Dobson. He had been a tad incredulous when I told him that the "don't leave the country" movie cop instruction was a done deal—that Thuan's lawyer had surrendered Thuan's passport and visa applications to me when he learned from Hollis that an APB was out on his

client. I had given Dobson the envelope and he had elected to sit tight on the documents pending further developments. The kid was learning.

Just as I turned the corner toward the restaurant entrance, my phone rang. The screen displayed "Unknown Number."

"Beaudry. Talk to me."

"This is a friend of a friend. You called about some Russian business?"

"Yes, I inquired if there were any dealings between both *companies.*"

"Where are you?"

I gave the caller the name of the breakfast place. He said someone would meet me in the next twenty minutes.

I had often passed by this place on my way home but hadn't gone in yet. I studied the menu. It was a colorful exercise on how many cute names and double meanings were possible using "egg." I went with the fruit eggsplosion. The service was fast, and the food eggsellent. I was savoring my second piece of blueberry-blackberry-smothered French toast when a man sat down at my table.

In his early thirties, he looked like a model from an Italian men's fashion magazine—even sported the currently in vogue three-day stubble look

and wore a tight-fitting mismatched suit jacket over a cold orange fine-wool sweater. From the corner of my eye, I saw a few women glancing our way. I was fairly sure my jeans-and-abused-leather-jacket look wasn't the draw.

Without looking down, I said, "Nice shoes."

He smiled and shook his head. "Discount Bruno Magli."

"You want coffee?"

He lifted a finger to shoulder height. The young waitress rushing to our table could have qualified for women's sprint at the national level.

"Green tea, one egg easy over, whole wheat, hold the butter."

"I'll take a cappuccino," I said.

As the dreamy-eyed waitress left, he said, "Cappuccino here is crap."

"Now you tell me."

"Our family has no direct dealings with the Russians," he said. "No partnerships."

"They have legit businesses here," I said. "Unfortunately for any unknowing financial backers or investors, Revenu Québec will be digging into transactions as part of an in-depth tax audit."

He took a small leather-bound notebook and slim silver pen out of his jacket and looked at me. I told him I wasn't in a position to give him details, but I gave him all the Korisky companies and

building projects I could remember from my conversation with Zafirah. I could call in favors from "friends of friends" only if I had earned and banked them before.

"I'll pass this on," he said. "You're well regarded as an honest and discreet person. I understand that you eliminated some Vietnamese problems a few days ago."

I shook my head. "An unfortunate and upsetting incident."

"Two contractors flew into town a week ago last Monday," he said. "Very professional, very polite— a Vietnamese and a Frenchman. They met a friend of the family and gave him a business deposit of forty K to ensure our noninterference."

"Noninterference in what, um, transaction?"

"Not in a position to give you details." He smiled. "They're in Montreal, searching for two *friends.*"

He nodded to me and left the restaurant without a good-bye.

I wondered whether Thuan had more reinforcements than just those that I had taken out of play. He was on the lam. It didn't make much sense that he would still be after Landry and his lady. Another strange fact to file away—a puzzle piece that might fit in somewhere down the line.

The first sip of cappuccino confirmed my mystery visitor's comment. I slit open the envelope from Landry's office and signaled the waitress over.

"Sorry, but the cappuccino is dishwater. Can you bring me back a coffee? Black."

"Your friend left in a hurry," she said. "I didn't have time to deliver his order. Was something wrong?"

"Late for a magazine shoot," I lied.

With a relieved grin, she fetched my coffee as I pulled out a sheaf of legal-size papers.

It was the detailed report from the private eye Vissani. The first part was the detective's log on his surveillance of Suzanne. At 2:15 p.m., subject left her apartment, drove to Claude Hairdresser on Such-and-such Street . . . At 4:10 p.m., left Hairdresser, went to blah, blah, blah . . . It was a boring read of a few days in Suzanne's life. It did, however, catch her at lunches with other men and in hotel assignations and late rendezvous. The male participants in her wanderings off the marital reservation were named and described, including home addresses, one of which I recognized as Thuan's. The report included each man's vehicle make and model, license plate number, office address, and banking and credit information. He even had a glossary identifying all the pictures he had taken, with dates, times, and

locations. No pictures were included in my file. Vissani may have been a crook, but his investigations were first rate.

The second part of the report was a more in-depth look at Thomas Thuan. It followed his daily activities in the same format as Suzanne's days. In a separate and smaller attached report were highlights of a meeting between Thuan and his lawyer, Phillip Yu. It read as if Vissani were in the room. I was sure it came from an illegal bug Vissani had managed to plant somewhere in Yu's office. The conversation was in French.

The bastard had snowed me with his bad English. The gist was that Thuan feared that some document created by Yu had a mistake in the figures and might lead to the discovery of missing funds from the family trust. If I were in a cartoon, a lightbulb would now be flashing above my head, with "BINGO!" written in my dialogue bubble.

\* \* \*

I didn't bother to walk home and get Colleen's car—just cabbed it downtown to headquarters.

I was ten feet around the corner from the captain's office when he barked, "Come in, Beaudry." His radar is downright scary.

"Jean, was your mother bitten by a bat when she was carrying you?" I said. "I swear, you can hear frequencies that humans don't."

His little mustache curled up slightly on the left. In all my years working with him, it's been the only clue that he may be smiling. I plunked the Vissani reports on his desk.

"I asked Landry to send me the report from Vissani, the private eye he hired to get the goods on his straying wife, Suzanne. Her affair with Thomas Thuan is what started the avalanche."

Jean rocked his chair back. "So far, I haven't learned anything new. You have something more exciting for me?"

"Patience is a virtue."

"Coming from a guy who's a minus forty-six on the patience scale, you're just flapping your gums to hear your own voice."

"Tough audience," I said. "The Vissani report contains a small addendum. Thuan has been embezzling funds for years—probably millions from the family trust, to support his racing habit and fast lifestyle. Based on Vissani's past performances, I'm guessing he must have tried to blackmail Thuan. It got him a shank in the throat. The next loose end was Paul Landry, and perhaps Angela, if Landry confided in her."

"Congratulations," Jean said. "You now have a motive."

"We still have to find Thuan," I said.

"There's no *we*. The fugitive-apprehension team have the ball. Move on to another game, Robert."

"No problem, boss. I'll let Ray's team grab Thuan. But, there's a cloud on the horizon: a team of hit men are in Montreal, looking to eliminate a problem. Not sure if Thuan wants to finish the job with Paul and Angela, or it's the Thuan clan, unhappy about getting ripped off by a wayward son."

"Bottom line, Beaudry?"

"I need a couple of days off. I'd like to hang around with Paul and Angela. I'd hate to read the headlines of their murder."

The captain dipped his chair forward. "I wouldn't want to see them hurt, and contrary to what you may think, it has nothing to do with headlines. My only worry is that little gunslinger goblin on your shoulder, whispering in your ear. I'll agree to your babysitting, but if somebody makes a move on them, you call SWAT. Don't jump in with guns blazing."

"*Gun,* not guns. And for once, I agree with you. I replay the scene with the Asians several times a day. I'm not happy with how that went down. I

give you my word, I'll call if things start going south."

The captain nodded my way, emptied the envelope onto his desk, and started to read the Vissani report. I got the psychic message that our conversation was over.

I went to my office, corrected a few of my reports, and sent them up the line. Then I did some research on lawyer Yu, got his home address and some background info through some Internet queries. There was nothing on him in our criminal database yet.

I called Dobson. He was in the midst of a crime-scene photo shoot. He told me to call back and he'd let the phone go to voice mail and that yes, he would appreciate an update. I did as he asked, then scrolled to Angela's cell number. She answered from somewhere with a lot of noise in the background.

"It's Lieutenant Beaudry," I said. "Sorry to disturb—just wanted to check up on both of you. Can I speak to Paul?"

"We're fine. I'm grocery shopping. Paul's at home. Call him there."

Angela gave me the number; I saved it and dialed out. Someone picked up, but no one spoke.

"Paul? It's Lieutenant Beaudry."

"I didn't recognize the number . . . thought it might be Suzanne."

"No such misfortune. I'm just checking up on you guys. Angela said all was well."

"Yes. Why are you calling me?"

"Well, I did have that invitation to see your car collection. I do have a couple of days off, so I was just wondering."

"Oh. No problem at all. I owe you a lot more than that. Tomorrow before lunch would be fine with me. I'm itching to get out to my country place in Hudson."

I thanked him for the Vissani report and rang off. Angela's mention of grocery shopping reminded me that my larder was at low tide. I scribbled a quick list of stuff to pick up on the way home. A few hours shackled to a desk was as much as I could tolerate in one day. Filled with the hopeful intention of working later this evening, I packed my old briefcase with non-confidential paperwork. Once in a while, I'd get an attack of tidiness and bring files home. More often than not, the briefcase went back to the office unopened.

I slipped out for a late lunch at a great Chinese restaurant close to headquarters, just north of the touristy "official" Chinatown district. Then I cabbed it back to my place.

My heart sank a little upon seeing Colleen's orange and black Cooper S in place of my GTO. It

stood out like a thumb splint on a concert violinist. It wasn't just the distinctive color scheme. It was parked at an angle some three feet from the curb. Feeling equal parts annoyance and trepidation, I climbed the stairs to my apartment. A piece of paper was peeking out from my mailbox. The note, folded into a pocket, held the spare house key and proclaimed in Colleen's bold script that she seemed to be missing some kitchen utensils.

*Hire a detective,* I grumped to myself. The extra key was useless. I had already decided to change the locks.

Everything in the apartment looked in its place. All was calm and peaceful. I dropped my briefcase on the kitchen table and pocketed her car keys. So far, so good.

The bedroom door was closed. Crackers woke when I opened it. He was sleeping on top of a pile of my sport coats, tossed on the bed. I guess they had been on her side of the closet.

I couldn't help smiling. He had won the battle to be let in.

Crackers unwound, stood up, and stretched to twice his length. After giving me an appraising look, he fell back onto a wool-and-cat-fur blazer.

A plate, rattled with fishy treats, solved my problem, and everything was back in its rightful place when Zee called.

"You free to talk for a few minutes?"

"Just got home. Colleen's emptied the closet. I hope it'll enhance my bedroom's appeal. What's up?"

"I just had to talk to you," she said. "I'm feeling terrible. I got called into my supervisor's office this morning."

"The ER incident caught up with you?"

"Yes. Her comments were so bureaucratic and stupid, I blew my top. Afraid I'm on bedpan duty. Supervisor said, if I wasn't happy, to stay home."

"That's nuts!" I said. "Why would they waste supernurse talent?"

"They don't care about supernurses. The administration isn't on board with reducing some of the doctors' work. They prefer adding young docs and low-wage nursing assistants."

"That makes zero sense," I said.

"Now you're getting the idea. Higher-wage supernurses are paid by the hospital; doctors are paid directly by the province; budgets look better."

"What are you gonna do, Zee?"

"Done it already. That's why I feel bad. I called a nurse friend in Miami and e-mailed her my CV. It's breaking my heart."

"Yeah, I'm sure you'll miss the winter fun up here."

"You big oaf, I'm going to hang up before I make a blubbering fool of myself."

"Hang in there, Super Zee. I may have an interim plan. It's my turn for the supper invite. I do the cooking tomorrow night."

"Working night shift a few days. I'll get Monday off. I need a long weekend to get my things together."

"Okay, I call dibs on Friday night. I could take Monday off to help you."

"That may make things worse."

"You can't disappear like a bail jumper in the night, Zee. I'd only hunt you down."

I managed to get a snickering laugh from the other end of the line.

"We agreed on free and easy," I said. "Let's keep to the rules."

"I guess I can't ignore a request from an officer of the law. Remind me: your address."

Zee said she would be here Friday at seven, after stopping at her apartment to change out of her work clothes.

I added to my mental shopping list. Since it might be our last meal together, I wanted to make it a feast. As I headed out to properly repark Colleen's orange racer, a plan was taking shape in the back of my mind.

# THIRTY-SIX

I woke to the sound of a breaking dish. I had rolled over, my fingers closing on the Walther's Hogue rubber grip, when I realized what was happening.

"Crackers stop that, you vandal!" I yelled.

He bounded into the bedroom and jumped onto the bed, a three-foot streamer of toilet paper trailing from his mouth.

"Aw, rats. I forgot to hide the roll last night, didn't I?"

Crackers gifted me with the chewed-up strip and proceeded to lick my forehead while purring like a trolling motor.

"Okay, I get the hint," I said. "I'm up, I'm up."

With breakfast done, I cleaned up in the wake of my in-house wrecking crew. I had given Crackers a treat last night and left the plate on the kitchen counter. He had knocked it down, probably while

trying to lick the smell off it.

I trashed what was left of the toilet paper roll and repotted the *Nephrolepis* fern, which, inexplicably, was flourishing despite the cat's regular attacks.

The weather guesser predicted a high of twelve degrees Celsius. My schooling had been in the Fahrenheit era. I still went through the whole cumbersome process—multiply by 1.8 and add 32—eventually transposing the forecast to sweater weather in the low fifties. Jeans, Irish knit, and sleeveless hunting vest seemed about right for a country stroll.

I had decided on a first stop before meeting Paul. Rising at my crazy cat's 5:50 a.m. breakfast hour did have the advantage of putting me ahead of morning rush hour. I made it to Phillip Yu's home just before eight. A short, stocky woman was standing on his front porch, rummaging through her purse, when I walked up.

"Good morning, I'm here to meet Mr. Yu," I said while doing a casual badge flip.

"*Su juste sa femme de ménage moi. Rien à faire avec des rendez-vous.*"

She told me in colloquial French Canadian that she was only the cleaning lady and had nothing

to do with his business meetings. She finally found the house key in her purse, opened the door, and told me to wait outside. I said yes but put a hand on the door so she couldn't fully close it. A minute later, she came rushing back and waved me in.

She shook her head side to side, saying that something was wrong, something was suspicious.

*"C'est pas normale, c'est louche, c'est pas normale du tout!"*

Yu's house was a mess. Not that it was ransacked, exactly, but furniture was out of place, a broken lamp lay on the floor, and suitcases were tossed haphazardly in the living room, one broken open with clothes hanging out. I pointed to her and then to the door as I pulled out my sidearm. She got the message and ran out to the front steps. True to my promise to Jean, I called 911 and requested backup. Later, I would have to explain my reasons for being here in the first place.

There must have been a doughnut shop around the corner—the patrolmen were at the door in under two minutes. I had my gun down by my leg, and my badge out as I signaled for silence. I waved them to my right, and we did our clearing manoeuvres.

No one was in the house. From the nearly empty medicine cabinet, open dresser drawers, and opened wall safe behind the nightstand, it was clear

to me that Yu had been warned of scary visitors on the way. He must have packed in a mad rush. The suitcases still in the living room, and the broken lamp meant his hurried preparations had ended on a sour note.

I gave the officers the short version of Yu's involvement in a potential embezzlement-and-murder case and told them to contact Dobson, who would get an APB out for Yu under a material-witness warrant. When they asked why I didn't do it myself, I told them I was officially on vacation and, besides, it was their district. I didn't have to tell them to take the initiative; they jumped at the opportunity of a big case. They called their desk sergeant and pulled in the housekeeper for questioning. One of them started taking pictures of the scene.

Back in the Cooper, I sent a long text to Dobson, laying out my hypothesis that Yu had been grabbed before he could make it out of the house. I felt bad for the guy, even though he probably deserved it. On the plus side, it seemed to confirm that Paul and Angela were probably not the targets of the French and Vietnamese hit team.

Sure enough, there *was* a coffee shop a minute from Yu's house. I treated myself to a muffin and coffee and called Paul Landry.

"I can pick you up in thirty minutes," I said.

"Angela won't be joining us," Paul said. "She's not much into boys' toys or hiking in the country."

I finished the muffin and fought off the temptation to have another. The morning traffic jams were ebbing, but navigating around closed streets and orange-coned construction zones added ten minutes to my trip.

Contractors were in a rush to finish roadwork, overpass construction, and sewer and water main repairs before winter set in.

Montreal was past due for a revamp of its infrastructure, but why they decided to do everything at the same time was beyond me. I just wanted to be the guy renting out the construction cones.

Paul Landry's hilltop mansion looked good with the sun shining on the stone walls and white woodwork. My last time here had been at night, in a much eerier setting.

Paul was waiting on the front veranda. We looked as if the same wardrobe consultant had dressed us both. A gorilla in a suit stood next to him. I supposed he was part of the security team that Naren Naidoo had recommended. I had to show my ID and give an estimated return time before he would let us leave.

Paul looked at the orange Mini. "Angela told me you drive a sixty-seven GTO."

I let him sit and adjust the seatbelt before explaining. "My ex borrowed the GTO. I have this for a few days."

"I thought for a minute you had started your own collection."

"Nah, just a temporary thing. She's emptying her stuff from my apartment—didn't have the room to fit everything in this."

"Sorry to hear about your separation," he said. "Lot of that going around these days."

His sad tone suddenly perked up. "This is a fun car. I used to ice race an eleven-hundred-cc Mini Cooper in my younger days."

We talked about car stuff and the silly pursuits of our youth as I motored us off island, west toward Hudson Village. The highway also led to Ottawa, and at each road sign announcing miles to- I couldn't help thinking of Colleen.

We stopped for a quick lunch at the Mega Centre Outlets in Vaudreuil, just off the tip of the island. Paul insisted on picking up the bill. I didn't fight him too hard.

Just before Hudson Village, Paul signaled me right, toward the lakeside. His house, a smaller version of the Montreal mansion, appeared after a bend at the end of a long gravel road. The Tudor

Revival style main house had two twin-car garages on one side, and a three-story stone tower on the other. Off to the left, a short drive led to a caretaker's house of similar half-timbered stone and stucco build.

"This must be your country shack," I said, grinning.

We unfolded from the Cooper, and I just stood there, admiring the property.

"It is a bit ostentatious, I admit," Paul said. "The house and six and a half acres, I inherited from a favorite uncle."

"I guess you were his favorite nephew, too."

"My father's gay younger brother, Jamie, had no kids. Dad never spoke of him. Several years ago, my uncle contacted me. He was in a pit of depression; his lifelong lover had developed full-blown AIDS."

"Ouch! Time to reach out for support."

"Yes, and I was on the board of a few hospitals. I had contacts in a US facility experimenting with new drugs. I arranged transport and treatment; it probably forestalled the inevitable by a year or more. I never expected that he would leave me anything—certainly not *everything*."

"The house was only part of it?"

"My uncle was a music producer—made a lot of money in the States and Canada. I kept the house

but used the money to fund an AIDS research grant in his name."

With a small bow, I said, "You, sir, are a gentleman, a bighearted philanthropist, and a fine judge of classic cars. I'm honored to have met you."

Paul smiled. "You forgot 'connoisseur of fine liquor.'"

"That remains to be seen."

As we walked on the gravel, our crunching steps caused skittering sounds from the boxwood border of the pathway. I pointed to a tree a few feet from where we stood, an annoyed squirrel hung from the trunk, head facing down, tail flicking at us.

"I think we've disturbed preparations for winter."

At the door Paul turned towards me, and out of context said, "Lieutenant, I can't thank you enough for your care—and for saving Angela. She's given me a new lease on life."

"Not 'Lieutenant,' please. Just Robert. I have some vacation time due. I daresay I was thinking of the yacht you have reserved in Miami—are you going ahead with that?"

"Next week. You want to join us? You're more than welcome. Plenty of room aboard. In fact, I insist." He fished a key from his jacket and turned his attention back to the door, an indication that the deal was done, we were on board. He made a phone

call before putting his key in the lock. "The alarm on the main house is connected directly to the police chief's phone," he explained.

The interior was dark, its baroque furniture draped as if on a horror movie set.

"Needs a bit of airing out," I said.

Paul opened a secret compartment in a wall panel and took out a ring of keys.

"I have little use for it, but the garages are perfect for storage. I have room for eight cars. If the economy picks up, I'll put the place up for sale."

We walked to the first garage. Paul inserted a key in the door frame, and the wide door slid up on a motorized track.

He gently lifted off a protective cloth cover, and I stood mesmerized in front of a gleaming yellow 1939 Cadillac LaSalle. With its flowing front fenders, and teardrop headlights, it was an avant-garde design for its time. The other two cars were Fords: a black rumble-seat 1933 coupe and a metallic-green five-window '34, both in museum condition. We stayed for the better part of an hour as he gave me the details of each car and when and how he had acquired them. I enjoyed every minute. We bundled everything up and headed to the second garage.

The door was halfway up when Paul let out the first swear word I ever heard him utter.

"What's wrong?"

"The Mustang's gone. Thuan's Mercedes is in its place."

"They must be using your small house," I said. "I'll have to call for backup."

"They're not here now," Paul said. "They must be using the Mustang, probably because you have a search out for his car."

"Yeah. Still a danger—they can be back any minute." I walked to the Mercedes and touched the hood. "Cold as a side of beef."

"They could have left the country," Paul said.

"I have Thuan's passport. He could be headed to another province, but the Mustang's too easy to spot. I'm guessing they'll hang here till Thuan can get hold of some cash and new papers."

"Let's check out the caretaker's house. I'll get a shotgun from my den."

"Paul, I think that'll head us both into trouble," I said. One of the few things I could imagine that would be worse than getting into another shootout was getting an innocent civilian involved in another shootout. He ignored my comment and headed to the main house. The Mercedes was unlocked. I popped the hood, thinking to disconnect the battery and impede Thuan's escape. I reached into the engine compartment and froze. An aluminium box, with a bunch of wires

snaking out of it, was attached to the driver's-side firewall. I backed out of the garage, then backed up another ten yards. For a few moments, I vacillated between calling for backup and going on my own. I decided, probably unwisely, that a SWAT team roadblock and a dozen black-clad cops would be seen a mile away and just scare Thuan off. Besides, one call for backup per day was pretty much my limit. I scrolled down my phone list.

"Tony, it's Robert Beaudry."

"Hey, thanks for the training," he said. "That was fun! Can we do it again?"

"Absolutely. I'm calling with a little problem you may be able to help with."

"Don't tell me you smashed your sweet muscle car and need a tow."

"No, it's your other skills I need. I have a Mercedes with what looks like a bomb on the firewall. I don't want to look like an idiot and call my people if it isn't. And, more important, I'm trying to be discrete and not scare off the guy I'm after."

"No problem. Where are you?"

I gave Tony the directions. He said to give him an hour. As I hung up, Paul walked up holding a double-barreled coach gun.

"Why are you hiding behind a tree?" he said.

"I think there's a bomb in the Mercedes."

Paul scampered over to join me behind the big oak. "Why would Thuan want to blow up my house?"

"Did you read all of Vissani's report?"

"Didn't need to—had more than enough in the first pages."

"Well, the punch line is hidden in the last pages. There's a bugged conversation between Thuan and his lawyer, discussing their embezzling of funds from the Thuan family trust."

"That's why Thuan wanted me eliminated," Paul said. "So I couldn't testify against him."

"I think he's more afraid of his own clan than of the law. They have two hit men after him. The bomb is for him."

"Good riddance. But I'd just as soon it blew somewhere else."

"Suzanne may be with him," I said.

"I'd like to say good riddance to her, too, but I might feel a little bad later."

"I have a friend who's coming to look at the device," I said. "Let's see what we can do."

Paul nodded toward the small house. "Let's go see if they're really holed up in the cottage."

As soon as we walked in, Paul said, "The furniture's a little out of place, as if someone searched and then put everything back."

"The bombing team were here looking for Thuan. Must have had a tracking device on his car, or someone who knows his plans has talked. His lawyer was missing from his home this morning."

"This is an ugly thought," Paul said. "They probably tortured him. I'm ashamed to admit I'm enjoying this adventure."

Paul told me to park the Cooper behind the house. We waited in the tower room, hidden from view.

The forty-minute wait felt like a full day wasted. I really wasn't cut out for stakeout duty. Paul pulled a book out of somewhere and seemed to be lost in the story. A matte-black Chrysler 300 rolled to a stop in front of the house. It idled for a minute or two. Paul checked his shotgun as I unholstered my pistol.

The person who finally stepped from the car was Tony, my friendly tow truck driver. I tapped with my knuckle on the tower window, got his attention, and signaled "one minute." Paul and I walked out.

"The place looked abandoned," Tony said. "Wasn't sure I took the right road."

Paul took over as if the judge had said, "your witness, Counselor." Shotgun cradled in one arm, he stuck out the other hand to Tony. "Paul Landry. I own the house with the, uh, *problem* in the garage.

I'd hate to see it blown up, and I'm hoping you can do something about it."

Tony shook hands with Landry but looked at me with question marks in his eyes.

I pointed to the caretaker's cottage. "The criminal I'm after is hiding here with Paul's ex-wife. He stole money from some powerful people. They aren't happy. The bomb's in his car."

Tony turned to Paul. "Hoo, boy, that's a doozy. Your ex-wife, huh?"

"Don't rub it in. What can you do about the bomb?"

Tony took a satchel from the passenger seat and pulled out some mesh gloves, a small mirror on a telescoping stick, and some kind of electrical meter. He walked to the garage as if on a leisurely stroll.

I gazed absently at the twisted bark on the big oak between us and the Mercedes.

A few long minutes later, Tony walked back, calm as before. "It's quite a nice job. Very professional, a sophisticated package. I'm impressed."

"I'm glad you approve," I said.

"Is it safe?" Paul added.

"Yes, it's safe. It won't arm until the ignition is on. The signaling unit is wired into the car's computer system and GPS navigation. Real neat."

"Signaling unit?" I said.

"The box on the firewall is the controller and firing mechanism. The two-plus pounds of C-four are under the driver's seat."

"Can you disarm it?" Paul asked. "How much damage will it do?"

"House should be okay—maybe some light shrapnel damage and broken windows."

"The garage?"

Tony made a sweeping motion with his hand.

"You didn't answer about the disarming," I said.

"Like I said, it's very sophisticated. From what I can see, this is a remote-controlled device. They can track the car from its GPS coordinates and set off the charge when and where they want. It's not on a timer and won't detonate when the car is started. But there may be some safeguards against removing it. Personally, I wouldn't take a chance."

"Like the cell phone bombs we see in the movies," Paul said. "So it won't blow up in my garage. That's good news."

"Tony looked at both of us. The bad news is, the guy with his finger on the button is certainly not far from here, probably watching us as we speak."

"Aw, rats. Let's get out of sight," I said. "Thuan may show up any minute. Tony, drive your car around back."

"We'll put everything back as if no one were here," Paul said as he handed me the garage keys. I handed them to Tony.

He shook his head but smiled. "Bunch of wussies."

We were back in the tower room. Tony had regaled Paul with some of his military adventures, and Paul had lent him a scoped bolt-action 7mm Remington Magnum.

"My dad's favourite moose gun. He came home with a deer when I was nine or ten. Never got his moose."

Darkness had fallen, and it was way past my supper time. There wasn't much in the house, but Paul scrounged up some soup and crackers and made a big pot of coffee.

"Thuan may be long gone, or the hit team may have got him," I said. "You guys up to taking shifts? We'll wait till morning. If he doesn't show, I'll call in SWAT."

Our ragtag little platoon settled in. It was going to be a long night.

# THIRTY-SEVEN

Something poked me in the chest "Stop it, cat!" I growled.

I opened one eye. Tony stopped prodding me and said, "What?"

"Thought it was my cat stomping me. What's up?"

Paul echoed me with a groggy "What's up?"

"It's close to two in the morning. There's a car coming up the road."

Crawling to the window, I lifted the heavy curtains just enough to peer out above the sill. Paul's classic '64 Mustang turned left in front of the house and parked down the road at the door to the caretaker cottage. The car's interior lights came on for a second or two, but with trees in the way, it was impossible to make out whether one or two people stepped out.

"What now, Lieutenant?" Tony asked.

"First, we don't know if Suzanne is with him. Don't want to put her in the middle of a firefight. Second, I don't want the little prick running off again. You guys cover me. I'm going to reconnoiter and let the air out of the Mustang's tires."

I borrowed Tony's black wool sweater, stuck my hand up the fireplace flue, and covered my face with soot. Paul cranked open a tower window.

"Don't shoot anything, Paul," I said. "Just signal if there's trouble headed our way. Tony'll cover me from the doorway here."

"You, uh, got another rifle in your collection?" Tony said. "Scope's no good at night."

Paul came back with a lever-action Marlin and a box of .35 Remington shells. "It's sighted in at a hundred yards," he said.

I cracked the front door and slid out into the chill. Stars were out, but the pale sliver of waning moon left the forest as dark as the devil's hoof. I did a low run along the side of the road, then a belly crawl across to the back of the Mustang, where I unscrewed the valve cap on the right rear tire and deflated it. I tried cupping my other hand around the valve. Although nothing moved, the hissing sounded as if it would wake up everything in the forest. I slithered around the car, flattening all four.

Once I finished nullifying the mustang as an escape option. I froze in place for a minute or so, listening to the night stillness. Nothing to worry about so far. I made a low run to the cottage.

No lights were on. I tried peeking into ground-floor windows, but all I saw was my eyes reflecting back at me. I tried the front door; it was locked. It wouldn't have been a wise move in any case. I hadn't gone through the entire house with Paul—we had scrammed once we saw the living room.

Back in the tower room, Paul asked if I had seen Suzanne.

"Pitch black, no lights in the house," I said. "Can't see anything from the outside. The front door's locked."

"Best bet is to ambush your guy when he leaves," Tony suggested. "If he has Paul's ex, it's safest. I can take him down with the scope from the top floor of the tower here."

"I think you're right." I said. "I'll get behind the Mustang with the Marlin. Thuan will be in a narrow crossfire—no room to move. Paul can cover me with the shotgun from the doorway if Thuan manages to make it around me."

"We have a few hours before dawn," Paul said. "I'll brew more coffee."

I cycled the action on the Marlin, emptied it, and then reloaded. I was itching to get to it, but first we had to endure another annoying wait.

# THIRTY-EIGHT

At false dawn, we took our positions. In the spruce tree behind me, a robin signaled the start of a new day. I had borrowed a down jacket from Paul, but it was a few sizes too small and I couldn't zip it up. I lay in wait on my left side, trying to keep my unprotected front off the cold ground. The Mustang's windows were frosted up, so my view of the cottage door was from behind the flattened left rear tire. After a half hour, my left leg cramped up, so I moved up to a crouch behind the car trunk. The taillight next to me shattered, and I heard a sharp snap from the forest. I dived to the side of the Mustang, pulled out my cell phone, and speed-dialed Tony. We had agreed to put our phones on vibrate and use them as walkie-talkies.

"Sniper, silenced rifle, maybe two hundred feet out, ninety degrees to the Mustang."

Tony's answer was to put two rounds in that general area. The sniper's reply shattered the window next to Tony. Not to be outdone, he countered with another two-shot volley.

I had circled the car and was heading as quietly as I could into the forest, to outflank the unknown shooter. I hoped Tony had seen my move and wouldn't mistake me for the bad guy. I tossed off Paul's too-tight red jacket—my tan sweater and Loden hunting vest were better camouflage. Taking care not to snap any twigs, I slipped from tree to tree. Tony kept up the suppressing fire, trying to pin the adversary down. The sniper responded every few minutes with a couple of shots to the house, probably moving as much as he could to avoid firing from the same position twice.

Some twenty yards out, I saw a dwarf juniper give a little shiver. I cradled my rifle in the crotch of a tree and waited. The sniper fired another shot at the house, and I saw the fume from the suppressor. I aimed a foot and a half behind the muzzle of his rifle, but he moved before I could shoot. Then his head and shoulder appeared between the branches a yard or so closer to my position. With him in my sights, I inhaled. At the end of my exhale, I squeezed the trigger. The top of his head bloomed pink.

I ejected the shell and levered in a new round, keeping him in sight as I warily approached.

The slumped body was Asian, dressed in deep-woodland camo. The hit team was now down to the Frenchman.

I left the body and weapon in place and headed for the gravel road and the house.

The road was just in sight through the branches when Thuan's Mercedes sped by. I saw a white flash and was instantly blown to the ground. Gravel, clods of dirt, branches, and scraps of metal fell soundlessly around me. I was on my back, looking up at my blood-covered hand. I felt something in one eye and couldn't hear a bloody thing. For several seconds, I couldn't figure out what had happened. Then I slowly realized that Thuan's car had exploded.

It took me another minute or two to get my bearings. I rolled to one side and managed to get up on all fours. Hanging on to an alder sapling, I worked up to a standing position. My eyes were tearing, and this washed the dirt out of my left eye. Vision and hearing were coming back bit by bit. A salty taste ran over my lips, and I wiped at it. The blood on my hand had come from my nose. Rifling the pockets of my hunting vest, I came up with a half packet of tissues. I packed the bleeding nostril and checked myself out. My nose and left cheek had begun to throb, and my left ankle was stiff and

painful, but that seemed to be the extent of my injuries. Picking up Paul's rifle, I staggered toward the road, my footsteps sounding like muffled drumbeats accompanied by a low hum.

My right ear popped, and sounds were suddenly crisper on that side. In the background, I heard crows complaining about the noise. I was pretty sure that the Frenchman having earned his pay was already headed to parts unknown, but just in case, with the Marlin to my shoulder I scanned right and then left, before I stepped out of the woods. Fifty feet down the road, the Mercedes looked like an eviscerated metal beast. The roof was peeled forward, and both front doors, all the windows, and the front seats were missing. The car's body was Coke-bottle shaped, the middle wider than the front and back. To my surprise, the car wasn't on fire. The backseat, a couple of yards behind the open trunk, was the only thing in sight smoldering. Not knowing if the gas tank was going to ignite, I stayed put and scanned around me. What was left of the twisted dashboard was covered in red, but no bodies were in sight.

I turned back toward the house. From a birch tree on the roadside hung a shredded nylon stocking containing a strangely unbloodied right calf and foot.

"Aw, crap," I said out loud as I turned to limp back to the house.

# THIRTY-NINE

Paul was sitting on the front steps, ashen and red eyed. Tony stood over him, holding a bloody dish towel over his left arm. He said, "You okay?"

"A piece of rock from the explosion caught me in the face. No big deal. What happened to you guys? How did Thuan get past you?

"Suzanne was with him," said Paul. "I couldn't get a shot. She's dead, isn't she?"

"I'm sorry," I said. "I don't know what else we could have done."

"Not your fault," he said. "I figured it would end badly. I knew it, I just knew it."

"Everything happened so fast," Tony said. "The sniper grazed my arm. I have a groove from wrist to elbow—stings like all hell. When the shooting started, Thuan ran out dragging Paul's ex with him. Took one look and zipped right by the Mustang, went straight for the garage. I couldn't get a shot from this angle, and I was bleeding like a

stuck hog."

"The sniper was one of the hit team," I said. "He must have mistaken me for Thuan when I popped up behind the Mustang—I had the hood over my head."

"Must've caught him off guard when I started shooting back," Tony said.

"Let's look at that arm. You were lucky you were shooting from the upstairs window. He couldn't see you for the branches. He was in a bad position and expecting Thuan to appear at tree trunk level."

"I have a good medical kit in my den," Paul said. "On another subject, I'd rather Angela not know what happened here. Can you do that for me, Lieutenant?"

"It's Robert, remember? And I'd prefer that *nobody* know what happened. But we do have a pile of twisted metal on your road."

"Not a big problem for a guy with a towing and salvage business," Tony said. "It can go straight into the compactor."

Paul went to get the medical kit. Tony and I moved closer, and I lowered my voice to a whisper.

"You okay with all this?"

"Hell, I haven't had this much fun in ages! Not that it's anything compared to Fallujah."

"We're going to need some help picking up

all the pieces," I said. "Let me make a call." I scrolled down my list.

"Hi, Naren, sorry to disturb. I have a little problem. How discreet are your mercs?"

"*Contractors,* please. More than discreet, if you need it. You may have to pay a bonus if it's too sticky—not that I would want to know any details."

"Fine. It's not something you have to worry about. I really appreciate your help with Paul. I owe you."

"A pleasure, no problem at all. And our bar's open till two a.m. should you feel inspired to buy me a drink."

"I'll call you back on that. Thanks."

Paul came back with the med kit, and I did a fair job disinfecting and bandaging Tony's arm.

"You have a number for your security people?" I asked Paul.

After giving me the number, he said, "They called yesterday asking why I was late. I told them all was okay, that we had decided to stay at the country place till today. Called Angela and told her the same. She expects me for supper."

"Is there another road out of here?" I said. "Your entry lane's a bit messed up."

"Old logging road behind the caretaker's house leads out to the highway. It should be

passable. What are you planning?"

"You don't want publicity on this, and neither do I. Tony will drive you back to your house, and I'm going to make all this disappear . . . if you're all right with this option."

"No problem. I had a great adventure that will stay with me as a secret memory. Suzanne's dad is her only family, and he's having chemo for late-stage lung cancer. He knows about our separation and her affairs. I'll tell him she ran off to Vietnam with Thuan. But I'd prefer not to have to answer to the legal system or to Angela. Do what you have to, and send me the bill."

"Is the Marlin registered in your name?"

"Actually, all the firearms belonged to my dad, acquired before those regulations came into effect. I never took the time to do any of the paperwork after he died."

I squeezed Paul's shoulder gently. "Enjoy a glass of wine with Angela tonight," I said. "I'll call you in the morning."

Tony drove an exhausted Paul back to the city and his Angela. He would return with the flatbed tow truck. I called the security guys, gave them the route to Paul's country estate, and told them I would explain the "sticky" situation on site.

The man on the other end of the line seemed

to understand me precisely. "We'll send some of our best people to clean up your problem," he said.

By the end of the day, their six-man crew, assisted by Tony and me, had turned the clock back to the day before yesterday. It was as if the events of this morning were merely the dark dreams of a troubled imagination. My part had been to help remove the Vietnamese sniper's body, wrapping him and the Marlin rifle up into one of the contractors' van. Some ten miles north, a farmer would discover a hunter who had tripped trying to climb a cattle fence with a loaded rifle in his hands. Regardless of all the safety training now given with hunting permits, there would always be a few accidents.

At day's end, I felt bad for Paul, who would forever carry the secret of Suzanne's grisly though rapid death. In all honesty, I didn't much care about her, Thuan, or his crooked lawyer, Phillip Yu. I did, however, feel some remorse about lying to my boss and Dobson.

I called the captain. "Jean, after I told you that a hit team may be after Paul and Angela, I had the inspiration to check on Thuan's lawyer, and I did call in backup. As you know, it looks as if he was snatched from his home"

"I didn't hear it from *my* lieutenant, as I should have. Heard it from a district captain."

"Sorry about that," I said. "My mind's a bit overwhelmed. Colleen is filing for divorce."

"*Calvase,* you should definitely have informed me of that. It could be a factor in the Viet shooting incident. *Sacramentos,* we better talk about you taking some time off. This stress isn't healthy."

"You're right, boss. I have at least six weeks accumulated. I need a break."

"You can take a month off, but I want to see you in my office tomorrow morning, request papers in hand. And I want to clear up a few loose ends."

"Not much in the way of loose ends here. My contacts tell me the hit men have left town. I don't think we'll ever find Thuan or his lawyer, and Paul and Angela are home safe and sound."

"My office, first thing tomorrow." The line went dead.

I stood behind Paul's house, my hand on the roof of the Cooper. The crows were still repeating their high-pitched, rapid-fire danger caw. Maybe they didn't like the color orange, or maybe it was my swollen face. Maybe they just wanted to give me fair warning of tomorrow's meeting with my boss.

# FORTY

I woke before the cat did. The pain in my face had me tossing and turning most of the night, and my pillow felt as hard as the rock that hit me yesterday.

When Crackers looked at me and shot out of my bed, I figured I'd better check out my appearance. The mirror on the wall *didn't* tell me I was the fairest. The left side of my face was a round-cheeked cherub with a shiner and a two-day beard. The right side was a sadder-looking version of me. I dumped all the ice-cube trays into the sink and filled it with cold water. Coming up for air every minute or so, I buried my pain in the cold until the swelling went down. It didn't help the purple around my eye, though. I shaved with a delicate touch, ate breakfast, refilled my hiding cat's automatic dispensing food bowl, and headed to the office.

* * *

"*Saint Simonaque,* what happened to you?"

"And a good morning to you, too, boss. I tripped on my cat in the dark last night—ended up doing a face-plant on the corner of my dresser."

"You have a cat? Is this new? Another one of your growing list of secrets that I'm not privy to?"

"I inherited a big Maine coon from Paul Landry. His girlfriend, Angela, is allergic."

O'Neil pointed to his ratty guest chair—a nonverbal command to sit. It also indicated that I'd be under the spotlight longer than I would have preferred.

"You get too personally involved in your cases, Robert. It's unprofessional, not to mention dangerous."

"That's exactly what my ex-wife used to say."

"What's the story on that situation? Combined with the shooting, it may warrant a trip to counseling."

"Gimme a break, Jean. Unless there's a tall blonde joining me, I don't recline on couches."

I spent the next ten minutes on my personal life, and the next twenty skating around the Landry case. Jean also went over the Bully Bauer incident. True, the video evidence showed that what happened wasn't a crime, but he didn't like my handing the

scene over to a beat cop.

"Bernie Phillips is a good cop," I said. "He's patrolled that area for years, knows the people involved.

He did a good job, got congratulations from his captain. I got a copy in my e-mail."

"I'm happy for him, but I sent *you.*"

"You keep on telling me to be more of a team player," I said. "I finally took your advice: spread the love around."

Jean's mustache twitched. "You delegated the lawyer Yu's disappearance to another team of beat cops. Is this going to be standard operating procedure from now on? You get to take only the part of your assigned case that you like, and leave the rest to uniforms?"

"It was their district, and not a homicide. Not my job."

Jean's mustache twitched again, and he clasped his hands together—probably to avoid the temptation to reach out and throttle me.

"First, when I give you a case, it's yours till the bitter end. Second, what were you doing at Yu's house?" Jean pushed papers to the side of his desk as if making room for my answer. He was in his come-to-Jesus speech mode, but so far he hadn't blasted me with a barrage of his subdued French swear words. I felt mildly relieved.

"You're supposed to be chained to your desk. Now your name is in another precinct's reports, in an incident reported miles from your office."

We did our verbal fencing match, each of us scoring a few points. It ended when I promised to be a better Boy Scout and when Jean had fully vented.

He finally signed my vacation request. The meeting was over when he turned to his computer to e-mail our personnel people about my time off.

I headed to Dobson's lab. I was going to miss working with him. Jean had said he was looking over candidates to be my new partner. Apparently, I was a difficult match for "normal" detectives. Jean was miffed when I took it as a compliment.

Dobson looked up from his monitor. "Holy moly! What happened to you?"

"You know, Tristan, you'd think nobody around here's ever seen a black eye."

"Yeah, I've seen a few, but that's a real beauty. Did you ice it?"

I nodded, sticking to my story. "Tripped over Crackers last night, had a blunt encounter with the corner of my dresser."

"Clean it off with water, no soap; then put some pure olive oil on it. It'll help healing and reduce swelling." He moved over and rummaged in a

desk drawer. "I have some makeup here that will make you look more human. You're still a few days from Halloween."

"I look that bad?"

"Considering the disparity between our ranks, Lieutenant, I'd prefer not to comment."

I gave Dobson my official version of where we stood with the Landry case. Lying to the boss was no great feat. Lying to Dobson, though—that was difficult. He listened patiently and, at some point, crossed his arms. I think he knew he was getting the sanitized version.

I rolled my chair closer to his. "I need a big personal favor," I said. "Please tell me if you can't help me. I'll understand."

"Depends on what you want," he said.

"I'm taking a few weeks' vacation to get my head straight. I need someone to apartment-sit and take care of Crackers."

"That's all? I was worried it might be something illegal. My pleasure. Your apartment's bigger than mine, and much closer to work than I am in the village. I'd stay with André, of course."

"Sure. Bring your boyfriend. And except for the bottom row, you can help yourself to anything in the wine rack."

"Wow, that's not *me* doing the favor."

Dobson gave me his wide, toothy grin. "Stay on vacation as long as you want."

"I'll be back in three to four weeks. My nurse friend has accepted a job offer in Miami. I'm helping her move and set up."

"That's a bummer. You just met her."

"My love karma is a roller coaster."

"Maybe the stars are saving you for the right person."

"Tristan, you're an even bigger romantic fool than I am."

I went over the logistics, and Dobson, true to his scientific nature, took notes and had questions on kitchen utensils, the days for recycling and garbage, the correct amount of cat food per day, and the name and number of my cat's vet."

I looked at him sheepishly. "Don't have one. Never even thought of that."

"I'll do research around your place and recommend one."

I told him about the car switch with Colleen, and to make sure to check the GTO for scratches or dents when it got back. He was to come to my place tomorrow for the house keys and final instructions.

I left the office, officially on vacation. With the Landry case behind me, my steps felt lighter, and the sky seemed a brighter, deeper blue.

# FORTY-ONE

I was hard at work preparing tonight's supper. I hadn't selected the appetizers yet, but the main course was my special meat loaf in twisty French bread. I added pinches of oregano and nutmeg to the recipe. I hadn't the time or the skills for flaky dough, so I cheated on dessert and picked up cannoli from my favorite Italian food emporium. A tawny port would go well with the sweet pastry and pink peppered strawberries.

My criminal cases had ended more or less to my satisfaction, my relationship with Colleen had ended rather less satisfyingly, and now I was losing Zee, which was not satisfying at all. This time, I had not settled for a needy and unstable significant other. We had a love affair between equals. I hadn't asked her to change her life for me, and she hadn't asked it of me. It was frustrating to think of her leaving due

to factors out of our control.

I cared for her and respected her decision to look for a better professional life south of the border. But, I also felt that our time together had been too short. I wanted, selfishly, to spend a few weeks of sun and fun with her before I had to return to Montreal and the craziness that was my life.

I had called Paul earlier this morning and assured him that all was professionally handled at his country estate. I could tell from the tone of his voice that he was relieved. He didn't ask for details. He confirmed that both Zee and I were guests on his corporate jet, and welcome additions aboard his rented yacht.

From our last conversation, it was obvious that Zee felt bad about our breaking up and would have preferred just to disappear south, with no tearful good-byes.

If I wanted a bit more, I had to sell the vacation package to Zee.

I hoped to provide an enjoyable meal while doing a good promotional job. Even with a damaged face, I had to act and look my best. Dobson's olive oil trick must be working—the bruise under the eye was less puffy, and the purple had paled and showed an attractive light-green tinge around the margin. I

was sure that nurse Zee had seen worse, but I would probably try Dobson's makeup just to be on the safe side. I hoped she wouldn't have too many questions. I'd have to keep to the script about tripping over Crackers—getting caught out lying to Zee would be a bad start to the evening.

My oven had reached 350 degrees. I slid the aluminum foil-covered loaf in and set my phone reminder for an hour and a half later. As I entered the last digit, the doorbell rang.

Danny, the locksmith, was forty minutes ahead of schedule.

"Finished a job early, took a chance," he said. "Who'd you piss off?"

"Ha! You should see the other guy," I said. I was tired of explaining.

"You wanted the Mul-T-Lock and four keys?"

"Pickproof?"

With a crooked smile, he said, "For anyone burglarizing *this* neighborhood."

"I want to keep the old brass door plate, so you may have to do some customizing."

"No problem. I'm used to these old houses."

He was still adjusting the new dead bolt an hour later, when Dobson arrived.

I gave him one of the new keys. "That's a strange-looking key," he said. "Pickproof lock?"

"You know everything, Dr. Watson."

"Not really, but I know what vet I'd recommend. They're in Outremont, and they specialize only in cats." He gave me a small printed file card.

I showed him around the apartment. "This side of the walk-in is empty. You can use it for your and André's stuff for the next four weeks."

"Nice old building. You could renovate this into a jewel."

"You're the second person to tell me that."

I gave him Colleen's phone number and the key to the garage behind my house.

"She's returning the GTO early next week."

Dobson left at the same time as Danny the locksmith. All was set. I had only to wait for Zee.

\* \* \*

I had worried for naught. Zee was in a great mood and complimented me on the food. I saved my speech for dessert.

I said, "I'd like to help you settle in Miami. I'm on vacation as of next week."

"Help me move? In exchange for what, more 'yoga' lessons?"

"Yes, and maybe. We said free and easy, but this is downright abrupt. I want to make and keep more fond memories."

"I have fond memories all the way back to 'you have no panty lines,'" she said, grinning. "'Free and easy,' by definition, meant one of us was going to leave someday. I would have liked more time, but I'm scared it'll make everything more difficult."

"We have to enjoy every moment. Worrying about the future just spoils it."

"The private clinic expects me in Miami in two weeks. Let me think about it."

I hadn't taken a restful vacation in years. Traveling with Colleen had been demanding: how much sightseeing and how many events and parties could we cram into each day was the ongoing challenge. I needed a break, and if my time with Zee was ticking down, I wanted to enjoy every one of our last minutes together in a relaxed, stress-free mode. When a woman says, "Let me think about it," it can sound a lot like "Give me some time come up with a good excuse to get out of it." I didn't want to give her the chance of opting out. I fired my best shot.

"Your ex-patient Paul Landry insists on thanking me for saving Angela. We're both invited as guests on his yacht. We fly out on his corporate

jet Monday afternoon."

"Oh . . . so *that's* the 'interim plan' you spoke of. I said you were a big spender when you showed up with hundred-dollar wine, but this is . . . wow."

"I'm not spending; he is. You can put the airfare toward new furniture."

"Even better," Zee said, putting out her hand to shake on the deal.

"One condition: no sad good-bye, no parting speeches—I wake up one morning and you're gone, that's it. Promise me."

I took her hand but, instead of shaking, moved closer and kissed her on the forehead. "You drive a hard bargain."

Zee stood up, and we held each other for a long time.

# FORTY-TWO

We had a three-hour-and-twenty-minute preview of the good life. Paul's Learjet landed us at Kendall Tamiami airport at 5:37 on a warm, hazy Monday afternoon. We were champagne primed for supper. I had brought a case of Veuve Clicquot for the trip. Paul scolded me in jest and accepted with a smile.

"I just phoned the crew," he said. "They're still preparing. By the time we finish supper, we'll be ready to cast off."

"What's the schedule?" I asked. "Zee has to start her job at the clinic in two weeks."

"I know. Angela told me. They've really hit it off, chatting away in the back of the plane like long-lost bosom buddies."

I looked aft. Angela had her hand on Zee's arm as she whispered something in her ear. I said to Paul, "Strange how women can do that."

"Miami to the Bahamas for a week, then back to cruise the island bays," Paul said. "I want to relax; we play it by ear."

The pilot dropped open the cabin door, and Zee and Angela moved up to the front seats.

"Zee, I left my cell phone in your purse."

She turned to Angela. "Not sure if Robert grasps the meaning of 'vacation' or 'relax' yet. Do you really need your phone?"

"N-no," I said. "You're right. I'm offline for the next three weeks."

Supper was close to the airport, at one of Paul's favorite spots.

The girls were still yakking away, both talking at the same time yet understanding each other perfectly—another feminine mystery. Paul and I had run out of intelligent conversation.

Thankfully, our meals arrived. Conversation waned as we enjoyed wine and food.

We arrived at the yacht an hour after sunset. After we settled into our cabins, Paul came knocking, to ask if we wanted a nightcap. I said yes, but Zee begged off and prepared the bed. I leered at her; she pursed her lips and made a brushing-off motion with both hands. I got the message. We had spent all Sunday and late into the night packing her apartment. Her energy tank was empty; she was running on nerve fumes.

The packing, combined with the stress of a new job, new city, new life, was taking its toll. She had accepted my vacation plan with some reticence, but last night she had admitted that this was what she needed. Her life in Montreal was boxed and crated. On my return and as soon as she found a new apartment, I would take care of shipping her belongings.

Paul and I lounged on the upper deck, drinks in hand, admiring the night sky.

"Angela's already sawing logs," Paul said. "Glad you brought Zee. I'll be able to do a bit of work without her thinking I'm neglecting her."

"Yeah, I saw you had a briefcase in your luggage. Me, I'm not even going to answer my phone."

We enjoyed the view, had a second nightcap, then both headed to our cabins.

\* \* \*

We spent a week in the Bahamas, hanging out, enjoying the night life, spending a day at the casino in Nassau, and attending a beyond-spectacular Halloween party at Stapleton Gardens.

As we danced, Zee whispered in my ear, "It's a difficult life, but with a bit of practice I could get used to this."

"No problem here," I said. "The SPF thirty notwithstanding, I now look like a beach bum who has always been here."

"Your cute butt is still white as Crisco."

"Speaking of tan lines, the other day, Paul and I accidentally noticed that Angela and you were sunbathing with only your bikini bottoms."

"Accidently, *sure*."

Back from the Bahamas, we docked for fuel and supplies in Key Largo, and I sneaked a text to Dobson, asking if all was okay and if my GTO had come home without a scratch.

Ten minutes later, he texted back that all was fine, the weather had dropped below the teens, and Crackers was in love with André. I smiled. His message also said he had no news on my car. My smile evaporated.

My call to Colleen went to voice mail: "Our understanding was that you'd need my car for a couple of days. I'd like it returned. I have to put it into winter storage. Get back to me, please."

We spent the next three days leisurely exploring secluded bays and mangrove islands from Key Largo to Big Pine Key. Paul, his yacht pilot, and

I tried our luck at baby tarpon fishing. Luckily, we had provisions from our restocking in Key Largo, or we would have starved.

The girls worked on their tans, and Angela discovered a passion for yoga—the actual health exercise version.

The last evening at Big Pine Key, I checked my phone. I had only one message from Dobson: a text of no-show on my borrowed GTO.

Again my call to Colleen went straight to voice mail. It was a little sterner this time, in both tone and wording: "Colleen, I left you a message about my car days ago. I'd really appreciate the *courtesy* of a return call."

We traveled down to Key West for another two days. Before heading back north to our base mooring in Miami, I left a nasty message on Colleen's phone: "Still no news from you. If I don't hear from you in the next twenty-four hours, I'm reporting my car as stolen. I won't call you again."

We arrived in Miami on Friday evening of the weekend before Zee was to start her new job. Paul and Angela were enjoying the breeze on the sundeck, Zee and I sat side to side, coffees in hand at the table in the front lounge, enjoying some private face time.

"Angela said they'll use the yacht as a floating hotel next week," Zee said. "Paul has to fly back for a daylong board meeting next Friday; then he'll be back with Angela for another two weeks of cruising."

I took a sip from my cup, "I still have two week of vacation," I said. "My plan was to stay on board, then get a hotel for my last week."

"Kathy has two apartments she scouted and wants me to look at, and she's offered her extra room if I need it. I'll stay at her place or come back here—not sure what my responsibilities will be, or my working-shift hours."

"I'm still in vacation mode," I said, "just hanging loose, giving tai chi lessons to Paul and Captain Hernández. Whatever you decide, I'm okay with."

"Your hair has grown long, unruly, and sun-bleached, and you're the color of brushed copper," Zee said. "I'd better take a few days on my own. I'm not looking forward to seeing you go, you overmuscled beach bum."

"I still have ten days," I said. "I'll help you get installed, then head back to Montreal. We have to take different paths in life, but no matter where we go, we take a little of each other with us."

Zee put her arms around my neck and hugged me hard. "That's so romantic," she said with a little sniffle.

"Not my line. It's a quote from a country singer named Tim McGraw."

\* \* \*

By Thursday, Zee had signed the lease on an apartment in the same building as her friend Kathy and had new furniture on order from our weekend shopping blitz. I was on the bridge, learning about navigation from Captain Hernandez, when Angela came up and handed me her cell phone.

"Zee's trying to reach you."

I took the phone. "Hi. Sorry, lost my cell somewhere in the cabin. What's up?"

"I have a staff meeting after work. I'm going to stay at Kathy's tonight."

"Ah, okay. How's everything at the clinic?"

"Fine—I love it, in fact. I think they're going to put me in charge of the diagnostic floor."

"Wow. Already! I'll miss you tonight," I said. "Call me tomorrow before work." We hung up.

After all this luxury, I wasn't looking forward to going back to work, but I didn't want to abuse Paul and Angela's hospitality. I went down to

the main cabin, returned Angela's phone, and told her I'd have supper ashore tonight.

Sometime after midnight, I staggered onto the gangplank. I wasn't sure whether the boat was rocking more than usual, or the wine and liberal after supper nightcap had anything to do with the sudden loss of my sea legs.

In the cabin I moved the cushions aside to make the bed and found my phone wedged behind a seat back. By instinct, I swiped the screen. I had eight voice mails and seven texts. I thumbed open the texts: two from my boss, Jean; three from Dobson; and two from Nico, my best friend from Vice. All the messages were worded differently, but the gist was the same: *Urgent, trying to reach you since before yesterday. Call me back.*

What the heck was all this about? That the Provincial Police had a change of heart and had decided to suspend me or press charges, was the only thing I could think of.

The only person I could call at this hour was my buddy Nico. He answered as if he hadn't been asleep.

"Roberto, where are you?"

"In Florida. I just opened my phone to a bunch of urgent messages. Sorry to call at this hour,

but what gives?"

"No problem, I'm on a stakeout. Nobody reached you? *Porca miseria.* I'm so sorry to ruin your vacation with bad news. Colleen is dead."

"*What!* What . . . happened, Nico?"

"Crashed your car into a concrete wall three days ago. Funeral is Saturday morning. I'll pick you up at the airport. Just text me your flight number. *Ti sono vicino.*"

"I don't understand."

"Nobody does. Provincial Police called you at home as soon as they ran the plates, then called your boss Jean as a courtesy. A late-night, single-car, single-occupant accident. Hit an overpass abutment at a hundred-and-thirty-plus kilometers per hour, somewhere between Ottawa and Montreal."

"Was she drunk? That's not like her."

"It appears not. Get your butt back here, Roberto. I'll meet you. So sorry."

"I'll call you tomorrow. Thanks for being there."

I sat, head in hands, on the edge on the bed. The professor's "what goes around comes around" from the Bully Bauer incident came back to me. I had done a few reproachable things recently. Was this karma coming back at me? I was too shocked to think straight.

I called Zee.

"Robert, what time is it?"

"Dunno. Past one. Sorry to wake you."

"Robert, what's wrong? Your voice is strange. Are you drunk?"

"No, my brain is screwy. Just found out that Colleen died three days ago. Crashed my car into a concrete wall at a hundred-and-thirty-plus."

"Oh, my God," she breathed. "That's *awful.* Doesn't make any sense."

"No, it doesn't. Funeral is Saturday morning. I'm going to hitch a ride with Paul in the morning. I feel really bad about leaving you. I promised to help you set up."

"You have to go, Robert. Don't worry. Angela and Kathy promised, too. I'll be okay. Remember what you said the other day: part of me is with you, and part of you is with me, forever. You can call me if you need to talk. Good-bye, my beach bum."

She hung up, and I started packing for home.

#

**MICHAEL KENT** is an international management and coaching consultant. Contrary to his technical writing, his fiction always has tinge of humor and a special twist to the tale.

A native of Montreal, he is fully bilingual, normally in the same sentence. Years as a private pilot, avid reading and extensive traveling, have generated a storehouse of plots and stories that still have to be shared with the world. A member of Canadian Crime Writers, and Sisters in Crime, he is also active with Writers on the net, Writers Village University and The Next Big Writer.

http://www.kentwriter.com/

**The Lieutenant Beaudry series :**

**Blood tail**
**Folded dreams**
**Twice dead**
**Tainted Evidence**
**Bank Shot**

Michael Kent

Manufactured by Amazon.com
Columbia, SC
10 April 2017

# JUST DUCKY

## USA TODAY BESTSELLING AUTHOR
## C.A. KING

*Jayne,
Happy Reading
C A King*

COVER DESIGNED BY RAVENBORN COVERS

EDITOR:
KAREN HRDLICKA

*If you believe this book is dedicated to you,
perhaps it is!*

*No ducklings were hurt during the writing of this book!*

This book is a work of fiction. Any historical references, real places, real events, or real persons names and/or persona are used fictitiously. All other events, places, names and happenings are from the author's imagination and any similarities, whatsoever, with events both past and present, or persons living or dead, are purely coincidental.

Copyright © 2024 by C.A. King

ISBN: 979-8-8833726-2-8

All rights reserved. This book or any portion thereof may not be reproduced or used in any manner whatsoever without the express written permission of the author and/or publisher except for the use of brief quotations in a book review or scholarly journal.

First printing March 2024

Look for other books by C.A. King,

The Portal Prophecies.

Book I-VI

Volume I & II

Tomoiya's Story:

Book I: Escape to Darkness

Book II: Collecting Tears

Book III: Stalked

Surviving the Sins:

Books I-VIII

Flower Shields: A Four Horseman Novel

When the Paint Dries: A Four Horseman Novel

When Leaves Fall: A Different Point of View Story

Miracles Not Included

Do Not Open Until Halloween

Truly Unfortunate

Serendipity's Debt

Hope After Death

From Alice to Malice

Tails Aways Wins

Hang On To Your Shirt Tails

Cupid's Connection

Evil Sushi Series

And more…

# JUST DUCKY

The border between supernaturals and humans is at risk. War is imminent unless a comatose princess wakes. It's only a matter of time before the situation turns violent. He's searching everyone and everything to find a cure and a peaceful resolution.

---

Unattached paranormals are on the prowl...

And who can blame them?

After being missing in action for quite some time, Vampire Lord Kobreon is in the limelight again. The competition is stiff to earn a place at his side. Who knows how long it will be before someone ends up owning a majority stake at the heart of the deal?

---

She studied his history—collected his memorabilia—worshipped him from afar. If only fate's favourable gaze would shine on her this one time...

The odds are stacked against her. Instead of fangs and claws, she has soft fuzz; replacing strength and agility are waddles and paddles. No one wants to talk to a failed shifter, let alone date one.

Can the only duckling on the water stay afloat, or will her dreams of a happily ever after sink forever?

Chances for eternal love don't come around often. She's praying this opportunity will turn out Just Ducky.

# THE FIRST VAMPIRE

THE KINGDOM OF HAMMERHEAD WAS BUT ONE OF MANY beautiful human nations. Only a vast terrain with unrealized potential lay between there and the Empire of Cliffside Castle. Still, few had seen how truly wondrous each other's side was. Traversing the land to make the transition between the two was as good as a death sentence. Not knowing exactly where the boundary between them lay was a problem for both growing nations.

For as far back as any one remembered, war plagued the world. Man and paranormal existed only to murder one another.

And for what?

At the root of it all was merely ignorance, prejudice, and greed. That was no way to live. Someone needed to extend the olive branch. Someone needed to take the first step. Who accomplished such a feat was of no concern, as long as both parties met in the middle. The only thing he hadn't expected was for the middle to be located at the farthest edge of a completely desolate area—a virtual wasteland of unused natural resources.

C.A. KING

The sun was beginning to make its descent on the horizon; the heat of the day dissipating along with it. They were in undeveloped territory—wide open with nowhere to hide or run to. There were no trees, no bushes. In fact, there was nothing to write home about as far as the eye could see.

Wasted potential.

The first sight of the man he was meeting almost made him break out in a bout of uncontrollable laughter. Insulting the pride of a king certainly wasn't the right way to start such an important meeting, even if it was the human's fault for setting up a pretentious, white, linen-clad table in the middle of nowhere, one meant for many to sit around, not just two. On it sat a lavish, well-laid-out meal fit for an army, albeit all the king's men were obviously not invited to the feast. His majesty alone was devouring the multitude of dishes. Perhaps that was the way of kings. Even his wardrobe was far too elaborately decorated for the setting. One aid stood to the crowned leader's left, hands folded behind his back, while, off to the other side, a servant held an umbrella over his head.

There was no rain. There was no sun.

No expense was spared.

"I am Drak Ula," he said, offering a hand to shake. "You can call me Drak." His lips curled upward for pleasantry sake.

The man across from him remained seated at the table, ignoring the offered gesture. "I am King Julius Hammerhead." A loud sigh accompanied his words. "You can call me King Hammerhead, or Your Majesty." The king motioned half-heartedly toward an empty chair, quite a bit smaller and less comfortable than his own.

"As you wish, Your Majesty." He held on to the back of his long-tailed jacket, bowing slightly as he accepted the invitation.

An array of well-groomed female servants rushed to cater to their newly seated guest's every whim.

Drak waved them off.

"The dead of night is an odd time to request a meeting," the king snapped, a turkey leg filling his mouth a moment before the words stopped. Teeth savagely ripped off an entire side, chewing it only enough to allow the meat to be swallowed without choking, after which wine trickled down from the corners of his mouth.

"Perhaps," Drak admitted. "It's a precaution on my side. In broad daylight, I'd be easily picked off by one of your soldiers." He nodded to the line of men standing a few hundred paces behind their regal leader. "That's quite a force you've brought along. Are they really necessary?"

"Ho. Ho. Ha!" the king sputtered, his fake laugh turning into a cough. His sleeve took the brunt of the damage, the remnants of food, drink, and spittle caking from the lower arm down to the wrist. "I also need to take precautions."

A plate of thin noodles in a butter sauce appeared on the table. "Oh!" Drac exclaimed, turning his head. "Please remove it." One hand covered his nose and lips. "I'm not a fan of garlic." A mouthful of bile gulped back. "It's the smell... I think."

"Take it away," the king ordered, the aid beside him rushing to remove the plate, despite it clearly not being in the man's job description.

Drak inhaled deeply, allowing the fresh air to push away the remnants of the scent which displeased his senses. "I assure you; no troops were needed. I am as vulnerable as you are at this meeting. Peace is the only thing on the agenda and on my mind."

Julius's brow rose. "If I were immortal, I wouldn't need military backing either. Alas." His sigh was as audible as any word. "I am not. I have a kingdom to think of. I would hate

to think what would happen should I be careless here and die."

"We may live extended lives, but I assure you we are not immortal," Drak said. "Drive a wooden stake through our hearts and we also will die."

"And who was it that granted you eternal youth?" the king queried. "Do you even have a god?"

"We have our own beliefs, albeit, they may not align with your own," Drak replied. "You won't find me stepping foot in one of your churches, or drinking holy water, anytime soon. That doesn't mean that I don't believe in a higher power."

"I'm not sure our priests will be happy to hear that," the king chuckled, one finger tapping on his glass for a refill. It came quickly. "Shall we get down to the reason for this rendezvous?"

"I am asking for a cease fire," Drak said. "I want humans and paranormals to come to an understanding and sign a treaty."

"How do you intend on making this peace happen?" the king inquired. "Nothing has ever worked before."

"Nothing has been attempted before." Drak shrugged. "I was thinking of making an official border between our lands." He pushed aside empty plates and bowls, laying out a map of the world. "Formal documents would be needed to cross from one side to the other, requiring valid reasons for entering... such as for work or schooling."

"Where would this border be located?" Julius asked.

"Draw a line," Drak answered. "We can start from there."

"Hmm." The king rubbed his chin, staring at the crude map. "Where we are right now might be a good location. Show me." A glimmer of light flashed in his eyes, boasting a portrait of glory days to come.

Drak pointed to a spot.

"Then put the line there," the king ordered. "If the first

JUST DUCKY

peace discussion took place here, I believe it should be commemorated." He turned to his aid. "Have a statue in my likeness erected, outside any buildings which may be needed."

"Are you sure this is where you want it?"

"Yes!" the king bellowed, standing. Three men stepped one pace forward, trumpets blaring. "Great men make great decisions in important places. I'll be remembered forever for this moment. I'll even take care of notifying the other human kingdoms that lie along the border. I'm sure they will fall into agreement. Let the records show we shall have peace because of King Julius."

All in earshot applauded. "Long live the King," they chanted in unison. The trumpets sounded in regal tones a second time.

"Draw up the papers and show me where to sign," the king demanded. "Erect a tent for me to wait in. We'll have this matter settled this eve."

The canopy went up before the shock wore off. He'd expected days of painstaking negotiating before anything was agreed to. Humans were reckless. He already knew that, but this was on another level.

Drak shook his head. How it happened wasn't of concern. A stop to the bloodshed was something to be thankful for. Now it was in his grasp, he wasn't letting go. He moved to a smaller table, carefully wording a treaty which hopefully would last for generations.

*MEANWHILE INSIDE THE TENT...*

. . .

C.A. KING

TWO LARGE LEAF-SHAPED FANS SWAYED, COOLING THE KING AS he rested on a plush couch, feet up, back supported by numerous pillows. The room had all the comfort of home; home being the royal palace.

No expense was spared.

"What do we know about them?" the king asked, opening his mouth for a servant to place a grape inside.

"They are faster, stronger, and more deadly than others of their race," his aid, Carlos, replied. "They really should have a name of their own."

"Tramp," the king snorted. "Did you see the way the servants gushed over him? It must be mind control. I saw the colour of his eyes changing."

"Tramps?"

"No," Julius waved off his aid. "That won't do. I can't have people knowing human females preferred him over their own king, now can I? It has to be something else... something original... something no one has heard of before."

"Maybe something that rhymes with tramp?" Carlos suggested.

"Mamp. Namp. Bamp." He paused, the alphabet running through his mind. "Lamp. No. Vamp. That's not bad. Vamp. We'll use that for now."

"That's a wonderful name, Sire!" Carlos exclaimed.

"It's weak, but in lieu of something better, it will have to do," the king answered, washing down his words with a large gulp of wine. Liquid dribbled from the corners of his lips, staining parts of his white beard at the tip of his chin red.

"I assume I can add to the list that these vamps have special mind control abilities, especially effective on women?" Carlos asked.

"Yes." The king nodded. "Put that in there."

"He also showed an adverse reaction to being within close proximity of garlic, daylight, entering churches, admitted

JUST DUCKY

they can be killed by driving a stake through their hearts, and never touched any of the food or drink we offered," Carlos added.

"Hmm," Julius grunted. "So they do have weaknesses which can be exploited. Good. Very Good." He laughed wholeheartedly. "If this paper agreement doesn't work out, we have other options. The kingdom will be safe either way. Share the information. I'll be known as the greatest king to ever live in any human domain."

"With everyone?" Carlos asked.

"Yes, but make sure you are discreet," Julius ordered. "Our kinds are supposed to be forming a peace treaty, not gathering intelligence to use against filthy animals, should the need arise. We don't want the vamps' ire to come down on us." His head tilted slightly; gaze focused on the dark horizon. "Vamps... ire. Vampsire. Vampire. I like that. Vampire. It flows off the tongue, yet still brings the essence of danger to mind. I think that's what we'll call them."

"Vampire," Carlos said. "I'll make note of the name and make sure everyone hears it and of your greatness. Your name will be revered for generations to come, commemorated in song, and praised by all."

*"You're only one step further from being an egg."*
—*Lita*

# 1

It was a rainy day in Shifters' Corner—the type no one enjoyed, especially not while wandering about in a human form. It was bad enough weathering drier days as a useless woman. Unfortunately, she had no choice but to persevere. No one actually needed her to do any real work. Why would they? Jobs went to the strongest, feisty, fiercest, fastest of the lot. Her shifted form wasn't any of that—not even close.

Simple and easy—that was all she was good for—like laundry.

"Ugh."

The overloaded bin of dirty clothes practically covered her entire face, making seeing where she was going close to impossible. Luckily, the route was one she knew well, having already taken it thousands of times before, in order to complete daily chores. Unluckily, it was also where her peers knew she'd be and the place they waited to torture her.

"Hey, Ducky," a girl laughed, sticking out her foot.

She fell for that one a lot.

Down went the laundry, followed by her clumsy body. "Ow!" She rolled over, staring at the prankster. There was

no use complaining; no one would listen. Even the adults were too busy howling and chuckling in a crude manner meant to further egg the instigator on. Nobody was on her side.

"And all the king's horses and men couldn't put Ducky back together again," the girl cruelly recited. Lita was the first daughter of the meanest, and most admired, wolf pack in the town—a future beta in training, who, with a lot of practice over the past year, finally had the family attitude down pat.

"That was an egg," Ducky blurted out. "It refers to the shell being broken."

"You're only one step further from being an egg." An extremely pink tongue popped out at her, followed by a lone middle finger sticking straight up. The gesture wasn't a recognizable one. Maybe the in-crowd knew what it meant. They were certainly laughing as if they did.

She wasn't one of them—the sort who were in on the joke. Her job was to be the punchline.

Ducky gathered her laundry. It was moot to try arguing. She was, in fact, barely a smidgen better than the egg. She was a duckling—a fuzzy yellow baby duck.

Who needed that?

Shifters were hired for a number of reasons: protection, mercenary work, travel guides, spies, and workhorses for a lack of a better term. Those ones weren't all horses, some were oxen, donkeys, or other large animals.

She wasn't a bear.

She wasn't a wolf.

She wasn't a beast of burden.

She wasn't able to fly, to spy, nor could she swim properly.

No one was frightened of her, and she stuck out like a yellow thumb.

JUST DUCKY

Add that all together and she was completely useless in a town when one's worth was decided by one's abilities.

She was just Ducky.

That wasn't even her real name. Someone, she was unable to recall exactly who, nicknamed her that in jest one day. It stuck. Even her own parents used Ducky, as if they chose it for her at birth.

"Hey, Ducky," Lita called out, holding up a pair of white panties. "You forgot these." She pinched her nose with her spare hand. "They stink. Are you sure these are clean? Maybe your stink is too strong for one washing."

Ducky's lips trembled, nerves fighting one another in her stomach to be the first freed. "Oh, no!" she exclaimed, knowing what came next: a big burp, followed by tiny feathers popping out everywhere. A second later, she was sitting in a pile of new laundry—her clothes. Her bill opened, emitting soft shrill whistles.

The youth of the town gathered, laughing while poking at her with sticks and throwing stones. That hurt.

It was waddling time.

Ducky hightailed it through yards and houses, taking every shortcut possible back to the safety of her home. She might have been a failure, but her parents were not. No one crossed them to their faces, even about their pathetic daughter.

"You've done it again, haven't you?" her mother, Chantelle, said, sighing heavily. "Where did you leave your clothes this time?" She glanced around. "And where is the laundry?" One hand scooped her daughter up, smoothing back ruffled out feathers. "You have to learn how to control your shifting. It's not normal for a paranormal creature to change at the first sign of anxiety or nervousness. We only shift when our talents are needed."

Except a duckling had no talents. There was no reason for

C.A. KING

her to change from one form to the other. She had no skills worth speaking of either way. A human wasn't meant to exist in the supernatural part of the world and a duckling wasn't either.

"Quack." She was on the floor again.

A woman entered the room unannounced, laundry falling from her arms. "I found this in the road." A storm brewed deep within the grey of her eyes, ending in a potent lightning strike as her gaze lowered to the floor. "Vampire Lord Kobreon is returning. We can't have these little incidents interrupting his arrival. Try to control your daughter. It's you who'll be the laughingstock, if he sees her like this."

"Lord Kobreon," her mother gasped. "Why now? Why here?"

The woman neared, whispering, "Word on the street says he's interviewing everyone, looking for a bride." She stepped back a few paces, waggling one hand at the wrist. "Well, that's just gossip, of course. Who knows what the real reason is?"

"Gossip," her mother replied. "When is this supposed to happen?"

"The day after tomorrow."

"Quack."

The woman's harsh gaze practically singed the ends of her feathers. "It might be best to keep Ducky indoors. We don't want anything embarrassing happening in front of His Lordship, now do we?" The smirk on her face insinuated she'd won some sort of competition. That was to be expected from the head of the feline shifters. Everything and anything was a chance to put down her peers. The cat mentality insisted upon them being held in highest esteem.

"No," Chantelle said, wringing her apron as the woman exited. "We don't." The answer wasn't actually needed. Only the two of them remained in the room. "Ducky." A painted-

on smile made her eyes slanted into thin slits. "Why don't you rest on your bed until you can manage switching back?"

Head hung low, she waddled away. There was no use arguing. Not even her mother spoke fluent quack, and even if she could, there wasn't much else to say. There was no point in meeting Lord Kobreon. It wasn't as if he was going to magically acknowledge her or anything.

Under a wooden dresser lay a box. A duck's jaw was just strong enough to pull it out, her beak then nudging off the lid. Inside was everything she'd collected over the years—clippings from papers, memorabilia from festivals. If it had his image on it, she bought it. That was her one iron-clad rule.

He was the epitome of warrior types—strong, confident, outspoken, stern. There was an air swirling about him, one which made him unapproachable by the norm.

He was beyond her reach, except inside that little box. She was just Ducky, after all. That wasn't going to stop her from taking a peek though.

*"Vampire Lord Kobreon has declared he will hold an audience with every citizen wishing to meet with him over the coming days and weeks."*
—*Dillinger*

# 2

JUST OUTSIDE THE TOWN LIMITS, PERCHED ON A HILL WAS THE biggest, most beautiful castle. Every child in the area, at one point or another, dreamed of living an entitled life there, albeit, no one had actually stepped foot inside. Now, there was a real chance of at least one of those dreams coming true.

It was only a few days ago gossip of his search for a partner reached their ears, yet the main road was spotless, townsfolk lining the sides of it, donning their best outfits and fancy accessories. Family crests flew high on banners born from pride.

No one knew exactly when the object of their affections would arrive. They simply stood there, waiting. Even if their legs hurt, no one sat. Even if the wind shifted, no one flinched. Hail from Hell could have fallen on them and they'd remain steadfast—all for a mere glimpse at his magnificence passing by.

Gender wasn't of concern. Shifter race didn't matter. Age wasn't even a factor. He was every paranormal creature's heartthrob and he was coming home.

C.A. KING

Vampire Lord Kobreon: the mere mention of his name sent shivers racing down her back, but not for unpleasant reasons. She wasn't afraid of him; she was in awe.

His draw was unavoidable, despite the fact she'd never actually seen him in the flesh before. Everything she knew about him was hearsay and few could actually put his grandeur into words. While attempting to envision him, his features were shadowed. If she dreamed of him, there would be no memory of it come morning. Still, she wanted to be the one he picked—the one allowed to stand by his side. It was nonsensical—a fairy tale in the making.

The crowd was thick, standing shoulder to shoulder. No one wanted to give up an inch. Carefully chosen spots were protected at all costs. Anyone showing up late was out of luck.

A black carriage pulled by eight white horses appeared, making its way slowly through the street, kicking up dust to the rear. They were all the finest shifters and volunteers. She'd read about it in an article. Lord Kobreon only hired shifters, never using wild or domesticated animals. That was his policy.

The fine gold etching adorning the sides and trim on the coach was a surprise and a sight to behold. Anyone could have stared at it for hours—the women fanning their faces, the flames dancing up the sides, snarling wolves staring right at her. She almost jumped out of her skin, turning away before unnecessary anxiety forced her into a feathery yellow ball again.

No expense was spared.

That wasn't how she imagined Lord Kobreon.

The blackened carriage windows remained closed. The cargo inside was too precious to allow commoners even a glimpse. The vampire so many worshipped was too important. Most of the townsfolk were oblivious to the true nature

20

JUST DUCKY

of his form. That was obvious the moment the carriage rolled to a stop beside the town square and a male stepped out.

He wasn't Kobreon.

She wasn't sure how, but a part of her knew it without even seeing his face. This man was an aide or devoted subject.

No one else seemed to notice or care. The applause simply began. The crowd parted, allowing him easy access to a stage, set up especially for a welcoming ceremony. Once the stairs were climbed, he came to a stop directly in the centre of the platform, giving his vest a strong tug to straighten it. A mist swirled around his feet, hiding them from view.

From there a complete view was clear. White hair, red eyes, a thin frame covered by an old-fashioned suit, and devilishly handsome: short of showing off a change in his form, he checked all the boxes for what a vampire was expected to be. If not for the expression plastered to his face, she might have swooned along with everyone else. As it was, he reminded her of someone seriously constipated.

"Ahem."

An announcement?

A horn blew.

Silence ensued.

Anticipation threatened to explode if something wasn't said.

"Vampire Lord Kobreon has declared he will hold audience with every citizen wishing to meet with him over the coming days and weeks." That was it. That was the whole message. They never even learned his name. He simply disappeared back into the carriage after speaking.

Kobreon never made an appearance. He might not have even been in the carriage. The whole festival vibe simply

C.A. KING

disbanded. The townsfolk had another agenda on their minds—meeting the vampire in person.

The rush was on. If she'd been in her duckling form, there was a good chance she would have been trampled. The whole town was in an uproar, pushing and shoving without a single thought for who might end up injured.

Sure, she wanted to meet him as much as the next person, but this was overkill. Vampires weren't gods after all. They were merely wolf and bat shifters, who earned their title from humans back when wars were brewing.

A wall became the support she needed to stay out of the way of the others. There was no need to be first in line to meet Kobreon. She merely needed to be somewhere close at hand... and maybe... just maybe... even hiding way at the very back, her turn would come. That was provided she controlled her shift and no one else noticed she was there.

*"We have done nothing wrong. Why should blame fall on us? Humans should take responsibility for human problems."*
—*Trishia*

# 3

IT WAS A CASTLE. IT WAS BIG. IT WAS ALSO MADE OF STONE AND had poor lighting. There was a chill in the air, which not even several oversized fireplaces could overcome and those were lit round the clock. In fact, a fire starter was one of the few servants the family kept. That position doubled as the official chimney sweep as well.

"All that fuss outside and I find my son cooped up in this dingy library," Trishia said. "So... when did you get back?"

"A few hours ago," Kobreon replied, without looking up at his mother. "If you experienced the same pleasures I did over the past few weeks, you'd understand why I'm taking a few moments for myself. Dillinger can handle the crowds for now."

"I take it things didn't go as smoothly as you'd hoped?" she asked, prying for answers and hoping to alleviate a bit of the weight off her son's shoulders. It was the least she could do.

He leaned back in his chair, gaze focused on the ceiling. "No. I spent much of the last part of the trip searching bogs

for a leech shifter. I can still smell the disgusting rot on my skin. Once that smell takes hold, it never lets go."

"No luck, huh?" Her upper lip arched.

"Oh," he chuckled. "I found him. He could cure any illness too. Unfortunately, ninety-nine-percent of the time his patients pass away from the treatment. What's the point in saving someone from one ailment only to have them die from being saved?"

"Right." His mother placed a teacup on the desk beside his notes. "That is a bit of a quandary, isn't it? Does this mean you are back to the drawing board?"

"I'm afraid so." Brilliant blue hues in his eyes turned golden, then red. The front two legs of his chair came down with a thud. "I'm running out of information. It's been weeks since even a unicorn sighting has been noted. I'm not sure we can meet the human king's demands this time."

"Then you'll have to talk through it," she suggested. "We have done nothing wrong. Why should blame fall on us? Humans should take responsibility for human problems. That's the way things are supposed to be."

Kobreon sighed. "It sounds easy enough, doesn't it? Honestly, I can't figure out why they think we are involved in all of this."

"Exactly." His mother nodded her agreement. "We don't hound them with our troubles, albeit, we probably could. We all need to take care of our own. It's as plain as the stench on your clothes. Maybe you should change. Have a hot shower... relax."

"I will," he replied. "I need to go through a few more books to see if I missed anything." He glanced over at her. "Whether we are involved or not, finding an answer is the fastest way to put an end to this whole saga. Our borders have been peaceful for a long time. I don't think anyone

remembers how truly horrible wartime can be. I'd prefer not to remind anyone."

"You really think it will come down to that?" she asked.

"I think we can't take any chances," he replied, a frown etching its way in his smooth skin. "That's why I've been working so diligently. Even if we aren't responsible, if we find an answer, it's problem solved. My time is better spent working on a possibility than contemplating what-ifs and whys."

"Perhaps," his mother sighed. "At least clean up. I'll draw you a bath and lay out fresh clothes. I think we'll burn the ones you are wearing... no arguments either. I can't see any way to remove that odour. Next time you go bog jumping, wear a covering of some sort to protect your outfit."

He chuckled. "You do have some strange ideas. Wearing disposable clothes over top of regular ones... that would be a sight to see. Let me know when you come up with the design."

"Is that a challenge?" One brow arched in anticipation of the answer.

"I know better than to issue a challenge to you," he replied. "A mother will always best her son in any provocation or dare. That's a fact I've come to understand and I care not to dispute in my lifetime."

"Fine words," she snickered, tying the straps of a fancy apron around her waist. "You're a good boy. Now if you'd only find a mate..."

"I have too much on my plate to worry about anything else, let alone a female," he snapped. "The opposite sex is the worst sort of trouble."

"I'll accept that for now." His mother flashed a quirky smile.

"But..."

"But when this is all over, there is no harm in peeking,"

C.A. KING

she replied. "You could take notes now. There are bound to be a few lookers in the lineup. You might want to remember them for later."

"Out!" he bellowed, grinning. "I can't be distracted at the moment." He paused. "Let me know when the bath is ready."

"Uh-huh," she hummed. "You need to look your best for the townsfolk, after all... and the ladies."

Paper crinkled in his hand, forming a ball. It launched through the air, hitting the door just as it closed.

Women—even his mother—were going to be the death of him. Then who would solve their country's issues?

*"No expense is to be spared."*
—*King Hammerhead*

# 4

*THE HUMAN KINGDOM OF HAMMERHEAD, LOCATED FOUR DAYS'
ride from the border.*

IT WAS BEAUTIFUL. IT WAS WARM. IT WAS INVITING. NOT A
penny was spared in the design of both the exterior and the
interior palace. The finest materials from around the world
were acquired and skilfully pieced together to royal specifi-
cations. A team of a hundred servants kept every inch of the
marble and gold decor polished and shining around the
clock. Another crew was responsible for keeping huge
braziers emitting light and heat day and night.

No expense was spared. It never was.

A deep red rug, edged with a finely embellished design in
gold thread led to the king's royal seat, splitting the room in
two. Carpets weren't the only thing with lavish borders and
embroidered fine patterns; the curtains and banners were
equally and precisely as detailed.

Fingers tapped impatiently, growing in speed and intensity, on the side of a cushioned throne made of the finest

C.A. KING

carved wood. Kings weren't accustomed to being made to wait. They rarely found the need to twiddle their thumbs for anything.

This situation was annoying and dire at the same time. The princess—the only heir to the throne—was gravely ill with a virus of unknown origins.

"Debouche," the king bellowed. "What is the latest report on my daughter? Has there been any change?" Only five minutes had passed since he last asked the same question. The answer was bound to be the same.

"None, my Lord," his advisor answered, hands folded neatly in front, head bowed. His underlings appeared on either side, kneeling. "She remains on death's doorstep. None of our doctors know what to do. I fear the worst, lest she waken soon."

"Find more doctors. No expense is to be spared," King Hammerhead insisted, his voice cracking. "There has to be a way to save her. I know there is. This situation is growing more and more dire by the day. My wife has sequestered herself in our chambers and refuses to open the doors. My daughter will not wake. I am at a loss as to how to help my family. Am I not the most powerful man in the nation?"

"Yes, Mi'lord" Debouche said. "I believe we both know that those responsible for her illness also have a cure for it. Maybe it's time we became a bit more forceful with them? I could make the arrangements."

"We will wait!" The king's voice shook the walls of gold and chandeliers made of the finest gems. "I gave Kobreon time. I am a man of my word. I can't go back on it now. That would leave a mark on my manhood."

"What time do you think we have, Sire?" Debouche's right-hand man, Charmichael retorted. "As you mentioned, your wife is secluded in your chambers and your daughter is unresponsive. No king should endure such helplessness in

his own castle. The whole kingdom is in upheaval. If our neighbours were to find out the details..."

"And how would they?" the king bellowed. He was young, one of the youngest to ever be crowned in his lineage. That alone was enough reason for his subjects to keep a watchful eye. Trust was hard to come by when times were rough and easily given in times of plenty. This year's crops were less than to be desired. He was already being scrutinized from the sidelines, even if he wasn't ready to admit it.

"He meant no disrespect, Sire," Debouche said calmly. "Only that time is of the essence for the well-being of the entire kingdom."

"Time is always of the essence," the king scoffed. "Humans are frail creatures. We live short lives and try to jam pack everything into them." He inhaled deeply through flared nostrils. "We were not blessed with the long lives of our neighbours."

"Exactly," Charmichael agreed.

The king flashed a stern glance. "It would do no good for us to rush. Kobreon knows what is at stake. If he procured the cure already, he would come. If he has not... a rush to arms would stop his pursuit of it. My daughter is the most important part of this equation. If there is even the slimmest chance for her recovery, I will take it."

"I fear it may be too late to save face, if we wait too long," Charmichael replied, bowing his head. "Please reconsider your position. I reiterate the concerns over this year's crops and trade. There are whispers in the shadows..."

A jewelled staff came down with a thud. "What whispers? Who dares to speak of their king in the back alleys? I'll have their heads."

"Your subjects are restless," Charmichael continued. "You cannot blame them for hoping for a better tomorrow."

"And you feel overthrowing the current regime would

C.A. KING

benefit the people?" Hammerhead snapped, standing. A light shone behind him, blinding his men. "Do you dare defy me?"

"No, Mi'lord," Charmichael replied, head remaining bowed, gritted teeth hidden from sight, as he backed away a few steps.

Debouche stepped in front of his subordinate. "What he means is simply that there would be no question as to your leadership abilities, if we were to take action. No one would blame you if war were to break out."

"Hmm," the king grunted, taking a seat in his throne again. "And we will have war... if a cure is not given. The Kingdom of Hammerhead will not instigate bloodshed unless it is absolutely necessary." His crown tilted slightly to one side of his head. That wasn't supposed to happen. It was meant to fit his head perfectly.

The royal head ornament represented power, glory, and sovereignty and was made from the purest gold, adorned with the rarest and most valuable gems and pearls, forming the family crest.

No expense was spared.

"Understood," Debouche said, walking backward toward a set of oversized double doors, while motioning for his underling to move in the same manner with a hand hidden behind his back.

No one was to see their king in a dishevelled state. The crooked crown was a bad omen, one which simply noticing could cost them their lives.

*"Quack...." And she was a duckling again*
—*Ducky*

# 5

IT WAS A BEAUTIFUL MORNING, DESPITE A FEW GREY CLOUDS. Rain might have worried others, but for a duck, even a duckling, it wasn't of any concern. She was, in fact, waterproof— or her feathers were and oddly enough hair. No matter how much it poured, liquid simply slid off. Clothes, of course, were a different story. They ended up soaked, but if she shifted, there was nothing to worry about. That was a big if though. Changing forms was a surprise, even to herself.

Gasp!

This was the closest she'd been to Lord Kobreon's estate. Tears welled at the beauty. Bees and birds hummed in the distance, bustling about the lush fields of crops surrounding the exterior walls. The abundance provided not only the manor's inhabitants with food all year round, but was also a large source of the entire town's provisions as well.

The centre point of the surrounding walls was a set of heavy, wooden double doors, in front of which a regular bridge traversed a small trickling river. At one point perhaps it had been meant to house a full moat, but peace saw no need for such a level of protection.

C.A. KING

This castle itself was a landmark, having survived for over a thousand years, but its sturdiness hadn't declined in the least. While other buildings crumbled, Lord Kobreon's roost withstood the test of time, outwitting the elements, and depriving them of victory. That alone was enough to warrant the trek across country to see.

Normally, most of the townsfolk weren't morning risers. Today was the exception. The lineup to see him was already insane, despite the hour being early. Every shifter and their mother was waiting for a chance to meet personally with Vampire Lord Kobreon, most of them still hoping he was actually searching for a partner, as the gossip and rumours suggested. That was, after all, the ideal ending for any love story, fictional or real: love at first sight, an arrow through the heart, swooning into each other's arms.

For her, hope was merely grasping at straws. Ducklings weren't allowed to fantasize about unattainable possibilities. There was no happily ever after waiting to pop out around the corner. The best life had to offer someone like her was the opportunity to watch from afar.

She wasn't giving that up.

"Ow!" A small thorn cut into a finger. Even the bush she was hiding behind had it out for her.

She ducked, licking her wounds. Being seen in such a state was her worst nightmare, one she'd never live down, and with the number of attendees, inevitable. She'd take what she could get, at least until someone noticed.

"Who's there?" a woman asked.

Ducky lunged forward, her straw-coloured hair catching on branches. "Ouch!" That was the second time she'd made a fuss.

"Are you okay?" The woman rushed to the backside of the bushes, staring down at her.

That was it! She'd been seen. There was no escaping the

JUST DUCKY

taunting that was bound to follow, even if she wasn't sure who the woman who found her was.

Poof!

"Quack..." And she was a duckling again. There was a good chance of becoming someone's lunch too. Most of the shifters in line hadn't had a bite to eat. Tummies were bound to be grumbling. Duck was delicious, or so she'd been told on many occasions.

"Oh, my!" the woman exclaimed, realizing the severity of the situation. "I better take you inside. This isn't a good place for someone like you."

"Quack." One was all that was needed.

It was of little concern if she agreed or not. There was no expressing her feelings while in animal form. Besides, she and her clothes had already been swooped up and were hidden inside the woman's dark cloak.

"Shush," the woman said. "It'll just be a minute."

Pulse, breath, the bumpiness of the ride... It all meant one thing: she was being saved. But for what purpose? Going inside the castle walls wasn't necessarily a good thing. Her would-be saviour might have been thinking about dinner too —one where she wasn't meant to be a guest.

"Don't worry," the woman cooed. "I won't let you get trampled by the rush. It's about to get very busy."

The rush?

She peeked her head outside the thick cloth of the cloak. There was indeed a stampede. Not the usual sort where animals panicked to escape impending danger. These were women, each wanting to be the first to be seen by the lord of this manner. Was it possible he'd come outside to address them already?

"Quack!"

She'd missed getting even a teeny glimpse of him.

39

"Ducky it is. I could use an emotional-support duckling about now."
—Lord Kobreon

# 6

THE INSIDE OF THE MANOR WAS A HUNDRED TIMES LARGER than she imagined, albeit, her vision range was impeded by her size. Being carried in the arms of a strange woman in duckling form wasn't how she expected, or wanted, to meet the lord. He certainly wasn't going to find the situation amusing. Her shifted form was loathsome.

It was better than being eaten though. Anything was. Bypassing the kitchen to a bedroom was a huge relief.

"Quack!"

Maybe it was too much of a relief.

Ducky landed on a bed, rolling off the side as she shifted back, naked.

"Oh, dear," the woman cried, dropping the garments she'd collected on the mattress. "You need to change quickly."

Ducky's head popped up, gaze surveying the room. One hand reached forward, grabbing her clothes and pulling them toward her. Dying of embarrassment before the castle occupants wasn't the way she planned to go out.

"And who might you be?" the woman asked. "There

C.A. KING

wasn't time to ask before. I was concerned for your well-being out there."

"Ducky," she whispered.

"Ducky?" One hand lightly slapped the side of the woman's own face. "I suppose that is an appropriate name. Can you shift back? Once the commotion settles, I'll take you to where I found you. I'm not sure sneaking you out in human form is a good idea at that point. Shifter emotions run high... especially jealousy. Anyone who sees you leave might take offence to you being allowed inside."

"Probably," she agreed. There was a lineup of females who would shred her to pieces, if they saw either of her forms emerging from Lord Kobreon's home. "I might end up eaten alive either way." She sighed.

"I'm Trishia," the woman announced. "I got you into this, so I'll find a way to get you out as well. I really thought you were just a cute duck who needed my help. I do love animals, especially cute fuzzy ones. I probably should have guessed from the clothes... It all happened so fast. So..."

"Mother!" a strong voice bellowed. "Where have you disappeared to?"

Gasp! Mother? Trishia was Lord Kobreon's mother? Did she really not know?

"I'm here," she answered, pressing one finger against her lips afterward. "It's not like I disappeared. So? Do you need something?" Attempts to head her son off at the door failed.

"What are you doing in here?" he asked, pushing his way in. "What are you hiding?" His eyes slanted, examining his mother's movements carefully.

"Nothing." Her arm intertwined with his, pulling his gaze away from the bed just as Ducky peeked up. "I was merely putting away some old clothing which I no longer fit into. I thought I'd save them in case they should become useful again."

44

JUST DUCKY

His laugh was genuinely warm. "Maybe you need to eat a few less pastries then?"

She lightly slapped her son's arm. "Is that any way to speak to your mother?" She broke out into her own bout of laughter. "Come on. Let's get something to eat before you have to face all the townsfolk again. Have you seen that lineup? I swear, it grows by the minute."

"I have seen it. You know I was outside to give a formal address a few moments ago. I'm giving them a few moments to calm down before I greet them individually." A mischievous grin covered his lips. "Now, I believe you are trying to distract me for some reason."

"I have no idea what you mean," she insisted, batting her eyelashes innocently. "You're being silly."

It was a battle which was never going to be won. The room they were in wasn't typically used. There was no reason to be in there. There was no reason for his mother to put old clothes away either. They always went to the less fortunate.

"You're lying to me," he sighed.

"What?!" she complained. "Why would you say such a thing?"

"I know you well enough," he smirked. "Is this a game?" The closet doors flew open, garments shifting to the side. "Hmm. Not in there."

"What in the full moon are you doing?" she asked, hands planted firmly on her hips. "Stop this nonsense before you make a mess."

"I am going to figure out what it is you don't want me to know," he replied, opening every drawer in a dresser. "Something is in here and I want to know what."

"Don't be ridiculous," she huffed, grabbing her son's arm. "Let's go have something to eat. There's fresh muffins and tea."

45

C.A. KING

He pulled away, racing toward the edge of the bed. "Ah-ha!"

"Quack!" She'd transformed just in time, her clothes hidden under the bed. The original plan was to join them and not be found. That failed miserably.

"A duckling?" He picked her up, cradling her in his arms. "What's this little fella doing in here?" Vampires weren't known for giving off heat. In fact, it was the opposite. They were downright cold. She felt no chill though. Perhaps it was the pleasant scent of woodsy musk which gently warmed her, or the rich blue colour of his eyes, partially hidden by long, thick, black lashes. A single bat from them was enough to send any living thing swooning—a family trait no doubt.

"Not a male... a she," his mother corrected, slowly inching closer, hoping to move near enough to snatch Ducky from his arms. That wasn't happening. "I found her outside. I think she lost her mother. I was worried with all the commotion she'd be hurt out there. It was silly of me to bring her inside. Here." Her arms opened wide. "I'll take her back to the water. I'm sure she'll find her family on her own. Animals are resilient after all. We all know that firsthand, don't we?"

"Nonsense," Kobreon said in a firm yet sensitive tone. "I could use some company. I think she'll make a good companion for me... and you when I'm away on trips." He turned away from his mother. "What shall we call you?"

"Ducky," Trishia blurted out. "I already named her."

"So you don't want to see her go either," he mused. "Ducky it is. I could use an emotional-support duckling about now." His genuine smile melted Ducky inside and out, turning her into a pool of soft feathers.

"Huh?" His mother tried again to take the little yellow duckling from him and failed. "I never thought of you as the pet type... especially not such an unusual one."

46

JUST DUCKY

"Think again," he smirked. "This little ducky might be my salvation."

"Quack."

Feathers ruffled. What was that supposed to mean?

*"I wasn't expecting my son to become quite so fond of you. I won't hear the end of it, if you were to disappear on my watch."*
—*Trishia*

# 7

TIME PASSED QUICKLY. AFTER A FEW DAYS WENT BY, SHE WAS
fully settled in—a seamlessly easy transition from normal
daily routines. The library, in particular, was the one place in
the castle she felt at home.

Lord Kobreon sat at his desk reading and doing paperwork nonstop, while she plunked down on a comfortable
pillow perch, overlooking his face as he worked. The down-
side was he only thought of her as a cute little duckling,
while she was falling deeper and deeper in love with everything about him.

When he moved, her heart skipped a beat.

When he spoke, her gaze carefully studied his lips.

When he stretched, her feathers ruffled at the sight of his
muscles pulling tightly on his clothes.

"I'll be gone for most of the day," Kobreon said.

"Quack." She glanced up from the ground. Even though
he was speaking to his mother, she, for some reason, felt it
necessary to add in her two cents' worth.

He dropped to a knee, one hand lightly petting the top of
her head. "I'll miss you too," he said, adding a wink. "Make

sure Ducky stays in the library. I don't want to come home and find her gone. Who knows what a pack of wolves might do to such a gentle creature? I'd rather she not find out." With a quirky grin, he stood.

"Of course."

"I'm sorry to leave you to deal with the line outside," he continued. "I'll try not to be too long. This lead is too good to be true. If it pans out, all our troubles will be over."

"I understand." His mother stood, smiling. "They'll still be there when you return." She moved closer, pressing her weight on her toes to gain enough height to plant a kiss on his cheek. "I hope you find what you are looking for."

Looking for? Ducky waddled around their feet. What are you looking for? Surely not a bride. No. It couldn't be. This is something else.

The sound of his footsteps grew weaker then vanished. He was gone to who knew where and she was left with a chance to leave. Surely someone noticed she was missing—at least her parents.

Poof! She was in human form again.

"I'll get you something to wear," Trishia offered, entering her son's bedroom from the adjacent door. "Here."

One of the Lord's silk robes hit her in the face. It wasn't exactly what she was hoping for and certainly wasn't an appropriate outfit for an escape.

"I was thinking about heading home," she mumbled. "My mother is probably worried about me. This might be my best opportunity."

"Sorry, I can't allow that," Trishia snapped rather hastily. "I wasn't expecting my son to become quite so fond of you. I won't hear the end of it if you disappear on my watch. We'll need to find another way, after he returns. Keep your eyes open. I'm sure a chance will come. For now..." She glanced

JUST DUCKY

around the room. "...there are numerous books to hold your attention."

Books.

The red silk felt cool against her skin. Pink filled her cheeks. This material wasn't something she was ever meant to feel. It was too luxurious. It was filled with his scent too. He'd worn it at some point.

"You can read, can't you?" Trishia asked, eyeing her with a best-say-yes expression.

Books, huh?

"Mostly," she replied. Reading and writing weren't everyday skills for those of supernatural descent. She was an exception. With no friends, and a lack of stable work, there was plenty of time to fill. Learning languages was a hobby she'd adapted, albeit, there was a severe lack of material. "I've never seen texts like this before."

"Hmm," Trishia grunted. "I suppose not. Well, there is no time like the present. Why not give one a try? I can help you out with anything you don't understand."

"I can't ask you to do that!" Ducky shrieked.

"Don't be silly." Trishia waved her off with one hand bending back and forth at the wrist. "I have loads of time with my son gone. Pick a book and I'll fix some tea."

The book she was interested in was a no-brainer. It was the one Lord Kobreon was reading—the one which was still open on his desk and bound to be filled with juicy information.

She inched closer, side-eyeing the published work as if it were a crime to be poking about in another person's affairs. There was no need to feel that way; his mother had offered her any book in the library to read. Still...

"EEK!"

Trishia chuckled, "Oh, my. Did I startle you?" A silver tray holding a floral design, fine china tea set settled on the desk,

53

C.A. KING

cups and saucers clanging. "That book might be a bit advanced for you. I find it's always best to start small and work your way up. Going big right out of the gate can lead to unnecessary frustration."

Her cheeks puffed out, filled with air; lips holding on to a defiant pout. The Lord's mother was right. There were only a few understandable parts at her reading level. Still, it was always possible to fill in some details with imagination.

"Why not try this one?" Trishia pulled a brown book with fading gold lettering on the cover from a shelf. "It might be a good place for you to start."

"This one is about fairies and elves," Ducky said, smiling triumphantly. "That means it's a fantasy, right?" One hand planted on her hip.

"I hope not." Trishia's previously joyful smile turned grim, the corners of her lips falling with her mood. "For all our sake's, I hope not."

*"And ruin a future soldier? Losing military might for a few gold coins isn't worth it. Besides, once hands are removed, someone would have to attend to the child constantly. He wouldn't even be able to wipe his own ass. That only serves to add to the problem we are already facing."*
—*General Debouche*

# 8

THE HUMAN KINGDOM OF HAMMERHEAD, LOCATED A FOUR
**days' ride from the border.**

WALKING THROUGH THE STREETS OF THE CAPITOL AT HIGH
noon was nearly impossible. Everyone and anyone was after
whatever merchants of the market were willing to sell. Prices
escalated hourly in accordance with the rate at which goods
diminished. By four in the afternoon, all stalls would be
empty. If food and necessities hadn't been procured by then,
those unlucky souls went without for the day. The streets
never emptied completely. Those who failed during the day
waited through the night for a chance at the next available
wares. Traversing the area was dangerous for anyone, but
more so for the rich who wore large targets on their backs
when it came to pickpockets and thieves.

"Tsk," Debouche complained, elbows serving as paddles,
pushing him through the sea of bodies. A simple trip to the
church and back was becoming bothersome. If the hour for

buying goods ever shrank, ending earlier, a riot would ensue. Changes in the land of Hammerhead needed to be made before that happened.

The ever-growing population meant a need for more housing. More housing meant building on farmlands. Reduced farmlands meant less food.

It was a never-ending cycle.

On top of that, the soil had been overworked. It lacked nutrients. Crops were beginning to fail. It was only a matter of time before fighting broke out in the streets and a revolution was put into motion.

"Tsk." He pushed to the side; a child narrowly missed bumping into him. No doubt the boy was new to the art of pick-pocketing. Had the tot actually made contact, there was no gold waiting to be stolen.

How could one hope to outsmart a kingdom without being able to outmanoeuvre a child?

Even from outside the gates, it was easy to see the palace was built with being admired at the top of the priority list. The structure boasted high walls, vaulted ceilings, and stained-glass windows in all directions.

There was no lacking in the depictions of religion in chosen pieces of art. Cherubs and angels were painted on the ceilings, immortalized by colourful glass, humbled as statues, and captured magnificently by grand fountains. No opportunity was missed to brainwash the masses into believing the king and his kingdom were blessed by the gods.

He nodded to the guards, passing through the first of several pillar openings. The final set were turrets used by the military to watch over all entering the Hammerhead domain. After that, there were a few steps before officially entering the inside of the castle. Technically, it was a cold breezy outer corridor, one in which no fire was able to remain lit.

JUST DUCKY

The windows were for show, definitely not for their functionality.

"Wait!" Charmichael called out, panting. "Why is it I am always stopped by the guards and you never are?"

"Tsk." Another stupid question he had no time or desire to respond to. The answer should have been obvious. Sometimes it seemed as if he was surrounded by fools. "Because I am the one who ensures they and their families are fed and clothed. Because of me, they don't have to fight in long lineups for their daily bread. That affords me their loyalty."

"But," Charmichael began, "the king was the one who approved those plans, was he not? It's his coffers that pay for the men's needs. Should he not be the one receiving said praise?"

Debouche turned around swiftly, one finger pressed against his lips. "Shh. What they don't know won't hurt them, or me."

A gust of wind blew shutters with the royal emblem painted on them open. Tapestries on the wall swung wildly, threatening to fall but stopping just short of disaster.

Carmichael barely moved a step before a group of servants raced by to rectify the situation. It took only a minute before the long hallway was back to normal. The only thing they hadn't fixed was his hair; the combed-over strands sticking up as if at attention. Decorative suits of shining armour made the messy do impossible to ignore.

"Damn." A pink tongue licked the palm of his hand, leaving behind thick saliva. Rubbing that on his head forced the mess of hair back into its proper state.

"In here," Debouche instructed, ducking in a room. "There are fewer eyes and ears behind closed doors. The last thing we want is for anybody to figure out certain plans. I'd like to keep things quiet as long as possible."

C.A. KING

Charmichael scurried after his comrade. "That's what I was trying to say. There might be a chance the king is already onto you."

"No," Debouche said in a stern voice. "He has no clue what we are planning. Luckily, our king isn't smart enough to figure out schemes created by his top aides and generals. That's what makes him controllable." Evenly paced steps landed him in front of a small bar made primarily of crystal bottles.

Pop!

A corked lid pulled easily from the top of one of the decanters. Amber liquid filled a similar-style glass. He lifted it, swishing the contents around before tossing the spirits back in one big gulp.

"You are planning," Charmichael scoffed. "I want change, but will have no hand in treasonous activities. My only guilt lies in agreeing war is inevitable, should suitable changes not be made."

"Spoken like a true coward," Debouche chuckled, his smile quickly faltering to an expressionless glare, fixated on nothing in particular. "Relax. I was kidding. Besides, we are simply taking advantage of a situation. There is no treason in preparing for the worst and reaping the benefits of success."

"I suppose not," Charmichael agreed. "As long as we agree to remain within legal boundaries, I am behind you all the way."

"I appreciate that." He'd never considered Charmichael to be completely in his corner. The man simply lacked the stomach needed to take on bloodier tasks. There were still other ways the aide could remain useful. Nothing was ever wasted in his plans. That was where his success came from. That was how he rose the ranks to general.

"ACK! My purse is missing. I've been robbed!" Charmichael shrieked. "That's a whole week's pay... gone."

60

JUST DUCKY

"Tsk. I told you not to bring your pocketbook along when we visit the church," he snapped. "Taking it out of the palace was simply asking for someone to steal it."

"It's those grubby little kids," Carmichael cursed, spitting in a golden spittoon to his left. "What are the guards doing?"

"Their duty," Debouche answered, swirling a new double dose of liquid in his glass before taking a swig. "Protecting the king and his palace. Nowhere does it say they need to arrest thieves."

"Someone needs to do something," Charmichael complained.

"What would you have them do?" Debouche snapped. "Remove the children's hands, perhaps? Would that be an adequate punishment for you? Hmm?"

"It would certainly deter others from stealing," Charmichael replied with an air of arrogance and egotism swirling around him.

"Ha!" Debouche stood, the legs of his chair scraping loudly on the floor. "And ruin a future soldier? Losing military might for a few gold coins isn't worth it. Besides, once hands are removed, someone would have to attend to the child constantly. He wouldn't even be able to wipe his own ass. That only serves to add to the problems we are already facing."

"Why isn't he making a move?" Charmichael sighed, switching back to the original conversation. "He's not taking the threat seriously. We may have to forfeit the plan." He peeked over his shoulder, glancing around for anyone who might have entered the room and been in earshot. "Maybe..."

Debouche let out a throaty groan. "Stop your fussing. We've planted the seed of mistrust. Let's wait to see if it grows the way we hope it will." He paused, looking off in the distance thoughtfully. "Or perhaps we can egg those emotions along a little."

C.A. KING

"And how, exactly, do you plan to do that?" Charmichael's brow arched inquisitively.

"Don't worry," Debouche huffed. "I think I know the perfect way."

*"I'd hate to see you lose your companions the way I lost mine. They aren't coming back. I am quite sure of it. That forest eats intruders alive."*

*—Max*

# 9

INCONSPICUOUS WAS THE ORIGINAL PLAN, ALTHOUGH HE wasn't sure how well it worked when put into action. A plain, tan, short-sleeved, cotton, knit vest covered a white, narrow-sleeved shirt, the ends of which rested just above his wrists and were cuffed with plain buttons. The matching pants were simple and wide enough to cover a pair of shiny boots. By the end of the trip their polish would be gone, a thick layer of dirt taking away the shimmer his mother worked so tirelessly to achieve. Appearances were more her thing than his. For as long as he could remember, she'd made sure he was viewed in the most favourable way while under the scrutiny of the public light. It was because of that he now had the authority which was needed to aid in stopping a war.

"Harold." He nodded to the brown-and-white patchwork coloured horse, who'd already shifted, and by the way things looked, it was some time ago. How early had he arrived? "It's good of you to come along."

"Neigh."

Horse wasn't a language he understood, but knowing the horse shifter, it was a pleasant greeting. In man form, Harold

was well-liked with a pleasant demeanour—a lover not a fighter. Well, perhaps not a lover or fighter so much as a hard worker. There was no job too tedious and if a horse was needed, Harold was always the first to volunteer for service.

He chuckled under his breath. "Shall we?" There was no need to squeeze or cluck, or even provide directional signals. This horse knew where they were going and understood the native tongue. That internal built-in map was drawn using years of experience. No one knew the land better than Harold. No one understood the terrain as well as the eldest horse in the country. Still, they were most likely heading into uncharted territory right after a necessary pit stop.

It was a long shot. Fairy and elf kingdoms were merely rumours—romantic fantasies of an era long past. There wasn't an ounce of proof they existed. Still, every prospect for a cure needed to be exhausted. A single report of a possible sighting was more than enough to dredge him out of the warmth of his home for a look-see, dragging a small party along for the trip.

The stop they needed to make along the way wasn't one he was looking forward to. Everyone had something he or she disliked. Taverns were, beyond a doubt, his least favourite places to visit. Everything about watering houses made him ill. Most of the time that included the patrons.

Stale beer, bad breath, and reeking body odour were enough nasty scents to kill any appetite. Still, small pubs usually offered lengthy menus made up of subpar foods, which customers ate without reservation. They were places where anything could be found, bought, or bartered for: a female for the night, a male for the night, drugs, alcohol— anything.

"What can I get you?" a barmaid asked, her smile just slightly smaller than her ample bosom. The dress she wore hung off her shoulders, low enough to accentuate their full-

ness, high enough to just cover perky nipples. It was obvious many of the male patrons came there to see her and most likely spread the word about services outside of waitressing.

"I'm looking for someone," Kobreon replied, holding out a piece of paper with a name clearly written on it.

"Ah," the waitress huffed, exasperated by a lack of attention. Once realizing he wasn't going to be an addition to a growing clientele list, her attitude changed, along with her tone. "Max is over there. The one hunched over at the bar. I don't know what you want him for, but buy him a beer and he'll give it to you."

"Thank you," he said, not thinking. It was a little too polite for a place so far removed from normal social statuses. Luckily, the barmaid was too concerned with delivering tankards of ale to other potential bar frequenters in need of a female escort to notice his manners.

This was no place for a Lord. Brawling was a waste of time, but inevitable, if the room found out his true identity. There was always at least one shifter in the room wanting to make a name for himself by attempting to dethrone anyone in a position of power. He took the stool next to Max, sliding in noisily, hoping that was enough to wake him from a drunken slumber.

It wasn't.

"I'll have a pint," Kobreon announced loudly, waving a few bills in the air. A bartender immediately took the bait. "And one for my friend here."

That worked.

"That's mighty kind of you, mate," Max said, raising his head, completely oblivious to the drool crusted on his face. "Have we met before?"

"No," Kobreon replied. "But I have heard of you. In fact, I was hoping to discuss the incident you had in the forest...

C.A. KING

you know the one where you saw," he drew in closer, whispering, "the ancient ones."

Drinks slid in front of them, froth running over the sides of the mugs.

"That's a long story," Max said. The first sip was more than half the contents of his tankard. "Ah." The sleeve of his shirt became a napkin, wiping away anything which escaped the long journey from mouth downward, as well as the remnants of his previous nap.

"Keep them flowing," Kobreon instructed the barkeep, laying down sufficient funds to cover more than a few rounds.

"I like your style," Max chuckled with a toothless grin. Whether from being knocked out or rot, more than a few were missing. "What would you like to know? Go ahead. Ask me anything."

"Can you tell me precisely where in the forest you encountered them?" Kobreon asked. Despite it being obvious the man was using the sighting for free drinks, he still wanted to investigate. "Maybe you could draw a map?"

"Hmm." The rest of the first beer disappeared in a gulp. "I suppose I could do that. I have to warn you, I'm not the best artist."

The barkeep placed ink and a quill before them, along with additional ale, as if ready for the situation.

"There's a clearing. It's a ways in," Max said, grabbing a napkin from beside another patron eating a meal. "That's where you'll find them." He pushed over the rough sketch. "It's not a place to tread lightly. There are creatures in them woods you won't see anywhere else... and the dead walk the paths cleared by those who enter. Things aren't right in them woods." He shook off a shiver. "It's frightening just thinking back."

"How did you survive?" Kobreon asked.

68

JUST DUCKY

"I don't know," Max admitted. "I found myself lost... separated from my party. While walking around aimlessly, I happened upon the clearing. It was dark, then bright. I remember squinting. That's when I saw them... figures in the light... shadows whooshing by." All that talk required an extra-long swig of ale. "Next thing I knew, I was lying by the side of the road. I haven't the foggiest how I ended up there, but I'm glad I did. Who knows what could have made a meal of me in there? I was lucky, that's for sure." The rest of his drink disappeared.

"Have you been back?" Kobreon motioned to the bartender to refill his confidant's tankard by curling a single finger.

Max took a swig of the fresh ale, this time emptying its entirety all at once. "No. I wouldn't go back there if you paid me." An empty gaze stared into the distance. "Not even for a year's supply of drinks."

"Where can I find the rest of your companions?" Kobreon asked. It was possible one of them might have additional information.

"Huh?" Max's expression went blank, matching already glossed-over eyes. "I wish I knew. We were seven strong. I haven't seen hide nor hair of any of them since that day." He paused waiting for a fresh pint to appear before him. This one disappeared twice as fast as the previous had. "I told the lot of them that going into that forest was a mistake. Plans for getting rich quick never work out. If it is too good to be true, it probably is." His head hung low, staring at the remnants of foam in his tankard. No more information was forthcoming.

Kobreon nodded his thanks, leaving additional bills on the bar. "You have been most helpful. I hope you find your friends."

"If you are thinking of going in there," Max called out

69

after him, "don't. I'd hate to see you lose your companions the way I lost mine. They aren't coming back. I am quite sure of it. That forest eats intruders alive."

Kobreon turned away. Maybe it was possible Max was telling the truth. At the very least there was a shred of hope.

*"I need your help. I am trying to stop a war."*
—Lord Kobreon

# 10

KOBREON STARED OFF IN THE DISTANCE IN SILENCE, STARING AT the changing scenery. Towns and small villages came and went. They passed fields and rolling hills covered in white flowers and lush clovers. Everything known was being left behind. Ahead was a foreboding darkness—an omen of dread. The Forest of the Forgotten was quickly nearing. Even he felt the air of ill intent flowing in their direction, as if the wind was issuing a warning to turn back.

"Here," Kobreon bellowed. Harold came to an abrupt stop. "We'll make camp." Originally, he'd thought about heading straight in, but after having some time to fully consider the possible consequences, leaving non-essentials behind was a smarter plan. There was no desire to lose any companions for what was possibly a ghost chase. The awaiting woodlands were like no other after all.

The whole region was one of the last remaining uncharted territories and was densely populated with thickets of thorny, jungle-like growth. A single prick could be deadly from undiscovered and untreatable toxins. Danger

C.A. KING

lurked around every corner. Even the sun, to a point, was frightened to enter.

"I'll take one man with me," Kobreon announced, nodding in agreement to the largest wolf in attendance—the obvious choice for the job. "Lead the way."

Gornen simply nodded.

There was no questioning a lord. Normally, there would have been a short stop for food and rest before departure on such a quest of that nature. Time was too valuable for that. They were pushing on immediately.

Despite removing the vegetation in their way, a glance over his shoulder showed no trace of where they'd first gained access. The forest was alive, closing in around them. With every step, the strangling effect became more noticeable.

According to the map Max made, they should have already arrived at their destination. Their location was much deeper in than he anticipated. The farther in they travelled, the more dangerous things were bound to become.

A sword sliced through thorny branches, continuing to clear a path through dense vegetation.

"This way, Mi'lord," a wolf in man's clothing said. "The clearing in the report must lie ahead. I fear this trip may be for naught though. Fantasy and folklore usually have no basis in truth."

"I want to be sure," Kobreon said, wielding his own sword. It wasn't the preferred method of exploration for any of their kind, but it was necessary, considering this particular location's reputation. Eyes were already on them, and not just scouts, either. These were the glares of the hungry seeing a meal after days, maybe weeks, of starving. "You should head back to the camp now. The reported sightings were allegedly all made by a singular party member who'd lost

74

sight of the rest of their party. If we are to recreate those events, I'll need to go it alone."

"I'd advise against it, Sire." He'd already picked up on the fact they weren't alone as well. "I have a bad feeling..." Goren plummeted backward, falling to a defenceless sitting position, hands on the ground behind him, while his sword remained stuck in some vegetation.

Blue eyes instantly turned golden, fangs descending. Kobreon's mouth opened wide, letting out a mighty roar. Chittering noises followed—the sound of many eight-legged creatures retreating.

"It'll be better for your health if you head back," Kobreon ordered, features returning to normal. "I can't guarantee your safety from here on out." The man's weapon came loose after a few good tugs. "Here." He returned it to its owner. "Stay on the path we made coming in and you'll be fine." He glared at the way forward—the place the most terrifying beasts called home. There was a chance even he was going to have a hard time of it.

"As you wish." Goren's head hung low—a man defeated. Regret of failure wasn't long lasting when coming face-to-face with death.

Kobreon chuckled quietly. Goren was gone before he even had a chance to turn around. That was the fastest he'd ever seen a wolf run away with its tail between its legs. Of course, it was hard to blame him. The forest was terrifying. Why ancient magical creatures made their home in its depths was mystifying.

From what he knew about fairies, they were simply smaller versions of elves but with wings. Their height was the big discrepancy as they stood no bigger than mice. Appearance wise, they were depicted in books and tomes as having upturned noses, puffed-out, pouty lips, and big, pointy ears.

C.A. KING

Elves had similarly shaped ears, albeit, theirs resembled certain leaves. The appearance varied in accordance with native foliage found in and around the location they were born. Ones in this forest were bound to have a rounded shape narrowing, to a needle-like point at the tip.

As for the rest of their guise, they were, in a word, flawless. Even the males were known to be unnaturally beautiful and extremely enchanting. No one ever saw a short, overweight elf. They were all slender and graceful—blessed by nature with keen senses and an ability to resist all types of illnesses and diseases.

That resistance was what he was searching for. If they had the power to ward off something potentially deadly, then perhaps curing the same ailment was within their power.

His blade sliced through undergrowth and bush, finally giving way to a circular clearing. Feet slid forward, a hand shading his face and eyes from what little sun there was.

Clouds were rolling in. Was that nature's doing, or was magic at work?

His jaw almost dropped. This wasn't at all what he expected to find in a dark, gloomy, ominous forest. Instead, it appeared as if he was standing in the middle of someone's well-tended garden. Even a true green thumb would have a hard time reproducing the flowery sights. It was almost perfect.

A tree trunk became a sofa, providing the perfect vantage point to daydream images of a certain duckling waddling through yellow bell flowers and daisies of varying pastel shades.

Kobreon quickly rubbed his eyes. That wasn't real. Ducky wasn't here and there was no possibility of ever taking her here. It was too dangerous. Even he was beginning to feel an air of regret for intruding in a place where he didn't belong and wasn't welcome.

76

JUST DUCKY

"Hello?" he called out. "My name is Kobreon." Finishing what he came there for quickly was imperative.

There was no answer.

Following the treeline, he circled the whole area twice.

There was nothing, except...

His gaze fell upon a series of miniature toadstools. Somehow, he'd completely missed them during his walkabout.

Whizzing.

The noise caught him off guard. He dodged to the right, turning to follow whatever zipped by him. Nothing appeared out of place. Perhaps it was the wind.

Whizzing sounds.

This time they came from the opposite side. A quick glance over the shoulder, caught a glimpse of a twig, which hadn't been there before.

"I'm not here to expose the fact you still exist," he announced loudly, without putting any thought into his words. "I am merely looking for some information. There are rumours... legends about your healing magic. This isn't for me." He paused briefly, wondering how much of the situation he should reveal. Would mentioning humans be a deterrent? "I need your help. I am trying to stop a war."

A rustle. A snap.

The wind? An animal?

One hand covered his forehead and eyes. He dropped to his knees.

"What am I doing?"

Hands banged down on the grassy ground, head lowering enough to provide a perfect vantage for watching the tops of each blade slightly vibrating. It was a sight to behold, one he hadn't bothered to notice before. In the distance, some odd colours caught his attention.

Toadstools?

These weren't the normal run-of-the-mill mushrooms.

These boasted colourful tops in red, blue, yellow, black, and purple—all gathered in one spot.

Crawling closer, eyes focused on the larger than normal but still tiny capped stems, brownish pots on which almost looked like doors and windows.

He gasped. A fairy village?

"Ow."

There was no whooshing this time, something straight-out hit his head.

*"I was worried what you needed to know might have been lost in translation. I always knew you were a smart Ducky."*
—Trishia

# 11

SHE WRAPPED HER ARMS AROUND HERSELF, TIGHTLY HUGGING her shivering body. The library was colder, less homey, without him. The grey stone, despite being lined with wooden shelves, made its presence known, creating a bleak, desolate atmosphere.

There were no banners with intricately woven family crests. There were no lavish rugs to cushion her feet.

As a duckling she hadn't noticed. In human form, however, inspired loneliness was very real. A woollen shawl closed around trembling shoulders. A cup of tea was the only reprieve. Even the candle, which in her duckling form offered ample heat, wasn't enough to stop her breath from becoming a visible fog.

If only there was a fireplace.

She sighed.

It was a silly thought. Of course there wouldn't be one in the library where there were hundreds, if not thousands, of rare and valuable books. One spark and it would all go up in smoke.

C.A. KING

The book Trishia suggested was tedious and quite a bit more boring than the fantasy one with rare information and facts about fairies, elves, and other creatures of lore and myth.

She already knew the basics behind the legends of her own species and humans, right down to where misunderstandings originally divided them. That was boring. Everyone knew those facts. She wanted something new, something exciting. The next few pages were skipped over. After that a few were skimmed, reading only every fourth word or so in a sentence. The search was on for something juicier to hold her attention, while still taking in bits and pieces she felt were relevant to both the current situation and the one her race was previously in. Undoubtedly, that was the reason why the book was forced upon her in the first place.

What was the point of learning about the past... unless the future was in jeopardy? Was there actually that big a threat? Were the humans causing problems for her Lord?

She shook her head. "No." If there was a threat, surely everyone would know.

So why then?

Her eyes narrowed to thin slits.

A way to better understand Kobreon's motivations wasn't necessarily a bad thing. Too bad there was nothing she was capable of doing for him in light of any situation he might have been in. Whether it was an opposition put forth by humankind, or the search for a viable marriage partner, there was no possibility of her being of any use in finding a resolution. A duckling was pretty powerless. She certainly held no sway over the other villagers. The whole topic itself was an odd thing to have thrust upon her by his mother. What was she trying to make her aware of? Why not just come out and say it?

82

JUST DUCKY

She sighed, reading on.

Vampire was simply a name for the elite of her kind—those born with the ability to shift into multiple forms. In summary, it was a fancy word humans gave those of their kind who could change into more than one creature. The most common shifted forms were the wolf and bat combination, which was similar to Lord Kobreon's abilities. There were other combinations—too many to list or bother reading through. She skimmed them like she had several chapters, right down to the last entry citing some combinations were still being discovered.

Vampires or Lords were usually able to control which parts of their bodies underwent the shifting process as well, appearing as a human with fangs, wings, or claws. From that, fear took over in the kingdom of men.

While it was true, fresh meat was a delicacy to many shifters, they hardly sucked the blood from the veins of their prey. A foundation based in altered facts led to the most ridiculous stories—a meeting in the dark all of a sudden meant they weren't able to go out in the sunlight—a pure blood who wasn't fond of the smell of garlic made the spice famous being cited as a way to ward off all of their kind. Then there were silver bullets and stakes through the heart; those would bring death to any living thing, regardless of their species.

That one night, eons ago, was how summit conferences were limited to being held at the border. Negotiations always had contracts, signed by both parties. Wars were virtually unheard of, along with incidents considered supernatural. Keeping the peace meant staying within the lines. The only crossings allowed were for sanctioned jobs and required the highest seal of approval.

The book closed, one hand resting on its cover. The world was in a horrible state in the past. It took a meeting of

83

C.A. KING

the minds to solve it... just two minds. Was anyone else aware of what was happening back then?

"Have you finished?" Trishia asked. "That was rather quick for an entire book. I'm not sure I could have read it in such a short time."

Busted!

"I-I," she stuttered. "I'm done." It was an obvious lie, but she wanted to discover those things she wasn't already aware of. An adventure awaited, even if it was a literary one.

"And... did you learn anything?" Trishia asked. "Was it useful?"

"Y-y-yes," she answered. It might have been a teeny fib. It might not have been. It all depended on what the woman was referring to. Unfortunately, Kobreon's mother wasn't exactly forthcoming in that matter and she wasn't a mind reader.

"Thank goodness." Trishia's arms folded over her chest. "I was worried what you needed to know might have been lost in translation." Her wrist waggled up and down, one finger extended. "I always knew you were a smart Ducky."

There was no going back after that statement. Her gaze drifted down, head hung low. "Is there actually a threat of war?"

Trishia inhaled deeply. "Ah." She paused as if collecting her thoughts. "You really are a smart Ducky." Her smile faltered, the corners of her lips pointing to her chin. "Yes. The possibility exists."

"I suppose that explains where he disappears to," she mumbled. "He's trying to stop it, right?"

Trishia's brow rose and fell quickly, the rest of her expression remaining sombre.

Few knew Vampire Lord Kobreon was the face of peace. That's what kept him from home for such lengths of time. Of course that's also what brought him home in the first place.

The rumours were wrong. He wasn't there looking for a mate. He was there hoping to stop a war—to save the lives of many.

*"But, after the animals fail to save the princess, after we wage war and take the land we so desperately need, I plan to miraculously find a cure. Once awakened from this long slumber, Kornelia's hand will be mine."*

—Debouche

# 12

THE HUMAN KINGDOM OF HAMMERHEAD, LOCATED FOUR DAYS' ride from the border.

FLOWERS, STUFFED TOYS, AND TRINKETS LINED THE CENTRE fountain base at the heart of the capitol city—all meant as offerings to heal Kornelia Hammerhead. Their princess wasn't merely the daughter of the king. She was a sign of purity, dignity, peace, freedom, and grace. Birds sat on windowsills to sing songs in her presence. Deer ate willingly from her hand. People smiled at her sight.

"A vigil?" Charmichael turned up one nostril to show his distaste for the idea. He shook his head at the gathering crowd. "You are asking for trouble this time. There are too many people involved. Mark my words; this will lead to an uncontrollable incident."

"Perhaps," Debouche chuckled. "But I have faith in our princess, or more so the people's love for her. Kornelia isn't merely adored by those residing in the palace. The whole kingdom cherishes her. This is merely a way for commoners

to offer their support." He held out a candle to the next person waiting in line. "Prayers can do wonders, after all."

"Sir," an attendant from the church said, feet stomping together. "I have come to aid you in the ceremony. The high priest is preparing his speech."

"Excellent," Debouche replied. "Make sure everyone has a candle. You can light one or two individual's wicks and have them share the flame just before the event begins.

"Thank you," a man at the front of the line said, bowing his head in gratitude for the candle. "If only there was something more we could do. I know I speak for all of us when I say we'd give our lives to help Princess Kornelia."

Debouche sighed heavily. "If only..." A wicked smile crossed his lips. He turned, moving back inside the first set of palace gates to watch the events unfold.

"That's what this is all about," Charmichael sighed. "You are planning on using the people's empathy to bolster your lines."

"You act as if I am manipulating them," Debouche commented. "I'm not a villain. I'm not forcing anything on anyone. You heard the man. He wants to do more to help the princess. You could even say he feels it is his duty."

"You're a sly one," Charmichael huffed, waggling a pointed finger. "I never would have thought of something this grand. Where did the candles come from? Did you pay for them all out of pocket?"

"Don't be absurd," Debouche replied. "The king was more than happy to supply them for his daughter. There wasn't the slightest hesitation to his commitment."

His aide leaned in to whisper, "I don't recall there being an announcement as to the King's involvement in this vigil."

Debouche gasped. "I must have forgotten. I feel horrible."

"Sure you do," Charmichael sighed. "It's a dangerous game

JUST DUCKY

you are playing. This could be construed as treason, if anyone were to find out."

"How so?" Debouche asked, hands clasped behind his back. "I am the King's right-hand man. No one cares more about this kingdom and its people than I do. I never said I provided the funds for any of this. There simply wasn't time to make an official announcement advising the king was behind funding it all. People will think what they want to, regardless of what they are told."

"Hmm," Charmichael groaned. "As much as you earn the trust of the people, you will never have royal blood."

"True," he sighed. "But after the animals fail to save the princess, after we wage war and take the land we so desperately need, I plan to miraculously find a cure. Once awakened from this long slumber, Kornelia's hand will be mine."

"A cure?" Charmichael repeated. "Do you already know of one?"

"Ah!" One finger scratched the left side of his chin. "I will find one. You can guarantee that." He'd almost revealed a little too much.

"And then you plan to force the king into an early retirement?" Charmichael asked. "It won't be that easy a task."

"With the new fertile lands, we will easily expand our domain," Debouche replied. "Finally, we won't have to worry about finding a way to use the mountain range of snow and ice to the north. People will rejoice that I, Debouche of Hammerhead, single-handedly saved the kingdom. I have no doubt the citizens will rejoice at my coronation."

"I certainly hope everything goes as you planned," the chubby man said. "I want an end to our nation's dilemmas, but I never thought you coveted the throne for yourself at the same time."

"And what do you plan to do now you know?" he asked.

C.A. KING

"As long as the people are fed, clothed, and housed... and there are no internal rebellions..." He shrugged. "...Nothing."

"Good!" Debouche clapped his hands together. "Then we have an understanding. I'll be counting on you when the time comes."

"Just don't lose yourself in fantasies of grandeur," Charmichael replied. "Things don't always go the way we want them to. Make sure you have a suitable plan B, should the need arise."

A plan B? An idea this amazing could go south, sideways, or turn upside down, and it wouldn't matter. There was no need for marking out a second path, just in case. He would see this through to the end, no matter what.

*"I might not have my ducks in a row, but that doesn't mean I'm giving up. I'll get them there one day. It's just going to take a little while longer."*
—*Lord Kobreon*

# 13

"I'm back!"

Ducky gasped. It was a voice she'd come to know well in a small amount of time. Lord Kobreon had returned early.

"Quickly," Trishia urged, pushing the small of her back toward a cupboard. "Get inside before he sees you."

There was no need.

Poof!

Stress handled the situation, instantly turning her into a fuzzy duckling once again.

Trishia shrugged. "Or that works."

"What works?" Kobreon asked.

Simply entering the room made it seem warmer—brighter. Heart pounding, she waddled in his direction before melting from his presence.

"Nothing. I was talking to myself. So how was the trip?" Trishia asked, hiding the robe she'd just picked up off the floor behind her back.

"It was bad intel," he replied, eyeing her suspiciously. Eyes veered over toward the tray on his desk. "How'd you know

C.A. KING

I'd be back for tea?" He picked up a china cup, taking a long deep inhale, before allowing taste buds their turn. "Mmm."

"Oh," Trishia chuckled nervously. "Call it a mother's intuition."

"Well," he returned the chuckle, albeit his was warmer, born of genuine happiness. "It's spot-on. I can really use this right now. My whole body is tense." He glanced down at the duckling by his feet. Crouching, he scooped her up, lifting her back to the usual perch on his desk. "I missed you most of all." A finger lightly patted the top of her head, before turning into a gentle caress.

"Quack."

"I wish I understood duck," he commented, smiling intensely.

"I'm sure she'd have a lot to say if you did," his mother said. "I bet she'd want to hear all about your trips."

"That would be boring," Kobreon replied. "I have little time left. If I don't find a cure for the princess in the next few days, I fear the worst."

"The humans really won't listen to reason?" Trishia asked. "They have no proof one of our kind was responsible for making her ill."

"They still believe it was a poison of some sort," Kobreon said, still staring into Ducky's eyes. "They want someone to blame. I suppose holding an enemy accountable is easier than an ally."

"Will you be okay?" Trishia asked.

"Quack." That was what she wanted to know as well.

"I might not have my ducks in a row, but that doesn't mean I'm giving up. I'll get them there one day. It's just going to take a little while longer."

"Quack." *How many ducks does he have?* she wondered. Wasn't one enough?

"Are you leaving again?" his mother asked.

96

JUST DUCKY

"Mm-hmm," he replied. "Soon."

"You'll both need to be vigilant while I am away," Kobreon said. "Look out for any signs of a coming invasion and sound the alarm if there is."

"We'll do our best," Trishia said with an obviously forced fake smile. "Won't we, Ducky?"

"Quack." She could sleep with one eye open, but what good was that? She was just Ducky, a powerless chick. If he wasn't there to watch over her, there was no one to turn to for help.

"I'll fetch some more tea," Trishia said, walking away.

The face he made the moment they were alone left her dizzy, threatening to haunt her every future waking moment. In that instant she saw the real Kobreon, and the image was now engraved in her thoughts forever. He wasn't at all the way she'd imagined—the way he'd been described.

The slight red blush creeping over his cheeks.

The blue of his eyes, deepening with embarrassment.

The loneliness written on his face.

She hadn't been prepared for this level of endearment.

She hadn't been prepared to fall even deeper in love.

"Thank you," he whispered, drawing her close, foreheads touching. His eyes slanted with a slight smile, before fully closing. "Thank you."

For what? She hadn't done anything. In fact, she'd spent most of her time lazing about. There was nothing to be grateful for.

"Thank you," he repeated. "For being here."

*For being here? That's it? He's happy just being near me?*

A warmth filled her chest, heart skipping beats. Would he feel the same if he knew she was a woman and not just Ducky?

97

*"Unfortunately, reason is often lost in the face of disaster."*
—Lord Kobreon

# 14

"THIS CAME FOR YOU," TRISHIA SAID, HAND AND ENVELOPE trembling as if permanently attached to each other.

"Oh," he yawned, candlelight illuminating his face and the bags forming under his eyes. "I must have dozed off." After a warm bath, it was hard not to. The moments he spent at home were relaxing, especially as of late.

He already knew what his mother was delivering. It was obvious, even without taking into account the amount of nervousness accompanying it. A letter sealed with bright red wax meant only one thing—humans.

They were tired of waiting. They were tired of excuses. Who stirred the pot and how it came to a boil was still a mystery to all. No one—not vampire nor shifter—had the ability to inflict the virus the princess was suffering from. Regardless, their whole species was being held accountable.

Not finding a cure was his failure.

He sighed. A single sharp claw grew from his otherwise perfectly manicured pinkie nail; a knife-like tip making fast work of the edge of the envelope. Reading the contents was merely a formality.

C.A. KING

They were on the brink of war.

All his searching and travelling was for naught. None of the ancient remedies were found. None of the creatures with healing abilities existed anymore, at least that he could locate.

Home was the final stop on his quest. Meeting with the locals was only a meaningless gesture. This was his backyard. If there was a legendary shifter living there, surely, he would have heard about them long before now.

"Well?" his mother whispered.

"I've been summoned before their king," Kobreon answered. "I doubt it is for pleasantries or a cup of tea." His smile remained, unfaltering.

"What will you do?" Trishia asked.

"There isn't much I can do," he replied. "I'll attempt to convince King Hammerhead one last time. Unfortunately, reason is often lost in the face of disaster. Even our kind is guilty of that... wanting someone to take responsibility for problems... hoping revenge will ease the pain of loss." He sighed heavily. "It won't though. I suppose some things people need to figure out on their own for them to hold any real meaning."

"When will you leave?" his mother asked in a saddened whisper.

"Immediately," was the answer. "There is no point putting it off."

"It's too dangerous to go on your own," Trishia complained. "At least take a few men with you this time."

"I can't," he replied. "If anyone goes, other than just myself, it could be construed as an act of aggression. That could spark an immediate war."

"But..."

"Don't worry," Kobreon said, eyes slanting simultaneously with the emergence of an obviously fake smile. "I'll be fine.

102

JUST DUCKY

They aren't going to kill me on the spot. That would make me a martyr. Trust me," he chuckled, "that's the last thing any strategist would want."

"How can you be so sure?" Trishia asked, following him into the library.

He tightened the sash on his robe before taking a seat at the desk. "Because." A blank expression took over his face. "Killing me won't get them any answers." He forced a smile again before turning to meet his mother's gaze. "They want a cure and a culprit. I can't give them either if I am dead."

"But if they know you don't have either," she cried, "doesn't that mean you are expendable? Won't that give them an excuse to murder you?"

"I don't believe it will," Kobreon answered. "No one will help them if they execute me. In fact, it would fuel the fire to wage war on our side of the border. They aren't going to want to give our people a reason to be angry. If they do, not only the princess will be in danger, but the whole of their kingdom as well. Both of us are between a rock and a hard place. I need to tread lightly, but so do they. Having said that, we still only have so much time before the king and his men will run out of patience and my death will only be the beginning. Men will march on Cliffside Castle and the surrounding towns and villages."

"Do you think you can extend the time before we reach that point?" Trishia asked.

"The point of no return, hmm? I don't know," he answered. "I don't know... but nevertheless, I have to try."

He'd only just returned and was off again, this time to answer the call of men. He had no answers for them either.

Who knew what the future would hold?

One hand reached out to stroke the pure yellow down of the little duckling sleeping on a pillow perch above his desk.

She gave him hope.

C.A. KING

She gave him a lifeline.

She provided the emotional support he needed to keep moving forward.

She was the one thing he could never live without. Everything he did from that point forward was for her, even if it meant forfeiting his own life.

*"Last I checked, generals do not make the orders. War isn't something leaders take lightly."*
*—Lord Kobreon*

# 15

THE BORDER BETWEEN THE HUMAN AND SUPERNATURAL LANDS.

"VAMPIRE LORD KOBREON," DEBOUCHE SAID. "I SEE YOU MADE good time. Come this way, the king awaits your arrival."

"Hmm," Kobreon grunted. He never liked the man's aide. Something about the way his face moved when he spoke drove trust straight into the soil beneath their feet, dirtying the treaty between their kinds. "I'd like a chance to freshen up."

"Are you suggesting King Hammerhead be made to wait?" Debouche asked, a single crooked brow arching to form a high peak, one which almost reached a severely receding hairline.

He bowed his head slightly. "I'd rather not sully his grace with filthy hands. It won't take but a moment."

"Quickly." One foot stomped on the ground, making the strength of the general's legs known. Debouche had obviously been training, but for what? "You have a minute of grace."

C.A. KING

Kobreon wasn't wasting time trying to figure out if the current meeting was actually meant to be a precursor to a death sentence. Whatever was meant to be, was meant to be. He'd searched high and low across the land for a cure. None surfaced. That was the best he could offer. His kind weren't to blame for the situation.

"Hurry up," Debouche demanded, foot tapping just outside a set of front tent flaps. "This isn't a public bath arranged for your leisure." When the man said a minute, he meant it. "This way." He turned his back on an advisor. That spoke volumes. The king's aide wasn't afraid of being struck down. He wasn't afraid of a vampire lord.

"Why are there so many men present?" Kobreon asked. "Am I to take this as a threat?"

Debouche stopped, turning. "Have you not thus far taken this as a threat? The king has been lenient until now, but his words must have been heard. What do you think will happen if his daughter, our princess, is not revived?"

"I believe that is between King Hammerhead and myself to decide," Kobreon replied. "Last I checked, a king's general does not make the orders. War isn't something leaders take lightly."

"Hmm," Debouche chuckled under his breath. One hand motioned toward a tent. "I hope you have good news for my king. He awaits you inside."

Kobreon pushed aside the heavy fabric, ducking to enter the lavishly decorated room. Magic, if it existed, could have been at work. There were rugs, furniture, tables filled with food and drink—a tent more comfortable than many homes.

No expense was spared.

"Kobreon," the king said without moving from his comfortable spot on a fully cushioned sofa. "I trust you are well."

"I am," he replied, bowing. "I hope you are doing as

JUST DUCKY

wonderfully as you appear." He took the seat directly opposite the king without being invited. "You summoned me and I have responded."

"And..." The king sat up, waving away numerous servants. "What news from the other side of the border?"

"None so far," Kobreon replied. "Out of courtesy, I won't stop searching, but I fear a cure may not be within my subjects' grasp. I am down to a few places to rule out."

"Two days," King Hammerhead declared. "I am willing to give you two more days to produce the cure and the guilty party."

"Thank you." Kobreon bowed.

It was better than nothing but useless at the same time. In all the months he'd searched, there'd been no headway. As for the guilty party, the king needed to calm down and look in his own backyard for that.

*"You're going in wolf form?"*
—*Trishia*

# 16

OPTING TO STOP AT HOME BEFORE VENTURING OUT AGAIN WAS
probably a waste of time. Ducky was the main reason he
longed to return. He needed to see her to keep the faith. Soft
yellow down provided the hope his resolve was missing. Of
course, he needed to change travelling partners as well.
Where he was heading was a little too cold for a workhorse.

Thump!

He was back in his usual seat. Ducky opened one eye but
remained silent. It was late. Too late to make a big ruckus.

The scroll unfolded on the desk before him. It was definitely some sort of map, one that led to yet another unexplored area.

The mountain range in Kaygnae was a dangerous place,
which only a few had attempted to climb, and no one was
reported to have descended from. If he was heading there, he
needed to plan out the details—go it alone or try to make his
way with a party. There wouldn't be many who could accom-
pany him.

"Quack?"

C.A. KING

He glanced up at the little duck, staring at the parchment. The intensity of her glare was felt and somehow understood.

"Ducky?" Trishia peeked in the room, holding a candle-lit lantern high in the air. "Are you... Kobreon! When did you get back?"

"Just now," he replied. "Was I too noisy? I'm sorry to wake you."

"Not at all," Trishia replied. "It was a certain quack that summoned me from a deep sleep."

"Quack."

"That's the one," Trishia teased. "What are you doing at this hour? I know you are fond of Ducky, but shouldn't you go straight to bed? You must be exhausted."

"Hmm." His gaze remained glued to the scroll. "Can you tell me what this says?" It was a crazy request. His vision was better than anyone else's in the kingdom. He turned to face a puzzled expression, forcing him to lie. "It's very faint. My eyes must be weary from the trip. I can't quite make it out."

"Quack?"

He avoided the duckling's stare this time. That little fluff ball already knew something was up. If ducks could speak, things might have been different. They couldn't though, and he needed to confirm what he suspected.

The space between mother and child closed, her face moving near the parchment, eyes narrowing to a forced squint.

"I don't see anything," Trishia said.

"Are you sure?" he asked. "Look again. Move closer."

"My nose is almost touching the paper," his mother complained. "It's blank." Her posture straightened. "Are you saying you can see something?"

"It's very faint," Kobreon replied, brow furrowing.

"Am I losing my sight?" Trishia gasped. "I can't see a single stroke."

114

"Hmm," Kobreon groaned. "No. I'm sure it's just the lighting." Once his hand moved, the scroll rolled itself back up. He returned it to the bag resting on the side of his chair. "I have to head out."

"Now?!" Trishia exclaimed. "You just returned and it's the dead of night. At least rest a bit before..." Words faded with the understanding time was of the essence. "What can I do for you? Shall I fetch Harold?"

"No," Kobreon replied. "I'll be going somewhere horses can't follow. I need you to place my bag around my neck."

"You're going in wolf form?" Her tone reeked of concern.

"I'll be fine," Kobreon reassured her. "I'm taking a pack with me. It's a fair distance to cover, but I doubt we'll be there long." He paused. "This is a last minute—last hope exploration. They will be coming soon."

She followed him outside, closing the door tightly. Losing Ducky was a problem her son wasn't in need of. He had enough on his shoulders already.

Feet dug into the ground, Kobreon falling to all fours. His back hunched, bones creaking. Blue turned to a golden hue in the centre of his eyes. Teeth elongated, sharpening, as did the nails on his fingers and toes. A beastly howl accompanied the transformation, long salt-and-pepper fur flowing as a breeze kicked up.

"Here." A reinforced strap went over his head. "Take care and come back quickly." If the humans arrived while he was away, it was likely all of the surrounding towns and villages would be destroyed, including Cliffside, herself, and Ducky.

A pack of six smaller wolves approached with caution. Kobreon let out another howl and they fell into line. A single bound and he and his followers were gone.

*"A heartless leader wins no favour."*
—*King Hammerhead*

# 17

*THE HUMAN KINGDOM OF HAMMERHEAD BORDER.*

DEBOUCHE PACED BACK AND FORTH, INSPECTING THE TROOPS. They were forty thousand strong—an army worthy of infiltrating, attacking, and claiming lands from the supernaturals. The enemy had fangs and claws, but the king's men had guns and bullets. If that wasn't enough, the cold steel of sharp blades would slice and dice their way to victory.

"Wooden stakes and silver bullets," he scoffed in front of his men. "These are wives' tales. We know better. These creatures are not immortals."

Grumbles.

"They merely live longer than we do," Debouche continued. "If you cut them, they will bleed. If you shoot them, they will die."

"Are you sure?" a shaky voice asked from the second row of soldiers. "Has it been tested?"

"Does it matter?" Debouche questioned, his lips curling downward, dragging along his moustache to form a

C.A. KING

pronounced frown. "The King's daughter... your princess... is ill because of them. They have provided no cure. They have captured no culprit." He straightened his posture, noting worry in the eyes of his men. "I've arranged for special arrows, made of the finest wood. If you are still unconvinced, arm yourself with crossbows and stakes. You can fire first on the enemy and aim for their hearts." Silver was too expensive to use for bullets, even if they would be recoverable after all was said and done. His voice rose. "Regardless of the weapon, we will be victorious!"

The men cheered; arms raised in a pre-battle victory celebration. Their general had erased the fear of loss from their minds and put a landslide conquest in its place.

Trumpets sounded.

"The king approaches."

Debouche bowed, allowing way for their kingdom's leader. He waited several minutes before straightening again.

"Are so many men needed?" the king asked. "Doesn't this seem like a bit of overkill? We are marching on a small village. They can't have more than a thousand residents in their command."

"I'd rather have too many men than too few," Debouche answered. "Once we cross the border, we are entering enemy territory. There is no turning back. Who knows what we might encounter?"

"Hmm," the king groaned. "I'd like to make one last appeal before we resort to violence. I am still hopeful we can resolve this without war."

"The time for negotiations is over," Debouche insisted. "These men have steeled their nerves and are willing to go the distance for their kingdom, their king, and their princess. If the enemy does not provide us with a cure, we will beat it out of them... for your daughter's sake."

"Um-hmm," the king agreed. "My daughter is the first

priority. I'd do anything for her. She will come home safely. But..."

"But?" Debouche repeated.

"But... no one is truly safe during times of war," the king continued. "People die needlessly. Hundreds if not thousands of lives could be lost. I'd rather not put my subjects through such pain and loss. A heartless leader wins no favour."

"Weak leaders are condemned and will ultimately find themselves replaced," Debouche replied calmly. "Revolutions have been started for less."

A number of attendants carried over a chair similar to the one in the palace throne room, placing it directly behind the king. He fell backward, pillows sinking beneath the weight. The travelling throne rose with him on it.

"Carry on," Hammerhead bellowed. "I'll let you take the lead for now."

"Thank you, Your Majesty." Debouche bowed. That was exactly what he needed the king to say. Giving him the power over the men was as good as handing over the keys to the palace. Without even realizing it, Hammerhead had given up his right to the throne. This wasn't just a war—it was a succession battle waiting to begin and the general had already taken a wide lead.

King Hammerhead was about to be blindsided. He had no idea what was coming.

*"Unfortunately, it seems others found this location long before we did."*
*—Lord Kobreon*

# 18

THE MOUNTAIN RANGE WAS ONE OF THE LAST AREAS remaining unexplored for a reason. The paths in, around, and up it were treacherous. The peaks weren't snow-topped; they were ice covered. It wasn't just a small layer of freezing drizzle either. This was a solid, slick coating which even thick, sharp claws had no effect on. One paw in the wrong place meant certain death.

Just being there was crazy. Still, an attempt needed to be made.

According to the map, there was an entrance to a cave approximately two-thirds of the way up. That was where they were heading. Every detail of the scroll had been memorized, knowing their party would only come to the end of their journey once he could freely unroll it again.

Muscles tensed, legs crouching in preparation for a single leap, putting him on a path above, one which rounded the side of the cliff, thinning precariously rather quickly. Stones and icicles tumbled down the side of the mountain, clanging and banging as they made their way to the bottom, or out of ears' reach, whichever came first.

The route wasn't made for large paws. His smaller companions were fairing slightly better.

Staying in wolf form was a choice made at the beginning of the upward trek, mainly meant to combat the cold. Changing into human form might have been a bit easier for the climb though. It was six of one, half a dozen of the other —falling or freezing. He chose the one which posed the best chance for survival, at least at the height they were currently at. Once they climbed higher, the stats evened out. It would be fifty-fifty from thereon out. As soon as the hidden entrance was located, things would hopefully go a little bit smoother.

That was wishful thinking.

The entrance wasn't so much hidden as it was close to impossible to reach. The path they were on was below an obvious opening, albeit, one was hidden from view from all other vantage points. Finding it came down to sheer luck and that was where the good sort ran out.

There was no ledge to leap to. The means for entry was obstructed by an iced-over doorway. Neither man nor beast had an advantage.

He sat, staring at the glossy cliff, colours changing from white to various shades of blue with the setting sun.

It was deadly.

It was beautiful.

It was a puzzle.

A front paw outstretched, banging on the side of the mountain, leaving an indent. How many steps would he be able to imprint without falling? Ten? Twenty?

A wolf's sigh was underwhelming. A howl was a better choice. It riled the pack up inside, the same as a bunch of humans yelling, "Chug," to a man downing beer in a drinking competition.

His voice spurred on the others.

JUST DUCKY

Hearing their support was enough to give climbing the best try possible.

A front paw came down on the mountain side a second time, shards of ice flying. The second foothold was in place. Then came the third, the fourth, and the fifth. That was where things became tricky. Simply climbing wasn't a problem. Placing new indents as he went up was. Even the slightest misstep was bound to end in a fall—one he wasn't necessarily coming back from.

The wind howled as loudly as the pack, snow beginning to fall. Within minutes, his fur was tangled with frost, eyes watering from the bellowing cold. None of it mattered. If there wasn't a safe place for her—for Ducky—what use was his life?

That soft down.

Those understanding glances.

The long nights they spent together by candlelight.

He'd never imagined having such feelings for a duckling. He'd never imagined having these deep feelings for anyone— even a partner.

His life hadn't been turned upside down. She'd managed to right side it up when he needed it most. Imagining a life without her in it was impossible. The thought of her suffering made his chest ache. Doing everything to protect her was the least he could do as repayment for all she'd given him without even knowing it.

The last foothold put him face-to-face with the door. A bright green glow came from his bag—the scroll. The blue of the ice mixed with the luminescence around his neck forging a calming teal colour. The doors opened, disappearing as he passed through.

Gone was the cutting bitterness of the wind. The farther in, the warmer it became. The need for wolf form passed. There were rooms up ahead which required searching. He

stopped, reining in fur, claws, and fangs. His long snout shortened, bones snapping back into place. Four legs turned to two—a naked man standing in a hallway of ice without shivering.

Kobreon removed the satchel from around his neck, fishing out a shirt and a pair of pants. If the others gazed upon his unclothed body, they'd be awestruck for far too long. That was the downfall of being a vampire lord.

The most beautiful beings.

The most adored.

The most sought after.

The ones who were never left alone.

The ones never treated as equals.

Maybe that was what he adored about Ducky so much. She never chased after him. She never put him on a pedestal. If anything, he put her on one.

She was in his thoughts again.

He shook his head. Now wasn't the time. The teal glow was lighting up one particular section of the parchment. He followed that path, peeking in different directions as he passed crevices and grottoes.

Ransacked.

Someone else had been there. But who? And what did they get away with? If there had been a cure at one time, was it still there?

Racing to the illuminated section on the map was useless. Whatever happened took place long ago, well before he existed. That didn't stop his feet from moving quickly enough to force a pant from laboured breathing. If his effort was for naught, peace was at stake.

Elves and fairies wanted to remain anonymous. He understood that now. This was their way of helping without involvement. No one was able to say if ancient races still existed. Not even he knew for certain. No one

JUST DUCKY

could say for sure where the scroll came from. Not even he knew that.

Apparently, he was the only one who could read it, or see anything, even the teeniest of details, other than a plain, blank parchment. There was no connection for others—just him. If the other races existed, they trusted him, and him alone, with this. Even so, those who placed their faith in him had a backup plan—should the need arise—should their trust be misplaced. He'd be deemed insane, if he tried to tell others, after all. It was the same as with the man from the tavern—a drunk no one took seriously—no one believed.

He stopped short, directly in the final cavern entrance, slipping slightly on the ice beneath bare feet. Body heat melted it just enough to make it slightly wet. Luckily, nothing stuck in the process. That was once again where the good part of luck stopped.

The whole cavern was a mess.

Overturned tables lay frozen in place, along with shards of glass from broken pottery and bottles. Water damage ruined shredded and torn pages of books. Empty ingredient jars lay where they'd been tossed on their sides.

Whoever was responsible was looking for something... but was that something found and was it the cure-all?

Most likely.

"Sir," Hans, a member of the pack accompanying him, said. "What orders have you for us?"

"Look for one of these." Fist still tightly gripped around the scroll which led them there, his arm rose. "And anything else which might be salvageable." That was a tall order for a few pack wolves. Still, he needed to make sure a cure wasn't hidden somewhere, that meant a thorough search of everything.

"I found one!" Hans exclaimed, holding up a scroll. "It's blank though."

"That's okay," Kobreon replied, snatching it away in a split second. "There may be magic at work." It even felt odd just saying that. Magic was the stuff legends were made of. Wizards and sorcerers weren't real.

"Seriously?" Hans asked.

"The past still dwells here," Kobreon answered. "If I am not mistaken, this was once a laboratory used by the elders... ancients. Unfortunately, it seems thieves found this location long before we did." He spread the new scroll out, glancing over the details only he was able to see.

Written on it were the directions to a second workshop, one which was likely harder for bandits to locate. There was a chance everything inside that location was still intact. Too bad the site was far to the north and in Hammerhead's territory. Humans weren't going to allow an expedition without a fight and reason.

They were already on the brink of war.

A blank parchment was hardly proof of anything.

He wasn't even sure exactly what he'd find there. There was no way to ask permission based on a hunch. Even if there were, humans had a reputation for their greediness. It was possible someone would try to jump the gun and ruin whatever chance there was to find a cure.

Everything was one problem after the other.

"My Lord?" Hans stared directly at his leader's expressionless face. "Do you see something?"

"Nothing." He released one end of the scroll. It rolled up with a snap. "It's nothing. Prepare to return home. I won't waste any more time here. We are needed elsewhere."

Hans merely nodded.

*"You're only hurting yourself by squirming."*
—*Lita*

# 19

ONE MORE RETURN. ONE MORE FAILURE.

He was out of time. It was over. The door slowly creaked open, allowing him to pass through.

"I'm back." The words weren't meant to be loud enough to be heard. Facing failure wasn't easy.

\*\*\*

The door hadn't fully closed yet. This was it. The great escape was on. She'd never waddled so fast in her life.

If she were being honest, the whole thing was actually planned. At some point, she'd realized there were momentary lapses between Lord Kobreon returning home and Trishia gushing over him, in which an opportunity was bound to arise.

Observation was a skill even a duckling possessed. With the right timing, they'd never know what zoomed past and was on the loose.

While being with Lord Kobreon on a twenty-four-hour basis was a dream come true. Living as a duckling day in and day out wasn't the way she'd pictured a life with him.

She wasn't his equal.

C.A. KING

She wasn't his partner.

She wasn't his lover.

She was nothing more than a pet.

That was worse than all the other abuse she'd endured. Being called the three-letter word was as low as a shifter could go.

No future was built on lies. No love was born from deceit. Her actions were for the best.

It worked like a charm, maybe a little too well. No one from the manor was following. She'd expected at least Trishia to give chase. Chest aching, she bolted forward.

What was this feeling?

Loneliness?

Regret?

She glanced back once more. This time her heart skipped a beat for a different reason. Being wound up inside over Lord Kobreon made her forget another very important detail. She was hated by some of the most ferocious half-beasts in the land.

There was no need to look twice. Someone other than the lord or his mother was behind her. The hate and blood lust aimed in her direction were stronger than they'd ever been before.

Out of the fire and into the pan, or vice versa. Which way it happened meant nothing. She was about to become one well-cooked goose. She'd made it out of the castle in one piece, but now someone else had a hold of her and the grip was terrifying.

"Quack."

"We've been wondering where you went." It was Lita. It always was. Her hatred for the duckling was first, foremost, and the most ferocious in the town. "Thought you could sneak in the castle disguised as a cute little duckling, did you?" She exhaled a throaty growl. "I suppose you felt you

134

JUST DUCKY

deserved to have Kobreon to yourself. Maybe, you even secretly hoped he'd pick you for his bride." Her upper lip rose, forming a predatory snarl. "That's not happening."

"Quack. Quack." It all sounded the same—help—ouch. Nobody else knew what she was saying; what she was feeling. No matter how much she struggled, or how many little soft yellow down scattered on the ground, no one was going to help her.

One good peck and she was free, waddling with all her might. It was a long way to safety. Her pursuers had the edge. They were leaps and bounds faster. Without the protection of family or Kobreon there was no hope for escape. Instincts demanded she make the attempt nonetheless. No one wanted to be cooked for lunch and served with a side of fries.

"Quack." It was only a few minutes before she was caught again.

"You're only hurting yourself by squirming," Lita said. "Stay still and accept your punishment. I have everything prepared." By prepared, she meant a small wooden shack no bigger than an outhouse, complete with chains and locks. "You'll be held in here until Kobreon announces his future partner. Hurry up." She wasn't alone. There were others helping her.

It was an underhand toss, except using a duckling as the ball. The side of the wooden shed was hard enough to leave a nasty bump, without breaking. There wasn't even a creak of a complaint for the rough housing. That meant, without extreme force, there was little chance for an escape. She was once again at the mercy of someone else. At least in the castle she was treated well.

Fists flew. Feet kicked.

There was no pain, still a small body could only take so much damage. Why was she hated so much? Why were they beating her senseless?

135

"Get in there, Tal."

Thud. The walls shook.

Eyelids grew heavy, a weight forced upon them. Her attackers were still yelling as they fully closed. Slurs, rude remarks, death threats: she heard them all before losing consciousness.

*"Flames from above. The sneaky devils are using fire to attack."*
—Debouche

# 20

A PART OF HIM WANTED TO LAUGH. HE'D NEVER SEEN A duckling waddle so fast before. The rest of him realized the speed at which Ducky moved was a direct result of fear—the fear of being chased.

An undeniable ominous feeling washed over him. There was a good chance she was going to run into deep trouble, if he wasn't the first to find her.

A tug on his heartstrings caught him off guard.

It was strange. They hadn't been together for a long time, but now that she was gone, there was an empty hole in his chest. Maybe it had always been there. Maybe he was only noticing it now because that little duckling had filled it effortlessly. Nothing else had ever come close.

He raced out the door. How long had she been missing? How far could she have gone? He was desperate for answers. An approaching sight stopped him in his tracks.

They were here and at the worst possible moment.

It was time to pay the piper.

King Hammerhead was coming with an army fit for a massive war in tow. Armour shone brightly the sun's rays,

bouncing off exquisitely polished chest plates, all together forming a giant mirror which reflected light in all directions.

His arm lifted, bent at the elbow, shading his face. The fact they were approaching in such large platoons was an eerie omen to itself. If he ignored them, the worst was sure to happen.

But, Ducky...

He turned to see a few pieces of yellow down leaving a trail in the general direction she disappeared toward. A gust of wind, or even a slight breeze for that matter, would gather all the clues up and scatter them throughout the land. If that happened, she'd be lost to him.

Trumpets blared.

Once again duty came first, personal feelings moved to the back burner. Duty came with his station—his abilities. He was a lord—a vampire.

The search for Ducky needed to halt until after the current conflict between two nations ceased. Those were the ugly truths of the world they lived in. Love and war weren't equal. One stole attention from the other.

Feet pounded on the ground—left then right, marching. He could hear every one of them; feel the vibrations they created.

Grand flags embroidered with Hammerhead's crest led the way. Behind them were white horses carrying specially dressed knights. In the middle rode the king himself, his outfit embellished in gold and jewels, specially made to match the crown upon his head, and seamlessly melding with the design of his luxurious travelling throne.

No expense was spared. It never was with humans.

Lavish items meant prestige. Prestige meant power. Power meant control. Control meant everything. It never made any sense to him or his people. Enjoying life was more

JUST DUCKY

important than possessions. Love was more important than life.

Kobreon sat on the same seat which he'd used to receive villagers outside his home over the past few weeks, waiting for the inevitable. Onlookers from the town stared at him for an explanation. There wasn't one, at least not yet. If he told them they'd been wrongly accused, it would only serve to make the situation worse. His own kind might take up arms against the humans without being asked. Before that happened, one last chance to negotiate was needed.

A line separated, making way for the human military to pass with their immaculate straight lines untouched. Their strength was undeniable. The lines reformed—four into two —one on either side forming a passage for precious cargo. A flat slab carried by eight guards neared, a few paces behind the king. On it lay a woman's figure, a veil covering her facial features.

They brought the princess.

They expected a cure.

There wasn't one.

Things were about to get ugly.

The pot was about to boil over and no one was watching. Racing to the stove at the last second wasn't going to save things from being burned.

Perhaps he should have concentrated on building their own army instead of searching for a peaceful resolution. Hindsight was useless now. Trouble was literally on his doorstep. A wicked ending to his story seemed unavoidable.

"Well," Hammerhead said, approaching. "Have you found a cure?"

Kobreon glanced to the king's side, noting the numerous lines of men. "Why have you brought such a large military force? Are you declaring war? Am I to assume you have given up on peace?"

141

C.A. KING

"Am I to assume you are not willing to save my daughter?" the king snapped.

"Willing?" Kobreon repeated. "I am most definitely willing. Able is another discussion entirely. We are not the ones who are to blame for the princess's illness, nor do we have a cure at this time. I have searched the countryside, far and wide, looking for something to help with your situation. I even went so far as to scour for magic. Of course, we all know that doesn't exist except in tall tales of fantasy. Even stories of creatures with healing abilities have proven fruitless. I continued probing with hopes the peace between our two nations could be preserved. I failed. For that, I am truly sorry."

He glanced up at a dire sky, home to both the sun and moon at the same time. In their world, such an event always foreshadowed doom. Flames burst between the two.

A falling star? A precursor to the apocalypse?

"Huh?" Kobreon stood, taking a few steps forward. Eyes squinted to make out the figure of a bird. "A phoenix?" Was he seeing things?

"What's that?" The king's head pointed upward. "A special bird of some sort. Is it on fire?"

"Be ready!" Debouche ordered, his horse rearing. "Flames from above. The sneaky devils are using fire to attack."

"Wait!" Kobreon yelled. "A phoenix's tears can cure all ailments." This was what he'd been searching for all along, but who sent it?

Elves?

Fairies?

A god?

Whoever it was might have just saved the day.

*"Who woke up fresh as a daisy, anyway?"*
—*Ducky*

# 21

BLURRY VISION—THAT WAS A NEW ONE FOR HER. WHO KNEW ducklings could need glasses? Not her, that was for sure. A shifter's senses were their lifeline. If one went, they were sitting ducks—pun intended.

Soft yellow down ruffled, her body moving to a sitting position. She was definitely still a duckling, despite the fact she appeared to have passed out at some point.

Running.

Her memory was as fuzzy as she was, but she was positive she was, at one point, being chased.

Lita! There were others too.

A fog surrounded her, coating everything in black soot. Not even she was immune. Bill open; abnormal panting, wheezing, and coughing began.

She was in trouble and in more than one way.

It was hot. The temperature was rising. A sizzling singe accompanied the fray, embers rising.

FIRE!

The wooden hut was on fire. The dry hay was on fire. She was on fire.

C.A. KING

Instinctively, her body rammed the side of her combined makeshift jail and coffin. Vibrations raced through her body, followed by pain. She lunged forward a second time, hitting with the opposite side of her body. Still, nothing changed.

Trapped!

The thought of death was worse than she imagined. Life flashed before her eyes. Actually, it was all Lord Kobreon from the bits and pieces she collected to the past little while they spent together.

He was all that mattered.

He was in as much, if not more, trouble as she was. If she died, who would he have to turn to? Then again, alive as a duckling was just as useless. He needed someone strong by his side.

The flames reached higher, the heat rising. She was surrounded, being engulfed. Pieces of the hut began to fall, narrowly missing her.

An opening!

It was too late. It was obvious from the surrounding massive inferno and combustion, she was dying, if not already dead.

So why was she still able to think? Why were her wings spreading? Ducklings couldn't fly, yet somehow, she was.

She glanced to the left and then the right. Long, sleek feathers flapped on each side, still burning. The hut below was completely gone, only a pile of kindling left to burn away to ash.

Ashes.

She'd read about a rare species in the library—a phoenix was able to rise from the ashes of its former self. That's exactly what was happening. That wasn't the only thing the bird was known for either. Its tears... her tears... were a panacea.

A soft sobbing noise turned into a song as the wind

JUST DUCKY

carried her over the lake. Ahead, the outlines of humans came into view. War was upon them and it was bound to be as violent as an active volcano. There was only one chance to save everyone—to save him. It all came down to putting herself between the two parties before any fighting erupted. She needed to find the right place.

There! A woman!

Being carried on a flat platform by six guards, the ghostly form resembled a sleeping beauty from one of the fairy tales in the library books. Even unconscious, her regal expression was undeniable—an aura of greatness shining brightly around her.

The perfect bride!

Every detail about her was glorious, from her pure white complexion to her small, thin body graced with ample curves, although that might have been a side effect of the lavish dress she was wearing.

White lace with diamond accents.

No expense was spared.

Even her light, soft pastel, yellow-coloured hair was soothing to the eye. This woman was a masterpiece, one capable of entrancing anyone laying eyes upon her, male or female. Even a duckling might have a problem, if not for having already fallen for another who was just as incredible, if not more.

This wasn't the time to be impressed. She was the only one who could help him save their world.

This was Ducky's first flight—first landing. There was no opportunity to practice. She was literally winging it, going on instinct alone. Messing up was bound to cause issues for her lord. That simply couldn't happen.

Wings flapped, her body slowly descending above the young woman's face. A tear dripped from her eye, falling into slightly parted, plump lips.

C.A. KING

Thick eyelashes fluttered, giving way to emerald green eyes. The heir to the throne of Hammerhead, beloved princess of the people, was awake.

Lord Kobreon's gaze filled with the princess and only the princess. Perhaps royalty, and in particular, the princess was to his liking. It would make sense. They were both beautiful beyond the normal spectrum.

*Who woke up fresh as a daisy, anyway?*

It was unheard of. It was unfair. Pure pain struck her heart, leaving her breathless.

Jealousy.

She'd felt it in smaller doses, but never anything on this level. It was undeniable. It was inescapable. The stupid ugly duckling had fallen in love with a stunning swan, who in turn had eyes for someone else. To make things worse, the silly yellow duck saved her rival.

Helping him hadn't made them closer. It was pushing them farther away from each other. In fact, all her hard work might have just tossed a princess into Kobreon's arms, rather than herself.

She took flight, looking for an escape, to stop further tears from falling. In the end, at least she'd been of some use to him.

*"Keep them close... for emergencies. You never know when someone might need a bit of healing."*
*—Trishia*

# 22

SIMPLY LANDING ANYWHERE WAS IMPOSSIBLE. THERE WERE TOO many things still mulling over in her mind, especially how the burn-up was controlled. Until that moment, nothing serious had happened. Setting a field or forest ablaze was counterproductive to the feat she'd just pulled off. It would be stupid to set fire to the town which had just been spared from war.

There were other considerations to take into account as well. She was bound to change from one form to the other and, in the end, a naked human was the most embarrassing. Giving the entire town, and the numerous soldiers in the human army, a free show was a frightening thought.

Trishia's hands waved frantically over her head.

Thank goodness.

That was the signal for her escape. There was no one near Kobreon's mother at the rear of the manor. Everyone was too busy with the events unfolding in the front. An open path was exactly what she needed; a friend waiting below was a bonus.

C.A. KING

She glided in, coming to a full stop, shifting as if on command.

"Quack."

She was a fluffy duckling again. Was it luck? Whatever the case, that form was easier for Trishia to hide, should the need arise.

"You figured it out," Trishia cooed. "Then the book I gave you was of some help? I am so relieved. I thought it might have been a bit vague."

"Quack."

The dreaded book. Was there something in it which was meant to help her shift? If there was, it must have been in the part she skipped or skimmed.

Shifting was still confusing. It felt spontaneous. It felt normal, as if it were a routine she'd gone through thousands of times. It was the how part which was still hazy. The past few shifts just seemed to happen on their own.

"Oh." A second change turned her into a girl. This time something was different though. There was no urge to cover exposed body parts. Instead, she stood tall, unafraid of her nakedness.

An elegant, full-length, yellow, feather-down dress appeared, covering her body like a well-fitting glove. One hand extended forward, bursting into flames then immediately extinguishing. This was what it meant to control abilities. That part she'd actually read about in the book, but never considered applying the knowledge directly to herself. It was all starting to make sense.

"Why didn't you just tell me?" she asked. "Why make me read books? I could have saved everyone from worrying." By everyone she meant Lord Kobreon.

"Some things we need to figure out on our own for them to hold any real meaning," Trishia answered. "And once you

JUST DUCKY

did, you needed the will to put things in motion. No person could give you that."

"Ow!" A pinch made her squeal. "What was that for?" A vial slid under one eye, collecting a few tears as they fell.

"I'd be willing to bet these will come in handy," Trishia replied. "Keep them close... for emergencies. You never know when someone might need a bit of healing."

"The princess is fine now." A puffy pout filled out her lips. "She's perfectly perfect in every way." Teeth gritted.

"Who said it was for the princess?" Trishia smirked. "She's not the only one here, you know."

That was true. It was stupid to leave before knowing everything was settled. She'd taken it for granted the humans would simply withdraw after their princess was cured. That wasn't necessarily the case. They might still want someone to take the fall for causing the king's daughter's ailment in the first place.

There was no choice but to hurry back.

*"You'll have all of our heads? Even if you managed to carry out such a feat, who would be left to follow your orders?"*
*—Debouche*

# 23

"Rejoice," the king bellowed. "Lay down your weapons. The princess has awakened from her slumber. All is well."

The men exchanged odd glances with one another, looks of confusion ran rampant. None took action as requested.

"I'm afraid we can't do that," Debouche said, moving to the front of the military line. "We have come a long way." One arm motioned for a group of archers to join him at his side. The weapons they wielded weren't ordinary bows and arrows. These were sturdy crossbows equipped with large, pointed, wooden stakes. "It's a little early for celebrations."

"You would defy your king?" Hammerhead snapped. "I'll have each and every one of your heads for this."

Debouche howled a sinister laugh. "You'll have all of our heads? Even if you managed to carry out such a feat, who would be left to follow your orders?" He motioned around. "Take aim."

Armaments pointed toward Kobreon.

"Wait!" Hammerhead exclaimed, stepping in front of their target with arms extended at his side. "I demand you put down the weapons at once."

C.A. KING

"Fire," Debouche said calmly.

A single arrow pierced the flesh of the king's shoulder, his body slouched to the ground at the feet of the one he protected.

"Father!" The princess sat, legs dangling off the platform, which had been her resting place since falling ill. "What have you done?"

"What needed to be done," Debouche said with confidence. "Your father has lost touch with the needs of his people." He grabbed her arm tightly the moment she tried to slip by him.

"Let her go," the king howled, voice shaking from pain. "I don't know what you are scheming, but it won't work. None of these men will stand for you killing my daughter after she has just been saved... perhaps me, but not her."

Debouche let out a hearty laugh, eyes enlarging wildly. "I have no intention of killing her. I'm going to make her my bride. Together we will rule the land, taking into account the needs of our subjects. And speaking of land... where we are standing will make a nice addition to what Hammerhead already possesses."

"Is that what this is about, the throne?" the king cried out. "You planned this from the start, didn't you? Were you the one behind the princess's illness as well?"

"Oh!" The princess looked up at him from where he pushed her to the ground, one hand covering her mouth. "Please stop this. It's madness."

"You should have gone along with the plan, old man," Debouche said, ignoring the woman begging him to reconsider his position. "Things would have been much easier." He moved forward. "I had no choice. The great line of Hammerhead kings has always been a troublesome lot, you see. Your ancestor is the whole reason we are in this mess in the first

JUST DUCKY

place... and they erected a statue of him. That's the real madness here."

"What are you on about?" the king asked.

"The original treaty," Debouche snapped. "That border-line was drawn where it never should have been put." His voice rose. "No thought went into it. Julius sold out his own people for fame."

"How so?" Kobreon asked.

"Of course, you wouldn't care," Debouche barked. "You lot ended up with the better end of the deal. What did we humans get? Huh?" He paused glancing around at the gathered paranormals huddled in groups. "I'll tell you what... ice and snow. The area to the north of the capitol is unusable by humans. We can't stand the cold long enough to build shelters. Nothing grows there worthy of being called food."

"That's not my father's fault," the princess cried out in a meek voice. Being shy was her downfall and what ultimately led to her becoming a target.

"It's his ancestor's!" Debouche barked back. "Great kings have always failed the people. It's time for a change." One hand grabbed Kornelia's arm, dragging her toward him.

"Let go!" the princess squealed.

Kobreon moved with the speed of a cheetah chasing prey. In one swift move, Kornelia was in his arms and away from danger.

"Fire a second round!" Debouche ordered.

Nothing happened.

"Give me that." The general snatched a crossbow from another man's hands, aiming it directly at Kobreon. "If you want something done right..."

"Stop." The king's arm lifted in front of him, the palm of his hand facing forward in protest. "Don't do this."

A yellow blur streaked between the two.

159

C.A. KING

A flash of flames erupted.

All of the remaining wooden bows stakes turned to ash in motion, including the single wooden stake which was already whizzing through the air.

*"Things could have gone completely different, had it not been for your pet."*
*—King Hammerhead*

# 24

AN ARROW STUCK OUT OF THE KING'S SHOULDER. IT WAS DEEP inside the flesh, but not visible from the rear. She wasn't sure if that was a good thing or a bad thing. Either way, it had to be removed before her tears would be of any use. She bent over his body, pretending not to notice the princess still in Kobreon's arms.

"Can you pull it out?" she asked, cringing at the thought of blood squirting everywhere. That was bound to happen, if she attempted the extraction.

A man fell to his knees at her side. "I am the doctor for this unit," he announced. "I can handle removing the arrow. It's a bad wound. Perhaps, your phoenix can provide a few tears."

It was as if Trishia had planned everything out from the start. There should have been no way to know healing tears would be needed beforehand. Still, they were collected and ready to use.

"Take these," Ducky said, handing over the small vial. "There should be more than enough in there for a full recovery." She stood, leaving the king and his men behind to head

C.A. KING

to where she belonged—at Kobreon's side—the princess exchanging glances and places with her

"Ducky?" Kobreon approached her slowly, allowing her advance to continue at a similar pace. "I should have guessed you'd come back. I'm sorry I didn't notice you right away."

"No. Not at all," she squeaked. "I should have said something... although I doubt quack would have been of any use."

"No," he chuckled, looking out over his domain from a small hill. "I suppose it wouldn't have." He stood tall, hands clasped behind his back, never once glancing her way. "Did my mother know?"

"Umm." That was a question worth avoiding.

"Never mind," he sighed. "I think I can figure that out on my own. I don't understand why she wouldn't tell me outright though."

"Some things we need to figure out on our own for them to hold any real meaning." They were Trishia's words from an earlier exchange, but somehow at that moment she was starting to understand the actual sentiments behind them.

"You sound like her," he commented. "My mother."

"To be honest, she said that to me earlier," she admitted.

"And things come full circle," Kobreon mused. "She's a rather profound lady, in her own way. Albeit, she has a roundabout, maze-like approach to things."

"That's true," Ducky laughed.

An awkward silence fell between them.

"It's been quite the day," he finally said.

"Yes. Oh. Are you hurt?" she asked, glancing at him from all angles. "I can help, if you are."

"No." Kobreon's lips curled up. "I'm fine."

"Better than fine," King Hammerhead said, nearing. "You are amazing." He held out one hand, a human gesture meant to strengthen bonds of some sort.

Kobreon accepted. "I appreciate your kind words, but

164

they are unnecessary. I am just happy the princess has recovered and there were no other casualties."

"Hmm," Hammerhead groaned. "I'm not sure that's true. I have a larger than normal number of traitors in my midst. Ah," the king grumbled. "What to do? What to do? This is a sticky situation, now, isn't it? I suppose first I owe you an apology. The culprit was right under my nose the whole time... my own race even."

Kobreon patted his back. "We all make mistakes."

"Still. Tsk." Tongue clicked in his royal cheek.

"Is this about your men?" Kobreon asked.

The king sighed. "It is a quandary. Normally, if anyone betrayed me, I'd simply take their head."

"Ah, but killing an entire army doesn't bode well for the nation, does it?" Charmichael asked, huffing and puffing from climbing the incline to reach the top. "If I may suggest, perhaps this whole ordeal was the fault of only one person. The other men were merely following orders. They believed their king had instructed their general."

"Hmm," the king groaned. "They committed treason. By all rights they should be beheaded." He sighed audibly. "But you have a point."

"A good one," Kobreon agreed. "Executing an entire army is a bit much for even a great king such as yourself. There would be a distinct lack of security in your nation... and possibly a backlash from friends and family of the deceased to deal with."

"No," Charmichael argued. "Normally, family members share the same fate." He paused, sighing audibly. "Now that I think about it, treating the military here as traitors would lower the population, which was the original problem. Of course, we'd have to retrain an entire army, which isn't a wonderful proposal either."

C.A. KING

"Wait!" Hammerhead held out one hand. "What do you mean population was the problem?"

"Surely you've noticed, My Lord," Charmichael continued. "Your land is overcrowded. There aren't enough houses. There aren't enough fields. There isn't enough food. Debouche planned to use this opportunity to steal back the land closest to the border." He took a step back, feet perfectly aligned with one another. "Perhaps this discussion is best left to a later date."

The king nodded. "Ah, but it's a good thing that phoenix of yours showed up when it did," the king said, changing the subject. "Things could have gone completely different, had it not been for your pet."

"Pet?" He glanced over at Ducky. "I don't have a pet. This is the first time that phoenix has appeared. I have a few thoughts on where it came from though."

"So luck was simply on your side today?" the king mused. "If only it were that easy for us to find a peaceful resolution to all our troubles."

"Ahem." Charmichael cleared his throat. "Might I suggest a union as a way to bridge the conflict between our races? The princess seems to have taken a shine to Lord Kobreon. They would make a fine couple."

Ducky gasped under her breath. A stake pierced her heart at that very moment. Even if it wasn't real, it hurt just the same. Questions swirled through her mind.

What if Kobreon had feelings for the princess as well?

What if he accepted the offer?

The only good thing about overhearing their conversation was her shifting remained under control, despite an onslaught of overflowing emotions.

"I'll leave you to your discussions," she said, politely excusing herself.

There was no use enduring pain unnecessarily. The

JUST DUCKY

princess and Lord Kobreon made a good pair. They looked good together. They came from similar social statuses. They had things in common and their union would serve to further strengthen the bond between two nations—two races.

*"I am seriously happy. I couldn't ask for anyone better to fall in love with my son. I mean, I knew you were attached to him, but I can see now it's the real deal. L. O. V. E. Ah, to be young."*
*—Trishia*

# 25

HAVING HER HAIR BRUSHED FELT NICE, SOOTHING. LORD Kobreon's mother was gentle too. Not even a single knot was felt. The golden brush returned to its place on the vanity.

"I think you'd look good in a braid," Trishia said, not waiting for a response before starting to separate three sections and intertwining them. "A single one." A playful smile crossed the woman's lips. "Two might be too girly."

"I am a girl," she replied. And a duck... And a phoenix...

"I happen to think you've grown into quite the young lady." Trishia yanked hard on fistfuls of hair. "You need to be more self-assured, especially now that you've found your third form. Luckily, things will be a bit easier now. Control should be next to second nature."

"What if it's not?" she whispered under her breath. "I mean it seems easier, but," She glanced up, fully taking advantage of the comforting gaze being returned.

Trishia sighed. "I'd hoped the book would be enough to help you fully understand. Hmm. I'm not sure how else to explain things."

There it was: the darned book. With every day that

C.A. KING

passed, her desire to carefully read through the whole thing intensified. It was clear there was so much more she needed to learn from it.

"You seem as if you have some experience in these matters," she muttered, turning to face forward once more, head hung low.

"Of course I do!" Hair tugged back tightly. A punishment for not understanding perhaps?

"Sorry?"

"Kobreon went through something similar," Trishia explained. "There." She added a bright yellow ribbon to the end of the braid. "That looks wonderful on you."

"Something similar?" Ducky repeated. "What do you mean?" There was so much about Kobreon she didn't know —so much she wanted to learn.

Trishia sighed. "What has you so troubled?"

Her head tilted up toward the sky. "Nothing. It's nothing."

"Spit it out," Trishia demanded, crouching at the side of the chair. "It has to do with my son, doesn't it?"

"Huh?" Heat filled her cheeks. "I never said..."

"You don't have to," Trishia chuckled. "I'm his mother. I can tell you have feelings for him." She stood, placing one hand on Ducky's shoulder. "How deep they run, and how long they continue, is up to you. You need to be more confident. You need to accept all the good qualities you have."

"Confident," she mumbled. That was a word she rarely thought of. How could she have confidence? She was just Ducky. "I'm..."

"A beautiful young woman," Trishia said, hands moved to her hips, forming a hero pose. "With rare talents that are worth sharing."

"But the princess..." Her words faded, head hung low. What was she compared to royal charm and exquisite flair?

"What about the princess? Hmm?" Trishia's strides had

172

the same grace as Hammerhead's beloved future ruler. "You don't think?" she gasped.

"They suit each other," Ducky replied, a pout puffing out her bottom lip. "She looks good by his side. Far better than anyone else I've seen." It was true. She'd seen it with her own two eyes. The slender yet curvy figure wearing a white dress and matching tiny flowers in her hair was more attractive than any bride could hope to be on their wedding day. Kobreon's suit of blue and gold matched perfectly. The sight of her in his arms was one she'd never forget, especially the slight blush overtaking beautiful pale skin. The princess was no doubt enamoured by him. Why wouldn't she be?

Trishia chuckled, hand smacking lightly over her mouth. "You're jealous." Her smile widened, eyes glistening. "I'm glad."

"Please don't make fun of me," Ducky begged, standing. The braid was finished. There was no need for anything else. Makeup was for human faces... for princesses.

"I'm not," Trishia snickered. "I am seriously happy. I couldn't ask for anyone better to fall in love with my son. I mean, I knew you were attached to him, but I can see now it's the real deal. L. O. V. E. Ah," she sighed heavily, "to be young."

"What?" She glared in horror. "I-I." The next words weren't there. There was no way to deny what was in her heart. He was too amazing to do that to. She was in love.

"My Lady," Dillinger said, announcing himself as he entered the room. "There are some townsfolk asking to see Ducky."

Her head snapped to face the messenger. Who wanted to see her and why?

*"I admit an arranged marriage seems the correct way to proceed. What are your thoughts, Kobreon?"*
—*King Hammerhead*

## 26

"I HAVE TO CONFESS YOUR OFFER IS APPEALING," KOBREON said, glancing over at the princess. "Your daughter is a beautiful woman."

"And you can't deny the political advantages for both sides," Charmichael added. "Now is the perfect opportunity to unite."

"Hmm." The king rubbed the stubble forming on his chin deep in thought. "I admit an arranged marriage seems the correct way to proceed. What are your thoughts, Kobreon?"

"There are other issues to consider," he replied. "While the political gain might be of some use for the moment, the future would not be without issues. Long term, things might not go as you'd like."

"What do you mean?" the king asked.

"It's simply... neither side would have an heir," Kobreon shrugged. "Our two species simply aren't compatible for mating purposes."

"I've never heard of anything of this sort," Hammerhead said in a firm tone. He turned to his aide. "Have you?"

Charmichael shook his head. "I know there are records of

C.A. KING

a few inter-species unions in the past, but not what happened to them, or the news of any children born from such unions. It is possible the information was lost or removed from most texts."

"That's more than likely the case. It was a dark time for both our pasts. Their offspring were classified as a new subspecies," Kobreon admitted. "They were bound to human form for the most part, but for one night every month they changed to a hybrid wolf-man form... one without the ability to process the intellect of either of their parents' species. They were savage with an insatiable appetite for killing and an unquenchable thirst for blood. From what I know, they were hunted to extinction prior to the border being formed."

"That is worrisome," the king admitted.

"You have only the one daughter," Kobreon continued. "It would be a shame if she bore no fruit to continue the Hammerhead name. I believe we can come to another under-standing, which will be equally beneficial."

"What did you have in mind?" the king asked.

"We have unused lands near the border," Kobreon said.

Gasp! "You'd give us the land?" Charmichael asked. "That's a generous proposal."

"Not exactly," Kobreon chuckled. "Think of it more as a lease."

"How much will this arrangement cost us?" the aide asked, eyes slanting in distrust. "We can't afford much."

"Nothing," Kobreon replied.

"Nothing?" Charmichael repeated.

"I am proposing a bit of an exchange," Kobreon said. "We have fertile land to grow crops on, and you have a world of ice and snow that you aren't using."

"You want the right to use the frozen lands?" the king asked, one brow arched. "Why not simply make an outright exchange? Tit for tat."

178

JUST DUCKY

"Because." Kobreon's brow arched. "The frozen land to the north of you is only accessible via your kingdom. We'd be cut off from it."

"I see," Charmichael chuckled. "This way we'd both be allowed access to areas within the other's territory. It would be fair."

"Precisely," Kobreon agreed.

"Why, exactly, would you want use of such a horrible terrain?" the king asked. "Is there something you aren't telling me?"

"No," Kobreon lied. He was keeping the location of the second ancient workshop a secret for the moment. If he turned up anything useful, then perhaps he'd consider sharing the information. "We have many who would appreciate the locale for hibernation purposes."

"But." Charmichael held up one finger. "We'd basically be developing unused land for you. There'd be farms and crops to consider."

"And we'd be developing what you consider wasteland," Kobreon argued. "You haven't built anything because of the temperature, correct? My people would construct buildings, resorts, and other amenities. The new infrastructure alone would be worth the deal."

"You have a point," Charmichael said, glancing at his king.

"Of course, we can enter negotiations to work out the exact details at a later date," Kobreon said thoughtfully. "We both will need to take time to consider all the advantages and repercussions. This isn't a deal to enter lightly. It will, no doubt, shape the future of the relationship between our two nations."

"For tonight, please feel free to set up camp by the lake," Kobreon offered. "Your men must be tired from marching all this way."

C.A. KING

"That's kind of you," the king replied. "I think we'll take you up on that."

"We don't have much prepared," Kobreon began, "but I'm sure we can throw together something to celebrate... some food... drink... and a few fireworks over the lake as the sun sets."

That sounds wonderful." The king's hands clapped together. "Charmichael, make the arrangements. Add whatever we have to the mix."

"As you wish," Charmichael replied, bowing. "No expense shall be spared."

"It never is," the king chuckled. "This shall be no exception." He draped his good arm around Kobreon's shoulders, turning him away. "Shall we make notes and meet again in a month's time when our heads are clear?"

"That is an excellent idea, Your Highness," Kobreon said.

"Call me Percival," Hammerhead insisted. "There's no reason for us to stand on formality after all we've been through together."

Kobreon smiled. "As you wish, Percival." He paused. "Can I call you Percy?"

"No," the king replied sternly. "Don't push your luck."

Kobreon backed off. "Percival it is."

*"I was jealous. You were the only one who made it inside and you did it as a duckling. It wasn't fair."*
—Lita

# 27

It seemed odd, being summoned, as if she were the lady of the manor. In reality, it was a fluke she was even there. So who was asking for her? No one should have known her whereabouts.

Dillinger was as much of a mystery as anyone else in the palace. He handled the appearances his lord wasn't able or willing to make. That much she'd confirmed when Kobreon first arrived. He'd been the one in the park that day, making the announcement. Other than that, he was an enigma. No one saw him. No one spoke of him. No one bothered with him. Yet today, he was playing butler.

"He's my other son," Trishia whispered in her ear. Reading thoughts must have been a pastime activity practised. "A year younger than Kobreon."

"Huh?" Her head spun, neck twisting as far as possible to the rear.

A brother? Why was she only just hearing of this? She thought she knew everything about Lord Kobreon, yet his immediate family was never a part of the equation. Origi-

C.A. KING

nally, it was only his face she became enamoured with. It was a fantasy.

Dillinger was just as attractive, albeit, in different ways. The younger brother might have been the hero in his own love story had he not been overshadowed. It almost wasn't fair. This family had good looks coming out the wazoo.

"It's true." Trishia nodded in the direction of her youngest. "Ask him yourself if you don't believe me."

"Apologies," he said, bowing diligently. "I should have introduced myself sooner. I am the second son of the family and Lord Kobreon's brother, Dillinger."

"No." Her arms flailed, hands waving fiercely in front of her chest. "Not at all. I-I am sure you must have been busy. Please raise your head. I am not deserving of your humbleness."

"You are most gracious," Dillinger replied, straightening. "I have, in fact, been quite preoccupied aiding my brother as best I can. It seems that duty is coming to an end though."

"Shouldn't you be outside with Lord Kobreon?" Ducky asked. "He might need your help. Not everything is wrapped up in ribbon with a tidy bow on top."

Dillinger chuckled. "I can see why now," he commented. "Don't worry. My brother is well versed in negotiations. He is the best choice for taking care of the rest. I can fulfill another duty simply by being here."

Another duty? What's that about?

Dillinger stopped just short of the front doors. "My job now lies with protecting those within the castle, at least until the humans have left."

"Oh dear," Trishia sighed. "You rascals do like to protect your family, don't you? It's almost embarrassing.

"How nice," Ducky muttered. Of course, it was their mother who was being protected. Why would anyone want to protect a duckling? Why would she be protected? She was

184

JUST DUCKY

always the victim. That was her role. No one was ever going to save her.

"The visitors are just outside." Despite the doors being unusually heavy, they opened for him with what appeared to be the slightest of effort.

"Lita!" she exclaimed, wanting to turn and run. Two hands on her back pushed her forward instead, urging her ahead while letting her know someone was in her corner. "What do you want?" Her arch-nemesis wasn't alone either. She'd brought reinforcements—both of their mothers—one standing on each side.

"I-I'm sorry," Lita muttered, head hung low. It sounded less like an apology and more like the forced statement of an employee being threatened with losing their job. It wasn't enough. Too much had transpired this time. There was a good chance it would never be enough.

"For what?" Ducky asked, arms folded over her chest.

Lita glanced up in surprise, eyes wide open. "For what happened," she replied. "I took things too far. I never should have..."

"Tried to kill me," Ducky finished the sentence. The faces in front of her all held the same expression; one she'd never seen before. Who knew what it meant? She certainly had no idea. It wasn't regret. It certainly wasn't apologetic.

"We rushed right over when we heard what happened," Lita's mother said. "You had already escaped the hut."

"Sorry," Ducky huffed. "I suppose your family was hoping to have a nice roast duck dinner. I guess I ruined it for you."

"That's rather extreme, don't you think?!" Chantelle exclaimed.

"Extreme?!" she bellowed. "I was chased, beaten, locked in a hut, left for dead, and if that wasn't enough, lit on fire."

Lita's hands rose in protest. "That wasn't my fault. We only found out about the fire when we returned. I swear."

C.A. KING

"I'm supposed to believe that?" Ducky huffed.

"It's the truth," Lita's mother said, as if pleading for forgiveness. What was with their change in attitudes? Were they intimidated by her?

"The fire was an accident," Chantelle said.

"How so?" she asked.

"I shoved Tal," Lita explained. "He wasn't thrilled about what we were doing. He wanted out. I got mad and gave him a good push in the chest. When his back hit the side of the shed, his glasses fell. None of us realized at the time. He ran off."

Ah... the shaking shack. That part she remembered. She often wondered why he wore glasses in the first place. Most of their kind had advanced senses, not the other way around.

"He's a bull shifter," Chantelle declared, as if reading her thoughts. Apparently, for some reason, all mothers were able to do that. "Their eyesight isn't good, no matter which form they take."

"The glasses landed on a bale of hay," Lita added. "The sun's rays must have hit the lenses and started the fire. It's the truth. I swear. I didn't want you to die."

"Just hurt a lot?" Ducky snapped.

"I-I." Red filled her arch-nemesis's face. "I was jealous. You were the only one who made it inside Cliffside, and you managed to do it as a duckling. It wasn't fair."

"That's all I was," she answered. "A duckling. That's all he thought of me too. I was trying to escape far enough away that shifting back wouldn't be a shock to anyone. That's when you jumped me. That's when my life flashed before my eyes."

"I'm truly sorry," Lita blurted out. "Please don't..."

"Arrest you?" Dillinger asked, twirling handcuffs that locked a person in their human form. "I'm afraid I have no choice. You've openly admitted to a crime. It will be up to

186

JUST DUCKY

Lord Kobreon to decide what fate befalls you now. He's rather fond of a certain little yellow duckling, so I can imagine you won't escape unscathed from punishment." A stern grip attached to her arm, the cuff locking in place. "I'll take care of this one and round up any accomplices." He glared directly at Ducky. "You should go enjoy the festivities. They aren't much, since we had no idea things would turn out the way they did, but there will be a few fireworks."

"Thank you."

The mothers had already disappeared, eager to avoid being arrested or further dragged into trouble. There'd been enough of that going around to last several lifetimes.

Colourful lights exploded in flower patterns in the sky. Behind them she could just make out both the sun and moon, positioned as if dancing together in celebration. There was nothing ominous about them. In fact, they brought a smile to her lips, a faint one, but a smile nonetheless.

*"Who would have thought a sweet little duckling would have such fire hidden inside her?"*
*—Lord Kobreon*

# 28

THE BREEZE WAS AMAZING, BLOWING HER HAIR GENTLY OFF HER face. It would have felt the same with duckling down, or even the fiery coloured feathers of a phoenix. Every aspect of her was in agreement. That was rare. The only other thing that aligned them all perfectly was their fondness of Lord Kobreon. The problem was how to express those feelings. There was always a chance, the moment he found out, he'd never want to see her again.

What if, after learning about her alter ego, he felt indebted to her for curing the princess? That wasn't what she wanted.

Wait!

She wasn't one-hundred-percent sure he was aware she was Ducky and the phoenix yet.

"Wow." Kobreon approached her, rubbing his head. A whimsical smile graced his lips. "You really saved me back there. I didn't want to let on in front of the king, but without your help, we'd definitely be waging war right about now."

Her trembling body froze. He was speaking to her so

C.A. KING

familiarly, as if they were long-lost friends, even though in human form, they were strangers. It made no sense.

She was just Ducky.

Of everyone there, she was the last one he should have been wasting time on. He was supposed to be with the princess, wasn't he?

"That was amazing," he continued. "Who would have thought a sweet little duckling would have such fire hidden inside her?"

"You knew?" she asked in a whisper, peering up at him directly for only a moment before casting her gaze back at the dirt beneath her bare feet. That was the first time she realized shoes had been left out of the equation when creating the fancy outfit.

He turned to her, reflections of fireworks from the celebration exploding in his eyes. "Hmm." He rubbed his chin, trying to look profound. "When we first met... not in the least."

Her head hung low. "Of course not."

"But..." He waited for their gazes to connect. "I'm glad we met."

"I am too." Her gaze automatically fell back to the ground between them again. What was she supposed to say? Nothing came to mind.

"Are you okay?" he asked.

"Yes. Umm. I met your brother." The words came out without thought—merely the only thing in her mind to keep the conversation going. Ending it now was far too depressing. Her heart was likely to break on the spot—something no one needed to witness.

"Oh?" His brow arched. "Which one?"

"Huh?" He had more than one? There was so much about him she didn't know—so much she wanted to learn. Before he'd merely been a pretty face on festival merchandise and in

JUST DUCKY

newspaper clippings. That image of him wasn't the real deal. The version of him she now knew was so much more. "How many do you have?"

"I have five siblings and I believe twenty-one half-siblings," he chuckled. "At last count anyway. Come to think of it, Dillinger is the only one at home right now. Is that who you meant?" His eyes shifted to watch her expression.

"Twenty-one?" she repeated, gasping.

"My father," he replied, not waiting for the question to be posed. "He enjoys travelling and variety. He gets a bit flustered when faced with strange offspring though and changes locale frequently."

"I'm not sure I understand," she admitted.

"Oh... first I should explain, my mother didn't mind his infidelity," he mused. "She was happy settling down and raising the six of us."

"Is that right?" She side-eyed him in disbelief.

"It's true," he insisted. "So off he went to see the world and leave his mark wherever he could."

"By mark you mean children?" she asked.

He shrugged, "I suppose. I even have a half-brother named Caspian living in a remote desert. I often worry about him, but I just can't bring myself to visit. The extreme heat of the sun and thought of sand in my eyes keeps me away."

Dry heat and sand, without the ocean, wasn't her idea of a good time either. "Can't he come here and visit you?"

He leaned into her ear, whispering, "He's a camel."

"A what?!" The heat of a blazing desert sun rushed to her cheeks merely for yelling so loud.

"Most of my siblings are odd," Kobreon mused.

"A camel isn't all that weird," she replied. "They are similar to horses. There are lots of those around here and nobody blinks an eye."

"Except camels live in deserts," he chuckled. "And those

C.A. KING

areas of our world aren't highly populated. He spends most of his time lazing around. Don't worry, I wrote a letter to tell him all about you. I'm sure he'll want to meet you, once he reads it."

Ah... the desert. What duckling wanted to waddle on hot sand? "Sounds... fun." She glanced away, hoping he wasn't able to read her words as lies.

Wait! He wrote a letter about me?

"Ah! You're amazing!" Kobreon blurted out.

Her eyes widened. There was that desert heat again, rushing to her cheeks. "What?" No one had ever said anything even remotely close to those sentiments to her before. Until that moment, she'd always been the one looked down on, treated as inferior—unworthy. "I-I..." Before another word came out, she was in his arms, head spinning as to how she ended up there. "Wha—"

"Shh." One finger caressed the outline of her mouth, his eyes searching hers. "There is so much more I need to know about you... things I want to share with you." His breath was hot with desire, gently scorching the side of her neck, the bottom of her earlobe.

It was all so sudden. How was she supposed to respond? The feelings were there. They were real. It was a way to describe them that was the problem.

She had zero experience romantically or otherwise. She'd never been in a relationship. She'd never even had a friend. This was too much to handle out of the blue. It was too much to ask of a Duckling.

Everything changed in an instant

"You don't have to answer," he said. "It's okay." The sadness in his eyes—his expression—was heartbreaking.

She glanced away, heart beating at triple its normal rate. What was he saying? He'd completely blindsided her. There

194

was no way anyone could have imagined those words coming from his lips—glossy lips which probably tasted delicious. This wasn't the way things were supposed to be. Sad wasn't a way she ever wanted to see him. There was only one way to fix things. Just as he let go of his embrace, she grabbed his arm, tugging him close again.

Lips collided.

Her first kiss and she'd initiated it, albeit, she hadn't the foggiest about how or what came after the initial locking of lips.

"Hmm?" He pulled slightly away. "Don't press your lips together so tightly. Open them for me when we kiss." The twinkling returned to his eye. "Trust me."

It wasn't an order, but she obeyed nonetheless, allowing him access to her mouth and he took it, swallowing her love whole, filling the rest of her body with yearning until her lips were swollen from kisses, her face was reddened with the heat of desire, and her lungs were panting for air.

One hand extended toward her gracefully, as if asking a lady for a dance at a fancy ball. "Come. Let's go home, Ducky."

He was so calm... collected. Her head was still spinning. This was really happening. He'd kissed her and she wanted more. Was that being greedy?

"You don't want to?" He peeked around her low hanging head, gazes connecting.

"I didn't say that," she mumbled, hand outstretching, fingertips gently resting in his palm. The grip tightened, pulling her in close.

"Let's go," he repeated, gently brushing his lips against the heat filling her cheek. "Now I have you, I'm never letting you escape again."

There was no need to argue. Everything was just the way

she wanted. She had her fantasy happily ever after and wasn't giving even a second of it up.

The End.

# A LOOK AT BOOK TWO IN THE WEIRD SHIFTERS COLLECTION:
## HAPPY HUMP DAY

*He's getting under her one way or another.*

Lazy, hazy, sandy days.
An expedition led by a beautiful woman with a secret.
A camel shifter lacking motivation.
An undeniable attraction.
A hero complex in the making.

Caspian is happy spending most days doing nothing, and only working as the need for money arises. Not that there is that much work for a camel shifter anyway. Most clients preferred using the real deal—one-hundred-percent hump. Animals don't negotiate terms of employment. They also rarely talk back.

When a pretty woman crosses his path, he's ready to make a few changes, especially when she goes missing, looking for some ancient ruins.
That's his cue and chance to find her and become the

A LOOK AT BOOK TWO IN THE WEIRD SHIFTERS COLL...

hero. After that, nothing will stop him from claiming her as his mate.

*Keep reading for a sample chapter.*

# BONUS CHAPTER
## HAPPY HUMP DAY

The Tanken Desert was unlike anywhere else in the world. Located to the far south of the human border, the risk of war was little to none, especially given the weather and environment. Wave-like dunes and squishy sand between the toes: that was it, the entirety of his stomping grounds summed up. The only thing missing from the description was the word hot.

Caspian sighed. He'd opened the letter from his brother and now it was all he was thinking about. Kobreon... Vampire Kobreon... Lord Kobreon... or maybe it was Vampire Lord Kobreon. He sat up, fingers tousling his already messy hair. He wasn't even sure how to address his own brother anymore, or if he should, for that matter.

Such a pain.

"But at least he found a woman," he chuckled to himself. No one else was around. No one ever was when the breeze was gently blowing. "Knowing him, she is some amazing beauty. He was probably kidding about the duckling part. Kobreon should know by now that isn't necessary. I'm happy with the way things are."

## BONUS CHAPTER

Happy probably wasn't the correct term. It was more content than anything else. He slept when he wanted to. He ate when he wanted to. He worked when he wanted to and for whom he wanted. Life was there for the wasting, and that's exactly what he planned to do with it. There wasn't much more to living for a camel.

If he was being honest, he worked when a job was available, which wasn't often. The majority of positions went to actual animals. They never complained about work conditions or wages. He, on the other hand, had a reputation for changing forms and arguing naked with his employers. That wasn't a great selling point when hoping to be hired for future desert trips.

The one thing he actually had going for him was knowledge. Inside his head he knew the ins and outs of every nook and cranny the desert had to offer. Even a severe sandstorm wasn't enough to throw him off a trail.

"Ah! Phooey!"

None of that actually mattered. He was single and that's the way he was going to stay. No one ever caught his eye before. So why change? Turning his head was too much of a pain anyway. Kobreon could keep his duckling. That was what his brother wanted, not what he wanted.

Regardless of what anyone else said, love was always going to be a four-letter word. Just as no one was going to choose a camel shifter for their mate, at least not anyone worthwhile.

So why bother to look? There was no point. Sleeping—daydreaming—that was more than enough to occupy the days and most nights.

Kobreon might have found himself a beauty queen, but she probably was nothing compared to the one in his mind. The best part was, his babe was waiting with bated breath

BONUS CHAPTER

every time he closed his eyes, willing to do anything and everything he asked.

What real woman was like that?

None that he knew of. And if they were, they certainly weren't going to live in a secluded outpost town in the middle of a desert. She'd have to have a screw loose to even consider visiting a place like that.

"Hello!"

Bang. Bang. Bang.

"Hello?"

He rolled on his side, slightly lifting a straw hat. If the breasts on the woman yelling where as big as her lungs needed to be to make such a commotion, it was worth opening one eye to have a peek. It was always good to refresh material for future fantasy figures, after all. He was a tits and ass guy all the way.

Bang. Bang. Bang.

The noise the woman's fist made against the camel rental office's flimsy bay door was annoying. A few more raps and the good mood he'd been working on was bound to be gone.

Bang. Bang. Bang.

"Can't you read?" He sat up abruptly.

"Read what?" she snapped.

"The sign," he answered, boasting an overexaggerated shrug.

"What sign?" she asked.

He stood, strolling over, hands hidden inside pockets. "That sign..." He removed his hat, fingers making a bigger mess of already tousled hair. "Well, that's odd. I guess they forgot to put it up. They're closed."

"Closed?" There was that lung power again. Up close, she had a set of bazookas on her to match and well worth remembering. "When will they be open again?"

"I don't know," he shrugged, chuckling under his breath.

BONUS CHAPTER

"I don't work for them." He returned to his seat, lying back with his face covered.

Brightness.

"What do you know?" she asked, his hat tight in her grip. Big brown eyes stared down at him.

"Ahem." He snatched back his property. "I'm not in their employ. If you are looking for a single camel, I can be of help."

"Single?" One nostril scrunched up, marring her otherwise attractive face. "No. No. No. That won't do." She retreated a few paces. "Do they usually close for long periods of time?"

"Yeah. Well, there aren't daily customers in these parts. Most folks call ahead and reserve camels, especially when they need more than one." He placed the hat back over his face. "Tape your contact information to the door. Someone will give you a call in a day or two, I'm sure."

"Right." She scowled. "Thanks for nothing. Where am I supposed to get a pen and paper, not to mention tape, in the middle of the desert?"

If she'd asked nicely, he had all of those items. Instead, she strolled away, huffing a few swear words under her breath. Still, that woman's figure was going to make a great model for his new and improved fake girlfriend, of course he'd give her a more pleasant demeanour.

The real one had a chip on her shoulder. As attractive as she was, no woman was worth taking on added emotional baggage. He had enough problems of his own. Now, if she had needed a single camel, that would have been a different story entirely.

202

# AUTHOR'S MESSAGE

I hope you enjoyed reading Just Ducky as much as I did writing it. Thank you for joining me on this journey. Watch for more in the weird shifter series coming soon, including, Lord Kobreon's half-brother, Caspian, in Happy Hump Day. While you are waiting, I hope you take a look at some of my other books and find more to enjoy.

Until next time... happy reading!

# OTHER TITLES FROM
# C.A. KING

GRAVE DIGGER ACADEMY

There is a reason why people don't believe in monsters and it's not because zombies, vampires, mummies, and ghosts don't exist...

Welcome to Grave Digger Academy—the last place anyone wants to end up.

---

Gravediggers actually do the digging. Grave Diggers, however, keep buried bodies where they belong—six feet under.

---

EVIL SUSHI

They aren't zombies.

They aren't the walking dead.

OTHER TITLES FROM C.A. KING

They are something else...

Just when you thought it was safe to go back for seconds...

Evil Sushi turns the tables, putting meat back on the menu.

───────

Two down-on-their-luck East Coast fishermen make the discovery of a lifetime—one that could solve world hunger once and for all. They find themselves fast-tracked on a quest to alter lives around the globe. Their discovery changes things, there's no doubt about it, but not in the way they hoped.

Is Evil Sushi fiction, the ramblings of a lunatic or a prophecy as to what may come to pass? Pick this one up and decide for yourself.

# ABOUT THE AUTHOR

C.A. King, a two-time USA Today Bestselling Author, is the recipient of several awards, including:

The Hamilton Spectator Readers' Choice Award for 2017, 2018 & 2019 in the Best Local Author category; The Brant News Readers' Choice Award for 2017 Best Local Author; Readers' Favorite award in the short story/novella category; the 2017 SIBA Award for Best New Adult; the 2017 SIBA Award for Best Novella; 2018 Readers' Favorite International Book Awards: Gold Medal in the Fiction—Supernatural genre; 2018 Readers' Favorite International Book Awards: Bronze Medal in the Fiction –-New Adult genre; 2019 Readers' Favorite International Book Awards: Gold Medal in the Fiction – Supernatural genre; 2019 Readers' Favorite International Book Awards: Gold Medal in the Young Adult – Fantasy – Urban Genre; City of Brantford Featured Artist February 2020; Burlington Post Readers' Choice Award in the Best Local Author Category 2020; Toronto Star Readers' Choice Award in the Best Local Author Category 2020; Cambridge Times Readers' Choice Award in the Best Local Author Category 2020; and Burlington Post Readers' Choice Award in the Best Local Author Category 2021.

Currently residing in Hamilton, Ontario Canada, she lives with her two sons. She began her writing career after the tragic loss of her parents and husband. Redirecting her

emotions through writing became therapeutic in her battle with depression and in 2014 she decided to publish some of her works.

You can sign up for C.A. King's newsletter here:
https://www.subscribepage.com/r8o8y3

Manufactured by Amazon.ca
Bolton, ON